EFFEMINATE ENGLAND

BETWEEN MEN ~ BETWEEN WOMEN
Lesbian and Gay Studies

Lillian Faderman and Larry Gross, Editors

BETWEEN MEN ~ BETWEEN WOMEN
Lesbian and Gay Studies

Lillian Faderman and Larry Gross, Editors

EFFEMINATE ENGLAND

Homoerotic Writing after 1885

JOSEPH BRISTOW

COLUMBIA UNIVERSITY PRESS
NEW YORK

Columbia University Press
New York
Copyright © Joseph Bristow, 1995
All rights reserved

Library of Congress Cataloging–in–Publication Data

Bristow, Joseph.
    Effeminate England : homoerotic writing after 1885 / Joseph
Bristow.
        p.   cm. — (Between men—between women)
    Includes bibliographical references and index.
    ISBN 0–231–10348–4. — ISBN 0–231–10349–2 (pbk.)
    1. English literature—20th century—History and criticism.
    2. Homosexuality and literature—England—History—20th century.
    3. Homosexuality and literature—England—History—19th century.
    4. English literature—Men authors—History and criticism.
    5. English literature—19th century—History and criticism.   6. Gay
men's writings, English—History and criticism. 7. Androgyny
(Psychology) in literature.   8. Homosexuality, Male, in literature.
9. Gender identity in literature.   10. Gay men in literature.
I. Title.   II. Series.
PR478.H65B751995
820.9'353—dc20   95–10836
                                                                          CIP

Typeset by Dorwyn Ltd, Rowlands Castle, Hants.
Printed in Great Britain by St Edmundsbury Press,
Bury St. Edmunds, Suffolk

c 10 9 8 7 6 5 4 3 2 1
p 10 9 8 7 6 5 4 3 2 1

BETWEEN MEN ~ BETWEEN WOMEN
Lesbian and Gay Studies

Lillian Faderman and Larry Gross, Editors
Eugene F. Rice, Columbia University Advisor

Advisory Board of Editors

Claudia Card, University of Wisconsin	Philosophy
Gilbert Herdt, University of Chicago	Anthropology, Sociology, Political Science
Barbara Johnson, Harvard University	Literature
Anne Peplau, University of California, Los Angeles	Psychology
Rhonda R. Rivera, Ohio State University	Law

Between Men ~ Between Women is a forum for current lesbian and gay scholarship in the humanities and social sciences. The series includes both books that rest within specific traditional disciplines and are substantially about gay men, bisexuals, or lesbians and books that are interdisciplinary in ways that reveal new insights into gay, bisexual, or lesbian experience, transform traditional disciplinary methods in consequence of the perspectives that experience provides, or begin to establish lesbian and gay studies as a freestanding inquiry. Established to contribute to an increased understanding of lesbians, bisexuals, and gay men, the series also aims to provide through that understanding a wider comprehension of culture in general.

To Jef Jones

Contents

Acknowledgements

In its earliest conception, this book aimed to provide a survey of the main strands of male homoerotic writing produced in Britain since the 1880s to the present day. Soon it became clear to me that this was an inadvisable task, since the scope and shape of such a study would mean that large quantities of material could only be given the most superficial treatment. In deciding instead to examine four distinctive formations – Wilde's dandiacal style; Forster's embattled treatment of effeminacy; Ronald Firbank's camp exoticism; and the politics of identity in male homosexual autobiography – I hope to have made some of the more prominent patterns in homoerotic writing after 1885 as clear as possible.

My thinking about homophile writing, as well as gay theory and history, gathered pace in the mid-1980s when I became involved with the Queory reading group that met intermittently in London over a period of 12 months or so. John Fletcher generously hosted these meetings, and Jonathan Dollimore, Mark Finch, Simon Shepherd, and Mick Wallis contributed to provocative discussions which certainly encouraged my academic research to take a more politicized direction. Never since have I been fortunate enough to participate in a forum that has had such a strong impact on my intellectual work. One person from Queory, above all, inspired me to progress with this and related projects. It is to Alan Sinfield that *Effeminate England* owes its largest intellectual debt.

Many colleagues have been generous in providing a supportive audience for sections of this book. Parts of my chapter on Oscar Wilde were delivered to members of the School of English, University of Leeds, and to the

Department of English Literature and Language, University of Liverpool. An early draft of Chapter 2, on E.M. Forster and his misspelled 'effeminancy', was the source of some heated debate at the Centre for Critical and Cultural Theory, University of Wales College of Cardiff. My thanks to Elleke Boehmer, Ann Thompson, and Jane Moore respectively for inviting me to speak at their institutions. Several useful insights into Wilde's works were gained from dialogues with Joel H. Kaplan and Sheila Stowell. Xiaoyi Zhou's doctoral dissertation submitted to the University of Lancaster in 1993 was a pleasure to examine, not least because it provided me with a richer context in which to comprehend Wilde's relations with consumer culture. Christina Britzolakis was characteristically munificent in the feedback that she gave on my first faltering attempts to articulate the homoerotic wishfulfilment shaping Forster's short stories and novels. In addition, I am grateful to Parminder Bakshi for permitting me to read her doctoral dissertation, submitted to the University of Warwick in 1993, on the 'distant desire' of male homosexuality in Forster's writings. John Birtwhistle kindly pointed me towards W.H. Auden's review of J.R. Ackerley's writings. Drawing on her own work on Victorian patriarchy, Trev Broughton referred me to useful materials connected with John Addington Symonds's memoirs. Ben Harker generously shared his resources on Alan Hollinghurst's fiction. And last – but, of course, by no means least – Nic Horsey thoughtfully guided me towards the fine autobiographical writings of Jocelyn Brooke.

Much appreciated help in locating various critical materials was provided by the interlibrary loan services of my former employer, Sheffield Hallam University, and the staff of the J.B. Morrell Library, University of York. Among my colleagues at York, Jacques Berthoud and S.A.J. Bradley did their utmost to assist me when my quota of interlibrary loans was exhausted. In addition, the London Library provided many of the books I required. Sigrid P. Perry of the Special Collections Department of Northwestern University, Evanston, Illinois, kindly arranged for copies of the T.E. Lawrence–Forster correspondence to be made for me.

Finally, thanks are due to my editors. At Open University Press, John Skelton has been at all times supportive of this project. My series editor in Britain, Kate Flint, made many helpful suggestions about the scope and shape of my argument. Ann H. Miller, at Columbia University Press, indicated exactly what an American audience would expect from a study such as this.

Joseph Bristow
University of York

Introduction

Effeminate England sets out to analyse some of the main patterns of homoerotic writing produced after 1885. This date has great significance in the history of male homosexuality, since it was in this year that the Labouchere Amendment – the eleventh clause of the Criminal Law Amendment Act – put a complete ban on acts of 'gross indecency' between men, not only in public, but in private. Nowhere after that time, for over 80 years, was male homosexual contact legally permitted in England and Wales. Nicknamed the 'Blackmailer's Charter' as soon as it went on to the statute book, this pernicious piece of legislation until very recently created a climate of secrecy and fear in the lives of men-loving men. Although the Wolfenden Report made extensive recommendations for legal reform in 1957, it was only 10 years later that the Sexual Offences Act partly decriminalized male homosexuality. Even then, there was an enduring inequality in law. Retaining a ban on male homosexuality in the armed services (a ban which is being vigorously contested as I write), the Sexual Offences Act put the age of consent for men engaged in same-sex practices to 21 when the law stood at 16 for heterosexuals. Only while I was completing work on the manuscript of this book, in February 1994, did the House of Commons vote to lower the age of consent for homosexual men to 18, once again maintaining an undue inequality in state legislation. It will probably take several more years before the British government succumbs to the pressure of the European Commission so that full equality between men involved in intimate same- and other-sex relations is observed in law.

This book, however, is not about legal reform. But it is impossible to understand many of the writings under analysis here without referring much of it back to the prohibitive and punitive conditions in which male homosexual writers produced their work. The key figure who became the most notorious victim of the Labouchere Amendment was Oscar Wilde in 1895. Not only did Wilde represent for the first time in public a celebrity who had committed sexual acts of 'gross indecency', he also came to emblematize a specific style of effeminate identity that represented a distinctly late nineteenth-century apprehension of the male homosexual. In calling this book *Effeminate England*, I aim to draw attention to the manner in which effeminacy became the main stigma attached to male homosexuality in the eyes of English society. So familiar is this queer stereotype that it is easy to forget that the connection between effeminate behaviour and same-sex desire was firmly established in the public imagination only after Wilde was sent to Reading Gaol for two years in solitary confinement with hard labour. Although effeminacy had always been a feature of sexual behaviour between men from the days of the 'molly houses' in the Renaissance, it is certainly the case that the meanings it connoted in the age of Wilde focused as never before on a specific understanding of a man's homophilia. Alan Sinfield has explored at length how and why effeminacy came to be indissolubly bonded to the figure of the homosexual man, after 200 years in which the implications of effeminate mannerisms modulated considerably – sometimes with suggestions of same-sex desire, and sometimes not.[1] The great virtue of Sinfield's researches – his work has inspired much of what follows – is that he adopts a model of uneven development to mark the shifts and changes in how the effeminate image of the queer nancy-boy emerged after the three trials that resulted in Wilde's imprisonment.

In emphasizing the uneven patterns that shape modern understandings of male homosexual desire, Sinfield is working with a set of assumptions similar to those which Mary Poovey outlines in her powerful study of the ideological work of gender in mid-Victorian Britain. Introducing her critical methods, Poovey stresses that any study of sexual ideology must be wary of the idea that changes in cultural understandings of sexual categories in the modern period can and do transform in a coherent and completed fashion:

> To describe an ideology as a 'set' of beliefs or a 'system' of institutions and practices conveys the impression of something that is internally organized, coherent, and complete . . . Yet it is one of [my] tasks . . . to reveal the other face of this ideology – the extent to which what may look coherent and complete in retrospect was actually fissured by competing emphases and interests. One of my central conclusions from this study is that the middle-class ideology we most often associate with the Victorian period was both contested and always

under construction; because it was always open to revision, dispute, and the emergence of oppositional formulations.[2]

Although Poovey's critical model attends to the divisions and contradictions within debates about masculinity and femininity in the middle-class sphere of the 1850s, her understanding of how sexual ideology is 'always under construction' can throw light on how gender relations were organized in the later period. This model of uneven development has a special leverage on how differing discourses operate to exert a range of pressures that finally alight – not always conclusively – on a specific stereotype of male homosexuality. Bearing this point in mind, Sinfield shows – to take just one example – how T.C. Worsley claimed to have no understanding of the words 'queer' or 'bent' when at school in the 1930s.[3] Just as 'queer' might not have any perverse significance for a public-school boy in the early decades of this century, so too might the term 'homosexual' elude his understanding. J.R. Ackerley, for one, would recall how surprised he was by the question 'Are you are homo or a hetero?' in the 1920s.[4] It was not that Ackerley was either offended or embarrassed to be asked such a personal question. It was simply that he did not know what it meant. Although the sexologists started using 'homosexual' as a clinical definition in the 1890s, it took some time for this designation to make its way beyond the specialized circles of the medical profession. Yet even if the word queer may have struck Worsley as odd some three decades after Wilde was serving time in prison, it needs to be borne in mind that there were groups of men – such as Henry James and E.M. Forster – who, in the 1890s and early 1900s, discreetly gave this epithet a homophile inflection. Cultural transformation in the naming and perception of dissident sexualities, therefore, is certainly uneven in the period that I am studying.

It follows that the labels I have chosen to employ in describing sexual attraction between men – as the preceding paragraphs illustrate – vary considerably, not least for the sake of avoiding stylistic repetition. At times using the adjective same-sex, I have on other occasions found that the words homophile or homosexual are more appropriate, depending on the context in which they appear. Where the term homophile accentuates the affectivity of desires between men, the label homosexual draws more fully on the specific identity that embodies the sexual subject of such desires. Every now and again, I find it helpful to draw on the epithet queer when its significance is appropriate for those materials that engage it on its own terms. But in deploying a quite flexible ensemble of labels, and by following the idea that labelling of this kind in any case reaches into different cultural contexts in an uneven manner, I am not disclaiming that distinctive patterns of homophilia do indeed emerge at specific moments of history. Indeed, it is here that effeminacy enjoys a central point of definition in comprehending these various namings of male homosexuality.

The writings of Michel Foucault and Jeffrey Weeks – the former in many ways shaping the historical and political considerations of the latter – show how and why sexological discourse played a special role in giving homosexuality a name. Most influential in this respect has been Foucault's axiomatic and persuasive (but now well-worn) statement that the invention of 'homosexuality' as a form of classification created the concept of a specific type of person that was altogether different from the earlier notion of the sodomite who manifested a form of sexual behaviour rather than sexual being.[5] Foucault's claims, however, have hardly gone uncontested. It was not only late-Victorian sexology that brought about changes in consciousness about what might be the precise identity of the man-loving man. In the mid-nineteenth century, there was a powerful intervention made on these questions by several eminent classical scholars who increasingly turned to the works of Plato and Plutarch to consider how same-sex eroticism was historically a part of male sexuality, on occasions suggesting that homophilia was not a form of eroticism that was necessarily distinct from other modes of affection.[6] Wilde, for one, fashioned his dignified models of male friendship from the protocols of Oxonian Hellenism, as it developed from the 1850s, to endorse his notion of 'Uranian' love. At the same time, however, an analogous term such as 'Urning' (deriving from Karl Heinrich Ulrichs's pioneering researches of the 1860s) would be employed by sexologists as they sought to ground their understandings of male homosexuality in a specific physiological type of person. But the most significant point to note is that the 'Uranian' and the 'Urning' – for all their diversity of sources and inflections – would become entwined by the mid-1890s in a particular notion of the effeminate man. There is no doubt that the sexual style that caused the greatest confusion and anxiety about homosexual identity in the late nineteenth century was its perceived attachment to femininity – and thus, by extension, to effeminacy. The chapters below explain how and why it remained difficult for homosexual writers to create affirming images of their own sexual preferences without referring – either with pride or with shame – to effeminate behaviour. Indeed, all the writers discussed in the present study are acutely aware of the gendering of their homoeroticism.

Here, too, Sinfield's work enables us to see why this should have been the case. His exemplary critical project insists that the meanings surrounding the idea of effeminacy underwent a huge shift of emphasis over the course of 200 years. 'Up to the time of the Wilde trials', he cautions, 'far later than is widely supposed – it is unsafe to interpret effeminacy as defining of, or as a signal of, same-sex passion.'[7] Aligned with luxury in the eighteenth century, effeminacy could at that time represent a disturbance within the discourse of civic republicanism that preoccupied many intellectuals writing about the relations between the individual and the state up to the time of the French Revolution. Linda Dowling identifies how the *effeminatus* in classical republican theory' represents 'the empty and negative symbol at once of civic enfeeblement and of the monstrous self-absorption that becomes visible in a society at just the moment at which . . . private interest begins to prevail against those things that concern public welfare'. That moment, Dowling observes, comes at the end of the seventeenth century, and she claims that this perception of *effeminati* is bound so much into understandings of the state that it is generally ungraspable to the modern mind which perceives effeminacy in primarily gendered terms.[8] By the end of the nineteenth century, as Dowling sees it, there was not necessarily any homophobic stigma attached to the young effeminate figure of Wilde as he courted the most fashionable company. His Hellenism, and its high-minded commitment to art, emerged from the Socratic ethos that had been fostered by his distinguished *alma mater* for the past half century after a period of rapid reform in which the teaching of Plato extended at last to the *Symposium*. In fact, from Dowling's perspective, Wilde's adopted style had a wholly comprehensible place in the move towards civic diversity that was sponsored by a broadening and enlightened liberalism. Even during the second trial, when Wilde made his impassioned speech about the 'love that dare not speak its name', his terms of reference were to the Bible and to Plato: texts to which he naturally turned to uphold forms of intimate homosociality which had long gained legitimacy among the Oxford faculty. 'It is, perhaps,' writes Dowling, 'one measure of the ideological potency of Victorian liberal Hellenism that it can in this moment [the second trial of 1895] speak without loss of persuasive power through the medium of precisely the most notorious dandy-aesthete-effeminatus of the day.'[9] Only after the trials would Wilde's persona become radically re-fashioned as that of a pathological being: a degraded degenerate whose effeminate bearing coincided with increasingly popularized notions of the invert who, according to some sexologists, contained a woman's soul within his male body. Hereafter, it would prove almost impossible to imagine Wilde as anything other than a congenitally womanly man. And, as Sinfield and Dowling in their respective ways show, it has proved very hard indeed for modern critics to return to the moments before the grisly trials of 1895 and resist assuming that homosexuality was always already effeminate because it was *not as yet* the 'homosexuality' whose categorical designation we have so fully – perhaps to the point of near-invisibility – assimilated into our own seemingly more emancipated culture.

To be sure, the fact that in the mid and late nineteenth century effeminacy could signify meanings that at times sound foreign to our ears should make any student of gender relations in the Victorian period pause for thought, and with good reason. It is not, after all, uncommon to assume that the Victorians established a paradigmatic framework of sexual difference whose familiarity is registered in the widespread belief that our own late twentieth-century struggles for liberation are defined against a repressive regime that – in the hands of the moral Right – always threatens to return its Victorian authoritarianism upon our minds and bodies with a vengeance. Time and again, we turn to the middle decades of the nineteenth century to examine how fixed ideas about the masculinization of the public world were set in place, just as the domestic realm was more decisively viewed as the proper sphere of femininity. Given that this inflexible and readily graspable model of 'separate spheres' retains such ideological power – even if social historians have now begun to argue that it is less rigid than previously imagined[10] – its enduring familiarity probably says more about current needs to hold on to solidified notions of gender difference in which clear-cut understandings of an oppressive patriarchy might be facilitated than it does about the awkwardnesses that the writers of conduct books from the 1830s to the 1850s were having in keeping men and women at opposite poles. The cultural ambivalence of Victorian effeminacy – its movement between a style of behaviour that could at times be acceptable and at others truly repugnant – must surely prompt us to think harder about how we locate ideas of manhood in many of the literary representations from the 1850s that appear furiously embattled in their virile expressiveness. A broad spread of examples could indeed be drawn from mid-nineteenth-century writings to show how effeminacy suggested all that the doctrine of manliness propounded by the Christian Socialists at midcentury so eagerly sought to condemn.

In this respect, Alfred Tennyson's poem, *In Memoriam* (1850), would at first appear to be an excellent case in point. This elegaic tribute to the poet's closest male friend has, to say the least, strong homoerotic overtones, ones which were promptly noted in the mid-Victorian press.[11] Even then, however, a major propagandist of manliness in its most muscular Christian mould would come to Alfred Tennyson's rescue to declare that this elegiac poem was espoused to a model of dignified friendship that respectably evoked the biblical legend of those comrades-in-arms, David and Jonathan, whose intimate affections were 'passing the love of woman'.[12] If we follow Dowling's lead – and, indeed, the manner in which she reads several of Tennyson's poems[13] – then it would seem that Kingsley's defence rests on the liberal attitude towards homosocial intimacy that gained greatest institutional legitimacy at Victorian Oxford. And there is, no doubt, a great deal of truth in this view. Yet in making this vigorous apology for Tennyson's manly sentiments, Kingsley was using an example that homophile writers themselves would in later decades employ to encode sexual attraction between men. This was indeed the Old Testament myth to which Wilde would refer when he found himself obliged in court to explain the nature of 'the love that dare not speak its name'. This reappearance of David and Jonathan, then, suggests that male homophilia lay in much closer proximity than we might have imagined to the manly love propounded by those whose ideals fed directly into the philathleticism of the public-school ethos for which the Christian Socialists are remembered.

There are other configurations of effeminacy from this period that are worth investigating for a moment, and here too Tennyson's poetry provides a rich resource. Not only in his writings can we see how the charge of effeminacy surrounds emotional ties between men. In 'The Marriage of Geraint' (from *Idylls of the King*, 1859), effeminacy also emerges as a symptom of nothing less than uxoriousness: his hero is so enamoured of his wife that he loses all resolve to fight in the manner of a true Arthurian knight. There Enid bitterly complains that her husband is 'melted into mere effeminacy' (l.107).[14] By drawing attention to this episode, I am not trying to suggest that 'The Marriage of Geraint' is strangely anachronistic in contriving effeminacy as the result of indulgent wife-loving. Indeed, it is a sign of the amplitude of the term in the 1850s that Tennyson could readily remark that effeminacy was the result of what we might now regard as a man's intense heterosexuality. But one thing is clear: it is proximity to – and identification with, rather than difference from – women that in this period is seen to bring about an effeminate weakening in the mind and body of a man, whether he shies away from women or indeed loves them too much.

Always responsive to the difficulties involved in making distinctions between masculinity and femininity, Tennyson would right to the end of his career – and for reasons that require much greater exploration – find himself puzzling over how he might 'prize the soul where man and woman meet'. The line, which is taken from 'On One Who Affected an Effeminate Manner', strongly echoes a well-known passage from *The Princess* (1847) which speaks of how 'in the long years' ahead of us men and women must 'liker grow': 'The man be more of woman, she of man' (VII. ll.263–4). But this short lyric, dating from 1889, takes pains to restrict the amount of likeness that can be accommodated in this blending of sexual differences. Even though it is surely 'Nature's male and female plan' (l.3) to fuse man and woman together – as if, perhaps, to return to the primordial being that unifies the sexes in the *Symposium* itself or to the 'statelier Eden' mentioned in *The Princess* (VII. l.277) – Tennyson's speaker reproves the 'one who affected an effeminate manner' by telling him: 'friend, man-woman is not woman-man' (l.4). Bearing this declaration in mind, Christopher Ricks observes that in a late notebook Tennyson writes: 'Men should be an-drogynous and women gynandrous, but men should not be gynandrous nor women androgynous.'[15] Such complicated reasoning no doubt suggests the limits to which Tennyson could take his idealistic desire to mix masculine and feminine qualities. Just at the moment he appears to be blending, fusing, and dispensing with gender, he underwrites that very idea with a fixed polarity between the sexes. By 1889, the effeminate man could be seen to embody an androgynous ideal and yet instantly betray it by seeming to be womanly. In other words, an effeminate manner expresses for Tennyson an admirable desire for a change in – if not a unification of – masculinity and femininity, only to witness the immediate reinscription of gender difference itself. Whether we regard the current of feeling in 'On One Who Affected an Effeminate Manner' (1889), however, as radical or reactionary (and such judgements remain open, I think), one thing is for sure: this effeminate man is not in any respect explicitly homosexual, or even implicitly so.

The effeminate man was not the only figure to present an unwelcome challenge to a culture in which writers and intellectuals were seeking for new sexual identities, and the 'woman-man' – as Tennyson styled him – needs to be seen within a much larger context in which gender relations were transforming in the late nineteenth century. The reconfiguration of the effeminate man as a perceptibly deviant sexual type occurred at the same time as ideas of femininity were themselves undergoing radical change, as the sphere of literary production clearly attests. Just as the 'Uranian' poets fashioned their innovative, eminently Hellenic, poems on boy-love, so too were feminist writers seeking alternative models for sexual relations. The 1890s witnessed the emergence of a distinctive, if diverse, canon of feminist writing, featuring headstrong and independent-minded female protagonists whose apparently masculine attributes were often satirized in the press. This new female type was not just present in the works of identifiably feminist writers, such as George Egerton and Sarah Grand. In fact, she appeared in novels as generically and politically different as Thomas Hardy's *Jude the Obscure* (1896) and Bram Stoker's *Dracula* (1897), among many others. Aiming at higher education, professional status, free union (not marriage), and the suffrage, the 'New Woman' was frequently viewed by conservative commentators as a figure of improper female sexuality, whose assertiveness threatened to undermine her femininity altogether. Examining the main points emerging from the cluster of periodical articles on the remarkable impact of the 'New Woman', Ann Ardis observes that the 'question of where sexuality figures into the whole of human character is . . . one of the most significant issues to emerge in the debate on realism and representation in the New Woman novel'.[16] Kate Flint, considering similar materials, remarks that by the 1890s a signal change had occurred in the moral danger into which the young woman reader might be led when encountering the lives set out in these pioneering narratives of female autonomy. 'Earlier in the century', writes Flint, the

> dangerous frissons she might obtain from reading certain texts rendered her vulnerable at best to accusations of frivolity . . . But by the 1890s, these anxieties and prohibitions were directed towards, among other things, attempts to control her conscious *knowledge* of sexuality; her understanding of its threats, and its role within patriarchal society.[17]

It is exactly in this period, too, that a young woman who read widely might encounter an increasingly self-conscious style of lesbian writing – in the poetry of 'Michael Field', for example. But the lesbian, as Terry Castle has shown, enjoyed an alluring spectral presence in a host of literary writings that predate her sexological designation at the turn of the twentieth century, and well before she was condemned outright during the obscenity trial against Radclyffe Hall's *The Well of Loneliness* (1928).[18]

Such shifts in consciousness about sexuality itself may wrongly imply that effeminate behaviour was incontestably subversive in much the same manner as the 'New Woman' and the lesbian were perceived to be. But, as the present study shows, the homosexual man of letters who displayed effeminophilia was not necessarily a sexual radical when it came to his representation of femininity. Even if Wilde and Forster differed markedly in their apprehension of effeminacy, they tend to define their preoccupation with a dissident masculine style against an often aggressive and despicable contempt for women. It is as if femininity is thought to embody a disturbing force that threatens to emasculate their chosen path of effeminate homophile resistance to imperialist definitions of the male norm. Such speculations suggest that by the last decade of the nineteenth century there was something more than a dualistic war of the sexes taking place between men and women. Taken together, the effeminate man, the 'New Woman', and the still spectral (since underresearched) figure of the lesbian complicate the pattern of erotic identifications and gendered identities that we may all too readily absorb into a hetero-normative model of sexual relations, as Sandra M. Gilbert and Susan Gubar may be reasonably thought to have done in their detailed investigations into literary patterns during this era.[19]

One further point about the period after 1885 needs to be taken into account. My frequent recurrence to the notion of empire in this discussion should have made it clear that it is hard to consider the decisive remapping of sex, gender, and sexuality in this period without bearing in mind the power of the state and its promulgation of a hegemonic ideal of Englishness. In an essay that takes its cue from Richard Shannon's view that 'all the oldest traditions were invented in the last quarter of the nineteenth century', Philip Dodd remarks on how a public-school ethic of combative masculinity – often enshrined in the word manliness – pervaded not just the political arena but affected many areas of cultural life. Dodd cites an 1872 essay from the Oxford journal, *Dark Blue*, that upheld this type of manliness, arguing that 'a nation of effeminate enfeebled bookworms scarcely forms the most effective bulwark of a nation's liberties'.[20] Countless other examples could be rallied to show how a specific ideal of the Englishman was being pressed into the service of empire: a man who was dutiful, self-sacrificing, and willing to go to the ends of the earth in a spirit of patriotic zeal. He was supposed to be physically and morally robust, becoming the complete antithesis to the introspective weakling confined to the ivory tower. By the Edwardian period, as Forster's liberal narratives show, the

troubling 'enfeebled' masculinity associated with the scholarly man of letters had become a figure of such internalized self-loathing that his own
homophilia drove him to despise the effeminate aesthete in much the same
way as the imperialists would. The stigma attached to effeminacy has more
or less remained intact ever since.

There is no doubt that effeminacy remains a considerable source of pro-
vocation, not least to gay men. The signs of effeminate behaviour frequently
conform so assuredly to the negative queer stereotype that countless men-
loving men do their utmost to disavow it, presenting to one another a
'straight-acting' demeanour. Effeminacy, as Daniel R. Harris remarks, finds
very few supporters among the ranks of oppressed minorities:

> In a society whose body language consists of firm grips and steely
> gazes, the gestural iconoclasm of effeminacy, its unconventional
> moves, sounds, and expressions, has more than just private and indi-
> vidual consequences. One only has to look at the media to appreciate
> the extent to which the quavering contralto voice and its accompany-
> ing mannerisms have been purged from public view on the grounds
> they are untelegenic in comparison with the sanitized corporate physi-
> ques and monotonously melodic tenors and baritones of most news-
> casters. The media are allergic to effeminacy.[21]

On this note, Harris proceeds to argue that this mode of bodily comportment is so abhorred in contemporary society that few effeminate people
would dare to uphold it as a positive identity – even when it is patently
obvious that a man's gestures and tonal range of voice are operating in a
non-manly repertoire of styles. If one thing becomes plain in the chapters
below, it is that self-consciously effeminate men, such as Quentin Crisp, are
in fact in a distinct minority among male homosexuals. So troubling were
Crisp's outrageous affectations for the best part of his life that he was
ostracized by his own community – to the point of sensing that he could be
the object of nobody's love. On one of the few occasions when a man
approached him for sexual favours, he came to the acutely painful realization that he himself was the limit of this lover's degradation. Effeminacy,
then, bore such shame that even homosexual men were driven to distance
themselves from it at any cost.

In each of the following chapters, my aim is to demonstrate that
homoerotic writing after 1885 constantly defines itself against the predominant assumption that to be a man-loving man necessarily meant that one
was weakened, morally and physically, by the taint of effeminacy. In Chapter 1, we can clearly see how Wilde's emergence as a dandified critic of the
arts came to embody the kind of individualistic and anti-social, not to say
narcissistic, characteristics that would in the light of his humiliation in court
serve as a convenient representation of a repugnant otherness completely
alien to all that English society believed should constitute normative manly

behaviour. Wilde, however, was determined to defend his name against the libel of being a sodomite. He went to court having convinced his barrister that he was a wholly respectable married man, entirely untainted by the calumny made by the Marquess of Queensberry. Subsequent events would decisively polarize late-nineteenth-century understandings of manhood. If the trials prove anything, it is that effeminacy and empire at this point stood in violent opposition. But Wilde's position within a predominantly imperialist culture shows that his audiences were magnetized as much as they were offended by his unorthodox style of posing. He and his public were not always enemies. Although it is unquestionably clear that Wilde set out to poke fun at the sexual double standards of the English middle and upper classes, he necessarily thrived on the support of the men and women whose social attitudes he had no hesitation in deriding. My analysis of Wilde, therefore, indicates that his work is much more compromised than has been claimed by previous critics whose attention has turned to the homosexual polemic in his writing. In fact, the general direction of my chapter is to demonstrate that there is a striking fatalism in Wilde's work that constantly suggests that the society that stigmatized his same-sex desires would eventually do its worst to him. In this respect, his writings possess an uncanny prescience of his eventual fate in Reading Gaol. One can, I think, regard this aspect of his work as a sign of considerable foresight as well as an indication of an element of self-loathing, if not self-oppression. But whether we conclude that Wilde was either heroic or foolish in his entertainment of a homophobic public (and the temptation to moralize is provoked by the rather moralistic vein we find in his work), one point is clear. It was Wilde who became the most influential figure of a specific homosexual style that would prove to be the most significant point of definition for practically every man-loving male writer whose work went into print after his death.

For many homosexual English literary men belonging to the next generation, the slur against effeminate masculinity was taken seriously, often with damaging consequences. The influence of the Wildean dandy-aesthete would be wholeheartedly repelled by Forster, in a series of fictions written across a period of seven decades. Chapter 2 examines Forster's faltering attempts to present idealized forms of male–male desire in plots that had, as a matter of obligation, to take a repressively heterosexual form. Time and again, Forster strives to devise scenes in which intellectual and physical kinds of masculinity can be erotically connected. He envisages how the man of mind can raise his muscular partner to higher levels of spiritual dignity, while being virilized in the process from the thundering loins in which he finds his wilting frame entwined. The contours to this covert fantasy never ceased to follow the same pattern in Forster's obsessional canon of work. Even in old age he was dreaming of the virile coupling of males who – in a science fiction scenario – could produce babies of their own, ensuring that the human race would comprise male homosexuals and no one else. This imperialist – not to say deeply misogynistic – narrative reveals how agonizingly Forster's own negative perceptions of male homosexual desire were shaped by his envy of what he continued to regard as the beneficial reproductive power of heterosexuality. Indeed, the hetero-normative imperatives shaping Forster's idealizations of erotic love between men appear to exert their influence so strongly in his work because he expressed a widespread loathing of the effeminate aesthete iconized by Wilde.

But not everyone repudiated Wilde's legacy in this manner. Chapter 3 considers how Wilde's aesthetic was taken to its logical and most extreme consequences by Ronald Firbank, whose experimental and courageous queer modernism still remains largely unacknowledged to this day. It is my conviction that Firbank's unswerving commitment to effeminizing the novel provides one of the most significant literary protests against the punishments meted out against male homosexuality after 1885. Relishing frivolity, despising the earnest plotting of realist forms, Firbank's fiction brilliantly mocks the assumption that effeminacy can ever be taken in any respect lightly. He is a pre-eminent exponent of the type of camp aesthetic that has always been associated with Wilde and his heirs, and its critical edge makes for a parodistic style that seizes each and every opportunity to satirize English smugness, especially where self-satisfied bourgeois family values are concerned.

The final chapter, however, returns to the late nineteenth century to see how sexological discourse influenced the self-perceptions of male homosexuals who saw themselves as having a place within the dominant social structure. Beginning with John Addington Symonds's pathbreaking memoirs, this discussion compares his account of his masculine identity with three subsequent autobiographers – Ackerley, Jocelyn Brooke, and Crisp – who were at times equally at a loss to define their necessary homosexual difference from heterosexual men. These particular auto-biographical writings have been chosen, not only because they represent some of the most incisive works of homosexual self-examination from this period, but also because they enable us to chart discernible shifts and changes in male homosexual consciousness from the 1880s to the 1960s.

As this book reaches its close, it becomes plain that from the time of the Labouchere Amendment to the passing of the Sexual Offences Act, homophile writers were constantly aware that erotic interest between men may be subject to such contemptuous treatment precisely because it discloses many resemblances to the male homosocial world that feels so threatened by it. To conclude, I focus on some of the main developments in gay politics since 1967, showing that a major work of fiction written in the contempor-ary brutal epoch of AIDS – Alan Hollinghurst's *The Swimming-Pool Library* (1988) – bears witness to the end of a tradition of homoerotic writing, both effeminophilic and effeminophobic, that came into its own after 1885. Constantly alluding to the likes of Wilde, Firbank, and Forster, Hollinghurst's erudite novel pays a disturbing tribute to a queer tradition whose literary achievements have frequently been disavowed as a central component of an England that could not bear to see the homosexuality of some of the nation's greatest cultural practitioners ever be mentioned in print. The power of Hollinghurst's exceptional novel lies in how it examines the lives of two generations of men – whose experiences, taken together, span the best part of the twentieth century – in an era of sexual liberation in which unprotected sexual activity became extremely inadvisable. Tracing, much as the present book does, the patterns of English male homosexual identity after Wilde, *The Swimming-Pool Library* returns us to the now distant moment just before we knew the full implications of an epidemic which still displays no signs of ceasing to claim thousands upon thousands of lives.

Notes

1 Alan Sinfield, *The Wilde Century: Effeminacy, Oscar Wilde and the Queer Moment* (London, Cassell, 1994). It would have been difficult to complete the present study without having absorbed many of Sinfield's insights. It is interesting to note that his main point of argument, that effeminacy only became recognizably queer after the Wilde trials of 1895, parallels many of the points raised in Linda Dowling's recent work (*Hellenism and Homosexuality in Victorian Oxford* (Ithaca, NY, Cornell University Press, 1994). However, my own project differs from Sinfield's and Dowling's respective researches in many of its methods, materials, and assumptions. For one thing, the following chapters give priority to literary form and technique in mediating changing perceptions of homosexual identity in a culture that remains altogether less at ease than our Victorian predecessors were about effeminacy.

2 Mary Poovey, *Uneven Developments: The Ideological Work of Gender in Mid-Victorian Britain* (Chicago, IL, University of Chicago Press, 1988), p.3.

3 T.C. Worsley, *Flannelled Fool* (London, Alan Ross, 1967), pp.40–1, cited in Sinfield, *The Wilde Century*, p.134.

4 J.R. Ackerley, *My Father and Myself* (London, Pimlico, 1992), p.117. I discuss this episode in more detail in Chapter 4.

5 Michel Foucault, *The History of Sexuality: An Introduction*, trans. Robert Hurley (Harmondsworth, Penguin Books, 1981), p.43. See Jeffrey Weeks, *Sex, Politics and Society: The Regulation of Sexuality since 1800*, 2nd edn (London, Longman, 1988).

6 A short essay by Dowling should be mentioned here: 'Ruskin's Pied Beauty and the Constitution of a "Homosexual" Code', *Victorian Newsletter*, 75 (1989), pp.7–10. For the adaptation of classical sources to homoerotic ends in this period, see Richard Dellamora, *Masculine Desire: The Sexual Politics of Victorian Aestheticism* (Chapel Hill, NC, University of North Carolina Press, 1990).

7 Sinfield, p.27.

8 Dowling, 'Esthetes and Effeminati', *Raritan*, 12(3) (1993), p.56. This essay is reprinted in expanded form in *Hellenism and Homosexuality in Victorian Oxford*. My disagreements with some of the general statements made about Wilde in Dowling's study are raised in Chapter 1.

9 Dowling, *Hellenism and Homosexuality in Victorian Oxford*, p.152.

10 For critical revaluations of 'separate spheres' ideology, see Leonore Davidoff and Catherine Hall, *Family Fortunes: Men and Women of the English Middle Class 1780–1850* (London, Hutchinson, 1987), pp.340–2, and John Tosh, 'Domesticity and Manliness in the Victorian Middle Class: The Family of Edward White Benson', in John Tosh and Michael Roper (eds) *Manful Assertions: Masculinities in Britain since 1800* (London, Routledge, 1991), pp.44–73.

11 For details of the ongoing debates about the same-sex desires of Tennyson's poem, see Christopher Craft, ' "Descend and touch and enter": Tennyson's Strange Manner of Address', *Genders*, 1 (1988), pp.83–101; Richard Dellamora, *Masculine Desire*; and Sinfield, *Alfred Tennyson* (Oxford, Basil Blackwell, 1986), pp.113–53.

12 [Charles Kingsley], '*In Memoriam* and Earlier Works', *Fraser's*, 42 (1850), pp.245–55, reprinted in John D. Jump (ed.) *Tennyson: The Critical Heritage* (London, Routledge and Kegan Paul, 1967), p.183.

13 Dowling reads two of Tennyson's poems, 'The Charge of the Light Brigade' (1855) and *Maud* (1855), within the martial ethic propounded by the civic republican ideal, and which was by the mid-1850s looking antiquated; thus the term 'manhood', which recurs in *Maud*, needs to be placed in this context (*Hellenism and Homosexuality in Victorian Oxford*, pp.48–56). This reading is offered as a corrective to those interpretations emanating from an unsuspecting 'gender criticism' that employs modern notions of masculinity to identify specific sexual crises at work within the poem. I, for one, have sought to explain the embattled male identity of Tennyson's maddened protagonist largely in terms of differences between bourgeois and aristocratic models of manhood: 'Nation, Class, and Gender: Tennyson's *Maud* and War', *Genders*, 9 (1990), pp.93–111.

14 Quotations from Alfred Tennyson's works are taken from *The Poems of Tennyson*, ed. Christopher Ricks (London, Longman, 1969). All line references appear in parentheses.

15 Ricks, p.1424.

16 Ann Ardis, *New Women, New Novels: Feminism and Early Modernism* (New Brunswick, NJ, Rutgers University Press, 1990), p.50.

17 Kate Flint, *The Woman Reader: 1837–1914* (Oxford, Clarendon Press, 1993), p.315.

18 Terry Castle, 'A Polemical Introduction; or, The Ghost of Greta Garbo', in Terry Castle, *The Apparitional Lesbian: Female Homosexuality and Modern Culture* (New York, Columbia University Press, 1993), pp.1–20.

19 A similar criticism is raised by Ardis, *New Women, New Novels*, p.186. See Sandra M. Gilbert and Susan Gubar, *No Man's Land: The Place of the Woman Writer in the Twentieth Century – Volume 1: The War of the Sexes* (New Haven, CT, Yale University Press, 1987).

20 Philip Dodd is citing Richard Shannon, *The Crisis of Imperialism 1865–1915* (St. Albans, Paladin, 1976), pp.12–13, and J.A. Mangan, *Athleticism in the*

Victorian and Edwardian Public School: The Emergence and Consolidation of an Educational Ideology (Cambridge, Cambridge University Press, 1981), p.189; 'Englishness and National Culture', in Philip Dodd and Robert Colls (eds) *Englishness: Politics and Culture 1880–1920* (Beckenham, Croom Helm, 1986), p.5. On aspects of Victorian manliness, particularly in relation to 'boy's-own' fiction, see Joseph Bristow, *Empire Boys: Adventures in a Man's World* (London, HarperCollins Academic, 1991), especially Chapters 1–2.

21 Daniel R. Harris, 'Effeminacy', *Michigan Quarterly Review*, 30(1) (1991), pp.72–3.

1

Wilde's fatal effeminacy

There is something tragic about the enormous number of young men
there are in England at the present moment who start life with perfect
profiles, and end by adopting some useful profession.
(Oscar Wilde, 'Phrases and Philosophies
for the Use of the Young', 1894)

I

Standing in the dock at the Old Bailey in April 1895, Oscar Wilde made a
characteristic public display of his inimitable wit, a style upon which his
career had flourished for nearly 20 years. Under rigorous cross-
examination by Edward Carson, Wilde was asked whether he had 'ever
adored a young man madly'. 'No, not madly', Wilde incautiously replied.
'I prefer love', he added, 'that is a higher form.'[1] This rather mocking
answer is altogether less clever than it may at first appear. For in making
his denial, Wilde was also confessing to the very crime that led to the
second and then third humiliating trials brought by the Director of Public
Prosecutions against him. Sufficient evidence was collected to ensure that
Wilde was sent to jail for two years in solitary confinement with hard
labour. This was the maximum sentence according to the terms of the
notorious Labouchere Amendment to the 1885 Criminal Law Amendment Act which prohibited 'gross indecency' between males either in
public or in private. So omniscient was this law in its punitive gaze that
Wilde's amused response to Carson courted great danger. But it is not as if
Wilde was unconscious of how the law set out to condemn his sexual love
for other men. He knew only too well how the institutions of power in
England sought to regulate sexual acts, and how indeed the nation, if not
the empire, was in part built upon the criminalization of what was still not
widely categorized as homosexuality. Young men with good profiles
were certainly not expected to solicit another man's erotic gaze. The

country demanded instead that they set about doing useful kinds of work, like administering the colonies.

Yet the sentiments expressed in 'Phrases and Philosophies for the Use of the Young' were not necessarily seen as the work of an immoral corrupter of youth before the débâcle of 1895. The crucial point about the trials is that, for all his displays of unmanly behaviour, few of Wilde's contemporaries suspected that he harboured same-sex desires. In fact, his barrister, Edward Clarke, represented him on the grounds that there was no truth whatsoever in the claim made by the Marquess of Queensberry that Wilde had been 'posing Somdomite' (*sic*). Wilde, after all, was taking the Marquess to court for an infamously misspelled libel. Few thought that this action would fail. But it did. And its failure opened up a series of events that forged, for the first time, a highly influential connection between effeminacy and male homosexual desire, one that would provoke the most appalling forms of abuse.

Let me cite just one example. Writing in the years following his mental breakdown in 1909 (after a successful career as poet and essayist), Arthur Symons – whose name is often read as synonymous with literary decadence – recalled his abhorrence of the effeminate Wilde. There is no doubt that the frequent incoherence that we find in Symons's recollections of the 1890s is the result of an unbalanced mind. But that is not to say that we should dismiss the homophobic tirade that he aims against the man who was called 'the High Priest of the Decadents' in the hostile Tory press:[2]

Wilde's vices were not simply intellectual perversions, they were physiological. This miserable man had always been under the influence of one of those sexual inversions which turned him into a kind of Hermaphroditus. That distress which he tried to express in his writings after his condemnation had nothing virile in it; and his best known tragedy *Salomé* reveals in its perversion of a legend his own sexual perversion. As he grew older the womanish side of him grew more and more evident. Lautrec saw him in Paris, and in the appalling portrait of him he shows Wilde, swollen, puffed out, bloated and sinister. The form of the mouth which he gave him is more than any thing exceptional; no such mouth ought ever to have existed: it is a woman's that no man who is normal could ever have had. The face is bestial. A man with a ruined body and a ravaged mind and a senseless brain does not even survey the horror of this hideous countenance in a mirror: this thing that is no more a thing gazes into a void.[3]

This single paragraph of contemptuous loathing shows how troublingly Wilde had come to represent all that was sexually other to the so-called normal virile man. No other account of Wilde from the early twentieth century could make it plainer to see the horror of the effeminate invert – with his womanish demeanour reducing him to nothing less than an animal. Assuming a decisive link between intellectual perversion and physiological disfiguration, Symons is here joining the ranks of those theorists of degeneration who would view the sexual invert as a racially regressive being. On this view, such is Wilde's apparent identification with the maniacal femininity of his own creation in the play *Salomé* (1892) that it seems his literary labours made him more and more womanly. In the end, as the French painter famed for his posters featuring dancing-girls would reveal, Wilde was indisputably a pathological figure: the sexual criminal had transformed by degrees into something of a gothic spectre, implicitly like the protagonist of Wilde's only novel, Dorian Gray, looking at the hideous thing that his immorality has led him to become.

But this image of the perverted homosexual – when both words gained their pathological inflections – only emerged once the trials had run their course. In 1897, writing to the publisher Leonard Smithers, Wilde would comment how, now that he was released from Reading Gaol, his life could no longer 'be patched up'. 'There is doom on it', he wrote. 'Neither to myself, nor others, am I any longer a joy. I am now simply an ordinary pauper of a rather low order: the fact that I am also a pathological problem in the eyes of German scientists: and even in their works I am tabulated, and come under the law of averages! *Quantum mutatus!*'[4] The very thought of turning into an example of special interest to sexologists struck Wilde as ludicrous in the extreme. Yet his drastic transformation from a dandified art critic whose plays entertained thousands of theatre-goers to a debased pervert gathered such momentum in the late 1890s that there seemed no way of reversing the process. Had he been recognized as a sexual invert before his personal life was exposed in court, there is no way in which he would have begun his fatal legal proceedings against the Marquess of Queensberry.

Only during the trials, as Ed Cohen's impressive and detailed survey of the press reports reveals, did Wilde – a married man, father of two children, distinguished playwright and man of letters – come to be represented as a 'grotesque' figure of abomination who, in one offensive illustration, was depicted with 'ponderous lips, monstrous nose, and bloated cheeks', features which served to 'body forth the physical degeneration that such non-"manly" practices portend'. Amassing much evidence of this kind, Cohen reveals how the press represented the Marquess of Queensberry 'both verbally and graphically as incarnating "neutral" masculinity',[5] despite this aristocrat's reputation for ill-mannered behaviour at many public functions. To journalists this peer of the realm became an icon of a wholly respectable manhood. So strange did Wilde's masculinity emerge in the face of these vilificatory press reports that columnists could not bring themselves to name the specific acts of 'gross indecency' with which Wilde had been charged. That the sexual behaviour Wilde had enjoyed proved to be glaringly inexpressible by the press meant that his sexuality became all the more horrifying. To say the least, the very thought of unnameable acts of 'gross indecency' assuredly excited a prurient public that consumed a diet of increasingly scandalizing journalism. No wonder it subsequently proved difficult for Wilde's own name to be spoken in polite conversation. One anonymous writer, reminiscing about his Edwardian childhood, states that 'when Oscar Wilde was mentioned at the table he was damned'.[6]

In the light of such information, it is not surprising that many critics – especially those of us committed to an anti-homophobic politics – have viewed Wilde as the ultimate victim of a culture that had, for quite complicated reasons, become more and more intolerant of male sexual types whose very being was thought to undermine the moral fabric of society. 'The feared cross-over between discursive and sexual perversion, politics and perversion', writes Jonathan Dollimore, 'has sanctioned terrible brutalities against the homosexual.' Such fears – exemplified by Symons's virulent diatribe – enable us to 'see why Wilde was hated with such an intensity, even though he rarely advocated in his published writings any explicitly immoral practice'.[7] In many ways, Wilde served as a convenient focus for a series of anxious displacements and projections about masculinity that were beginning to escalate as sexuality itself became a discrete area of psychological and medical inquiry. The 1890s, as many commentators have shown, marked an era in which sexual desire looked increasingly anarchic, degenerate, and dangerous. Wilde's appearance in court crystallized many emerging fears of ungovernable and abnormal sexual varieties of person who would corrupt the nation. Given these circumstances, it would be easy to assume that Wilde was an entirely oppositional figure, one whose socialist politics, Irish national identity, and homosexuality – all prominent features of his dissidence – were entirely antithetical to the dominant order of the day.

But this chapter concerns a rather different, more compromised, aspect to Wilde's writing. I set out to show how and why the homoerotic inflection to much of his mature work is defined against – rather than flatly opposed to – a world governed by the kind of entrepreneurial and utilitarian form of manliness that was regarded as respectable, and which the pugilistic Queensberry (who, after all, devised the rules of modern boxing) would come to embody during the trials of 1895. Unquestionably, the fighting-fit athletic masculinity championed by the late Victorians is a sure sign of how far ascetic evangelism, stemming from Christian Socialism in the 1850s, shaped the precepts of ruling-class authority. No wonder that the last two decades of the nineteenth century struck Wilde, in *The Picture of Dorian Gray* (1890, revised 1891), as a place where 'the soul grows sick with longing for the things it has forbidden to itself, with desire for what its monstrous laws have made monstrous and unlawful'.[8] Aesthetics were being crushed by athletics, as young men put their energies into training for the empire, rather than posing – as does the eternally youthful Dorian Gray

– as a beautiful object whose perfect profile is ready to be transformed into an avowedly useless art (as Wilde insists in the preface to *Dorian Gray* (p.17), even if art is, at the same time, 'the only serious thing in the world' (p.1203)). If one point emerges clearly from so many of Wilde's sharp turns of phrase, it is his acute awareness that the dandified man of letters is likely to be defeated by the puritanical attitudes of late Victorian England that sought to transmogrify many a forbidden pleasure into a form of monstrosity. My attention to this prominent feature of his writings – which are doom-laden from the start – somewhat runs against Dowling's confident assertion that 'in the cultural moment before the Wilde disaster there was no implication of an impending doom, only the gradual emergence into visibility of a new system of values and attitudes, associated with a variety of movements in art and society, having in common their relation to the inchoate counterdiscourse of "homosexuality" '.[9] Much as I would like to believe, as Dowling does, that mid-Victorian liberalism provided the generous terms, if not the latitude, to accommodate transformations and subsequent eroticizations of the Oxonian homosocial context in which Wilde developed his aesthetics, his canon of writing – like the memoirs of John Addington Symonds – demands that we confront hostile forces that are indeed impending, and which were anticipated in plays, novels, and poems that regarded sexual desire between men as frustratingly inexpressible. The tide of Victorian masculinity had in any case long been turning against the Oxonian aestheticism in which Wilde was immersed during the 1870s.

In the face of what was a widespread public-school ideal of manhood – one that found its most powerful propaganda in a work such as Thomas Hughes's *Tom Brown's Schooldays* (1857)[10] and which had reached to the heart of many institutions – Wilde launched his career as a flamboyant art critic by adopting an outrageously effeminate manner that instantly caught the public's rapt attention. He named himself, within a matter of months of his first appearance, as the 'Professor of Aesthetics'. His chosen style was, in the late 1870s and early 1880s, a daring mode of self-exhibition, concerned not only with turning out phrases that were eminently quotable in their capacity to shock, but also in transgressing dress codes to stage an alluring form of spectacle. Max Nordau's influential attack on anti-social and genetically regressive types, *Degeneration*, gives a good summary of the cultural meanings with which Wilde's name had become associated by the mid-1890s, although these are not, we should note, viewed as homosexual. Nordau claimed that the aesthetes' 'predilection for strange costume' was a 'pathological aberration of racial instinct'.[11] Developing this eugenicist line of thought, Nordau would add that such behaviour was 'no indication of independence of character'; instead, it stemmed from 'a purely anti-socialistic, ego-maniacal recklessness and hysterical longing to make a sensation'. Nordau's polemic shows that Wilde was by far the most prominent of several *fin-de-siècle* artists who, according to George L. Mosse, were 'following their own reveries, withdrawing into a life of the senses, always in quest of artistic beauty'. The so-called 'decadents', whose work was characterized by a sensuous eroticism, were engaged, according to Mosse, in a form of 'passive protest' against an imperialist ethic that championed principles of duty, sacrifice, and self-sufficiency.[12] Mosse's comment accentuates an enduring difficulty in Wilde's artistic practice. The languid aesthete's political opposition to what he identified as the puritanical elements of late Victorian society hardly involved the revolutionary subversion of the dominant culture. In Wilde's hands, the aesthete – for all the controversy he aroused – became what I shall call an insider dissident: a figure who provoked the commonsensical mentality of bourgeois England by entertaining it from within its ranks.

But if such a tactic proved successful in terms of Wilde's career, this task was undertaken with not a small modicum of fear. The aesthete's decision to taunt a potentially hostile public's gaze meant that he had to negotiate forces that could all too easily spell his doom. And it was a doom that constantly allured Wilde, and which his work – right to the end – never hesitated to embrace. Even though Wilde's critique of an imperial England that would finally send him to jail is always charged by his memorable parodistic wit, the narrative shape he frequently gives to his work repeatedly tends towards fatalism. Tragedy, to be sure, is his enduring mode, and it often takes a moral – if not moralistic – turn. This feature comes out strongly in Wilde's prompt response to the scurrilous review of *Dorian Gray* that appeared in the *Scots Observer* in 1890, and which claimed that he was writing for 'outlawed noblemen and perverted telegraph-boys' (a thinly veiled allusion to the Cleveland Street affair of 1889, where young male workers at the Post Office made up extra cash by performing sexual favours for wealthy men).[13] In the face of such calumny, Wilde remarked: 'For if a work of art is rich, and vital, and complete, those who have artistic instincts will see its beauty, and those to whom ethics appeal more strongly than aesthetics will see its moral lesson.' It is not as if this fatal narrative of a young man with a beautiful profile dissents entirely from moral prescriptions. As Wilde stated in the same letter, many reviewers of the book believed he was a 'moral reformer'.[14] Such was the impact of this tragic tale.

This chapter reveals how and why Wilde took so many of his writings to their tragic limits. My discussion falls into three parts, each with the intention of examining what I call his fatal effeminacy. By focusing first of all on some of the main tropes of fatalism that recur in his writings, I then proceed to a sustained discussion of Wilde's most problematic masculine types: his effeminate dandies. Ostensibly figures whose well-turned maxims subvert the stuffy upper-class ethos in which they move, such men are often revealed as hardly heroic in their luxurious worlds. In fact, Wilde's dandiacal men – if at times approximating to a particular homosexual ideal of male vanity – are on several occasions shown to be ruthless philanderers who treat the women in their lives with appalling disrespect. Their mocking attitudes towards their own aristocratic world often appear to be no better than those apparently conventional male protagonists whose contemptible behaviour becomes clear as the plots of his Society comedies unfold. Having explored how and why Wilde's witty dandies do not necessarily embody a political or sexual ideal, I move on to examine the plangent and maudlin notes of tragedy that sound throughout many of Wilde's best-known works, including those with a clear homophile inflection, such as 'The Portrait of Mr W.H.' (first published in 1889). By the time we arrive at *The Ballad of Reading Gaol* (1898), it becomes clear that the doom-laden mottoes that resonate so memorably from that poem do not mark a major transition in Wilde's dominant modes of thought. Instead, by the end of his career, we begin to see that the refrain declaring that 'Each man kills the thing he loves' has the resonance of a troubling wishfulfilment.

II

Nearly all of Wilde's writings and essays engage with doom or fate, often of the most unlikely kinds in the least plausible conditions. One only has to look at the plotting of *The Importance of Being Earnest* (1895) to see how an interest in predestinarian forces shapes what is structurally a quite conventional farce. *The Picture of Dorian Gray* stands as the work which most obviously displays his perennial anxiety that the Hellenic ideal enshrined in a boy with consumingly beautiful looks must, in the end, face inescapable tragedy. It could be said, then, that the trials that led to Wilde's imprisonment uncannily enacted the fatalistic narrative structure that even casts its shadow across his comedies. Lest there be any misunderstanding, I am not claiming that the trials should be interpreted as the fulfilment of prophecies laid down in works whose strong sense of foreboding can hardly pass our notice. Instead, the trials throw into sharp relief a knowledge about the violent interdiction against homosexual desire that provides one of the predominant figurations in Wilde's aesthetics. Those who transgress, in Wilde's art, are at the mercy of a higher unassailable law.

But that is not to say that his work is wilfully self-negating in the face of such fatalistic forces. The point is that he seeks to subvert the dominant order fully aware that systems of bourgeois authority will, ultimately, maintain their hegemony. One memorable biographical incident persuades us to this view. Undoubtedly, Wilde allowed himself to go through the second and third trials when the opportunity to leave the country was his for the taking, as W.B. Yeats observed in his memoir of these events.[15] He could have deserted England for Paris, as his lover Lord Alfred Douglas had done. Instead, Wilde waited at the Cadogan Hotel for the police to arrest him.

John Betjeman's poem on this episode captures the popular image of Wilde as the dandified aesthete who

> . . . sipped at a weak hock and seltzer
> As he gazed at the London skies
> Through the Nottingham Lace of the curtains
> Or was it his bees-winged eyes?[16]

Although some may argue that Wilde's decision to face another gruelling interrogation in court indicates that he was determined to see if he could honourably defend his reputation, and so emerge from the proceedings as any gentleman would have wished, he had already experienced sufficient intimidation from the press for him to know that to remain in London was singularly unwise. Like a tragic hero, however, he went to meet his fate. 'I shall stay', he informed Robert Ross, 'and do my sentence whatever it is.'[17] 'To have altered my life', he declared after his release from prison, 'would have been to have admitted that Uranian [i.e. homosexual] love is ignoble. I hold it to be noble – more noble than other forms.'[18] Such a defence of homosexual superiority – its 'higher' form, not its degenerate status – simply could not pass muster with the English judiciary.

Given the abuse that Wilde experienced from each and every quarter of English society in 1895, it is not surprising that he casts himself into a tragic mould throughout *De Profundis*, the title posthumously given to the letter he addressed to Douglas from his prison cell after he had pleaded for months with the Home Office for books and writing materials. 'I blame myself,' he tells Douglas, 'for the entire ethical degradation I allowed you to bring on me' (p.877). This statement, typifying much of the remorseful stance adopted in this long recriminatory document, shows exactly how determined Wilde was to fashion himself as a man who had consented to his own ruin. But, in fact, the whole trajectory of this epistle has a striking continuity with his earlier work, not least in the innumerable phrases it recycles from his established canon. It is as if his life has become one of the scripts he has already written, and in this drama of his own making he takes centre stage to contemplate his grisly predicament. In the opening paragraphs of this letter, he refers to the four years he had spent with Douglas as 'Our ill-fated and most lamentable friendship' (p.873). Later, he remarks that, even as 'the Fates were weaving into one scarlet pattern the threads of our divided lives', he never the less knew that Douglas 'really loved' him (p.893). This truth can be told all the more surely since, Wilde claims, Douglas had also suffered 'a terrible tragedy' in his life (p.893). As the tone of this anguished item of correspondence becomes more and more sentimental – squeamishly so, as Eve Kosofsky Sedgwick puts it[19] – Wilde adopts the voice of the hero laid low in an extravagant rhetoric that is assuredly theatrical. Praising Ross's loyalty, Wilde observes that his devoted friend's letters have been a source of consolation – 'little messages between me and the beautiful unreal world of Art' – since they are reminders of his former glory where once he 'was King, and would have remained King' (p.909). Yet, as he states earlier, the 'gods are strange'. Ushered into a narrative almost as relentless as *Oedipus Rex*, he experiences a moment of revelation when confronting these punitive deities: 'They bring us ruin through what in us is good, gentle, humane, loving' (p.889). His ruin, he adds, is not 'Destiny merely, but' – and the word vibrates with agony – 'Doom' (p.889).

Wilde's sustained account of his own downfall, however, does not draw exclusively on Greek tragedy. Other universal laws define the fated pattern of his life. Haunting his narrative as well is the biblical lesson of the Fall. Like Adam tempted by Eve, he regrets how he let himself be 'lured into the imperfect world of coarse uncompleted passions, of appetite without distinction, desire without limit, and formless greed' (p.909). This Christian notion of sin plagued his imagination, and often it would consort with the unpredictable wrath of the classical gods when one of his famous aphorisms was taking shape. Lord Henry, for example, advises his protégé, Dorian Gray, that the 'only way to get rid of a temptation is to yield to it' (p.29). So far it should be clear that these classical and Christian forms of authority provide some of Wilde's main narrative tropes, and these repeat – like so many of his aphorisms – from one text to another. In fact, the biblical Fall and classical tragedy do not just impose a fatalistic power over the shape of his writing, they also set an intellectual limit on it. 'I thought life was going to be a brilliant comedy', he tells Douglas, 'and that you were to be one of many graceful figures in it. I found it to be a revolting and repellent tragedy' (p.892). Such pat phrasing shows how Wilde structures his vision of life in a bleakly dualistic fashion, and it makes for a type of absolutism in his fiction, essays, and drama. Little wonder, then, that Dorian Gray maintains his youthful beauty as long as his hidden portrait grows increasingly corrupt. The superficial comedy of the one implies the gruesome tragedy of the other. And while Dorian, like Jack and Algernon in *Earnest*, yields to the temptations offered by many an unnamed pleasure, the beautiful boy turns into a homicide, while the hedonistic bachelors meet their fates as conventional married men. This is surely the serious outcome to this most trivial of comedies – as suggested by the subtitle to *Earnest*, *A Trivial Comedy for Serious People*.

Such observations surely imply that some caution needs to be exercised when estimating the radicalism of Wilde's writings. Before claiming that Wilde's career was one of ceaseless experimentation and transgression – particularly where the emergence of a homosexual tradition of writing is concerned – it has to be remembered that nearly everything he wrote and said was set within the very terms, genres, and grammar that he desired to contest. His work is structurally much more orthodox than we might at first assume. As Josephine Guy points out, it is confoundingly 'difficult to find evidence of formal innovation in Wilde's work'. 'His writing', adds

Guy, 'is too derivative, too free in the formal conventions it borrows' for any reasonable claim to be made for his originality.[20] This point becomes most clear when we bear in mind Wilde's innumerable and often unacknowledged borrowings from other sources. Even the briefest of comparisons make it clear that *Dorian Gray* draws very fully upon Joris-Karl Huysmans's *A Rebours* (1884) (notably in Chapter 11),[21] and that the Society comedies take many of their dramatic features from contemporary plays in the West End. Kerry Powell, who has conducted painstaking research into the writer's use and abuse of dramatic precedents, remarks: 'What we sometimes assume to be Wilde's voice *par excellence* is really that of another, lost to memory, speaking through him.'[22] If subversive wit was one of Wilde's distinctive textual strategies, so too was plagiary. Ian Small observes that Wilde's essay, 'Pen, Pencil, and Poison' (1889), lifts whole sections of other authors' accounts of the Regency poisoner, Thomas Griffith Wainewright.[23] In any case, stealing of this kind had been something of a notorious habit with Wilde for many years. The painter, James Abbott McNeill Whistler, was among the first who loudly complained that the young Wilde, propounding his theories of art in fashionable company, had brazenly stolen his own catchphrases.

Yet this snatching away of his contemporaries' property is double-edged. If looking at times unashamedly derivative, Wilde's plagiarisms are a significant sign of his outlawry, especially in a literary culture that was placing increasing emphasis on the sanctity of copyright. Forgeries and fakes were carried out in the spirit of individualism: the term he used in his utopian treatise, 'The Soul of Man under Socialism' (1890), to champion the significance of self-development for each and every person in a non-authoritarian system of social relations. What he stole from others was offered back to the public as a unique gift on which his extraordinary identity had been stamped. Everywhere we look in Wilde's canon of writing there is this often confusing mixture of conformity and insubordination. This characteristic double movement shows how he worked both within and against the society in which he fashioned his career. In making this point, I am not suggesting that there was a free space in which he could have invented utopian ideals fed by republican fervour and homophile politics. (His socialist contemporaries, such as Edward Carpenter, were none the less engaged in ambitious projects to create visions of an altogether more egalitarian England outside the metropolitan centre that Wilde inhabited.) It is simply to claim that any analysis of his writings needs to bear in mind this contradictory pattern of his readiness to exploit and antagonize English cultural conventions.

His parodistic critiques of the prosaic English imagination that enshrines its moral values in worn-out proverbs are not solely the province of the dandy-aesthete. Given the recent critical interest in the radicalism of Wilde's sexual politics, perhaps one of the less obvious aspects of Wilde's

career that accentuates this divided and ambivalent stance towards the
fashionable world in which he developed his art concerns his Irishness. In
writing that the 'English are always degrading truths into facts' (p.1203),
Wilde was largely speaking from the perspective of a colonized and subju-
gated culture. Like the young Stephen Dedalus contemplating Shakespeare
in James Joyce's *A Portrait of the Artist as a Young Man* (1914–15), Wilde
knew what it meant to be cast 'in the shadow of his language'.[24] Few of his
contemporaries picked up on this specific angle to his assault on English
values. It would take an Irish writer such as George Bernard Shaw, when
reviewing *An Ideal Husband*, to claim that Wilde 'plays with everything:
with wit, with philosophy, with drama, with actors and audience, with the
whole theatre'. Such playfulness, argues Shaw, is the surest sign of Wilde's
Irishness. 'Ireland', he claims, 'is of all countries the most foreign to England.'[25] Considering his place as an Anglo-Irish writer who, like Joyce, saw
how the experience of colonization resulted in a wholehearted rejection of
the manly imperial ideal, Declan Kiberd draws attention to the 'extraordinary feelings of jeopardy and threat evoked for British playgoers and readers
by the womanly men of Wilde and Joyce'.[26] This is not to argue that
Leopold Bloom, Joyce's chief protagonist in *Ulysses* (1922), falls into the
tradition of the dandiacal man who absorbed Wilde's attention. It is instead
to show that Anglo-Irish writers working at the time of the nationalist
movements made an important political response to militarist authority by
frequently feminizing their male figures. What is more, according to Kiberd, such potentially androgynous beings had the capacity for liberatory
self-invention. Effeminacy, then, was in Wilde's hands partly shaped by his
own distinctive republican concerns, ones that recognized that the Irish
critic of art would fly in the face of the jingoistic triumphs of empire. But
that should not encourage us to disregard the fact that like the gods, the
empire maintained its own punishing system of authority, not least when it
came to legislating against male homoeroticism. Wilde's writings, however,
provide no visionary alternatives for his effeminate men to transform the
upper-class ethos upon which their wit thrives. So, in a general sense,
Wilde strove to amuse the English, just as much as he wished in the process
to prove that – as Gilbert puts it in 'The Critic as Artist' (1890) – 'the
English mind is always in a rage' (p.1057). Terry Eagleton makes very
much the same point when he writes that

> If [Wilde's] concern with rhetoric, humour, self-irony, the mask,
> theatrical display are at one level the fruits of an Irish lineage at odds
> with middle-class English moralism, they are also preoccupations that
> can play straight into the hands of the English aristocracy.[27]

Wilde's fatalism suggests that this is indeed the case.

So great was the shaping spirit of fate in Wilde's aesthetics that on occasions he took to a comic defence against its all-consuming power. In 'Lord

Arthur Savile's Crime' (1887), for example, the protagonist discovers from a
'chiromantist' that the lines on his palm reveal that he shall shortly commit a
murder. His plight is the selfsame one into which Wilde would cast himself
in *De Profundis*. There Wilde repented for indulging in 'feasting with pan-
thers' (p.938), before proceeding to recycle sections of 'Lord Arthur Savile's
Crime' so that he could blame the gods for his downfall. Lord Arthur is
among several of the many vulnerable young men of Wilde's invention
whose 'beautiful boyish insouciance' immediately indicates that he will be
defeated by powers beyond his control. Having learned that he shall commit
a violent crime, Lord Arthur 'for the first time' becomes 'conscious of the
terrible mystery of Destiny, the awful meaning of Doom' (p.173). So he
decides to act upon this situation by poisoning a maiden aunt. The amusing
ruse of this story is that Lord Arthur is foiled in this and later attempts at
murder. For exactly the same thing happens when he arranges for a bomb to
be sent to his uncle. Utterly despairing of his inability to commit the predicted crime, he finds himself wandering along the Thames Embankment.
And it is there that he sees, for the first time, his true victim. It is no less than
Mr Podgers, the palm-reader himself, whom Lord Arthur promptly drowns.
'For the next few days', we are told, 'he alternated between hope and fear.
There were moments when he almost expected Mr Podgers to walk into the
room, and yet at other times he felt that fate could not be so unjust to him'
(p.190). The gods happily do not send him to his own grave, since he was
their instrument, not their object. Although there is a comic outcome,
predestination has managed to work its narrative magic upon him.

Just as intriguing in its ironic manipulation of fatalism is *Earnest*. Here
both the young dandies, Jack Worthing and Algernon Moncrieff, at different times and for different reasons, adopt the imaginary identity of
'Ernest'. Like Lord Arthur, they try to control their destinies, each using
the alibi of 'Ernest' as a ploy to obtain what they want. For Jack, 'Ernest'
enables him to live another life in the city, far from the claims of his
dependants at his country estate. As he reveals to Algernon, 'my name is
Ernest in town and Jack in the country' (p.325). His excuse for his innumerable visits to the city involves going to see his 'wicked' brother Ernest
whom no one in Hertfordshire has ever met (p.343). Algernon, meanwhile, plays a practical joke upon his friend by arriving at Jack's country
seat as no less than the dissolute 'Ernest' himself. Little does Algernon
realize that, in taking up this imaginary identity, he is already in another
implausible plot, one devised by Cecily Cardew, Jack's ward of court. In
this dramatic universe, everyone is making up their own fictional narratives, from a three-volume novel to the story of the Brighton Line. So it is
not surprising that the thought of Uncle Jack's 'wicked brother' has made
Cecily focus all her romantic energies upon him – even to the point of
writing the scripts of their love-letters. And if the fatefulness involved in the
writing of romantic plots were not sufficiently made clear by Cecily's

invented correspondence with 'Ernest', then there is another entangled tale. With all the implausibility of a sensation novel from the 1860s we discover how Miss Prism was so obsessed with the manuscript of her three-decker novel that she accidentally put the baby in the handbag that ended up on the train that was bound for the seaside resort that – in this breathless chain of events – gave Jack his adoptive name.

Jack's and Algernon's respective fates become almost symmetrical once the plot – which is several plots, each one fatalistically entrammelling the other – hurtles towards the final dénouement where the story of Miss Prism's handbag testifies to Jack's true origins. He is, after all, Ernest Moncrieff, and the revelation inspires this spirited remark: 'it is a terrible thing for a man to find out suddenly that all his life he has been speaking nothing but the truth' (p.383). The upshot of the comedy is that the part he has been acting is in fact the one into which he was cast at birth. But rather than make a tragedy of this almost Oedipal plight, Wilde lightheartedly teases his audience with the brilliant technical device – the blatant pun on e(a)rnest – that enables these young men's 'double life' to fall into an aesthetically satisfying shape.

Yet there is more to this pun than the fatalism that makes the once feigned 'Ernest' the man he truly is in 'E(a)rnest'. As the subtitle to the play reveals, this *'Trivial Comedy for Serious People'* is operating at two reversible levels where fatalistic emplotment is constantly being exposed as a sham. The plot alone demonstrates that this is a comedy shaped by tragedy, and that the gods bear the heaviest of burdens upon the homoerotic interests that this play is trying to disclose. For what Wilde was seeking in this, his last and most significant drama, was a form that could articulate, as legit-imately as possible, same-sex desire. Timothy d'Arch Smith has pointed out how 'earnest' served as a codeword for homosexual among the 'Uranian' poets who belonged to the subculture in which Wilde moved. Even if this deceitful piece of word-play eluded the large majority of Wilde's contem-poraries (to the degree that some critics believe that this 'Uranian' pun may not have been known to Wilde himself),[28] the comedy is full of sexual innuendoes. Food, from cucumbers to crumpets, signals the most erotic of appetites. Yet several of these jokes come close to making the homosexual inflections of the drama more than a little obvious. Addressing Cecily Cardew, Gwendolen Fairfax – the object of Algernon's fated affections – makes the following telltale remark:

> The home seems to me to be the proper sphere for the man. And certainly once a man begins to neglect his domestic duties he becomes painfully effeminate, does he not? And I don't like that. It makes men so very attractive. (p.362)

Exploiting his well-tried technique of reversing received opinions, Wilde is using Gwendolen to underscore two points about Victorian ideals of manhood, and both play with the idea of effeminacy that roused his public to either applause or censure. In making the home the 'proper sphere' for men, Gwendolen is turning the Victorian doctrine of 'separate spheres' for the sexes on its head. But in her second sentence, Gwendolen's delight in the man who neglects his duties reveals that the respectable individual had become altogether too domesticated. The most attractive man, on the basis of these finely turned phrases, exists outside the home in all his 'effeminate' glory. Yet, as Wilde's manipulation of the effeminate dandy reveals, there is not necessarily an escape from the social pressure to conform to proper codes of masculine behaviour. Let us look, then, at Wilde's manipulation of his dandiacal style of wit, first in person, and then in a number of his narcissistic personas.

III

On 20 February 1892, after the curtain had dropped on the final act of *Lady Windermere's Fan*, Wilde presented himself before his audience to make some characteristically witty remarks on what had been a highly successful opening night:

> Ladies and gentlemen: I have injoyed [*sic*] this evening *immensely*. The actors have given a charming rendering of a *delightful* play, and your appreciation has been *most* intelligent. I congratulate you on the *great* success of your performance, which persuades me that you think *almost* as highly of the play as I do myself.[29]

According to the painter, Louise Jopling, the comedy was indeed 'gorgeously put on stage, and splendidly acted'.[30] More memorable still was the pose that Wilde struck when addressing his enthusiastic playgoers. He delivered his short and amusingly condescending speech while smoking a cigarette. Jopling observes that, at the time, Wilde's 'smoking of the cigarette was put down to a deliberate insult', although she herself attributes Wilde's behaviour to 'sheer nervousness'. Smoking in such a public manner, to be sure, caused several influential members of the audience considerable offence. The arch-conservative critic, Clement Scott, in a review published in the *Illustrated London News*, regarded Wilde's gesture as a complete affront to good manners. Imagining Wilde turning over in his mind how he might test the limits of propriety, Scott puts these arrogant words into the playwright's mouth: 'The society that allows boys to puff cigarette-smoke into the faces of ladies in theatre-corridors will condone the originality of a smoking author on the stage.'[31]

An increasingly fashionable item, the cigarette by the 1890s was superseding the hand-rolled cigar and the working-class clay pipe. In *Dorian Gray*, it features as a sure sign of aesthetic indulgence. Informing the painter, Basil Hallward, that he must not light a cigar, Lord Henry Wotton insists that he should smoke a cigarette. 'A cigarette', remarks Lord Henry, 'is a perfect pleasure. It is exquisite and leaves one unsatisfied' (p.70). No sooner has Lord Henry spoken these words than he assures Dorian Gray of the hedonism represented by the cigarette-smoking man. 'I represent to you', he says, 'all the sins you have never had the courage to commit' (p.70). Set alongside Scott's indignation at Wilde's public behaviour, Lord Henry's remarks suggest that these recently machine-rolled items were the focus of an unsettling shared interest in unrespectability among those who belonged to different classes. On his opening night, Wilde appears to be adopting the vulgar discourtesies of young men who engaged in rituals of resistance against those who wanted them kept at a safe distance. And it is doubtless the case that the hostility Wilde aroused on this occasion related to wider anxieties about the social and moral standards set by the theatre as a whole. As John Stokes has shown, the music-halls had gained greatest notoriety in the mid-1890s for allowing an undesirable traffic between respectable and unrespectable types, and it was in places such as the Empire in Leicester Square that people of a great diversity of social classes could mix.[32] In *Earnest*, Jack and Algernon promise to indulge their life of un-named pleasures by considering a ten o'clock visit to the Empire (p.337). So intolerable was the situation at these kinds of theatre that purity cam-paigners such as Mrs Ormiston Chant petitioned for their closure. In Scott's eyes, Wilde's flagrant lack of decorum no doubt suggested that the middle-class St James's Theatre might be heading in the same direction. Blowing smoke in the public's face simply served to compound Scott's distaste for what had been a despicable drama, one that displayed a wholly con-temptuous attitude towards 'that holiest and purest instinct with women': motherhood. Not only had Wilde presented himself before the public as no man of his class should have done, he had also produced a comedy in which it was acceptable for a young wife to desert her newly-born child and rush into the arms of a '*roué* admirer' because 'she has learned from the tittle-tattle of her friends that her husband has been false to her'. No doubt Lady Windermere struck him as repugnant as Nora in *A Doll's House* by Henrik Ibsen. In his review of the English production in 1889, Scott condemned Nora for 'doing a thing that one of the lower animals would not do'.[33]

A month after *Lady Windermere's Fan* had opened, *Punch* took the oppor-tunity to lampoon Wilde's outrageous act of smoking in the public's face. Representing him in a manner similar to that of Jellaby Postlethwaite – the so-called 'Professor of Aesthetics' created by George du Maurier in the 1880s – the playwright in this 'Fancy Portrait' by Bernard Partridge is depicted in a languid pose, leaning against a pillar (see Figure 1). At his feet lies a toppled statue of the Bard, set next to an open box of cigarettes. Rising above the author's head are three 'puffs' of smoke, each one making a neat pun that satirizes Wilde's reputation for arousing the unwarranted

QUITE TOO-TOO PUFFICKLY PRECIOUS!!

Being Lady Windy-mère's Fan-cy Portrait of the new dramatic author,
Shakspeare Sheridan Oscar Puff, Esq.

["He addressed from the stage a public audience, mostly composed of ladies, pressing between his daintily-gloved fingers a still burning and half-smoked cigarette."—*Daily Telegraph.*]

Figure 1 Bernard Partridge, 'Fancy Portrait', *Punch* 1892

enthusiasm of his audience – here pictured as nothing more than the puppets, as Wilde had called them in the letter he published in the *Daily Telegraph*. This remark would prompt Charles Brookfield and J.M. Glover to stage a satire of Wilde entitled *The Poet and the Puppets* (1892). In Partridge's picture, underneath a caption imitating Wilde's camp style with the words 'Quite Too-Too Puffickly Precious', there is a short extract from a review in the *Daily Telegraph* drawing attention to the way in which 'his daintily-gloved fingers' held 'a still burning and half-smoked cigarette'. Like those illustrations by du Maurier that chide the arrogance of aesthetes such as Wilde, this 'Fancy Portrait' attacks the arrogance of a self-styled demi-god who exhibits a dandiacal narcissism that shows complete contempt for anyone but himself. Here he is indisputably the ego-maniac later to be despised by Nordau.

But if Wilde was incensing some sections of the theatrical establishment with his elegantly mocking pose of superiority, he won in equal proportions a great many admirers. A.B. Walkley, one of the most enlightened late Victorian drama critics, was only too aware that *Lady Windermere's Fan* drew many of its incidents from 'half a dozen familiar French plays'. He observed that 'its plot is always thin, often stale; indeed, it is full of faults'. Yet, in spite of his reservations, Walkley claimed that what distinguished Wilde's play from its contemporaries was its 'sparkling dialogue'.[34] This quality alone drew the crowds, breaking with the rather predictable exchanges that take the equally popular plays of Arthur Wing Pinero and Henry Arthur Jones to melodramatic fever pitch. Even if this comedy is not particularly 'good', argues Walkley, it is at least 'diverting'.

Three years later, Ada Leverson attended the premiere of *Earnest* on 14 February 1895. In her memoirs, Leverson recalls the air of anticipation among a 'rippling, glittering, chattering crowd'. Even if the play were to have unexpectedly failed to amuse them, she says, the audience could rest assured that the author was bound to make his mark during the evening's entertainment. 'Would he', Leverson remembers them asking, 'perhaps walk on after the play smoking a cigarette, with a green carnation blooming in his coat' or 'would he bow from a box and state in clear tones, heard all over the theatre, that Mr Wilde was not in the house?'[35] By this time Wilde was not just an author but also an integral part of the performance. Indeed, his whole reputation dating from the late 1870s, when he entered fashionable society as the chief protagonist of the 'Aesthetic Movement', was based on the idea of the male critic as an artist in his own right. This doctrine would come into its own in 'The Critic as Artist' where Gilbert insists that 'the highest Criticism, being the purest form of personal impression, is in its way more creative than creation' (p.1027). When Wilde's comedies were staged in the early 1890s, he accomplished yet another categorical shift, making the dramatist into a performer. Endlessly promoting his spectacular personality, Wilde brought about a signal change in the relations between the artist and his audience. No longer was the artist the producer of culture, he was now an embodiment of it. In other words, he became the artwork while art itself, like the writings of the Bard, toppled over at his feet.

Wilde's calculated self-exhibition, however, had a much wider aim than simply drawing attention to his superiority to those he entertained. He was, as Scott observes, involved in gaining the admiration of a society whose values he never ceased to mock, often at the expense of his observers. Nothing was more to the point in this respect than the buttonhole Wilde wore while smoking in front of his audience in 1892. Although Scott was infuriated by the cigarette, he makes no mention of the green carnation, which a number of Wilde's associates sported on their lapels on the opening night. This is not so unexpected given that this unnaturally coloured bloom was, so the legend goes, the secret symbol of Parisian homosexuals.[36] Most spectators probably viewed this flower as yet another 'aesthetic' eccentricity, since Wilde had worn lilies and sunflowers ostentatiously when dressing up for the fashionable circles he moved in during the 1880s. Lillie Langtry, the famous actress, remembers Wilde's appearance at the opening night of one of his plays (she does not specify which one); he was 'wearing a black velvet jacket, a white straw hat in one hand and a lighted cigarette in the other'.[37] There are several similar accounts of Wilde's couture. Although it is common for critics to claim that Wilde's dress sense transformed from the unconventional exhibitionism of his early career to gentlemanly sobriety when his work reached the height of its popularity, descriptions such as Langtry's show that, right up until the time of the trials in 1895, Wilde did not present himself on important occasions in clothes that would allow him to pass as an ordinary man. Even when he had been embraced by the establishment, he remained a poser – true to the Delsartean tradition on which, according to Moe Meyer, he modelled his public persona.[38]

Ada Leverson, recalling Wilde's appearance at the close of *Lady Windermere's Fan*, states that 'he was dressed with elaborate dandyism and a sort of florid sobriety'. Like Langtry, she itemizes his garments, but draws attention to different details:

> His coat had a black velvet collar. He held white gloves in his small pointed hands. On one finger he wore a large scarab ring. A green carnation – echo in colour of the ring – bloomed savagely in his buttonhole, and a large bunch of seals on a black moiré ribbon watch chain hung from his white waistcoat. This costume, which on another man might have appeared perilously like fancy dress, seemed perfectly to suit him; he seemed at ease and to have a great look of the first gentleman in Europe.[39]

If Leverson's judgement that Wilde appeared like 'the first gentleman of Europe' is anything to go by (this was, in fact, the sobriquet given to the

Prince Regent in the 1810s), then it would appear that Wilde's distinctive style involved taking a given form (such as comedy) and a given style (that of the gentleman) and renovating them. His ability to make exceptionally familiar things seem new depends on an aesthetics that is unavoidably vicarious. Sedgwick identifies this 'vicariating' impulse as a part of a sentimentalizing of the male body that underpins Wilde's homoerotic project.[40] This is a useful formulation for comprehending Wilde's late Victorian adaptation of a dandiacal style both in person and in writing. His work, argues Sedgwick, engages with a campness and an archness that ridicule the moral codes of respectable Victorian masculinity. These obviously theatricalizing aspects of Wilde's life and *oeuvre* served to question the founding categories in which the late bourgeois sphere understood the organization of gender. Appearing before his public, with all the appurtenances of the modern dandy, Wilde drove at the heart of the multiple denials and disavowals upon which respectable society was built. If too excessively dressed to be a gentleman, he none the less had the ingenuity to look like the only one in the house, reminding everybody else of their ordinariness.

Yet, as the outrage that always attended Wilde's career makes perfectly clear — most vividly, of course, in the trials of 1895 — his position as a mocking dandy was a hazardous one to maintain. In making himself so original, Wilde worked in perilous proximity to those conformists who so brutally accomplished his downfall. For not only did Wilde deride respectable society, he also needed its support to underwrite his success. In many respects, his performances in person and in print bear all the hallmarks of the endangered parodist, since parody was, by and large, Wilde's intellectual mode. Through a suave and incisive manipulation of proverbial sayings, he turned innumerable platitudes on their heads to lay bare the spurious assumptions upon which accepted moral wisdom was based. The most striking lines from his fiction, essays, and plays all adopt this parodic attitude. 'Only the shallow know themselves' and 'Industry is the root of all ugliness' are two of the more obvious 'Phrases and Philosophies for the Use of the Young' that exemplify a technique in rhetorical legerdemain that repeats throughout his *oeuvre*.

Nothing could bear out his distinctive dandiacal style more than his closing remarks to his audience in 1892 where he turns back their flattery upon themselves: 'I congratulate you on the *great* success of your performance.' Reversing roles, Wilde takes himself the customary voice of his appreciative theatregoers, making them realize that they too are also performers, ones who rarely see how they are acting out already scripted parts. 'Being natural', as we are told in *Dorian Gray*, 'is simply a pose' (p.20). Yet the denaturalizing poses that Wilde struck as an unrivalled parodist proved to be far less durable than one might be led to believe, particularly by those critics who view Wilde as a precursor of postmodern thought. When his

pithy maxims, which brilliantly derided middle-class pieties, were set before him in the Old Bailey as evidence of his immorality, his ability to
sustain his parodic style suffered immeasurable strain. A substantial difficulty
for Wilde was that the pose he developed in the early 1880s was altogether
too closely defined against the middle-class respectability he wished to
flout. As Eagleton has said, he left a deep impression on his privileged
public because it was making fun of what was only too familiar to them.
His critique, in other words, was bound into – if not presupposed by – the
very terms it wished to attack.

Let me explain this point more fully by taking issue with one of the most
powerful analyses of Wilde's key rhetorical manoeuvre. In his wide-
ranging study of sexual dissidence, Dollimore argues that Wilde's aesthetics
and politics engage in a radical revision of received orthodoxies, and he
implies that this process of inversion may be related to the sexual inversion
classified by sexologists, such as Havelock Ellis and Richard von Krafft-
Ebing. Inversion provides an account of how femininity defines the psyche,
if not physiology, of an anatomically male body, and how, by comparison,
masculinity shapes the psychological contours of a body identified as
female. In his account of Wilde's 'transgressive aesthetic', Dollimore warns
that 'inversion is only a stage in a process of resistance whose effects can
never be guaranteed and perhaps not even predicted'.[41] But, in seeking to
align rhetorical strategy with sexual taxonomy, this series of suggestions
about '(in)subordinate inversion' compounds some of the main protocols of
post-structuralist thought, ones which have been immensely enabling in
undoing binary oppositions, with an idea about homosexual desire that
does not necessarily apply to Wilde. Rather, it is an elegant form of parody
that operates within the very institutions that he so punishingly critiques.
And the force of Wilde's parody is not, as Dollimore might be indicating,
one in which the world, in terms of the carnivalesque, is readily turned
upside down.

But that is not to say that postmodern paradigms are irrelevant to Wilde's
aesthetic practice. Recent theorizations of the parodic have a useful bearing
on those aspects of his work that mock those cherished middle-class values
which – as Dollimore himself shows – privilege depth over surface, and
make specious claims on authenticity. In her powerful study of theories of
sex, gender, and sexuality, Judith Butler stakes a large claim on the political
advantages that may be won through strategic forms of parody. Although
Butler recognizes that parody may on many occasions be the result of
despair and hopelessness, she generally takes an optimistic view of its trans-
formational possibilities. Butler points out how highly self-conscious gender performances such as gay male drag may disclose how the apparent
'original' is just as much a construction as the parodic 'copy' upon which it
is modelled. 'The performance of drag', writes Butler, 'plays upon the
distinction between the anatomy of the performer and the gender that is

being performed.' It follows that the 'notion of parody' that Butler defends 'does not assume that there is an original which such parodic identities imitate'.[42] Parody may, in Butler's terms, serve to undermine the naturalizing assumptions that so often support our ideas of what constitutes a correct sex, gender, or sexual preference. But, as a number of commentators have remarked, Butler's argument that gender is a performance – something which comprises a set of props including dress, tone of voice, and styles of bodily comportment – lacks a social theory that would adequately explain the power differentials that necessarily obtain when men and women act out their genders.[43] Without an account of power in its structural, discursive, and institutional forms, this idea of 'gender performance' suggests that one could, as if by an act of will, change one's gender.

This objection has hardly escaped Butler's attention. She recognizes how gay male drag has often served to reinforce the very forms of misogyny that are often displaced on to male homosexuality. Experimentation with gender performance, then, necessarily operates within a field of constraints and opportunities. Wilde's career surely testifies to the intractable problems in finding a political space in which one might successfully mount a cultural critique through parody, not least when it comes to devising visual and verbal forms where male same-sex desire could, at some intelligible level, be expressed. So let us be clear about one point. In Wilde's career, homosexuality remains, not in the field of sexological inversion and theories of the 'third sex', but within the realm of the simulacrum, the feigned, and the forgery. Once we recognize how much of Wilde's work depends on ideas and acts of theft, it is possible to see how the criminality of same-sex desire is all the more outrageous because it could prove to be attractive to the very society that created 'monstrous laws' to ban it in public and in private. It should not surprise us, then, that the imperative to police male homosexuality intensified so alarmingly at this time because this type of desire threatened to expose the naturalized – that is, not natural – structure of respectable relations between the sexes. In asserting, much in the manner of Charles Baudelaire, that 'Dandyism is the assertion of the absolute modernity of Beauty' (p.1204), Wilde was partly trying to fashion homosexual desire in a guise that could be passed off as something else – the bachelor, the artist, the poser, the forger.

But, as *Earnest* shows, his dandies and their associates are rarely in control of their destinies, and only in one work do they emerge as men with discernibly homoerotic interests. Early on in *Dorian Gray*, the painter Basil Hallward states regretfully that 'there is a fatality about all physical and intellectual distinction' (p.19). This is 'the sort of fatality', he adds, 'that seems to dog through history the faltering steps of kings' (p.19). The premonitory force of these words leads not only to his own death but also to the high gothic tragedy of the beautiful Dorian Gray whose portrait Hallward had so faithfully painted. Between these two men stands the arch figure of the dandy, Lord Henry Wotton, whose hedonistic philosophy casts a baleful influence upon them both. Lord Henry is the knowledgeable wit who draws on a rhetorically persuasive hoard of well-turned phrases. Yet the more we see of Wotton, the clearer it becomes that his desires are closely attached to crime. But his praise of the 'Hellenic ideal' exists only in theory. Lord Henry, after all, does not practise what he preaches. He finds in Dorian Gray the material he needs to conduct a practical experiment, to see if the beautiful boy will become either 'a Titan or a toy' (p.41).

The dandy, then, hardly exists on the front line of transgression. His crimes remain the substance of theory rather than practice. Indeed, the force of his political insurgency is blunted because of his class position. Although the dandy's identity had passed through several transformations in Victorian England, he still occupied a special place in the upper echelons of Society. As Victorian writers on the first and most influential dandy have made clear, Beau Brummell's career during the Regency depended on entering the aristocratic order from below. In this period, then, the dandy was a figure of ascendancy. When fashioning Lord Henry as his chief spokesman for the pursuit of pleasure, Wilde was bearing Baudelaire's definition of the dandy in mind. In claiming that 'Dandyism appears above all in periods of transition, when democracy is not yet all-powerful', Baudelaire regards this figure as one who is making a bid for those aristocratic values that dispense with work and money. In some respects, the dandy could be seen as the last bastion of the *ancien régime* before the 'rising tide of democracy . . . invades and levels everything'. That is why an apocalyptic tone issues from this style of man. 'Dandyism', writes Baudelaire, 'is a sunset' – brilliant but inevitably fading.[44] He is all the more fading when we remember that Wilde's dandies are generally men who are not on the ascendant, gaining entry into the most exalted circles. They are, instead, men who were born into the landed classes, and yet who have the prerogative to mock the idleness of the rich.

No one has made this point more forcefully than Regenia Gagnier whose pathbreaking study of Wilde examines the complex dynamic of his interaction with the Victorian world of cultural consumption. Tracing the genealogy of Wilde's dandiacal affiliations, Gagnier claims that Baudelaire 'sees the dandy as an auracular artwork' – an artwork that, in Walter Benjamin's terms, strives to defend itself in the face of mass society.[45] Undoubtedly, this ideal fed directly into Wilde's aesthetics. But so too did Baudelaire's fatalism. Everywhere Wilde's dandies are at once aristocratic in their bearing, and yet in jeopardy of losing their reputations. This is certainly the case with the Regency poisoner, Thomas Griffith Wainewright, the subject of 'Pen, Pencil, and Poison'. Wainewright was, we are told, a 'young dandy', one who 'sought to be somebody, rather than do something' (p.995). Yet in making his mark, Wainewright was compelled to thrive upon crime. Not without coincidence, so too does Wilde violate the

protocols of authorship by thieving substantial portions of his essay from
unacknowledged sources. Bent on self-invention, Wainewright powerfully
suggested to Wilde that there was a mode of life that could exist outside
'the vulgar test of production' (p.995). Flatly opposed to the utilitarian
values that had come to regulate the Victorian middle classes, Wilde extended Matthew Arnold's view that culture should be promoted as the
alternative means through which social relations may be improved. That is
why Lord Illingworth, who flaunts his mocking phrases in *A Woman of No
Importance* (1893), resolutely declares that 'the future belongs to the dandy'.
'It is the exquisites', he argues, 'who are going to rule' (p.459). But this
confident speech is delivered to a young man who will soon discover that
he is Lord Illingworth's illegitimate son. Worse still, the son will come to
reject his newly-found father once the dandy's treachery in siring a bastard
comes to light, for Lord Illingworth is finally humiliated by the woman
whom he once cruelly betrayed. The triumph of this drama assuredly goes
to the mother, Mrs Arbuthnot, who strikes Lord Illingworth across the face
with his own glove before returning victorious to her son and his fiancée.
And it is in the woman who shall become Mrs Arbuthnot's daughter-in-
law that the dandy comes up against his greatest rival in terms of both moral
and dramatic power.

Ironically named Hester, this puritan from New England enshrines those
fiercely retributive values that branded the scarlet letter on the heroine of
Nathaniel Hawthorne's celebrated gothic novel. And it is this young
woman's high-minded propriety that scorns the hypocrisy of Society which
produces the main challenge to the dissolute dandy. What is more, Hester
represents an insurgent force that is making an equal, if not greater, bid for
power within what is left of the English aristocracy. Hailing from the
entrepreneurial class, Hester is one of the *nouveaux riches* from the United
States whose presence here produces an animated conversation – one satu-
rated with anti-American sentiment – in the pages of *Dorian Gray* (see
pp.42–3). Lord Illingworth, for example, does not hesitate to remark that
'American women are wonderfully clever in concealing their parents'.
Spending their money on haute couture, these young women are, according to the Lady Hunstanton, 'very pretty'. No wonder they 'carry off', as
Lady Caroline Pontefract observes, 'all the good matches' (p.436).

One can see from both scenes that the English dandy and the daughter of
an American entrepreneur are making competing claims on the fashionable
round of parties comprising the upper-class 'Season'. Tightening their grip
on the same forms of social power, these antithetical figures incline not
only to differing national and class origins, they also point to new formations of gender. Hester, like Lord Illingworth, speaks her mind, and her
forthright manner is a source of some consternation in the decorous ambience of Hunstanton Close. In this sense, she has something of the status of
the New Woman whose prominence in the 1890s witnessed a spate of

feminist novels where the protagonists are notable for their strong-minded opinions. It was not uncommon for conservative critics to see the New Woman and the aesthete as two sides of the same decadent culture, where the genders had been unnaturally reversed. To some conservative commentators, argues Dowling, the aesthete and the New Woman were perceived as 'twin figures of apocalypse'.[46] Like her dandiacal antagonist, Hester deplores the otiose rituals and the stuffy hypocrisy of the English aristocracy. She believes – like the dandy himself – that her values are superior to those of everyone around her. But her unrefined class origins emerge in her vulgar lack of tact when she rounds on her host, Lady Hunstanton:

> With all your pomp and wealth and art you don't know how to live – you don't even know that. You love the beauty of the life you can see and touch and handle, the beauty you can destroy, and do destroy, but of the unseen beauty of a higher life, you know nothing. You have lost life's secret. (p.449)

Even if marked out as a socially clumsy prude – one who causes needless offence by referring to Lord Henry Weston as 'a man with a hideous smile and a hideous past' in front of her host, who is in fact the brother of the man in question – the incisiveness of Hester's critique remains almost on a par with that of Lord Illingworth (p.449). He, however, approaches the shortcomings of Society in an altogether more poised manner. 'People today', he declares, 'are so absolutely superficial that they don't understand the philosophy of the superficial' (p.459). While Hester indulges in an assault on English aristocracy from the position of a righteous puritan, Lord Illingworth mockingly celebrates the absurdities of upper-class behaviour as a member of that privileged class.

This opposition between the American puritan and the lordly dandy is a telling one because it points to a central problem in Wilde's work when it comes to reproaching this life of luxury. Keen to expose the stupidity of the upper classes, Lord Illingworth speaks with greater authority than Hester because he stands on the inside of the culture he is attacking. 'The English country gentleman galloping after a fox' strikes him as 'the unspeakable in full pursuit of the uneatable' (p.437). Such memorable remarks are allowed to pass without question because he has the specific class and gender prerogatives to be dissident within this élite. Each of his elegant well-turned phrases causes a frisson, not an offence. Take, for example, how he informs Kelvil, an MP, that those who, like himself, serve in the House of Lords 'are never in touch with public opinion'. 'That', he adds, 'makes us a civilized body' (p.437). He is altogether too aware of the power of irony ever to make a gaffe as gross as Hester's. And his sentiments here exemplify his particular place within the refined echelons of English Society. Rather than reject the redundancy of outmoded institutions, Lord Illingworth revels in them. Why?

Because to do otherwise would be to capitulate to the earnest, moralistic, and ascetic values espoused by the likes of the American puritan. 'Exalting in appearance over essence, decoration over function', argues Rita Felski, feminized heroes like Lord Illingworth voice 'a protest against prevailing bourgeois values that associate masculinity with rationality, industry, utility, and thrift'. Felski adds that the dandy's mockery of middle-class puritanism remains 'implicated in, rather than dissolved by, the espousal of a self-reflexive and parodistic consciousness'.[47] This point could not be borne out more clearly by the way in which the dandy maintains his arch posture, not only by deriding the follies of the middle-class Philistines and the landed classes, but also by dissociating himself from women.

In *A Woman of No Importance*, the realm of moral propriety is significantly attributed to an outsider who is also a woman from the trading classes. This division of interests between Lord Illingworth – who represents insider dissidence – and Hester is worth pursuing further, not only because it clarifies the class values that support the dandy's critical pronouncements, but also because it derogates a whole cluster of despicable bourgeois qualities to the feminine. There is, however, an additional reason for this ranking of outspoken and morally superior femininity with the 'rising tide of democracy', as Baudelaire calls it. If the dandy is going to have a monopoly on aesthetic values, then his main rival is likely to be a carefully qualified kind of female identity. And that is because the late Victorian dandy, such as Lord Illingworth, is always potentially like a woman, especially where his narcissistic attention to dress is concerned. 'A well-tied tie', declares Lord Illingworth, 'is the first serious step in life' (p.459). He enshrines those self-regarding qualities, ones that mark out the dandy as a figure of sheer affectation, that only women were legitimately expected to exploit. As one writer remarked in an essay published on the dandy in 1890, 'Devotion to women demands too great a sacrifice of his own independence, and moreover, in every Dandy, it may be said, a woman lies more or less deeply buried.'[48] It is this feminine aspect of the dandy that at times – but by no means always – avails him as a figure of homosexual definition in Wilde's writings. But it serves another far more explicit function. Since dandiacal femininity, and thus effeminacy, often rivals women for social attention and admiration, it is the case that this kind of man's narcissism frequently encourages him to voice a virulent misogyny.

Such woman-hating comes into its own in Wilde's depiction in *Dorian Gray* of Lord Henry Wotton, a dapper figure who stylishly 'tap[s] the toe of his patent-leather boot with a tasselled ebony cane' (p.23). Having taken 'a cigarette from his case, and producing a gold-latten match-box' (p.83), he proceeds to inform Dorian Gray how foolish it would have been for a young man to have married the hack actress, Sybil Vane. Women, declares Wotton, 'are charmingly artificial, but they have no sense of art' (p.85) – sentiments that Wilde would repeat in the axioms he published in the

Saturday Review in 1894 (p.1203). Femininity for Lord Henry relies on 'primitive instincts' (p.86), it belongs to the market, and it is tied into the fripperies of the commercial world. Time and again, he deplores 'that awful memory of woman' (p.85). 'Women', he says, 'never know when the curtain has fallen. They always want the sixth act' (p.85). Here the relentless misogyny lends clearer definition to the homoerotic interests of Wilde's narrative. Just as women are routinely condemned for their 'entire lack of style' (p.84), Dorian is esteemed for his eternal 'good looks' (p.23).

Such considerations of the superiority of male beauty are validated by the repeated allusions to the 'Hellenic ideal' espoused by Lord Henry, and which derive much of their force from the works of Walter Pater (notably *Studies in the History of the Renaissance*, 1873) and Wilde's more general Oxonian inheritance. But it is not just the idealized homoeroticism of ancient Greece that underwrites the noble lineage to Dorian's desires. Wilde's novel contains another discourse – one perhaps less visible to modern eyes – to define the homosexual man as a 'higher' being. Throughout Wilde's writings there is a persistent strand of hereditarian thought that emerges from the forms of social Darwinism – the 'wild struggle for existence' (p.25) – that Wilde also encountered at Oxford in the 1870s, and which the editors of his undergraduate notebooks have traced in detail.[49] The idea that heredity is a controlling force shaping same-sex desire appears where Dorian progresses through a gallery of family portraits:

> What of George Willoughby with his powdered hair and fantastic patches? How evil he looked! The face was saturnine and swarthy, and the sensual lips seemed to be twisted with disdain. Delicate lace ruffles fell over the lean yellow hands that were so over-laden with rings. He had been a macaroni of the eighteenth century, and the friend, in his youth, of Lord Ferrars. (p.113)

Apart from taking a specifically Victorian interest in physiognomical signs to new extremes, this vignette presents Dorian Gray as the direct descendant of the flamboyant macaronis who came into the public eye in the 1770s. Such men, writes James Laver, adopted a style of dress that 'might be described as the last flourish of eighteenth-century artificiality before the dandy revolution' took shape in the figure of Beau Brummell.[50] Reading the macaroni as a man of excessive effeminacy, Wilde here identifies this style as a homoerotic one, since George Willoughby and Lord Ferrars were, we must infer, lovers at one time. Passages such as these, therefore, refer the dandy back to a privileged past rather than a world of 'absolute modernity'.

The dandy, then, is by no means an idealized figure in Wilde's fiction and Society comedies. Excepting Lord Henry in *Dorian Gray*, there is little in Wilde's *oeuvre* to indicate that his dandiacal men possess anything but other-sex desires, no matter how much they relish a feminized identity which frequently throws them into misogynistic tirades against their female rivals for social attention. Even if we accept the suggestion that in Lord Illingworth we see a homosexual stereotype lurking in his role as a 'surrogate father',[51] this figure is remembered for his flamboyant style that marks him out as a philanderer who does not hesitate to make a pass at the puritanical Hester. So, all in all, the dandy had the potential for Wilde to demonstrate a man's unconventional sexual desires – for women and (to a much more limited degree) for men. But whereas in the Society comedies the dandy was employed as a figure who, if running against social mores, never the less embodied understandable heterosexual desires, he would turn out to be a wholly unacceptable figure when his effeminate narcissism was attached to male objects of love. All of which is to claim that still, by the early 1890s, Wilde's dandies were not exclusively men-loving men. Only in the light of the Wilde trials was it the dandy's fate to become a recognizable homosexual type of man.

IV

Carson's strenuous cross-examination of Wilde did not allude to the Society comedies. They were clearly not an obvious source of evidence of Wilde's corrupt nature. But the scandal attached to his name meant that they could not run their course. Playing to packed houses at the beginning of the first trial, An Ideal Husband and Earnest were never the less promptly closed down, and Wilde's name removed from the hoardings. Apart from Dorian Gray and the 'Phrases and Philosophies' Wilde published in an Oxford undergraduate magazine, Carson took the author to task with 'The Portrait of Mr W.H.' The first version of this story had appeared nowhere less respectable than the conservative journal, Blackwood's, in 1889.

Just after Wilde carelessly declared that he had never 'adored a young man madly', Carson asked him if he had 'never had that feeling'. 'No', replied Wilde. 'The whole idea', he provocatively added, 'was borrowed from Shakespeare.' But Wilde's playful recourse to the Bard only provided Carson with another cue for his interrogation. 'I believe', he declared, 'that you have written an article to show that Shakespeare's sonnets were suggestive of unnatural vice.' 'On the contrary,' Wilde remonstrated, 'I have written an article to show that they are not. I object to such a perversion being put upon Shakespeare.'[52] To be sure, the charge against the morality of Shakespeare's sonnets was familiar to the Victorians, most memorably in the words of Henry Hallam who in 1839 declared that 'it is impossible not to wish that Shakespeare had never written them',[53] and whose disgust at the sonnets is mentioned in the 'Portrait' itself (p.1176).

Now Wilde's courtroom defence of the 'Portrait' was more than a little ambiguous. Although his libel charge obliged him to deny that 'unnatural vice' featured in this work, the 'Portrait' does not let desire between men submit to Carson's legalistic calumny. It is not that in the 'Portrait' there exists what Douglas had called in a published poem the 'Love that dare not speak its name',[54] and which had also been cited in court. This novella instead suggests that there is no name for same-sex desire. Sexual attraction of this kind, Wilde implies, has no essence of its own. If it did, as Carson's cross-examination demonstrates, such love would be immediately labelled, condemned, and sent to jail. The 'Portrait', by contrast, frames homoeroticism in altogether more confounding terms. Indeed, Wilde's narrative subverts the homophilia of the sonnets through a fraudulent theory claiming Shakespeare, in fact, had a boy lover.

So the plot of this 'Portrait', like Wilde's axioms, shifts between denying and affirming a truth. It is one of the tricks of Wilde's parodic style to expose the hollowness of pietistic proverbs while not substituting an alternative substantive claim to truth. In this novella, the unnamed narrator learns from Erskine how Cyril Graham invented a theory to prove that Shakespeare had dedicated his sonnets to Willie Hughes. This was the boy actor 'for whom [Shakespeare] created Viola and Imogen, Juliet and Rosalind, Portia and Desdemona, and Cleopatra herself' (p.1156). In making his case, Graham was following the clues that first led Thomas Tyrwhitt to advance this theory in 1766. Graham rallied his evidence quite plausibly, examining how the puns in the poem spell out this young player's name. But when Erskine demanded ocular proof of the boy-actor, he found that the portrait of Mr W.H. owned by Graham was forged. Once this fraud has been exposed, Graham takes his life. 'His faith', states Erskine, 'was fixed in a thing that was false, in a thing that was unsound, in a thing that no Shakespearean scholar would accept for a moment' (p.1161). The unnamed narrator, meanwhile, became entranced by Graham's theory, and desired to make 'everybody recognize, that Graham was the most subtle Shakespearean critic of our day' (p.1161). 'Every day', he writes, 'I seemed to be discovering something new, and Willie Hughes became to me a kind of spiritual presence, an ever-dominant personality' (p.1169). He went so far as to suggest that Masilio Ficino's fifteenth-century translation of Plato's *Symposium* could well have influenced the Sonnets, for in Plato there were 'curious analogies . . . between intellectual enthusiasm and the physical passion of love' (p.1174). Yet further research, as he informs Erskine, revealed that Graham's theory could not be substantiated. On receiving the narrator's letter, Erskine recovered his faith in Willie Hughes, declaring that he too would take his life as a sign of his conviction. But when the narrator tried to prevent Erskine's suicide he found that his friend had knowingly died of consumption. So Wilde has produced, as Lawrence Danson puts it, a 'self-subverting narrative' that 'enlists a tale of scholarly detection in the service of the indeterminate'.[55] One peculiar consequence of such theoretical indeterminacy was Douglas's wish to defend Willie Hughes long after

Wilde had died, going to lengths as extreme as those represented in the
'Portrait' to uphold Tyrwhitt's theory. In the archives of Canterbury Cathedral, Douglas unearthed a reference to one Will Hewes, apprentice to
shoemaker John Marlowe, the father of Christopher Marlowe.[56] In so
doing, Douglas was compelled to insist that Wilde was 'no homosexualist'.
That such a denial should be made in the very process of affirming the
theory undoubtedly points to the problems of representing male
homoeroticism that characterize the 'Portrait' itself – although we should
be cautious, as critics have warned, in assuming that such indeterminacy of
meaning signals either an evasion or resistance on Wilde's part.[57]

If confounding in its theory of Willie Hughes, there is one undeniable
feature of his forged portrait: its effeminacy. Mr W.H. himself has 'quite
extraordinary personal beauty, though evidently somewhat effeminate'
(p.1151), while Cyril himself 'was always cast in the girls' parts' at Eton
(p.1153). The son of Lord Crediton, Cyril thought his 'father a bear, and he
thought Cyril effeminate' (p.1152). So there is an important link between
Graham and the man whose portrait he has forged. Erskine remarks that
Graham, once he had left Eton, was 'wild to go on the stage'. But both
Erskine and Lord Crediton did everything to discourage him, and took him
to the theatre to see Shakespeare's plays performed instead. On reflection,
Erskine thinks that this 'good advice' was 'absolutely fatal' (p.1153). It is
clear, then, that Cyril Graham was denied what he wanted in life. In
forging the identity of Willie Hughes, he was in effect trying to liberate his
own desire. The same could be said for Erskine, who wishes to repeat
Graham's gesture, pledging his life on a theory that they both knew could
not be proved. The 'Portrait', to say the least, provides an exemplary
instance of transference. In this triangular circuit where evidence is perpetually exchanged, each player in the narrative would like to take up the
position of the other man. Just as Graham wishes to project himself into the
imaginary world of Mr W.H., so too do Erskine and the narrator want to
vindicate Graham. Once the effeminate forger has passed away, then the
identity of Willie Hughes – who, of course, resembles Graham – stands at
the centre of a life-and-death struggle between Erskine and the narrator.
Never in this network of scholarly research, extravagant forgeries, and
suicide notes can they save each other's lives. Their fantasy of Mr W.H.
instead ceaselessly circulates as a mystified form of knowledge on which
they cannot for one moment all agree. 'Like Lacan's formulation of the
purloined letter of Poe's story,' observes William A. Cohen, 'the theory
passes through and locates the subject, but continues ever on its trajectory.'[58] The effeminate young man of Graham's invention constantly mes-
merizes them, only to become the object whose insistence thwarts their
desire.

Written four years after the 1885 'Blackmailer's Charter' placed a strategic ban on sexual contact between men, Wilde's 'Portrait' signals only too

clearly that its subject concerns '*l'amour de l'impossible*' that preoccupied the unpublished memoirs of his contemporary, the art critic, John Addington Symonds.[59] Symonds, who to many also presented the aesthetic temperament, found *Dorian Gray* 'a very audacious production, unwholesome in tone, but artistically and psychologically interesting'. Clearly apprehending Wilde's homoerotic codings, Symonds none the less resented the 'unhealthy, scented, congested touch which a man of this sort has on moral problems'.[60] So although Symonds and Wilde shared the same project in attempting to make sexual desire between men as visible as possible, they were at odds with each other when it came to their ethical standpoint. Both knew that '*l'amour de l'impossible*' dare not speak its name, lest it led its lovers to prison. But Symonds, unlike Wilde, was exceptionally keen in his private writings to take up the models of inversion devised by the sexologists where Wilde most definitely was not. In other words, where Symonds was eager to label his homosexual identity through sexological classification, Wilde showed a persistent interest in disclosing in public that sexual identities could not be so readily named. In this respect, the elusive and tantalizing quality of the 'Portrait' surely marks an ironizing response to the legal prohibitions that exerted brutal pressure on male homophilia. To fix, to name, and to classify 'homosexuality', as the sexologists were attempting to do in the 1890s, was for Wilde to sign its death warrant. And yet the need to forge it was, as the 'Portrait' shows, a component part of those entranced by the effeminate young man. The 'Portrait', therefore, performs a remarkable sleight of hand. In suggesting that the proof of a sexual truth leads to death, this story also discloses that a homoerotic 'Portrait', like Wilde's own, must be forged in two senses. On the one hand, it must escape an authenticating identity that would give licence to the state to criminalize it even further. Yet, on the other, unless such love gains some form of public representation, as in *Blackwood's*, then young men like Cyril Graham will be driven to take their lives – or, at least, sent to jail.

V

The Ballad of Reading Gaol (1898) brings Wilde's enduring interest in deathly desire to its most celebrated close. This was the only full-length work that Wilde completed after 1897, during his years of exile and penury in Italy and France. In style and form, this poem was far removed from what his public once expected from his pen. It bore no traces of his axiomatic wit. Instead, it directed its polemic in a tone of harsh realism. Here he was petitioning for an end to capital punishment. In one of his letters, Wilde deplores 'the lack of imagination in the Anglo-Saxon race that makes the race so stupidly, harshly cruel'. His Irish sense of justice forces him to add: 'Those who are bringing about Prison Reform in

Parliament are Celtic to a man.'[61] To emphasize its point, the *Ballad* strikingly resembled the triumphal nationalism associated with W.E. Henley's and Rudyard Kipling's poetry. In adopting their heavy rhythms and memorable refrains, Wilde recognized that he was perhaps colluding with the bards of empire. Indeed, while ceaselessly emending his drafts, he declared he would 'never again out-Kipling Henley'.[62] But, in modelling his work on that of the jingoists, Wilde was once more resorting to parody to remind the imperialist English of the violence committed upon the minds and bodies of their criminals. And it is in this strongly muscular style that he cleverly implants a homoerotic rhetoric that spells out the fatalistic notes of desire that preoccupied him from first to last.

At first simply signed 'C.3.3.' (Wilde's cell in Reading Gaol), this hugely successful poem passed into five editions in as many weeks. But the critical reception was divided. No doubt seeing his own style invoked in its rousing stanzas, Henley rudely remarked that it sounded like 'sentimental slush' that falsely elevated its subject above the 'herd of lags'.[63] More damning still was the *Pall Mall Gazette* which claimed that 'with all its feverish energy' the *Ballad* seemed 'unmanly'.[64] The enduring taint of Wilde's aestheticism and subsequent 'gross indecency' no doubt informed such a hostile response. Elsewhere, however, the *Ballad* drew attention because of its biographical interest, and Wilde's supporters felt its excellent sales showed the public's remorse at his wrongful term in prison. Implicitly, for some, Wilde's two-year sentence had toughened him up. Arthur Symons welcomed the *Ballad* as a 'turning-point' in Wilde's career since this 'extraordinary talent', once 'fantastically alone in a region of intellectual abstractions', was at last engaged with 'real things'.[65] This is, undoubtedly, Wilde's only work that draws directly on an event from real life: the execution of Charles Thomas Wooldridge ('C.T.W.' in the poem), a trooper in the Royal Horse Guards, for murdering his wife. Wooldridge's death on 7 July 1896 provides the starting-point for an ever-widening meditation on the disavowals that tightened the hangman's noose. 'For', as the refrain to the *Ballad* insists, 'each man kills the thing he loves'. 'Yet', unlike Wooldridge, 'each man does not die' (p.844).

The world, Wilde insists, makes criminals of us all. The bare number of the author ('C.3.3.') bears a stark resemblance to the initials 'C.T.W.' honoured in this poem. Whether free to roam or locked up in solitary confinement, argues 'C.3.3.', 'each man' knows the desire for one thing shall lead to the death of another. If not 'with a bitter look', then 'with a flattering word' shall this universal crime be committed (p.844). No one can escape the bitter truth that in 'C.T.W.' they see an image of themselves that they cannot bear to claim as their own. In this respect, Christian hypocrisy proves most disturbing of all. 'The chaplain,' writes the poet, 'would not kneel to pray/ By his dishonoured grave', even though Wooldridge was among those 'Whom Christ came down to save' (pp.856–7).

Such is the contempt for the murderer that he is placed in an unmarked grave. But the prisoner who 'had to swing' (p.849), as the poem insists, is part of the all-embracing 'we' that chants its abhorrence at a system that reduces a man to the number of his cell – the place from whence this protest issues. 'C.T.W.' – like 'C.3.3.', like 'each man', and, finally, like all those subsumed in the poem's universal 'we' – is ultimately subjected to the deathly love that resides at the core of everyone. 'Each narrow cell' addresses not only the life of the inmate, but all of us who are metaphorically locked up in 'Humanity's machine' (p.858): a machine that legitimates its ritual violence in capital punishment. Here 'the crimson stain that was of Cain' is indissolubly linked with 'Christ's snow-white seal' (p.859). The profane transubstantiates into the sacred, reminding us that in every sinner there may well be a saint.

The poem, then, addresses more than 'a community of men who kill the thing they love and their banishment and divorce from society', as Gagnier claims.[66] The prison, in Wilde's typically mocking parody, becomes the shaping figure for human life itself. Gagnier, however, points specifically to the homosexual as one of many 'outcast men' whose profoundest passions fly in the face of social mores (p.847). Only through transgression, such as murdering one's wife, can this urgent truth be told. She argues that the *Ballad* closely resembles *Salomé* (1891) in its 'open rebelliousness' against the law. Both works, of course, focus on incarceration and the violation of legal authority. Salomé's defiance of the divine authority of Jokanaan and Herod's secular rule has encouraged gay and feminist critics to believe she is an icon of erotic resistance against patriarchal culture. In particular, Aubrey Beardsley's extraordinary illustrations for the edition commissioned in 1894 by John Lane have put the multiple perversities of the play into very sharp focus. 'Both in dramatizing a rebellious woman and in portraying male–male desire,' writes Richard Dellamora, '*Salomé* puts normal masculine representation under pressure.'[67] But, like the *Ballad*, Wilde's sacrilegious play adapts a familiar repertoire of images to make its derisory protest clear. Salomé's rebellion is certainly set against tragedy: one in which her desire to kill is pushed up against the limits of an equally murderous injunction on those who seek to transgress.

It is worth pausing over Wilde's representation of this *fin-de-siècle* female stereotype to consider more closely how the transgressive sexual impulse expressed in this play is in fact incarcerated in specific cultural paradigms. To begin with, Salomé is recognizably one of the innumerable *femmes fatales* who preoccupy the masculinist practices of *fin-de-siècle* artists. Like the Medusa, Salomé is the cynosure that draws all onlookers into her mortifying stare, and she is associated throughout the drama with the 'dead woman . . . looking for dead things' that the Page of Herodias first witnesses in the moon (p.552). 'You must not look at her', declares Herodias, reproving Herod's insatiable desire for Salomé. He answers by observing

how the 'moon has a strange look to-night' (p.561). Yet where Herod sees
the moon as a 'mad woman who is seeking everywhere for lovers' (p.561),
Salomé regards her as a 'virgin'. 'She has never defiled herself', insists
Salomé (p.555). Like the moon, she will not submit to any rule of law,
especially her stepfather's. Prophets and kings cannot conquer her, and her
desire spells disaster for all who are caught by her mesmerizing 'look'. Just
at the moment when Jokanaan cries from his cistern for this 'daughter of
Sodom' to cease her amorous advances towards him, the Young Syrian
who adores her commits suicide (p.599). The Page of Herodias breaks into
tears, bemoaning the death of the man he loves. Homoerotic desire is
destroyed, rather than unleashed, in this minatory act. This catastrophe,
says the Page, would not have occurred had he hidden the prophet
elsewhere. Salomé's intense obsession with Jokanaan's body cannot be
assuaged, least of all by Herod, who fears the prophet's words. So when
asked by Herod to dance, she insists on having Jokanaan's head served on 'a
silver charger' (p.570). Her only wish is to defile the virginal prophet by
repeatedly exclaiming her desire to kiss him on the mouth. Yet to capitulate to her wishes would cause confusion in Herod's kingdom, especially as
the Jews have been demanding the prophet's release. Such is her import-
unity, however, that he complies with her murderous obsession only to
execute her in the final scene. Her orgiastic energies, which threaten to
wreak anarchy upon the state, and which culminate in her tantalizing dance
of the seven veils, lead to her destruction. This demonic woman, like so
many late Victorian *femmes fatales*, has her sexuality avenged. For all its
subversive intent, the play strikes Dellamora as 'complicit to a degree with
the male power that it satirizes'.[68]

The same might be said about the *Ballad*, for there too it is a dead
woman who provides the premise for the contentious argument of
Wilde's refrain. It is she who stands as the nameless 'thing' that at no point
enjoys any identity whatsoever, while 'C.T.W.', like 'C.3.3.', if reduced
to his bare initials, remains one of a gendered community comprising
'outcast men'. Even if this poem represents a society of criminals wrongly
punished for their love of the body, that love subsists on the invisibility
of the murdered woman. In examining how the *Ballad* sets up a chain of
identifications where 'the reader becomes gay – joins a community of
outcast men – by reading Wilde, as Wilde became gay by commiserating
with C.T.W.', Wayne Koestenbaum hesitates about the construction of
gay identity that he sees emerging in the poem. 'Does a pact between a
gay male writer and reader', he asks, 'depend on erasing the slain wife and
justifying her death?'[69] This is one of several significant questions that
Koestenbaum leaves unanswered, suspending his critical reflections in
parentheses. It is perhaps a painful recognition for modern gay readers to
confront Wilde's political proximity to the dominant sexual ideology that
his work undoubtedly challenged. Both the *Ballad* and *Salomé* belong to a

larger pattern that suggests there is no escape from the doom-laden consequences of desire. Eroticism, here and elsewhere in his writings, is
almost always fated.

But Wilde's fatalism need not be ours. In *Who Was That Man?* Neil
Bartlett embarks on a brilliant meditation about the meaning of Wilde's life
and work for those men who since the Gay Liberation Front of the 1970s
have been able to celebrate in public our sexual identity. Offering itself as a
'present' to Wilde, Bartlett's book places its scholarly gift between two
photographs of Wilde's grave in Père Lachaise. On the tombstone, some
graffiti represent a heart, a Cupid's arrow, and the names of 'Jo and Dave'
entwined. Like 'Jo and Dave', Bartlett adds his own name to those for
whom Wilde symbolizes the long history of gay men's oppression. Our
history, however, is necessarily distinct from Wilde's. Invoking Gilbert's
remark in 'The Critic as Artist' that 'The one duty that we owe to history is
to re-write it' (p.1023), Bartlett emphasizes how gay men, nearly a century
after Wilde's death, 'articulate a challenge that Wilde could not'. 'We
suggest', he adds, 'that a gay culture is something to be struggled for, not
dreamt or bought.' Given the capitalist resources now in our hands – gay
publishers, gay businesses, gay pubs and clubs – 'our rewriting of history
becomes a truly dangerous activity'.[70] In other words, although Wilde
stood at the beginning of a political struggle that has for over a hundred
years witnessed the slow but sure development of a metropolitan gay
subculture that enjoys a thriving and expanding commercial scene, the
historical distance between his life and ours is immense.

So the impulse to heroize Wilde – if an understandable part of reclaiming
the gay past in a period of sexual liberation – should be conducted with
some circumspection. Although his life and work went far towards fashioning a familiar modern queer identity, Wilde's achievements also exemplify
the high costs involved in doing so. It is not that Wilde's emergence from
Reading Gaol a broken man sounds a warning to us all, for it does. But one
other troubling thought remains. Wilde established his homosexual difference in a marketplace that ultimately used him more than he could
comfortably manipulate it. His adoring audience ultimately held the power
that could banish him from sight. To make this claim is not to underestimate his achievement or to dismiss his pain. It is simply to comprehend
how he negotiated the severe cultural prohibitions that sought to eliminate
his desires. In this way, it remains hard not to notice how his remarkable
canon of writing seemed only too uncannily aware that this would and
should be the case. On that note, then, let me close this chapter with the
prescient words of the painter, Basil Hallward, who has poured his lifeblood
into creating the picture of Dorian Gray, only to die for his taboo desires. 'I
had a strange feeling', he remarks, 'that Fate had in store for me exquisite
joys and exquisite sorrows' (p.21). Much the same could be said for the
fatalistic pattern of Wilde's own work.

Notes

1 H. Montgomery Hyde, *The Trials of Oscar Wilde*, 2nd edn (New York, Dover, 1973), p.112.

2 *National Observer*, 6 April 1895, cited in H. Montgomery Hyde, *The Trials of Oscar Wilde*, p.156. Hyde notes that 'it is possible that the article was written by Charles Whibley'.

3 Arthur Symons, 'Sex and Aversion', in *The Memoirs of Arthur Symons: Life and Art in the 1890s* (University Park, PA, Pennsylvania State University Press, 1977), pp.146–7. No date is given for this memoir.

4 Oscar Wilde, 'To Leonard Smithers', 11 December 1897, *The Letters of Oscar Wilde*, ed. Rupert Hart-Davis (London, Rupert Hart-Davis, 1962), p.695.

5 Ed Cohen, *Talk on the Wilde Side: Toward a Genealogy of a Discourse on Male Sexualities* (New York, Routledge, 1993), p.139.

6 'A Priest's Life', in Kevin Porter and Jeffrey Weeks (eds) *Between the Acts: Lives of Homosexual Men 1885–1967* (London, Routledge, 1991), p.49.

7 Jonathan Dollimore, *Sexual Dissidence: Augustine to Wilde, Freud to Foucault* (Oxford, Clarendon Press, 1991), pp.67–8.

8 Oscar Wilde, *Complete Works*, ed. J.B. Foreman (London, Collins, 1966), p.29. Further page references appear in parentheses. This text is not wholly reliable. A fully annotated edition of Wilde's collected works is forthcoming from Oxford University Press.

9 Linda Dowling, *Hellenism and Homosexuality in Victorian Oxford* (Ithaca, NY, Cornell University Press, 1994), p.132.

10 I have written elsewhere on the growth and development of public-school stories and the types of masculinity they promoted: *Empire Boys: Adventures in a Man's World* (London, HarperCollins Academic, 1991).

11 Max Nordau, *Degeneration*, translated from the second edition (London, Heinemann, 1895), pp.318–19.

12 George L. Mosse, *Nationalism and Sexuality: Middle-Class Morality and Sexual Norms in Modern Europe* (Madison, WI, University of Wisconsin Press, 1985), p.43.

13 Charles Whibley, *Scots Observer*, 5 July 1890, cited in H. Montgomery Hyde, *Oscar Wilde: A Biography* (London, Eyre Methuen, 1976), p.118. I discuss this imputation of sexual immorality at greater length in 'Wilde, *Dorian Gray*, and Gross Indecency', in Joseph Bristow (ed.) *Sexual Sameness: Textual Differences in Lesbian and Gay Writing* (London, Routledge, 1992), pp.44–63.

14 Wilde, 'To the Editor of the *Scots Observer*', 31[?] July 1890, in *The Letters of Oscar Wilde*, p.268.

15 Yeats remembers calling on Lady Wilde and Willie Wilde during the course of the trials. Willie Wilde is reported to have said, in intoxicated tones: 'He [Oscar] could escape, O yes, he could escape – there is a yacht in the Thames, and five thousand pounds to pay his bail – well, not exactly in the Thames, but there is a yacht – O yes, he could escape, even if I had to inflate a balloon in the back-yard with my own hand, but he has resolved to stay, to face it out, to stand the music like Christ' (*Autobiographies* (London, Macmillan, 1955), p.288).

16 John Betjeman, 'The Arrest of Oscar Wilde at the Cadogan Hotel', *Collected Poems* (London, John Murray, 1970), p.18. The poem was first collected in *Continual Dew* (1937).

17 Wilde to Robert Ross, cited in Richard Ellmann, *Oscar Wilde* (London, Hamish Hamilton, 1987), p.429.

18 Wilde, 'To Robert Ross', 18[?] February 1889, *Letters*, p.705.

19 Eve Kosofsky Sedgwick, *Epistemology of the Closet* (Hemel Hempstead, Harvester-Wheatsheaf, 1991), p.148.

20 Josephine Guy, *The British Avant-Garde: The Theory and Politics of Tradition* (Hemel Hempstead, Harvester-Wheatsheaf, 1991), p.139.

21 On the larger cultural context informing Wilde's handling of Huysmans' 'fatal book' in *Dorian Gray*, see Linda C. Dowling, *Language and Decadence in the Victorian Fin de Siècle* (Princeton, NJ, Princeton University Press, 1986), pp.170–4.

22 Kerry Powell, *Oscar Wilde and the Theatre of the 1890s* (Cambridge, Cambridge University Press, 1990), p.6.

23 Ian Small, *Conditions of Criticism: Authority, Knowledge, and Literature in the Late Nineteenth Century* (Oxford, Clarendon Press, 1991), pp.122–3.

24 James Joyce, *A Portrait of the Artist as a Young Man* (Harmondsworth, Penguin Books, 1992), p.205.

25 George Bernard Shaw, Review of *An Ideal Husband*, *Saturday Review*, 12 January 1895, pp.44–5, reprinted in Beckson, p.177.

26 Declan Kiberd, 'Introduction' to James Joyce, *Ulysses*, annotated student's edition, ed. Declan Kiberd (Harmondsworth, Penguin Books, 1992), p.xvii. Kiberd elaborates many of these points in 'Wilde and the English Question', *Times Literary Supplement*, 16 December 1994, pp.13–15.

27 Terry Eagleton, 'Foreword', *Saint Oscar* (Derry, Field Day, 1989), p.x.

28 Timothy d'Arch Smith explores the possible homosexual pun on 'earnest' in *Love in Earnest: Some Notes on the Lives and Writings of English 'Uranian' Poets from 1889 to 1930* (London, Routledge and Kegan Paul, 1970), pp.xviii–xix. For a reading of Wilde's play that explores the homophile valences of 'earnest', see Christopher Craft, 'Alias Bunbury: Desire and Termination in *The Importance of Being Earnest*', *Representations*, 31 (1991), pp.19–46. On reflection, I now feel that in my earlier work I have probably been a little too enthusiastic in identifying some of the punning pleasures of this play; for some of the suggestions I have made, see Wilde, The Importance of Being Earnest *and Related Writings*, ed. Joseph Bristow (London, Routledge, 1992).

29 E.H. Mikhail (ed.) *Oscar Wilde: Interviews and Recollections*, 2 vols (Basingstoke, Macmillan, 1979), II, p.398. The quotation is also recorded in Hesketh Pearson, *The Life of Oscar Wilde* (London, Methuen, 1946), p.224.

30 Louise Jopling, *Twenty Years of My Life* (London, John Lane, 1925), reprinted in Mikhail (ed.) I, p.205.

31 Clement Scott, review of *Lady Windermere's Fan*, *Illustrated London News*, 27 February 1892, p.278, reprinted in Beckson, p.125.

32 John Stokes, *In the Nineties* (Hemel Hempstead, Harvester-Wheatsheaf, 1989), pp.54–93.

33 Scott, 'A Doll's House', *Theatre*, 14 (1889), pp.19–22, reprinted in Michael Egan (ed.) *Ibsen: The Critical Heritage* (London, Routledge and Kegan Paul, 1972), p.114.

34 A.B. Walkley, review of *Lady Windermere's Fan*, 27 February 1892, pp.257–8, reprinted in Beckson, pp.119–20.

35 Ada Leverson, 'The Last First Night', *The New Criterion*, January 1926, pp.148–53, reprinted in Mikhail, II, p.268.

36 Like many pieces of received wisdom about the homosexual codings associated with Wilde's life and art, the specific status of the green carnation has not as yet been verified. Research on this topic is currently being conducted by Joel H. Kaplan and Sheila Stowell for their forthcoming performance history of Wilde's dramas.

37 Lillie Langtry, *The Days I Knew* (London, Hutchinson, 1925), reprinted in Mikhail, II, p.257.

38 Moe Meyer, 'Under the Sign of Wilde: An Archaeology of Posing', in Moe Meyer (ed.) *The Politics and Poetics of Camp* (London, Routledge, 1994), pp.75–109. Meyer notes that the influence of Francois Delsarte's stylized rhetoric of bodily gestures can be first felt in Wilde's writings in the review of Whistler's work, 'The Relation of Dress to Art', that appeared in 1886.

39 Ada Leverson, in Mikhail, II, p.270.

40 Sedgwick, *Epistemology of the Closet*, p.152.

41 Dollimore, p.66.

42 Judith Butler, *Gender Trouble: Feminism and the Subversion of Identity* (New York, Routledge, 1990), pp.137, 138.

43 Ed Cohen, for one, observes how Butler's exploration of 'gender performance' suggests that 'subversive bodily acts', such as drag, could be viewed as 'voluntaristic': 'Who Are "We": Gay "Identity" as Political (E)motion (A Theoretical Rumination)', in Diana Fuss (ed.) *Inside/Out: Lesbian Theories, Gay Theories* (New York, Routledge, 1991), p.83. Butler herself defends many of the controversial claims about 'gender performance' made in *Gender Trouble* in a subsequent collection of essays: *Bodies That Matter: On the Discursive Limits of 'Sex'* (New York, Routledge, 1993).

44 Charles Baudelaire, 'The Painter of Modern Life', in *The Painter of Modern Life and Other Essays*, ed. and trans. Jonathan Mayne (New York, Da Capo, 1989), p.28, 29.

45 Regenia Gagnier, *Idylls of the Marketplace: Oscar Wilde and the Victorian Public* (Aldershot, Scolar Press, 1987), p.82.

46 Linda Dowling, 'The Decadent and the New Woman', *Nineteenth-Century Fiction*, 33 (1979), p.447.

47 Rita Felski, 'The Counter-Discourse of the Feminine in Three Texts by Wilde, Huysmans, and Sacher-Masoch', *PMLA* 106 (1991), p.1096, 1099.

48 A. Forbes Sieverking, 'Dandyism', *Temple Bar*, 88 (1890), p.534.

49 See Philip E. Smith II and Michael S. Helfand (eds) *Oscar Wilde's Oxford Notebooks: A Portrait of Mind in the Making* (New York, Oxford University Press, 1989).

50 James Laver, *Dandies* (London, Weidenfeld and Nicolson, 1968), p.17.

51 Ian Small and Russell Jackson make the suggestion that Wilde mediates his homoerotic interests in the paternal attitude that Wotton and Illingworth take towards Dorian Gray and Gerald Arbuthnot respectively: Oscar Wilde, *Two Society Comedies: A Woman of No Importance and An Ideal Husband*, ed. Russell Jackson and Ian Small (London, Benn, 1983), p.xxv. Compare Sinfield, ' "Effeminacy" and "Femininity": Sexual Politics in Wilde's Comedies', *Modern Drama*, 37(1) (1994), pp.36–7.

52 Hyde, *The Trials of Oscar Wilde*, pp.112–13.
53 Henry Hallam, *Introduction to the Literature of Europe*, III, pp.501–4, in *The Poems of Tennyson*, ed. Christopher Ricks (London, Longman, 1969), p.861.
54 The memorable reference to the 'Love that dare not speak its name' comes from Alfred Douglas, 'Two Loves', *Chameleon* (1894), reprinted in Brian Reade (ed.) *Sexual Heretics: Male Homosexuality in English Literature from 1850 to 1900* (London, Routledge and Kegan Paul, 1970), p.362.
55 Lawrence Danson, 'Oscar Wilde, W.H., and the Unspoken Name of Love', *ELH*, 58 (1991), p.980.
56 Rupert Croft-Cooke, *Bosie: The Story of Lord Alfred Douglas* (London, W.H. Allen, 1963), p.337. Douglas details his defence of Wilde's 'Portrait' in *The True History of Shakespeare's Sonnets* (London, Martin Secker, 1933), p.34, and *The Autobiography of Lord Alfred Douglas* (London, Martin Secker, 1929), pp.61–2. I am grateful to Kate Chegdzoy for this information which is contained in her doctoral dissertation on modern adaptations of Shakespearean myths, University of Liverpool, 1993.
57 Danson's suggestion that 'the deferral of meaning' in 'The Portrait of Mr W.H.' 'was a necessary act of resistance' (p.997) has been contested by both Sinfield and Dowling. Sinfield notes that this idea of 'resistance' may 'be a strategy for our time; it might involve claiming same-sex eroticism without accepting the terms and conditions, social and psychological, of being "gay". But Wilde, whatever his wishes, could not simply discover a queer precursor in Willie Hughes because "Mr W.H.", the plays, the trials, and the whole package that we call "Oscar Wilde", were key sites upon which a modern queer identity has been constituted' (Alan Sinfield, *The Wilde Century: Effeminacy, Oscar Wilde and the Queer Moment* (London: Cassell, 1994) pp.20–1). Dowling makes a slightly different objection – but one with the same target in mind – when she writes:

> In recent years, this critical approach [i.e. a gay-themed criticism influenced by Foucauldian paradigms of resistance] has supplied a predictable interpretive context in which Wilde's failure in *Mr W.H.* or *Dorian Gray*, for instance, to *name* the 'love that dare not speak its name' as 'homosexuality' or 'inversion' or some other name will always be found to constitute either a sign of his ideological erasure from a dominant discourse that denies public forms of expression to male love or, alternatively, the sign of his opposition to that very discourse, the play of indeterminate or deferred naming in *Mr W.H.*, for instance, constituting in Lawrence Danson's view 'a necessary act of resistance' (p.997). Yet not to see that Wilde's very lack of specificity may itself constitute an aesthetic choice wholly independent of the mechanics of repression and resistance is to make the mistake of reductionism. (Linda Dowling, *Hellenism and Homosexuality in Victorian Oxford*, pp.126–7)

Even if Danson's analysis perhaps too readily assumes a 'resistance' that is anachronistic given the fact that there was no specific sign for a countercultural sexual identity to be mobilized (such as homosexual, gay, queer, or whatever), both Sinfield and Dowling are blunting the political edge to 'The Portrait of Mr W.H.' – not least its interest in turning to history for models of same-sex desire – by suggesting that the whole issue of homoerotic representation could hardly be operating within perceived forms of censorship (expressed, for example, in Henry Hallam's well-known hostility towards Shakespeare's sonnets). Dowling, in particular, wants us to view Wilde's independent and liberal choice of material as yet another sign of his affiliation to Oxonian Hellenism, and its 'genuine expressiveness' (p.127). Surely the slippery elusiveness of Mr W.H.'s identity, in the light of Hallam's contumelious remarks, demands that we consider how there may be some difficulty for Wilde in representing what we – for all our misguided twentieth-century prejudices – might think of as male homosexuality: the name that could not speak itself because it had yet to be spoken at this time. Readers will be able to assess for themselves whether my own analysis of 'Mr W.H.' stumbles into the selfsame 'reductionism' of which Danson's important essay has been accused.

58 William A. Cohen, 'Willie and Wilde: Reading *The Portrait of Mr W.H.*', *South Atlantic Quarterly*, 88(1) (1989), p.229.

59 The phrase *'l'amour de l'impossible'* occurs in both Symonds's poetry and in his *Memoirs*, ed. Phyllis Grosskurth (Chicago, IL, University of Chicago Press, 1984), p.190. I discuss Symonds's *Memoirs* at length in Chapter 4.

60 Symonds, 'To Horatio Brown', 22 July 1890, in *Letters and Papers of John Addington Symonds*, ed. Brown (New York, 1923), 240, reprinted in Beckson, p.78.

61 Wilde, 'To Georgina Weldon', 31 May 1898, *Letters*, p.751.

62 Wilde, 'To Robert Ross', 1 October 1897, *Letters*, p.649.

63 W.E. Henley, 'De Profundis', *Outlook*, 5 March 1898, p.146, reprinted in Beckson, p.216.

64 Unsigned 'Comment', *Pall Mall Gazette*, 19 March 1898, p.4, reprinted in Beckson, p.221.

65 Arthur Symons, Review of *The Ballad of Reading Gaol*, *Saturday Review*, 12 March 1898, 365–6, reprinted in Beckson, p.221.

66 Gagnier, p.173.

67 Richard Dellamora, 'Traversing the Feminine in Oscar Wilde's *Salomé*', in Thaïs E. Morgan (ed.) *Victorian Sages and Cultural Discourse: Renegotiating Gender and Power* (New Brunswick, NJ, Rutgers University Press, 1990), p.249.

68 Dellamora, 'Traversing the Feminine in Oscar Wilde's *Salomé*', p.252.

69 Wayne Koestenbaum, 'Wilde's Hard Labor and the Birth of Gay Reading', in Joseph A. Boone and Michael Cadden (eds) *Engendering Men: The Question of Male Feminist Criticism* (New York, Routledge, 1990), p.186.

70 Neil Bartlett, *Who Was That Man? A Present for Mr Oscar Wilde* (London, Serpent's Tail, 1988), p.229.

2

Against 'effeminancy':
The sexual predicament of
E.M. Forster's fiction

I

Adopting a deliberately self-mocking tone, E.M. Forster's narrator opens the sixth chapter of *Howards End* (1910) with these rather condescending, distinctly Arnoldian words:

> We are not concerned with the very poor. They are unthinkable, and only to be approached by the statistician or the poet. This story deals with gentlefolk, or with those who are obliged to pretend to think that they are gentlefolk.[1]

To all intents and purposes, this declaration is perfectly true, since Forster's early novels pay scant attention to anything other than cultured society. By and large, his fictional universe concerns the English and Anglo-Indian bourgeoisie on whose territory working-class men and women only occasionally make their presence known – either in the form of the tragic autodidact, Leonard Bast, whose fate it has been to stand 'at the extreme verge of gentility' (p.43), or in the altogether more alluring shape of Alec Scudder, the seductive gamekeeper of the posthumously published *Maurice* (1971), who figures as an 'untamed son of the woods'.[2] Scudder inhabits England's remote idyllic pastures that lie at the farthest reach from the metropolitan centres and their extensive suburbs that increasingly intrude on the English greenwood. At a time when England had become the most urbanized nation in the world, Forster's Edwardian narratives emphasize how the sprawling city defines the worst aspects of social and political change.

No one can fail to see how Forster's novels – as demonstrated by the various film adaptations of them made under the directorial guidance of David Lean, James Ivory, and Ismail Merchant – celebrate an affluent society that avails itself easily to the kinds of costume drama that became popular in the 1960s and 1970s, with television series such as the BBC's *The Forsyte Saga* (from Galsworthy's epic) and ITV's *Upstairs, Downstairs* achieving impressive audience ratings. It is precisely this genre that has fuelled a late twentieth-century nationalist nostalgia for a class-divided Edwardian England where everyone seemingly knew their station in life. But, as Forster's tactful narratorial reminder makes clear, his fiction is not entirely at peace with the bourgeois values he feels obliged to represent. Indeed, Forster's fictional world is uneasily shaped and directed by the inheritance of the high Victorian novel aimed at those members of the leisure class who can easily identify with the men and women depicted in his works. Especially influential on Forster's apprehension of this ostensibly charming middle-class culture are the novels of George Eliot and Henry James, whose writings he knew intimately.[3] So in acknowledging the 'unthinkable', Forster is not only pointing out how his own writing is involved in a disquieting repression of working-class life. He is, at the same time, suggesting that his chosen genre is addressing itself to people who bear little relation to other social commentators. Attending solely to 'gentlefolk', even 'pretend' ones, *Howards End* – like many of Forster's narratives – self-regardingly ponders the social limits in which it is operating, and with which it is displaying not a little dissatisfaction. Bearing this aspect of Forster's ironizing narratorial self-consciousness in mind – one that accentuates the modernist tendencies of *Howards End* – Michael Levenson observes that this writer's 'formal experiments, which are by no means negligible, often appear as involuntary expressions of his own sense of loss'.[4] No longer, it seems, can the novel represent class differences in the unapologetic manner of Forster's literary ancestors. The very idea that the novel must face up to the 'unthinkable' certainly suggests the inadequacy of this literary form in the face of unwelcome transformations in the social structure of the nation.

This chapter begins by investigating how Forster's troubled plots manipulate a specifically middle-class domain where the best possible kind of culture finds itself obliged, time and again, to confront 'unthinkable' things. The first part of this discussion concerns the gendering of the voice of cultural authority that arbitrates what may and may not be 'thought' in such a drily ironic manner. Here I argue that Forster's novels constantly return to the impossibility of depicting social forces that are anything but gentle. If his work has one purpose in mind, it is to contest the imperialist masculinity that was keenly intolerant of the intellectual artistic type of leisure-class aesthete with whom he clearly identified. His abhorrence of imperial manliness, however, is exceptionally conflicted. Defying it, he at the same time recognizes that the imperialist's robust physique embodies a set of regenerative values that those aesthetes fashioned on the model of Wilde can only weakly mock. Even if displaying a repugnant brutality, the imperial male struck Forster as possessing an eroticized physical power that could both ennoble and maintain the race. Yet the zealous athleticism of such fighting-fit men could not, as he saw it, be left to its own inhuman devices. To resolve this dilemma, he seeks to synthesize the aesthete and athlete, trusting that the intellectual man can and should refine the sensibility of the cricket-playing son of the empire, while the vigorous hearty type may reciprocally virilize the scholarly fellow.

Much of Forster's anxiety about the status of the effeminate man of letters and the need to masculinize him forms part of a fairly longstanding polemic about the virtues and vices of Matthew Arnold's definition of culture. In each of his Edwardian novels, Forster attempts to include empowering social-sexual structures for the well-off community that inhabits this particular milieu, on each occasion with the purpose of giving firm physical shape to culture in its most elevated form. To achieve this end, his sensitive male protagonists – together with the intellectual women whose femininity often represents delicacy of insight – are made to benefit from taking a few rough knocks from strongly masculine types. To be sure, his Edwardian novels demonstrate that culture can have little influence unless it acquires strength from the robust qualities that are for him embodied in muscular styles of manhood – working-class, imperial, non-European – all of which are diametrically opposed to the rather feminized, if not troublingly effeminate, sensibilities of 'gentlefolk'.

Everywhere we look in Forster's fiction there is an all too visible dialectic between a perspicacious aestheticism that appreciates high art, on the one hand, and sources of brute strength that can be found in the military, in business, in the proletariat, and in the native peoples of Asia and Africa, on the other.[5] In practically all his fictional narratives, he strives to bring these antithetical presences into a productive tension. It is precisely this quality that made Forster the icon of the 'liberal imagination', according to one of his first and finest critics, Lionel Trilling.[6] Margaret Schlegel's memorable reflections in *Howards End* point directly at this persistent narrative desire:

> Only connect! That was the whole of her sermon. Only connect the prose and the passion, and both will be exalted, and human love will be at its highest. Live in fragments no longer. Only connect, and the beast and the monk, robbed of the isolation that is life to either, will die. (pp.183–4)

Connection clearly emphasizes the combination of opposite attributes. But such connection is – as the telltale nouns disclose – also of a sexual nature. The rapacious beast and the ascetic monk are to intertwine in an act of 'human love'. In other words, a liberal impulse to 'connect' carries with it a homoerotic dynamic. As Richard Dellamora suggests, this passage articulates Forster's 'anger at the violence done to him and his resistance to compulsory heterosexuality'.[7] But we should not be led to believe that these two masculine types can combine in their liberal homoerotic union by themselves, as if they were entirely free from what we have come to call, *pace* Adrienne Rich, 'compulsory heterosexuality'.[8] Framed by insistent imperatives, this well-known excerpt is characteristic of a larger pattern that we can discern in many of Forster's fictions where the blending of two contrasting male subjects is imagined by a woman. Margaret's much-cited 'sermon', therefore, shows that this urgently desired connection involves three – not two – people. So in considering the integration of brutish and cultured styles of manhood here, Forster is exploring what may be rightly called a love triangle: the classic structure for generating intriguing forms of emotional turmoil in the modern novel.

Margaret Schlegel's insistence on what we must 'only connect' draws attention to a general feature of Forster's plots where sexual desire is woven into complex triangulated structures of the kind influentially explored by René Girard, and then rethought by Eve Kosofsky Sedgwick in relation to dominant patterns of male homosocial desire. In revising Girard's 'schematization of the folk-wisdom of erotic love triangles' – where male suitors intensify their rivalry over a desired female object – Sedgwick suggests that 'the bond between rivals' appears to be 'even stronger, more heavily determinant of actions and choices, than anything in the bond between the lovers and the beloved'.[9] But that is not to argue that in the love triangle male homosociality always becomes explicitly sexualized. According to Sedgwick, the violent mechanisms of homophobia and misogyny in western cultures frequently serve to regulate, and thus disavow, any homoerotic connection. The love of these men, after all, is ostensibly aimed at a woman. Yet, simultaneously, these men know for sure that they are superior to the female object who shall, in the end, become the property of one of them. Such imbalances of power between the sexes only too clearly imply that male suitors of this kind must, subliminally or otherwise, admit that their male rival has a higher value than the female beloved. Given the intensities of feeling that this relay of erotic interests can create between men, Sedgwick's specific interest is in how precarious the divide between homosociality and homosexuality can prove to be.

Now this system of social and sexual relations is, to some degree, turned inside out in Forster's narratives. Instead of fending off the homoeroticism that these love triangles produce almost in spite of themselves, his plots seek to exploit it. And they do so by making women into powerful agents who preside over the connection between 'the beast and the monk'. Yet, as with all erotic triangles, no matter how they are inverted, the romantic conjunction of two lovers is both *enabled* and *inhibited* by a third party. Forster's lifelong narrative problem – which stretches from his earliest stories of the late 1890s to his fragment of science fiction produced in 1961 – is how to discover a public and plausible form in which male homoeroticism could benefit from feminine authority without becoming effeminate. Although in Forster's work effeminacy signals degeneracy, femininity often implies intellectual sensitivity. Between the two, however, there runs an ambivalent identification with the cultured side of the feminine and alienation from the taint of its vitiating influence on masculinity. Not only that, feminine authority – if voicing the desire of male–male connection – all too often threatens to impair the potency of love between men. To grasp this complex point, it is useful to look at the gendered meanings attached to the late-Victorian ideal of culture. The polemic attending Arnold's ideal of culture can enable us to see how the kind of homosexual connection that Forster envisaged was regulated – if not, by necessity, mystified – by profoundly hetero-normative assumptions. Forster, a homophile writer, was perpetually fascinated by the gendered difference between the prose of the middle-class novel and the romantic passion that lay at its core.

II

At the start of his career, Forster's chief political and aesthetic obsession concerned the emergent and widely disputed question of 'culture'. This preoccupation arose because the idea of 'culture' had become, by the late 1860s at least, a feminized concept. What has rightly been called the feminization of the literary sphere in the last quarter of the nineteenth century sent shock-waves throughout Britain.[10] As I show in Chapter 1, the loosely defined Aesthetic Movement – where Oscar Wilde features as the leading protagonist – characterized the foppish arrogance of the oversensitive writer, painter, or critic. Wilde's provocative posing was – to draw a somewhat long perspective – the consequence of controversies that date from the late 1820s about the need for 'dynamism' to combat the Utilitarian 'mechanism' stemming from the expanding lower middle classes. This famous opposition comes from Thomas Carlyle's influential polemic, 'Signs of the Times' (1829), and it would undergo considerable transformation in Matthew Arnold's *Culture and Anarchy*, published 40 years later.[11] Far from being a work of any explicit kind of sexual politics, Arnold's treatise enjoined an altogether new debate about the gendering of the very 'dynamism' that Carlyle believed would restore an increasingly secular nation to new spiritual heights.

Although in 1935, after the bulk of his fiction writing had been completed, Forster would nervously remark that 'Culture is a forbidding word' (he was thinking of how Germany had troublingly given birth to both aesthetic criticism and National Socialism),[12] it was a term whose prohibitive connotations maintained a decisive grip on his work. To comprehend Forster's perception of culture, it cannot be stressed sufficiently that

Arnold's *Culture and Anarchy*, together with the 'Arminius' letters that
preceded it, was sometimes read as the pompous rhetoric of an impotent
don. Lacking the hearty robustness of the Utilitarian dogmatism that it
systematically denounced, Arnold's desire to improve the sensibility and
intellect of the trading and commercial classes through such vague offices as
'sweetness and light' often met with derision. Not only directed against the
middle class, Arnold's assault on divisive social values also frequently focuses
on the love of 'athletic exercises' and 'games and sports' by the sons of
middle-class Philistines. 'Culture', he proclaims, 'does not set itself against
the games and sports . . . but it points out that our passing generation of
boys and young men is, meantime, sacrificed.'[13] In several short essays
published in the 1860s, Fitzjames Stephen pokes merciless fun at Arnold's
precepts: 'To bid us to follow culture . . . is like the sterile admonition of
the moralist to follow virtue.' Deploring Arnold's lack of practical instruc-
tion, Stephen makes this pointed demand: 'Present to us the fruits of
culture in forms . . . that may help us to realize the methods and the ends in
something like bodily shape.'[14]

Many shared this view. W.H. Mallock would depict Arnold in almost
identical terms in *The New Republic* (1877), a brilliant Tory-minded satire
on the intelligentsia of the day. Mallock represents the prophet of culture in
the 'supercilious-looking' Mr Luke:

> 'Culture', said Mr Luke, 'is the union of two things – fastidious taste
> and liberal sympathy. These can only be gained by wide reading
> guided by sweet reason; and when they are gained . . . we are con-
> scious, as it were, of a new sense, which at once enables us to discern
> the Eternal and absolutely righteous, wherever we find it.'

Mr Luke continues his amusing disquisition by pontificating on which
aspects of the New Testament 'culture' will deem to be variously 'grotesque, barbarous, and immoral'.[15] Mocked from this perspective, Arnoldian culture was sent up as an irreligious doctrine.

The clear-cut divide between Arnold's seemingly weak-minded culture
and the Utilitarian demand to give it physical shape appears in another of
Stephen's articles, and it is here that his line of thinking sets a distinctive
pattern for the main preoccupations of Forster's novels. Stephen is com-
menting on the witty objections to Arnold raised by the positivist philo-
sopher Frederic Harrison in the *Fortnightly Review*, and he believes that the
dialogue between the two exemplifies a 'divergence' between modern
types of masculinity:

> The divergence is one which is to be seen every day in the world
> around us, and especially in the younger generation that is growing
> up. Disbelief in the established ideas in which they have all been
> educated appears, in the case of some men, to lead to a species of

delicate conservative scepticism. Everything seems to them noisy and unsettled and out of tune, and they come to the conclusion that there is nothing like the comfortable quiet of their own libraries, and the pursuit of their own intellectual tastes and pleasures. Others, who begin with a similar disquietude and uncertainty, find refuge in a species of revolutionary faith, a passion of action, and a hope and belief in the future which appears to compensate for their disbelief.[16]

This 'divergence', without doubt, is a schematic one. Confronted by the ever-increasing secularization of Victorian moral standards, the young college student of the 1860s is said to be faced with two alternatives. Either he may go into the world and try to change it or he can timorously retreat into his ivory tower. Out of this inflexible dichotomy would spring – most urgently for Forster – the opposed interests of the sociable sportsman and the smug intellectual. (This is a pairing that Alan Sinfield, more than anyone else, has analyzed at length.)[17] But rather than dispose of culture and the unmanliness associated with it by surrendering to the imperialist masculinity championed by the 'Khaki Election' of 1900 (it occurred right in the middle of the second Anglo-Boer War), Forster's earliest fictions more and more point towards a world that derives its ethical and spiritual authority from specific forms of femininity that may enable the connection between opposed types of men. The wilting aesthete may gain in stature and the strapping athlete prove poetical in an environment where an idealized womanhood can influence the needs and desires of these men for each other.

The main outline of this pattern arises in the 'Plot' of the novel that Forster sketched out in 1904, and which he remodelled when drafting *The Longest Journey* (1907). The 'Plot' comprises 14 points, each one a stage in a projected *Bildungsroman*. Although this material neither falls into a logical sequence nor adds up to a fully rounded structure, the first and most expansive item suggests a definite beginning:

> 1. Renée and Mr Aldridge – a practical, unsuccessful, man – paid a visit to Humphrey [*blank*], in his second year. They are old friends: but Renée for the first time 'realizes' him – that he [is] clever in the first place, and that something might be 'made' of him. She disapproved of his effeminancy [*sic*], and of his friends – notably the brainy uncouth undergraduate soaked with the idea of mutability, Ford, and of a don who wished to run him also.[18]

Composed one year before Forster's first novel, *Where Angels Fear to Tread*, enjoyed appreciative reviews, this synopsis reveals that already some of the main ingredients of his celebrated early fiction are firmly in place. The scene is a Cambridge college, the protagonist is a weak young man prone to external influences, and there is a scheming woman ready to take advantage of his vulnerable nature. The 'Plot' angles its gaze at a complex sexual predicament that is reworked, not only in *The Longest Journey*, but also in nearly every other story that Forster wrote before and after the First World War.

The salient features of the 'Plot' can be quickly laid out in turn. First of all, there are Humphrey's intellectual camaraderie and his blossoming creativity at college. Next comes 'a year of cramming for the Civil Service', and the 'increased . . . interest' of the woman who wishes to 'realize' him. Their engagement is swiftly followed by a honeymoon in his Uncle Basil's home at the exotic location of Ponte Molino. Enter the previously unknown Pasquale whom the uncle – presumably creating the first major crisis in the 'Plot' – introduces as Humphrey's illegitimate brother. Panic understandably ensues. And so the young couple, troubled by the stigma attached to this new-found relation, are divided about whether to accept or reject him. The remainder of this rather elliptical tabulation of events shows Humphrey awkwardly caught between the competing affections of his calculating wife and his talented peers at Cambridge. To some extent, the story witnesses Humphrey's triumph as a writer of fiction – if in the face of no uncertain tragedy. Humphrey perishes in the fire with Pasquale before his book has been published. Quite what happens afterwards to Humphrey's wife, Renée, and his college friend, Ford, is unclear. The 'Plot' focuses more or less exclusively on Humphrey's passage from effeminacy – or, as Forster tellingly misspells it, 'effeminancy' – through the convention of marriage to his suggestive immolation with an outcast of his own sex. This narrative design stands as something of a prototype for Forster's completed works of fiction, in which Humphrey's yearnings and final burning would re-emerge.

From the outset, Forster's impulse is to make the effeminate boy into a manly man. This is blatantly the case in his earliest piece of sustained fiction, 'Nottingham Lace' (as his editors have named it), which amounts to 20,000 words and was probably drafted in 1899. In the story, a weakly teenager named Edgar Carruthers has been left in the charge of his aunt and uncle, the Manchetts, while his altogether distant father explores obscure 'Topes' in the East. Edgar's adoptive family represent the most despicable traits of Home Counties snobbery. Mrs Manchett styles herself as a society dame, adjudicating who among her neighbours shall and shall not be deemed worthy of a 'visit' in Sawstone, the imaginary town that reappears as Sawston in *Where Angels Fear to Tread* and *The Longest Journey*. The Manchetts – as their family name implies – stand for fighting-fit public-school morality. The father is a cricket-playing outdoor type who embodies the aggressive ethic of industry and empire promulgated by the New Liberalism that emerged in the mid-1890s. This is hardly a hospitable environment for young Edgar, as he whiles away his time reading the works of Walter Pater, A.C. Swinburne, John Keats, and the soporific incantations of Alfred Tennyson's *In Memoriam* ('like dull narcotics numbing pain').[19] Early on we are told that Mr Manchett's attempts to 'make a man' of Edgar have been entirely in vain. The reasons why are only too obvious for a boy who has until recently been overdomesticated by an indulgent 'maiden aunt'.[20]

The aim of this paradigmatic narrative is to 'make a man' of Edgar by means somewhat different from those which the imperialist Manchetts have proposed. The boy's salvation appears in the figure of Sidney Trent, 'brown, athletic, and good looking' (p.15). Trent is an active sports-loving schoolmaster in his early 20s whose family has recently settled in the neighbourhood. If Edgar is an outcast because of his literary tastes, then Trent is excluded from the upper crust of Sawstone because of the impecunious life enjoyed by his lower middle-class mother and sisters. Similarly, Edgar and Sidney, in different ways, are fatherless men. In this respect, the story opens up a field of mutual recognition between them. But class, as always, marks the most painful social divisions. No sooner has Mrs Manchett learned of the 'common things' that have been moved into the Trents' new home (p.7) than her husband declares Sidney Trent to be 'vulgar', 'ill-bred', 'a rough diamond', and 'one of nature's gentlemen' (p.17). Both young men, therefore, are excluded from this imperial stronghold.

Roughness, athleticism, and strength from humbler social origins have a magnetic pull on Edgar Carruthers. Through his encounters with Sidney Trent, who kindly teaches him how to ride a bicycle, Edgar learns to blend his aesthetic sensitivity with physical and moral courage. When, for example, Edgar's strapping young cousin is caught smoking with one of Trent's sisters, the guilty Jack Manchett approaches Edgar for comfort. The newly beefed-up aesthete tells him: 'Things aren't wrong because people say they are. You must rely on yourself: no one else'll do' (p.64). Echoing Ralph Waldo Emerson's *Essays* (1841–4) – a significant resource of authority for Forster – he adds: 'One must be self-reliant' (p.65). Edgar, in fact, is now playing to Jack the role that Sidney Trent had formerly adopted in relation to himself. Having achieved this startling transformation from Edgar's aesthetic lassitude to where Jack can proclaim that his cousin is 'strong', 'Nottingham Lace' comes to an abrupt halt. Why?

The reason for the sudden termination of 'Nottingham Lace', lingering on the aesthete's independence of mind, is open to a good deal of conjecture. Possibly it ended on this note because Edgar's triumph occurred too early, pre-empting any further narrative development. Perhaps in the light of the Wilde trials – which had occurred only four years earlier – Forster felt the story was heading in a direction that might incriminate him. Such, after all, was the impact of the trials, that T. Fisher Unwin withdrew from publishing Edward Carpenter's idealistic treatise on the 'third sex', *Love's Coming-of-Age*, in 1895. Only the Labour Press of Manchester would print and circulate his controversial writings the following year.

It was in this profoundly homophobic climate that Forster suppressed his short story, 'Ansell', drafted in 1902 or 1903. There the narrator returns from university where he has been completing a 'dissertation on the Greek optative'. At the station to meet him is his gamekeeper, Ansell.[21] Immediately a clear contrast is established between the physical attributes of both men. The 'slope' of the narrator's 'shoulders', like the 'contraction' of his 'chest', is assuredly characteristic of the erudite weakling (p.4). Calculating Ansell's imposing 'chest measurement', the narrator consoles himself by thinking about the man's low intelligence (p.5). Yet just at the point where the scholarly narrator has weighed up his mental strength against Ansell's physical bulk, their horse-drawn carriage goes out of control. To save themselves, they have to shed the weight of the scholar's heavy box of books. Almost driven insane at the loss of these precious belongings, the university-educated man comes round to his senses by declaring: 'Ansell has appropriated me' (p.8). At the end of the story, the scholar is more concerned about the bruise on his shoulder and the rawness of his grazed knee than he is about his copy of 'Liddell and Scott's Greek Lexicon' that still lies open on the ledge where they nearly met their fate. Across the wind-blown pages of this learned tome, he imagines an 'unembodied searcher after knowledge' whose 'ardour . . . in the damp' begins to flag (p.8). The practical outdoor world that Ansell so obviously enjoys clearly stands superior to the narrator's cloistered life of scholarship.

Materials from 'Ansell' would find their way into *Maurice* some 10 years later. But if both the story and the novel featuring manly gamekeepers were censored by Forster for fear of publicly exposing his homosexuality, he none the less remained determined to find a legitimate form in which sexual desire between men might be glimpsed. 'Albergo Empedocle' is about as explicit in its homoerotic interests as any work of fiction Forster published in his lifetime. Appearing in the periodical, *Temple Bar*, in 1903, this disturbing story is narrated by Tommy about the insanity of Harold, 'the man I love most in the world'.[22] During a vacation in Sicily, Harold begins to think, feel, and even speak like an ancient Greek. Touring the island with his fiancée and her family, Harold disturbs Sir Edwin Peaslake with his strange account of how he cures his recurrent attacks of sleeplessness. 'You pretend you're someone else', declares Harold, 'and then you're asleep in no time.' 'It's so queer', he tells his father-in-law (p.39). But when Harold's susceptibility to adopting another identity in this manner is influenced by Mildred's desire that he should imagine himself a Greek in the ancient city of Acragas – now modern Girgenti – his behaviour becomes even odder. Little wonder that when Harold displays signs of increasing physical and mental weakness Sir Edwin declares: 'I'll have no queerness in a son-in-law' (p.19).

By now the homosexual codings are fairly clear. The young man, who has the capacity to turn Greek and who repeatedly strikes his companions as 'queer', proceeds to inform Mildred that in his ancient life he 'loved very differently' (p.25). This 'different' form of loving makes itself most evident when, at the peak of his distress, he cries out 'Tommy' (p.32). In the closing section, Tommy reports on how the Peaslakes have abandoned Harold, leaving the two men together – one completely psychotic, unable to communicate in any language, ancient or modern; the other delighted that his friend, now placed in a mental asylum, has at least on one occasion 'got up and kissed' him 'on the cheek' (p.63). Solely in madness, it seems, can one man express homosexual 'love'. But such 'love' can be realized only because a woman, in spite of herself, has enabled them to do so. Here Mildred's insistent romantic longings – 'Today you must imagine you are a Greek' (p.15) – provide a powerful figuration of how heterosexual wish-fulfilment can drive the homosexually inclined man to lose his sanity. The eerie irony of this story is that Mildred's and Harold's shared yearnings to become 'Greek' have entirely opposed objects in mind. No one, at all three corners of this tragic circuit of desire, can in any way connect. All that is left is Tommy's unrealized 'queer' desire. It was this epithet – one that increasingly enjoyed a homoerotic inflection after the turn of the century – to which Forster would return in *A Passage to India* to signal the impossibility of representing sexual desire between men.

If 'Nottingham Lace' and 'Ansell' are shaped by a wishfulfilment to align the aesthete and the athlete, and if 'Albergo Empedocle' seeks a means to this conjunction through a woman, then *Where Angels Fear to Tread* attempts to combine both models. But it does so only by allowing a quite traditional heterosexual romance to be established in the first half of the narrative. At the start, the novel ostensibly concerns a 33-year-old widow, Lilia Herriton, her small daughter, and a dissatisfied set of arrogant in-laws. Sent off to Italy to improve her knowledge of the arts, Lilia falls in love with a younger, highly attractive Italian man. But within a matter of chapters the focus turns more and more upon the bodies of the two contrasting male protagonists. Her cousin, Philip Herriton, is the archetypal aesthete; he is 'a tall weakly-built young man, whose clothes had to be judiciously padded on the shoulder to make him pass muster'. Although 'both observation and sympathy' are 'in his eyes', his Ruskinian powers of discrimination are offset by the 'confusion' that lies 'below the nose and eyes'.[23] Lilia's husband, Gino Carella, is by contrast 'very good-looking'. 'All his features are good, he is well-built', if noticeably 'short' (p.18). Let us see, then, how this novel strives to force the much-desired connection between these two men.

Pompously jibing Gino for having become engaged to Lilia without the Herritons' permission, Philip receives an 'aimless push' from his Italian counterpart which 'topple[s]' (p.29) the cultured Englishman over. This is the first of several struggles that ensue between them. That their physical contact should supersede the consummation of Gino's marriage to his English wife is suggested as much by the following passage which indicates that women prove to be a block to socially – if not sexually – satisfying relations between men:

Italy is such a delightful place to live in if you happen to be a man. There one may enjoy that exquisite luxury of socialism – that true socialism which is not based on the equality of manners. In the democracy of the *caffè* or the street the great question of our life has been solved, and the brotherhood of man is reality. But it is accomplished at the expense of the sisterhood of women. Why should you not make friends with your neighbour at the theatre or in the train, when you know and he knows that feminine criticism and feminine insight and feminine prejudice will never come between you! Though you become as David and Jonathan, you need never enter his home, nor he yours. (pp.35–6)

These carefully measured sentences take special pains to exhibit their bourgeois authority. Repulsed by a politics based on 'equality' and the dissolution of class, Forster's liberal ethic transcodes 'socialism' into a homosocial frame of reference where differently gendered characteristics can be played off against one another. The more we examine this extract the more it appears that what is at stake is not so much the difficulties of Italian women's lives – their silencing under Roman Catholic patriarchal rule – but the problem of women to men in their differing English and Italian contexts. In middle-class England, where women visibly enjoy domestic 'sisterhood', they are constantly interposing their quarrelsome femininity between men. Such feminine behaviour is a particular source of irritation since English women possess those qualities of 'criticism', 'insight', and 'prejudice' that the narrator would assuredly like to think belong solely to the province of men. In Italy, by contrast, the home is not a place in which men may be so close. But they can at least enjoy their loving comradeship in public. That is why the loaded biblical reference to David and Jonathan is crucial. In alluding to the love that was 'passing the love of woman', the novel is signalling the steps it is about to take to purge itself of the obstructive, interfering, and no doubt prattling voices of women before a particularly powerful form of femininity can be ascribed to the men. Very promptly, then, Lilia dies in childbirth. Her baby, however, survives. The remainder of the story is taken up with Philip's and Gino's competing claims upon the child, and their rivalry brings about a configuration of homosexual desires that is cleverly contained within an ostensibly heterosexual framework.

Having removed Lilia from the scene, and thus eradicating the dominant heterosexual romance, the novel fixes its attention upon another woman who can facilitate sexual desire between its male protagonists. Once again, the narrative demands that the two men shall only connect if there is a female presence to act as a catalyst. The intervening figure is Lilia's former chaperone, Caroline Abbott, who returns to Italy to recover the baby. In a moment of high drama, she and Philip Herriton are involved in a tragic road accident in which the child is killed. Once Philip has reported the death ('Your son is dead, Gino. He died in my arms'), he immediately petitions the Italian: 'do what you like to me'. Given this invitation, Gino strikes first, and Philip returns an astonishing blow, crying 'You brute! . . . Kill me if you like!' (p.135). Immediately realizing that Gino is broken with grief, Philip forgivingly approaches his adversary. 'He managed', the narrator tells us, 'to raise him [Gino] up, and propped his body against his own. He passed his arm around him. Again he was filled with pity and tenderness' (p.136). David and Jonathan would appear to have secured their bond. But Gino revives and almost manages to break Philip's windpipe.

How, then, can these acts of violence be resolved? How can the physical connection be transformed into one of comforting intimacy? Like a harmonizing 'goddess', Caroline Abbott sets the men apart (p.138). At this moment, Perfetta, the negligent housekeeper, appears with the baby's milk. Tenderly, Caroline kisses Philip's sweating brow, and he undergoes an implicitly religious 'conversion' whereby he sees in her the magnified 'greatness in the world' (p.139). She persuades Gino to feed Philip the milk, and once the Englishman is replete, the Italian consumes the rest of it. Desire between men of differing masculine types, therefore, figures within an almost cinquecento scene of the madonna nourishing her beatified child. And it is a woman who, like a spiritual guide, has set the stage for this tableau. Despite the narrator's earlier championing of the Italian male comradeship enjoyed in the *caffè*, the novel demonstrates that it is femininity – for all its 'criticism', 'insight', and 'prejudice' – that finally allows these men, in this domestic space, to come together. In other words, without women – without the love, nourishment, and intimacy figured by the maternal body – male homoeroticism could not become visible.

Although we may wish to account for the structuring of this compelling scene as a result of the tactful negotiations that Forster had to undertake when struggling to find a legitimate context in which to represent male–male desire, the ambivalent attitude towards femininity that we find here is very much a part of the rest of his fiction. In fact, his succeeding novels operate within a complex dynamic that works *for* and *against* those values that he constantly associates with middle-class women. Time and again, Forster concedes considerable authority to the cultured, intellectual, and altogether sympathetic qualities that he identifies with femininity. But, simultaneously, his plots recognize that women are forever subtracting from the erotic attraction between men that he is seeking to represent. This perpetual difficulty arises because Forster continually imagines circuits of sexual desire in primarily gendered terms where connection is seen as the complementarity of feminine and masculine virtues. In other words, it is as if this wished-for homoerotic coupling were itself structured by the assumptions of the dominant heterosexual ideology of the day. The picture that slowly begins to emerge in Forster's continued attempts to find adequate configurations for this rather hetero-normative apprehension of

sexual love between men makes one thing clear. If femininity is the medium that achieves the desired connection between men, it also has the
power to break it as well.

III

Forster's next novel, *The Longest Journey* – which he regarded as his finest
work[24] – does everything within its power to remove the taint of effeminacy
from the aesthete. To accomplish this end the narrative presents a wholesale
vilification of femininity, since here we discover an erotic triangle where the
woman and the scholarly young man are tragic competitors in their shared
desire for the same athletic male. Many aspects from the 'Plot' drafted in
1904 reappear in the disastrous marriage of the orphaned Rickie Elliot to his
cousin, Agnes Pembroke, and from the outset she proves to be an impedi-
ment to his desired connection with other men in his Cambridge college.
Together they manage to frustrate each other's sexual needs. To make matters worse, Rickie is depicted in terms that take their cue from the deterministic plotting characteristic of George Eliot's and Thomas Hardy's
respective fictions. Social Darwinism of a very instrumental kind shapes the
struggling ambitions of Forster's intricate cast of characters. Rickie – a sickly
mother's boy, unloved by his father, with no remaining family support –
strikes one of his college friends at Cambridge as 'effeminate' (p.79). He
suffers from a congenital disability – he is lame. 'Weakly people,' we are
told,'if they are not careful, hate one another, and when the weakness is
hereditary the temptation increases' (p.121). Absorbing those influential discourses of 'degeneration' that controlled much thinking on homosexual
desire at the time of the Wilde trials, Forster's novel does its utmost to kill off
this refined scholar. In slowly destroying the sickly aesthete, Forster reaches
out to a new ideal which can embody those complementary masculine and
feminine qualities without any loss of mental or physical strength. What we
find here for the first time is Forster's appropriation of the notion of comradeship propounded by the socialist and homosexual emancipationist,
Edward Carpenter. In large part, Carpenter's aesthetics were drawn from the
controversial writings of the American poet, Walt Whitman.[25]

The tripartite movement of the novel – from 'Cambridge', to suburban
'Sawston', and thence to the great outdoors of 'Wiltshire' – moves along a
vector that deserts scholarship for liberty, domesticity for adventure, and
effeminacy for manliness. But the path that opens up before Rickie Elliot is
one which shows that he is not fit to travel its complete length. The man
who can undertake this 'longest journey' – as it is worded in Percy Bysshe
Shelley's *Epipsychidion* (1821, ll.149–59) – is not the complete antithesis of
Rickie but he is certainly of hardier stock. It is Rickie's illegitimate half-
brother, Stephen Wonham, who combines the poetical and the pragmatic

in a robust body of the kind that Forster first imagined in Sidney Trent in 'Nottingham Lace', and which – for some undisclosed reason – he could not flesh out into a full-length draft.

Right from the outset, Rickie's desires for other men are thwarted by the thought of marriage:

> He was thinking of the irony of friendship – so strong as it is, and so fragile. We fly together, like straws in an eddy, to part in the open stream. Nature has no use for us: she has cut her stuff differently. Dutiful sons, loving husbands, responsible fathers – these are what she wants, and if we are friends it must be in our spare time. Abram and Sarai were sorrowful [see Genesis 16–17], yet their seed became as sand of the sea, and distracts the politics of Europe at the moment [i.e. the Dreyfus affair]. But a few verses of poetry is all that survives of David and Jonathan . . . [H]e wished there was a society, a kind of friendship office, where the marriage of true minds could be registered. (p.64)

Here, to be sure, is a vision of a minatory Mother Nature, definitely – in the words of In Memoriam – 'red in tooth and claw' (LVI. l.15). In fact, it is as if a monstrous form of femininity were controlling the social imperatives imposed on young men to go forth and multiply as good husbands and responsible fathers. She, above all, prevents any kind of Platonic arrangement where there might be a male marriage – as it were – of true minds. (The friendship office, needless to say, echoes the registry office.) Rickie's patent unsuitability for this social institution is made clear by the Hegelian idealist, Stewart Ansell, whose sexual desire for Rickie drives him towards reproving his friend.'You should not marry at all', insists Ansell (p.83). Struggling against his better judgement, Rickie offers this fatalistic reply:

> You've written to me, 'I hate the woman who will be your wife', and I write back, 'Hate her. Can't I love you both? She will never come between us, Stewart . . . because our friendship has now passed beyond intervention. No third person could break it. (p.83)

Agnes does, however. When she and Rickie first embrace, he ambiguously remarks: 'I prayed you might not be a woman' (p.73). (Strictly speaking, he was hoping she would turn out to be a dryad – a product of his poetical imagination.) Hereafter, the doors of the 'friendship office' are closed firmly behind him. But, then, the narrative does not even want us to think that such a man could ever be fit enough to participate in Greek love.

Everything goes wrong for Rickie. His effeminate impotency in all fields of endeavour emerges most saddeningly in the 'supreme event' that awaits him (p.183). Hoping that his first child will be a boy, he is a broken man when he discovers that Agnes has given birth to a daughter. Not only that, the baby is also lame. The symptoms of this family illness are diagnosed most clearly in Rickie's similarly afflicted aunt – whom Forster rather clumsily calls Mrs Failing – a condescending society lady who takes delight in belittling others, since she regards herself, and no one else, as 'cultured' (p.123). By the central 'Sawston' chapters, it has become only too clear that the metonymic links between culture, snobbery, degeneracy, and effeminacy are tightly interwoven. Since he has been contaminated by all these things, Rickie's painful fate is to wither out of the book.

It is the appearance of Rickie's half-brother, Stephen Wonham, that re-directs the narrative towards a Whitmanian conception of a hybrid masculine type who has only been barely witnessed so far in Forster's novels. Whit-man's 'Calamus' poems had been the source of much homophile interest since William Michael Rossetti published a selection of *Leaves of Grass* for English readers in 1868. The 'Whitmania' – as Swinburne called it – that excited homophile campaigners such as Symonds would be the source of controversy in the late-Victorian periodical press.[26] In the spirit of the mus-cular men of nature whose virile bodies glisten in the noonday sun of Whitman's American epic, Wonham is a sensitive man of action. Raised in Mrs Failing's care, this roguish, illegitimate, and ill-educated man is for some time Rickie's object of fear. Even if drinking and swearing like a trooper, Wonham turns out to be anything but a cad. Instead, he is strongly associated with a rich array of values directly opposed to the Elliots' introspective and altogether too cultured, feminized world. A product of the passionate union between Rickie's mother and a robust farmer, Wonham roves the coun-tryside with a strength and beauty that overwhelm his half-brother:

> He stood, not consciously heroic, with arms that dangled from broad stooping shoulders, and feet that played with a hassock on the carpet. But his hair was beautiful against the gray sky, and his eyes, recalling the sky unclouded, shot past the intruder as if to some unworthier vision. (p.252)

Unconstrained, enjoying life to the full – even when, as is often the case, he is abused by his relations – Wonham demonstrates a resilience that marks him out as a figure of both moral steadfastness and magnificent eroticism. After he has been turned out of Mrs Failing's home, Rickie offers him refuge, and immediately Wonham generates a force field of desire which ultimately leads to the breakdown of Rickie's marriage to Agnes. If despis-ing his intrusiveness, Agnes is none the less drawn to Wonham's athletic build ('for one terrible moment she desired to be held in his arms' (p.260)). He resembles only too clearly the man she once loved, the rugby-playing Gerald Dawes, who received a fatal injury on the sports field. Indeed, Wonham sets Rickie and Agnes at loggerheads precisely because he is the kind of muscular brute the married couple either want to be or to have.

Yet Wonham – even if he has the girth and bulk of Gerald Dawes – is much more than a beefy sportsman. 'He was', the narrator reports, 'the child of poetry and of rebellion, and poetry should run in his veins. But he lived too near to the things he loved to seem poetical' (p.242). It cannot go unnoticed that even when praising Wonham to excess the narrator still hesitates in positing his 'poetical' quality. By the Edwardian period it was impossible for Forster plausibly to aestheticize the athlete. Aiming to ennoble Wonham in one sense, the 'poetical' threatens to vitiate him in another. Poetry, like Arnoldian culture, connoted effeminacy. That is why the novel makes such a pronounced appeal to Walt Whitman – section 31 of 'Song of Myself' is cited in Chapter 29 (p.237). Whitman's effusive evocations of male 'adhesive love' offered Forster an almost exclusively masculine model of poetry that could also be – in a covert sense – homosexual. So rather than 'make a man' of Rickie in the manner of Edgar Carruthers in 'Nottingham Lace', *The Longest Journey* elects instead to locate the 'poetical' in the 'villainous young brute' that Wonham appears to be (p.245). In proposing that 'poetry should run' in Wonham's veins, Forster would seem to be recovering some ground on which to stake an aesthetic ideal that had been debilitated by the consequences of Arnoldian precepts of culture. Here we discover the potent 'poet' who sires a healthy daughter to Agnes, and who is seen in the closing moments taking the child outdoors to spend a night sleeping beneath the stars.

In a rapturous finale, Wonham is said to have 'believed that he guided the future of our race' (p.289). The withering and fated aesthete, in the meantime, has accomplished two things that complement but cannot supersede Wonham's eugenic prerogative to be a 'poetical' survivor whose progeny shall strengthen the future of humanity. First, Rickie proves his nobility of character by saving his half-brother from being run over by a train – a feat that tragically results in Rickie's own death; and second, he enjoys posthumous success as a published author (in the final chapter, Rickie's brother-in-law and Wonham are arguing about how to split the percentage of Rickie's short stories). Both men, therefore, achieve varying proportions of the contrasting masculinities they initially represent. But Wonham is the one who benefits, by virtue of natural selection. Yet if the effeminate Rickie has disappeared by the end, what place might there be for femininity, given that it is Wonham's destiny to reproduce the race? It is a sign of the unease with which this novel regards feminine influences that the woman these half-brothers have both loved, at different times, almost disappears from view. Agnes, the mother of their children – one lame and deceased, the other alive and perfectly formed – diminishes into an overheard voice.

IV

One main consequence of *The Longest Journey* is the difficulty it has in locating a place for feminine authority in face of the Whitmanian embodiment of the masculine 'poetical' type. The lame and weakly Rickie dies, Wonham stays largely unaware of his poetic nature, and Agnes fades out of sight. *A Room with a View* (1908) tries to find a dignified role for female influence in relation to the redefined aestheticism embodied in Wonham. As the title suggests, this novel is preoccupied with the organization of domestic space and the cultured 'view' that such a feminine domain might be able to provide. Indeed, its 'view' opens up a perspective on how athletic manhood can be softened without losing any of its robust potency. Here, however, in an apparently more caring and nurturing context where men are to some degree compliant with womanly demands, the male 'desire to govern a woman' remains strong, even if there is the admission that 'men and women must fight it together'.[27]

It does not take long for the novel to compare and contrast its two differing types of men, and it is clear that the aesthete shall act in a condescending manner at no uncertain peril. Said to possess 'beautiful manners', Cecil Vyse has no hesitation in 'prais[ing] one too much for being athletic' (p.85). In other words, he belongs to that despicable and regressive species of mocking intellectuals who would like to be proper men but who hardly find courtship easy. Hopeless in making his advances towards Lucy Honeychurch, he wonders: 'Why could he not do as any labourer or navvy – nay, as any young man behind the counter would have done?' (p.108). Instead, he looks at her through the aesthete's Paterian lens. Here the vampirism of La Gioconda, haunting the stylized cadences of Walter Pater's *Studies in the History of the Renaissance* (1873), displays the cold misogyny invested in the sphinx-like secrecy that so many *fin-de-siècle* writers ascribed to female sexuality. 'She was', Cecil thinks to himself, 'like a woman of Leonardo da Vinci's, whom we love not so much for herself as for the things that she will not tell us' (p.88). Patronized by his supercilious 'chivalry', Lucy breaks off the engagement.

Cecil's athletic opponent is the young, seemingly withdrawn, but preeminently sexual George Emerson. His socialist father, hailing from the skilled working class, insists that 'love is of the body; not the body; but of the body' (p.202). The father's rather Whitmanian philosophy is put into practice by his impulsive son. Even if from the start he has 'lacked chivalry', later emerging '[b]arefoot, bare-chested' and 'radiant' after a healthy swim (pp.44, 133), George Emerson is not all brawn. Devoted to the writings of Schopenhauer and Nietzsche, with a 'rugged' face that could spring 'into tenderness', he is a serious-minded, if highly sexual, man (p.24). In a sense, George Emerson marks a median point between the high-mindedness of the cultured snob and the brute strength of those navvies and boys at the counter whose uninhibited manner threatens Cecil Vyse. The narrative takes pains to outline the suspicion with which the Emersons are treated by middle-class English society. Rumours abound about Mr Emerson's 'advantageous' marriage, an idea which prompts the elderly tourists staying at the *pensione* to suggest that he reputedly 'murdered' his wife (pp.53–4). In the Emersons, Forster was experimenting with an idiosyncratic blend of cultural interests and class specifications where the appreciation of art and 'love . . . of the body' are not separate.

This 'love . . . of the body' seems to be so impetuous – since George embarrasses Lucy twice with an indiscreet kiss – that the brooding ruggedness of his pulsating Nietzschean loins threatens to subordinate her in much the same manner as Cecil Vyse's repellent condescension. So the narrative undertakes to give pride of place to two figures of female authority in its closing pages. The first – and quite unexpected – agent of change is Lucy's cousin and former chaperone in Italy, Charlotte Bartlett. Having infuriated Lucy by gossiping to another tourist about George's indiscreet behaviour, Charlotte returns much later into Lucy's life to display previously unnoticed skills in social engineering. Having brought Lucy across George's path, Charlotte witnesses an exchange where George explains why he, and not Cecil Vyse, should be Lucy's lover. It is her role in enabling them to elope that preoccupies the final chapter. Now once more with Lucy in the *pensione*, George's thoughts are governed by Charlotte's desire: 'from the very first moment we met, she hoped, far down in her mind, that we should be like this' (p.209). Being in love – 'like this' – prompts them to understand how this other woman has brought the two of them together. Preoccupied with Charlotte's interventions, Lucy playfully chides George for acting like a 'baby'. Lying on his bed in the Pension Bertolini, demanding her affection, he protests: 'Why shouldn't I be a baby?' (p.205). Wanting to be mothered by his lover, George observes that Charlotte 'is not withered up all through' (p.209). His sexual connection with Lucy, then, has been facilitated by one whom both of them may have mistaken for a resentful spinster. (Spinsters, after all, were routinely described as 'withered' in contemporary discussions of 'old maids'.)[28] Like Philip Herriton and Gino Carella, George is placed under the aegis of feminine forms of care and nurturance, since Caroline represents an interceding goddess and Lucy tends him like a mother would a small infant.

Neither of these female identities is in any respect innovative, in the way that George Emerson's unusual masculinity surely appears. Although he internally connects the erudition of the monk with the passion of the beast, George achieves this improved state of masculine being only by virtue of Lucy transforming from an object of courtly attraction in the eyes of Cecil Vyse to a source of maternal nurturance that ministers to her lover's every need. So it might be said that the beneficial feminization of this 'connected' man can be achieved only as long as his woman partner moves from one traditional female role to another. Exactly the same could be said for Charlotte Bartlett, since she moves from being a spinster to a 'goddess'. There is, all in all, no positively regendered position of strength *for women*. Effeminacy, in this novel, has been disavowed at the expense of denying women a form of cultural authority that might exist outside conventional sexual roles.

It is precisely this problem that *Howards End* (1910) attempts to overcome, and its solution drives Forster's urgent desire to combat imperialist brutality to limits that exert almost unbearable pressures on the feminized power of Arnoldian culture. The novel provides an intellectual form of femininity that refuses to capitulate to the effeminate identity that English society so easily associates with the world of the arts. In this ambitious narrative, Forster decides to abandon the aesthete such as Cecil Vyse and replace him – not with a Nietzschean male whose scholarly interests refine his working-class origins – but with a high bourgeois woman who may more successfully connect with the forthright muscularity enshrined in the public-school ethic first voiced by the Manchetts in 'Nottingham Lace'. Addressing her maiden aunt, the fatherless Margaret Schlegel remarks:

> I suppose that ours is a female house . . . and one must just accept it . . . I don't mean that this house is full of women. I am trying to say something much more clever. I mean that it was irrevocably feminine, even in father's time . . . our house – it must be feminine, and all we can do is see that it isn't effeminate. (p.41)

Descending from a distinguished German line, Margaret Schlegel is – as the drafts to the novel make explicit – 'a distant relative of the great critic', Friedrich Schlegel.[29] Representing not only the virtues of the articulate Arnoldian culture but also some of the traits of the New Woman who rose to fame in the 1890s, she demands equality in marriage, if not 'free union' outside it. She displays selected aspects of this type of educated womanhood that is 'clever' enough to see how an 'irrevocably feminine' household must take pains not to grow weak, just as she knows equally well that a similarly 'masculine' one must be careful not to become 'brutal' (p.41). Effeminacy certainly retains a background presence in the high-minded world of the Schlegel family – notably in their younger brother, Tibby, who languishes in his rooms at Oxford. Like Wilde, he relishes the art of 'epigram' which, 'with its faint whiff of the 'eighties, meant nothing' (p.250). Tibby serves as a passing reminder that effeminate manhood should be consigned to the rarefied atmosphere of a former generation. According to Margaret's younger sister, Helen: 'Men' like the imperialist 'Wilcoxes would do Tibby a power of good' (p.2). So a cautiously defined form of women's liberation serves to challenge Tibby's effeminate leanings. At no point, however, are the Schlegel sisters called feminists, and the only mention of that polemical term – one that was increasingly at issue during the campaign for women's suffrage – occurs in a disparaging allusion to the 'crude feminist' who supports Helen during her illegitimate pregnancy in Munich (p.291). Yet their proximity to feminist ideals emerges in Helen's remark about Henry Wilcox and his family, whom she has met while touring the cathedrals of

Germany: 'He says the most horrid things about women's suffrage, and when I said I believed in equality he just folded his arms and gave me such a setting down as I've never had' (p.3). If the Schlegels have enjoyed an enlightened education – to travel where and as they wish, to attend concerts at their own choosing – then the Wilcoxes are designed by the narrative to make these intellectual women altogether more practical. Likewise, the Wilcoxes are shown to benefit – albeit in limited ways – from the judicious pleas for equality against the most 'brutal' kinds of 'setting down'.

So this plot, like its predecessors, is once again rehearsing how differently gendered elements within English society may be productively conjoined. But this time the historical significance of Forster's narrative is much more in the foreground than before. 'What Forster attempts in *Howards End*', as Peter Widdowson points out, 'is to establish a defensive position through individual "connection", against the breakdown he already senses but does not fully comprehend before the First World War.'[30] Without doubt, the dynamic of this liberal narrative aims to mark not only a symbolic synthesis between competing social forces, but also to establish an imaginary pact of peace between two nations – Britain and Germany – approaching what must by 1910 have felt to be the probable onset of war. Yet the pacifist spirit of '[t]emperance, tolerance, and sexual equality' insistently figured in the Schlegel sisters fails to provide them with the physical power granted to their sexually potent opposites (p.25). Having discovered and then forgiven Henry Wilcox's infidelity in his first marriage, Margaret points to his hypocrisy in chasing her adulterous sister from his home. 'You', she declares, 'have had a mistress – I forgave you. My sister has a lover – you drive her from the house. Do you see the connection?' (p.305). Margaret and Helen, therefore, emerge as admirable aesthetes because they have freely – one might say liberally – been able to engage with the decisive 'setting down' of empire-building zealotry, and in the process learn how to chasten it. No sooner are Margaret and Henry married than his pugilistic son, Charles, is led to think that his father's uncharacteristic 'petulant touch' makes him 'more like a woman' (p.325).

Howards End demonstrates how the Schlegels' ethical strengths can only be realized through their instinctual attraction to robust physicality, and Forster's persistent Darwinism provides the rationale for this desire to connect. Their sole guardian, Aunt Juley, exhibits similar traits. Glancing 'stealthily' at one of the younger men from the Wilcox clan, her 'feminine eye' notes 'nothing amiss in the sharp depressions at the corners of his mouth, nor in the rather box-like construction of his forehead'. Bearing all the trademarks of the bullish athlete, he is 'dark, clean-shaven', and seems 'accustomed to command' (p.14). No wonder that, with such bodily bulk in mind, Margaret informs her sister that there is an 'outer life' which neither she nor Helen has experienced. If 'obviously horrid', that unknown realm is at least 'real' – for there is 'grit' in it, as well as 'character' (p.25).

Similarly, Margaret's own 'feminine eye' travels with equal fascination across the Wilcox physique. Even if advanced in years, Henry is redoubtably the product of hardy stock, as the narrator – while entering Margaret's consciousness – makes clear:

> His complexion was robust, his hair receded but not thinned, the thick moustache and the eyes that Helen had compared to brandy-balls had an agreeable menace in them, whether they were turned towards the slums or towards the stars. Some day – in the millennium – there may be no need for his type. At present, homage is due to it from those who think themselves superior, and who possibly are. (pp.158–9)

Embodying the 'outer life', exploiting his rubber plantation in West Africa, Henry keeps the wheels of industry in motion, if with an eye that strikes 'superior'-minded persons of culture as wholly imperceptive. Yet the connection between the Schlegels and the Wilcoxes is bought at a considerable price. Just at the point where femininity has been given far greater influence than anything previously encountered in Forster's novels, another point of historical antagonism comes into view. This is the emergent Labour Movement that was increasingly threatening the hegemony enjoyed by the Liberal Party in the early 1900s. Henry's ruthless business sense ruins the life of another, less prominent, male figure in *Howards End* – the working-class autodidact, Leonard Bast.

Bast becomes the vehicle through which the limitations of Arnoldian culture are subjected to the most punishing scrutiny. Enchanted by people who could 'pronounce foreign names correctly', this disciple of the high arts burningly desires the Schlegels' company (p.37). Hoping to 'come to Culture suddenly', he immediately takes the advice of the Schlegels, who inform him – on Henry Wilcox's authority – that his employer is likely to go bust (p.48). This is bad advice. In duly moving to an insurance company with supposedly better prospects, Bast finds himself betrayed. Although finally crushed (with heavy-handed irony) under a bookcase, he retains an instrumental role in the narrative. Even if disadvantaged by his class, he shares the Wilcoxes' 'primitive good looks', ones that have a fundamental physical strength that will ensure that the Schlegels shall not remain in a weakened effeminate condition. True to his truncated surname, he fathers Helen's baby outside marriage. In the closing pages, the baby frolics at harvest-time in the garden of Howards End. There, too, Helen is nourished by the milk brought to her by the farm-boy, Tom. It is in this domestic space – where this madonna-like sustenance is one vital sign of the maternalism that shapes the heavily symbolic design of the novel – that femininity has full rein.

Undoubtedly, *Howards End* enshrines a vision of England that aligns the Schlegels with a lineage combining cultural sensitivity, dissenting politics, and liberal egalitarianism – all of which implicitly refer to the Parliamentary Acts of 1870 and 1882 that granted married women legal rights over property. Shortly before her death from cancer, Henry Wilcox's first wife, Ruth, bequeaths the house that she inherited from her own mother to her new-found friend, Margaret Schlegel. Aghast at Ruth's wishes, the indignant Wilcoxes ensure that Margaret hears nothing of the piece of paper on which Ruth Wilcox's will has been lightly pencilled. Howards End, her family home, is where – as Ruth's elderly housekeeper remarks – 'Things went on until there were men' who came to occupy the female domain, and promptly erected signs with the warning: 'Trespassers will be prosecuted' (p.271). These divergently gendered traditions, which point up Ruth's feminine compassion and Henry's masculine imperialism, relate directly to the marked distinction – one that was still prominent in the late nineteenth century – between differing Christian sects. Ruth, we are told, 'came from Quaker stock', while Henry's forebears – although 'formerly Dissenters' – had risen through the ranks, and were 'now members of the Church of England' (p.88). Clearly under threat from business-minded imperialists joining forces with the Establishment, Howards End, therefore, emblematizes far more honourable English values, ones that are associated with modesty (not bombast), the pastoral (not the Stock Exchange), philanthropy (not capitalism), and maternal influence (not patriarchal rule). The narrator explains how this distinctly feminine home lies – in terms of class, geography, and importantly, politics – in the settled, calm, and distinctly 'Liberal' middle of England:

> The chestnut avenue opened into a road, smooth but narrow, which led into the untouched country . . . Having no urgent destiny, it strolled downhill or up as it wished, taking no trouble about the gradients . . . The great estates that throttled the south of Hertfordshire were less obtrusive here, and the appearance of the land was neither aristocrat nor suburban . . . 'Left to itself', was Margaret's opinion, 'this country would vote Liberal'. (p.265)

This type of romantic vision, where neither landed lord nor city professional rules the country, evokes several of the most lyrical passages in the novel. But it is, as the larger design of the narrative indicates, very much an ideal. 'Howards End, which is meant to signify England,' writes Levenson, 'is contained and threatened by England; the symbolic vehicle sputters; the house is now, again, merely a house, jeopardized by the appetite of the suburbs and the smoke of cities.'[31] Indeed, Margaret Schlegel's perspective on middle England often has to face up to the fact that her outlook is utopian. It is not just that she can see the sprawl of encroaching housing developments upon the horizon. On several occasions, she is led to question the very forms of feminization that characterize the liberal ethic idealistically embodied in Ruth Wilcox's former home.

Precisely because it places so much emphasis on the anti-imperial aspects to this feminine realm, the novel at times finds it difficult to maintain the gendered oppositions from which it derives its narrative momentum. In one or two places, the country that lies before Margaret's admiring gaze is set within a framework that attempts to do away with the defining features of gender. What begins to open up in front of her is a liminal space where the dialectic between aestheticism and athleticism may be sublated into a new ideal form. Observing that the tree outside Howards End was 'neither warrior, nor lover, nor god', Margaret considers how its mixture of 'tenderness' and 'girth' makes it into a 'comrade', and how the intimate touch of its finger-like branch around the house 'transcend[s] any simile of sex' (p.203).

At this juncture, Carpenter's homophile rhetoric of comradeship comes fully into its own. Viewed as superior type, the comrade – an emergent androgynous being with its distinctive capacity for cross-gendered understanding – provided Forster with the opportunity to imagine the mixing of masculine and feminine qualities in a 'third' or 'intermediate' sex. In 1908, Carpenter would sketch out his perceptions of how gender relations had shifted radically by the turn of the century:

In late years (and since the arrival of the New Woman amongst us) many things in the relation of men and women to each other have altered, or at any rate become clearer. The growing sense of equality in habits and customs – university studies, art, music, politics, the bicycle, etc. – all these things have brought about a *rapprochement* between the sexes. If the modern woman is a little more masculine in some ways than her predecessor, the modern man (it is to be hoped), while by no means effeminate, is a little more sensitive in temperament and artistic feeling than the original John Bull. It is beginning to be recognized that the sexes do not or should not normally form two groups hopelessly isolated in habit and feeling from each other, but that they rather represent the two poles of *one* group – which is the human race.[32]

Fuelled by utopian zeal, Carpenter's socialist and feminist-inspired vision of a world where sexual difference could be eradicated by racial unity is in fact somewhat less radical than it might at first appear. In making high claims for the sensual and sentimental capacities of the Uranian temperament, Carpenter readily saw how the charge of effeminacy had to be repudiated in the very process of advancing this noble being in the face of a pugilistic John Bull. Forster shared exactly the same difficulty: namely how to make the sensitive man of Uranian genius seem strengthened, not weakened, by feminine qualities. Yet the impulse in *Howards End* to unite the Wilcoxes and the Schlegels under the banner of Uranian comradeship quickly comes up against political obstacles that run altogether against the current of Carpenter's thought.

Margaret's repeated yearnings to coalesce with a 'comrade' fail to achieve the androgynous vision that Carpenter upheld, and for one good reason. Carpenter, renowned for his work with the Independent Labour Party, espoused the very forms of socialism and feminism that proved intolerable to the narrator of *Where Angels Fear to Tread*, and with which *Howards End* displays a similar unease. In *Howards End*, Forster defensively modifies Carpenter's ideal of comradeship into an exclusively middle-class affair, one that is freed from any ignoble adulteration from below. Pondering Helen's sexual liaison with Leonard Bast, Margaret concludes that her sister 'could pity, or sacrifice herself, or have instincts'. At the same time, however, she questions whether Helen 'had . . . ever loved in the noblest way, where man and woman, having lost themselves in sex, desire to lose sex itself in comradeship' (p.309). Yet that is not to suggest that she fails to consider her own limitations when confronting the issue of how one might 'lose sex'. 'In dealing with a Wilcox', she reflects, 'how tempting it was to lapse from comradeship, and to give him the kind of woman he desired' (p.226). No doubt we are expected to see her concern to 'transcend . . . any simile of sex' as influencing Henry's gradual change into a figure who 'is more like a woman'. So, to reiterate, the sexual scenario haunting this novel relates to the moderately feminized male obtaining, not the 'woman he desire[s]', but a 'comrade' like himself – a member of the 'intermediate sex' that provided a powerful model for theorizing the homosexual as an 'invert' in the 1880s and 1890s. In making this point, I am not claiming that Margaret is, in fact, the masked figure of the aesthete as homosexual, or that, indeed, she is a new hybrid type of 'third sex'. Instead, what needs to be underlined is that Margaret's desire for comradeship is predicated on her femininity. The need to 'lose sex', in this context, represents a feminine – not a masculine – desire, since it emerges from the cultured ideals of Forster's liberalism and their effeminate origins from which he was still trying to dissociate himself.

If shifting away from effeminacy, the novel none the less struck some of his readers as distinctly feminine. In 1910, one reviewer regarded *Howards End* as expressing 'a feminine brilliance of perception'.[33] Even if attempting to use a particular form of refined femininity to 'lose sex', Forster had not entirely managed to transcend it. The spectre of Edgar Carruthers certainly haunts the figure of Margaret Schlegel as she looks out across an England that she knows can only be improved by positively encountering, learning from, and judiciously tempering the imperial spirit that roused the populace. But in rejecting the dissatisfying 'degeneracy' of the effeminate young man – abandoning him to a narcotic poetry that implicitly ruined Wilde and his coterie – Forster was finally driven towards acknowledging that desire to 'lose sex' is caught up in the very problem of the curiously misspelled 'effeminancy' from which his sequence of Edwardian fictions sought to disentangle itself. This idealized vision of England – domesticated, fertile, maternalized, liberal, and comradely – is indissociable from a feminine principle that absorbed and ultimately obscured virile masculinity from view. Hereafter, his two remaining fictions – one suppressed, the other published to great acclaim – break with the earlier obsession with the wilting man of letters troubled by the feminized culture which promised to establish the liberal condition of England.

V

'Home emasculated everything', remarks the narrator of *Maurice* (p.44), the novel Forster originally wrote in 1913–14, and redrafted in 1932 and 1959, and which was published (with various errors) posthumously 58 years later.[34] Here, once again, Forster's project is to banish those deeply loathed forms of effeminate intellectuality of the kind that he identified with himself, and which Carpenter – the guiding influence over the narrative – assuredly disliked in him. 'I knew him fairly well', Forster wrote of Carpenter, 'and I was perhaps too intellectualized and mentally fidgety quite to suit him.' The problem lay in Forster's cultured background. 'He had escaped from culture by the skin of his teeth – he had been a don, a clergyman, and a University Extension lecturer – and he was naturally suspicious of anyone who might seem to drag him back into prison.' Carpenter never hesitated to tell the implicitly effeminate Forster to 'sit quiet' rather than make 'some intelligent if useless remark'.[35] Forster's novel seeks to abandon this style of cultured masculinity, focusing instead on how two men overcome the class barriers set between them by obeying an unstoppable impulse to love the body. Here the intrusive femininity that has so far interposed itself between the male lovers is finally eradicated from the plot, and with misogynistic consequences.

The narrative moves from the domestic realm governed by women via the collegiate world of Cambridge to an English 'greenwood' where comradeship between men flourishes according to Carpenter's utopian model (p.236). The plan of the story, as Forster's 'Terminal Note' of 1960 makes clear, was written up immediately after meeting Carpenter at Millthorpe, near Sheffield, in 1913. It was there that Carpenter's lover, the working-class George Merrill, made a lasting impression on Forster by touching him 'on the backside – just above the buttocks'. So startling was the effect of Merrill's physical intimacy that Forster explains how the 'sensation . . . seemed to go through the small of my back into my ideas', to the degree that he had, as it were, 'conceived' (p.235). Equally taken aback by the psychical resonances of this event, John Fletcher remarks that here we are witnessing a Freudian 'primal scene of masculine love in which by a strange displacement the male partners combine to touch and to inseminate the watching third'. It is, as Fletcher observes, the 'continuing and seductive power of the primal scene' that 'derives from what remains untranslated, enigmatic, or repressed for the adult participants in that scene as well as for its childish witness'.[36] So the narrative stages – in a more focused manner than before – Forster's compulsive need to grapple with what was for him the enigmatic psychology informing sexual desire between men. Yet the novel has rarely been interpreted in this way. Few of its earlier readers were willing to credit the narrative with much, if any, artistic or intellectual complexity. Philip Toynbee, for example, found it 'novelettish, humourless and deeply embarrassing'.[37] (One might indeed add that the embarrassment to which several commentators have admitted when analyzing *Maurice* has only too often appeared as a displaced form of homophobia.)[38]

To realize this form of what Maurice himself calls 'masculine love' (p.221), the novel sets up a straightforward contrast between the respective fates of its male protagonists. The narrative juxtaposes Maurice Hall – a man of average intelligence, athletic good looks, and possessing the willingness to obey his bodily desires – against the intellectual, arrogant, and upper-class Clive Durham. In this stark contrast, one point is obvious. The comrade who accomplishes the democratic homophile ideal may accomplish his happiness only when the Cambridge-educated Platonist weakly opts for an unconsummated marriage with a spouse who has never been taught the facts of life. But this novel intersperses the divergent destinies of these two men with incidents that explore Maurice's psychological landscape – notably his recurring dream of the garden boy where the enigmatic signifier of homosexual desire both obscures and awakens the memory of the dead father. Entranced by 'masculine love', the novel not only rages against Clive's moral and physical failure to obey his erotic attraction to other men, it also has two other targets under attack. If the female characters are not being subjected to appalling abuse (the narrator observes that both men are 'misogynists, Clive especially' (p.91)), then women are – figuratively speaking – objects to be killed off. One incident makes this clear. At the height of their passionate affair at Cambridge, Clive climbs into the side-car of Maurice's motorcycle 'without demur'. Maurice then 'turned the machine into a by-lane and travelled at top speed. There was a wagon in front of them, full of women. He drove straight at them' (p.52). Were this purging of feminine presences not enough, the narrative is impelled to dissociate itself entirely from the effeminate homosexual identity of the 'Oscar Wilde sort' (p.145). The figure of the society wit, Risley – modelled on Lytton Strachey – embodies the worst traits of the 'aesthetic push' (or company) in which Maurice finds himself plunged at Cambridge (p.29). It is highly significant that the scholarly world that must during college tutorials grapple with 'the unspeakable vice of the Greeks' completely inhibits the physical realization of homoerotic desire (p.42). Not without irony, Clive takes a vacation in Greece where he enters the temple of Dionysus only to remain 'untouched' so that he lapses into 'sterility' to spurn his homosexuality (p.106). This central turning-point of the plot suggests that Carpenter's democractic body shall supersede the Platonic intellect and the Wildean aestheticism accompanying it. In the end, Maurice Hall turns his back on his job in the city and faces the risk of escaping into the 'greenwood' with a working-class man. 'Physical love', observes the narrator, 'means reaction, being panic in essence, and Maurice saw now how natural it was that their primitive abandonment at Penge [Clive Durham's estate] should have led to peril . . . Not as a hero, but as a comrade, had he stood up to the bluster' (p.211). The virilizing power of Whitman's poetry oozes from the primordial, if not Edenic, fantasy projected in these paragraphs.

For all its discontinuities with the feminine idealism of the publicly admired *Howards End*, the suppressed *Maurice* has political aspirations similar to its predecessor. The love affair between Maurice and Alec which 'overleap[s] class' resides in an idealized England that belongs to the unpretentious world which the Schlegels finally claim as their own (p.191). Once Maurice has bidden farewell to Clive, he disappears 'leaving no trace of his presence except a little pile of petals of the evening primrose' (p.230). He and Alec belong – as Forster puts in the 'Terminal Note' – to an 'England where it was still possible to get lost' (p.240). There is regret in these words. By 1960, the English 'greenwood' was not only covered over by increasing acres of suburbia, but also governed by an intensely homophobic state that would take another seven years to enact in law the recommendations made by the Wolfenden Committee in 1957. No sequel was drafted to tell us how Alec and Maurice fared. Strachey, for one, 'prophesied a rupture after six months – chiefly as a result of lack of common interests owing to class differences'.[39] Perhaps it was the painful thought that these comrades only too obviously risked being placed in the dock on charges of gross indecency which convinced Forster that his homosexual lovers should vanish into obscurity. Possibly, too, this utopian ending signals Forster's inability to relinquish an implausible fantasy in which he had indulged. But even if we find *Maurice* overflowing with too many wishfulfilments about virile comradeship, his protagonist none the less accepts that his sexuality is not a morbid condition that needs to be treated any longer by doctors and hypnotists. 'England', remarks Mr Lasker Jones, 'has always been disinclined to accept human nature' (p.185). So Maurice's destiny is to return to a state of 'primal being' of the very kind that D.H. Lawrence felt Forster's homosexuality continually 'dodge[d]'.[40] In *Maurice*, Forster brought himself up against the fact that the comradely life to which his lovers had been making their way could remain only in the imagination. His subsequent writing of male–male desire showed little or no faith in the consolations of pastoral England. Nor would he seek any further to engage with the need to strengthen Arnoldian culture. The comradeship he craved would from now on form a prominent part of his dystopic outlook on the violence of imperial rule.

VI

'Are the sexes really races, each with its own code of morality?', asks Margaret Schlegel, contemplating Henry Wilcox's ruthless business mentality (p.237). Given the strong eugenic inflections in those descriptions that classify the social and cultural differences among Forster's cast of characters, her query arises quite naturally in a world where the 'belief in comradeship' keeps being 'stifled' (p.237). By 1924, with *A Passage to India*, Forster tries once again to see what kinds of connection can be made between opposing parties. But this time the narrative does not lead to the comradely 'greenwood' where Maurice and Alec may rest eternally in each other's arms. Even though it culminates – as do all Forster's novels – in a scene thematizing regeneration (the Hindu festival of Gokul Ashtami), the process of rebirth goes strangely awry. Here there are no frolicking children, maternal goddesses, or dreams of an English Eden. Instead, the Rajah who should have stood as a figurehead during the seven-day ceremony unexpectedly dies. What is more, the whole festival is washed out by torrential floods. Everywhere, indeed, the story makes its potential harmonies discordant. The comic manner that Trilling praised in Forster's Edwardian *Bildungsromane* takes on a sardonic tone.[41] Given the persistent negations that structure so many aspects of this narrative (the word 'nothing' features prominently throughout),[42] there is little hope from the outset that comradeship will breach the imperial divide that stands at the centre of the plot.

Forster's representation of imperialist violence has prompted widely varying responses to the political direction of this novel. Although the story eventually exposes the Anglo-Indians' foolish readiness to incriminate an Indian doctor for the attempted rape of a member of their own community, this patent critique of empire does not always extend to paying due respect to emergent Indian demands for independence. The novel, after all, was largely completed in the wake of the appalling Amritsar Massacre in 1919, one of the very worst attacks on the native population since the violent suppression of the Sepoy Rebellion in 1857. Edward W. Said draws attention to one passage where Forster's narrator remarks demeaningly on how the Cambridge-educated Hamidullah nostalgically recalls his undergraduate days. For Hamidullah there is a stark contrast between the golden age of Edwardian England and the world of contemporary India intent to free itself from British rule. 'There, games, work and pleasant society had interwoven, and appeared to be sufficient substructure for a national life. Here was all wire-pulling and fear.'[43] Not surprisingly, Said states that Forster's 'view of Indians as a nation contending for sovereignty with Britain is not politically very serious, or even respectful'. So it follows that Forster's 'presumption is that *he* can get past the puerile nationalist put-ons to the essential India;

when it comes to ruling India – which is what Hamidullah and the others are agitating about – the English had better go on doing it, despite their mistakes: "they" are not ready for self-rule'.[44] Undeniably, Forster's liberalism condescends to what it deems the political inadequacies of a country that is dissatisfyingly divided between fragmentary groups, such as the 'Hindus, Moslems, two Sikhs, two Parsis, a Jain, and a Native Christian' who gather together with Hamidullah in a 'worrying committee of notables' (p.96). In this instance, Forster's putative anti-imperialism subscribes to the very forms of imperial rule that he is criticizing. Much the same could be said of several other narratorial interventions, not least where Forster insists that '[s]uspicion in the Oriental is a sort of malignant tumour, a mental malady, that makes him self-conscious and unfriendly suddenly; he trusts and mistrusts in the same way that a Westerner cannot comprehend' (p.26). Needless to say, the omniscient narrator is unlikely to succumb to any such kind of incomprehension himself.

Incomprehension baffles much of the narrative from beginning to end, however, to the point of becoming a thematic preoccupation. If one issue continues to tax readers of Forster's *magnum opus*, it is its nescient indeterminacy. 'Forster', writes Trilling, 'refuses to be conclusive. No sooner does he come to a conclusion than he must unravel it again'.[45] Yet that is not to say it is a nihilistic work. Instead, the narrative explores the conditions in which truths are rendered possible. Paul B. Armstrong has made the most exacting case for what Trilling first apprehended as this 'double turn' in Forster's thought:

> A work of much greater epistemological complexity than its seemingly conventional narrative form suggests, this novel invokes the ideal of non-reified, reciprocal knowledge of other people and cultures only to suggest that interpretation invariably requires distancing, objectifying prejudgements. The novel insists that truth and justice can be determined unequivocally – Aziz is innocent [of sexually assaulting Adela Quested], and India must be liberated from the yoke of British oppression – but its manipulation of point of view demonstrates the difficulty (perhaps impossibility) of attaining a lasting consensus about any matter or of discovering a final, uncontestable meaning to any state of affairs.[46]

If we were to locate the impossibility of 'uncontestable meaning' anywhere in the novel, it would be in the discordant 'Boum . . . bou-oum . . . ou-boum . . . Boum' echoing from the heart of the Marabar Caves (pp.138–9). To the very end, it remains unclear what made Adela Quested flee their eerie darkness. Such is their enigmatic status that we might infer that Forster is here defying his earlier impulse to 'only connect'. In the caves, things are not linked in such a complementary way. Instead, they are violently condensed, as Homi K. Bhabha observes:

Such words as 'Ou–Boum' are not naturalized and primitivistic descriptions of colonial 'otherness', they are inscriptions of an uncertain colonial silence that mocks the social performance of language with their non-sense; that baffles the communicable verities of culture with their refusal to translate.[47]

'Ou-boum', however, addresses other silences as well, especially those that render sexual desire 'unspeakable' (p.178).

If *A Passage to India* is trying to 'only connect' anyone or anything, it is through a carefully coded pattern of erotic attraction between the two male protagonists: Dr Aziz and Cyril Fielding. To a limited degree, this is Forster's well-tried conjunction of the athletic with the aesthetic male. But if Aziz indubitably represents athleticism, Fielding shows no taint of a weakening effeminacy that needs to build up its strength with the aid of a virile partner. Instead, Fielding is an educated man, one who easily grasps the narrow-minded attitudes of the British expatriates who gather together in their club to perform light entertainments such as *Cousin Kate*. His outsider status makes him warm to Aziz's friendly advances. It is hard not to notice how the final chapter tries to bring the two men together – no less than 'half kissing' – as they issue from the 'gap' at the end of their 'last ride' in the Mau jungles (pp.307, 312). But Forster's focused interest in the virile body of Aziz has been read as just as damagingly imperialist as his rather high-handed treatment of Indian nationalism. Sara Suleri, for example, finds in those passages that dwell on Aziz's attractive physique and the alluring physical beauty of several other Indian men a 'hidden tradition of imperial looking in which the disempowerment of a homoerotic gaze is as damaging to the colonizing psyche as to that of the colonized'. Suleri's general point is that this 'troubling' novel of 'cultural self-examination' must constantly face up to the fact that same-sex desire cannot be legitimately expressed in the public domain. Forster, she claims, is acutely aware of how his homoeroticism has to hide beneath the cover of an admissible imperialist surveillance: a punitive gaze used to classifying racially otherized bodies in line with eugenic thinking. In fact, Suleri goes so far as to argue that the whole novel belongs to a tradition of Anglo-Indian fiction where the 'familiarity of the tropologies' remains an 'undiminished embarrassment to post-colonial discourse'.[48] The most familiar trope, she claims, is that of friendship, where the colonizing subject reaches out to heal the wounds inflicted by empire on the native population. In this respect, the exemplary embodiment of this imperial figure is the 'Little Friend of All the World': the eponymous boy-hero of Rudyard Kipling's *Kim* (1901). Certainly, *A Passage to India* continually refers to the desire for friendship between Indians and English people, while contemplating its enduring impossibility. Near the start, the Indians are 'discussing whether or not it is possible to be friends with an Englishman' (p.5). This much-repeated theme reappears in the disillusioned ending: 'Friends again, yet aware that they would meet no more, Aziz and Fielding went for their last ride in the Mau jungles' (p.307).

The trouble with Suleri's provocative analysis is that she fails to observe the homophile inflections to this insistent emphasis on friendship. The title of the novel is taken from an addition to *Leaves of Grass* that Whitman made in 1871. Although Whitman's 'Passage to India' has frequently been mentioned in commentaries on *A Passage to India* – to the point of being cited at length – the dissident homosexual politics implied in this choice of title have generally gone unrecognized.[49] This is not to say that Whitman's poem provides a straightforward gloss on the homoerotic attachment that we occasionally glimpse between Aziz and Fielding. In fact, one might argue that Forster's *A Passage to India* is to some degree disputing the imperialist ambitions enshrined in Whitman's 'Passage to India'. Whitman's poem, after all, was written to celebrate three technological achievements: the laying of the Atlantic cable in 1869; the joining of the Union Pacific and the Central Pacific railroads at Promontory Point in 1869; and the completion, in the same year, of the Suez Canal. Such feats of engineering are celebrated in these typically expansive lines:

> an earth to be spann'd, connected by network,
> The races, neighbors, to marry and be given in marriage,
> The oceans to be crossed, the distant brought near.[50]

'In this image of the earth literally "spann'd" by advances in technology', writes Betsy Erkkila, 'Whitman found a fitting symbol for his vision of history as a unitary and spiritually infused process evolving toward a global democratic community.'[51] But this was not a vision that Forster shared. The closing words of his novel – 'Not, not yet . . . No, not there' (p.312) – signify at least two related things. First, the narrative concludes by showing how Aziz and Fielding cannot exist in Whitmanian comradeship. And second, these negative phrases emphasize that the time has not yet come for a 'global democratic community'. Indeed, some readers would take an altogether more favourable view than Said of Forster's anti-imperial politics here. At this point, we may detect how comradeship – between men and between nations – can only come about with the end of empire. So if the novel has a strong interest in the virile masculinity associated with Whitman's name, it also revises the political idealism enshrined in 'Passage to India'.

A Passage to India does its utmost to realize homophile intimacy from the moment when Aziz first makes a visit to Fielding's home. But Forster has a very limited space in which to signal these sexual interests, as we can see from the initial encounter between the two men. When he first hears Aziz's greeting, Fielding is getting dressed behind a ground-glass screen. Symbolizing the opacity that often comes between them – no matter how hard they try to consolidate their friendship – the partition becomes the subject of an amusing guessing-game about their respective bodily features. Fielding declares that Aziz must be 'five feet nine inches high', and the Muslim doctor jokingly asks: 'Have I not a venerable white beard?' (p.58). Surprisingly informal for an encounter of this kind, their conversation takes an even more intimate turn when Fielding exclaims that he has stamped on his collar-stud. What follows, according to Suleri, is 'the most notorious oblique homoerotic exchange in the literature of English India'.[52] Loosening his own collar, Aziz discreetly unfastens the stud, and pretends it can be spared. Now this small gift signals several things. The stud represents 'the rapidity of their intimacy' (p.58), it symbolizes exploitative imperial rule, and it is an obscure emblem of homosexual desire.

But it is not so easy to enfold each aspect neatly into an anxiety-inducing 'imperial erotic', as Suleri would have it.[53] The collar-stud, if a humble token of Aziz's servility, also represents his sexual potency: a feature that emerges most forcefully in later descriptions of Aziz's body. It is he, after all, who inserts it into the 'shirt back's hole', which he remarks is 'rather small' and that 'to rip it wider [were] a pity' (p.59). Inscribed, therefore, in the subaltern male's servile behaviour are the caring words of an active sexual partner who wishes not to damage the 'back . . . hole'. Although race places Aziz as Fielding's inferior, he none the less embodies a form of sexual authority which in itself is very quickly associated with imperialism. No sooner has Aziz cried out 'Hooray! Stud's gone in' than he starts recalling his daydreams of the 'Mogul Empire at its height and Alamgir reigning at Delhi upon the Peacock Throne' (p.59). So the contradictory sexual and imperial features to this exchange accentuate two things. First, Aziz's erotic power – pushing the potentially punning 'stud' neatly into the 'back . . . hole' – emerges in a scene that emphasizes his subservience. And second, the embarrassing lengths to which Aziz goes to please the English ruling class are intertwined with his own fantasies of imperial power. Forster's 'imperial erotic', then, is not only conditioned by violence and despair, as Suleri would suggest. Even if this exchange is necessarily arranged from a Western perspective, the line of its gaze is persistently interrupted by devices as opaque as the ground-glass screen where yearnings for imperial domination and homophile comradeship coalesce and dissipate at once.

This incident assuredly points to the ambivalent manner in which homophile longing and dreams of empire meet and part. Without doubt, Aziz's body provides the template for the highly conflicted desires experienced by the European liberal author whose homoeroticism often must have felt uncomfortably close to the dominative violence meted out by imperial rule. Most commentators concur that Aziz is moulded by Forster's two romances with oriental men: Syed Ross Masood and Mohammed el Adl. Yet biographical information alone cannot adequately explain the erotic and political forces shaping Aziz's restive sexuality. If the drafts to the novel are anything to go by, then it would appear that Forster was unsure about how to account for the muscular attractiveness of Aziz's physique. Initially, Forster wrote that Aziz 'was a small but well developed man, with broad shoulders and strong arms. He had fenced in Germany, loved riding, and did dumb bells every morning.'[54] Here it is almost as if Aziz's physical strength is modelled on the English public-school 'blood' or 'hearty'. In the published version, however, Aziz is reduced in stature: 'He was an athletic little man, daintily put together, but really very strong' (p.13). Suleri observes that this description is one of many that serves to belittle this idealized Indian subject. But Aziz's 'really very strong' body suggests that his virility is not entirely subjected to imperial condescension. In fact, the novel goes to considerable lengths to show how the most appalling kinds of imperial prejudice can attach to an Indian man's sexuality. Aziz's daydreams about 'an evening with some girls' whose 'vague jollity would culminate in voluptuousness' frequently come to our attention (p.92). This is not at all to suggest that he is a potential rapist. The narrative makes it patently clear that Aziz is not attracted to Adela Quested. Indeed, she repels him: 'he wondered how God could have been so unkind to any female form' (p.61).

So it is truly shocking when Aziz is accused of sexually assaulting her. This criminal charge is based on presumption, rather than evidence. Since explicit details of what happened to Adela are strategically occluded in the narrative, all we can assume is that she was terrified by the 'ou-boum' that echoed from the centre of the Marabar Caves, and that she escaped as fast as she could. Jenny Sharpe points out that Forster takes pains to configure the purported rape of Adela Quested within the colonial memory of the Sepoy Rebellion of 1857, an event so traumatic to the British Raj that rumours of Indian sexual assaults on Englishwomen were credited as factual in the press.[55] 'The crime', remarks the narrator when the Anglo-Indians hear of Adela's plight, 'was even worse than they had supposed – the unspeakable limits of cynicism, untouched since 1857' (p.178). Thereafter, they can only bring themselves to mention the young woman and her presumed assailant by way of an evasive 'periphrasis' (p.173). It is, indeed, the 'unspeakable' nature of sexual acts that creates such confusion in the courtroom. Only there does Adela for the first time break her silence to make it clear that Aziz did not follow her into the caves. Consequently, she is excommunicated by the Anglo-Indian community at Chandrapore, and she has to suffer Aziz's understandable wrath as well. An untold amount of damage, after all, has been done to him. In some respects, it is tempting to agree with Brenda R. Silver that 'rape' operates as the most powerful trope in the novel, since it is the nodal point where imperial violence and an unbending 'sex/gender/power system' interconnect.[56] On this view, Aziz is 'raped' by the imperial authorities, just as Adela has been subjected first to her dreadful experience in the Marabar Caves, and then 'raped' once again by the community that ostracizes her. But we need to bear in mind that the novel does not treat them equally where such violence is concerned. Far less attention is given to Adela than to Aziz once the trial is over. The crisis enables the two men to come together more closely than ever before.

From the beginning, Fielding has defended Aziz against the unsubstantiated charge of rape. So when '[f]orced to choose sides', as Silver observes, 'Fielding chooses Aziz, and in doing so, he reaffirms the discourse of sexuality, a discourse in which their shared gender mediates – at least potentially – racial difference'.[57] In other words, male homosociality accomplishes connections that can and must override racial differences. But this is done at a cost, as Christopher Lane has argued: 'Forster's essential defence of Aziz against the charge of rape is . . . a considerable humiliation for Adela Quested', and it 'raises questions about his support of feminine sexuality and its structural abuse by men.' Pursuing this point, Lane adds:

> this potential 'alliance' between European author and Indian protagonist may usefully foreground the complex political stakes between colonial homophilia and misogyny at the turn of the century, for narratives that set out to 'promote' intimacy between men at that time and simultaneously critique heterosexuality and phallocentrism are now almost impossible to detach from an accompanying contempt for femininity.[58]

This astute comment identifies the structural exclusions on which the narrative is based. By now the novel has done everything within its power to eradicate the two women who attempt to create a bridge between Britain and India. It finally exposes Mrs Moore's religious impulses as 'spiritual muddledom' (p.198), and renders Adela's search for the '*real* India' as fatally myopic (p.19). Having dispatched Mrs Moore and Adela to England, the novel concludes with the two men taking their zestful 'last ride' together where the galloping pace of their conversation heightens the intensity of their 'knock-about' jibes (p.311). Yet if emphasizing the emotional intimacy between these two men, the final chapter also stresses their alienation from one another. The ground-glass screen that initially came between them retains its symbolic power to the end.

No one can help but notice how the confusions that have often set Aziz and Fielding plainly at odds are compounded during their eroticized 'last ride' through the jungles of Mau. At every level, the novel refuses to resolve their differences. In this respect Forster goes against the regenerative principle that features at the end of his Edwardian fictions. Lashed by rain, the discordant rebirth of Krishna in Gokul Ashtami that provides the backdrop to the final 'Temple' section could not contrast more sharply with the pastoral hay-making concluding *Howards End*. Now that the earth mouths 'myriads of kisses' as it draws off the floodwaters, there are more than slight hints of 'colonial intimacy'. But separations occur when Fielding asks Aziz: 'Do you know anything about this Krishna business?' (p.309). Aziz protests that he has nothing to do with Hindus. This is an extraordinary disavowal. As Frances B. Singh has pointed out, Aziz's nationalist sentiments are voiced in 'the overwhelmingly Hindu atmosphere of Mau', and she adds: 'The confidence that Aziz manifests is what Gandhi hoped to instil among Muslim politicians.'[59] Singh sees Aziz embodying Gandhian ideals of Hindu–Muslim unity – ideals that were not realized by the time of Indian independence in 1947. So the political configurations of this final chapter remain complex, at best. Pursuing his confused response to Hinduism, Fielding remains disappointed because he cannot understand the peace of mind it has brought to his wife and her brother. 'I wish you would talk to them,' he urges Aziz, 'for at all events you're an oriental' (p.310). To Aziz, this is a 'clumsy' remark. It is, however, a forgivable one because he recognizes that Fielding is once again trying to breach cultural misunder-standings, if only serving – at the same time – to compound them.

The 'last ride' focuses on two related issues that inevitably divide them: nationalism and women. Their lively banter grows increasingly serious when Fielding lightly mocks the feminism that he detects in Aziz's poetry. Aziz, articulating the voice of a progressive Islam, has declared that an independent India must be accompanied with women's liberation. Such sentiments strike Fielding as hopelessly idealistic: 'Free your own lady in the first place, and see who'll wash Ahmed, Karim and Jamila's faces' (p.311). He continues this polemic by making fun of Indian independence: 'India a nation! What an apotheosis! Last comer to the drab nineteenth-century sisterhood!' (p.312). Such mockery is ambivalent. Even if it jokingly impersonates the voice of empire, Fielding's badinage simultan-eously utters the fear that a 'conference of oriental statesmen' may turn as imperialist as the British Raj. Yet – as this intricate conversation gathers pace – in implying that nationalism has its dangers, Fielding makes him-self understood through a disparaging image of femininity: the nations of Europe for him comprise a 'waddl[ing] sisterhood'. It is a revealing image. The wished-for connection between these Whitmanian comrades is de-fined against a loathing of femininity and a contempt for the authoritarian power identified with the nation state. In the end, too many obstacles lie between these men: the inestimable violence of imperialism, together with the Lawrentian demand for the homosexual Forster to 'take a woman and fight clear to his own basic, primal being'. In this respect, *A Passage to India* finishes on a loud protesting note against those forms of imperial masculine power that once promised to strengthen the effeminate man of culture.

To contest those punishing types of authority, this novel offers its own 'queer' perspective on why its male partners cannot 'only connect'. This epithet, which already signalled its homophile interests in 'Albergo Em-pedocle' in 1903, recurs on countless occasions in the narrative, not least during the 'last ride'. At one point, the narrator remarks that to Fielding the scene at Mau 'was as park-like as England, but did not cease being queer' (p.308). Queerness, in its official usage at the time, pointed to those incongruous, uncanny, and peculiar aspects of experience that often left one with a feeling of bewilderment. This is, indeed, how the word operates every time it arises in the novel. After Adela has gone missing from the party visiting the caves, Fielding 'felt at once that something had gone queer' (p.148). Discussing how a snake escaped into the college, Fielding ends his day in 'a queer vague talk with Professor Godbole' (p.166). Later, just after the charges against Aziz have been dropped, the narrator uses indirect speech to express Fielding's opinion that '[i]t was a victory, but such a queer one' (p.222). When it looks as if Adela shall have to pay compensation for the trial, Fielding 'couldn't bear to think of the queer honest girl losing her money and possibly her young man too' (p.237). And it is not just Fielding who has this 'queer' consciousness. Imploring Fielding to '[r]ead any of the Mutiny records', McBryde informs him that 'when an Indian goes bad, he goes not only very bad, but very queer' (p.160). Later still, in the courtroom, Adela remembers Mrs Moore, and the conversation both of them enjoyed 'before the old lady had turned disagreeable and queer' (p.208). But this epithet is also tinged with a strong sense of sexual disharmony, where 'queer' perceptions do not square with the heteronormative culture that thwarted Forster's dreams of comradeship. Eternally divided, the sexes remained very much like races, as Margaret Schlegel speculated in *Howards End*. But in the small amount of fiction that he wrote after *A Passage to India*, Forster never ceased from devising different scenarios in which his comrades could 'only connect'.

VII

The posthumous publication of *The Life to Come and Other Stories* (1972) brought most of Forster's suppressed homoerotic short fictions to light. Nearly all the work in this collection has homosexual subject-matter, and it comprises the main part of what survives from a larger body of writing, much of which Forster consigned to the fire in 1958. If one thing characterizes the stories written after 1924, it is their preoccupation with generational differences between men. Time and again, he associates potency with a form of youthful manhood envied by his older male characters. Entries in his *Commonplace Book* disclose how urgent this issue was for him as he began sketching out a possible plot for another full-length novel. 'Robust alert character of 50 – ', he writes in 1927, 'not sympathetic with the 20s except through duty or lust. Not hard on the young or consciously thwarting them, but unable to adopt their attitude. Which was? Well he isn't very clear.' Nor, for that matter, is Forster. Whatever he might have had in mind for this middle-aged man swiftly meets with his disappointment, as he protests: 'no this doesn't satisfy me. I must get nearer myself, but how? how get out my wit and wisdom without this pretence that it is through the young and on behalf of the young.' So rather than celebrate 'life's mellow wisdom' of middle age in his 'robust alert character', he decides that he had better make him 'lecherous' – 'still capable of a carnal meal'. But such musings typically come up against one enduring obstacle: 'How [can I] get down the first hand experiences of my life?'[60] By 1927, it was still not possible to find a public arena in which to give a representative shape to the many and flourishing homosexual experiences that Forster knew 'first hand'.

In the same year as he was considering an appropriate role for his middle-aged 'robust alert character', he drafted a short story about a country squire who was equally hungry for a 'carnal meal'. 'Dr Woolacott' focuses on an eerie sexual fantasy that ultimately leads to death. Suffering from an un-named 'disease', Clesant initially hallucinates and then imagines having intercourse with a strapping young farm-hand who has been 'patch[ed] up' after serving in the First World War.[61] But the story makes it difficult to tell where reality ends and fantasy begins. This was one of the points that Forster raised in his lively exchange of letters with T.E. Lawrence, who had first consulted Forster on the drafting of the controversial memoir, *Seven Pillars of Wisdom* (1926), which described Lawrence's participation in the Arab Revolt of 1916. 'Yes I know', Forster informed him, 'Dr Woolacott is the best thing I've done and also unlike anyone else's work . . . I want to know, among other things, when you first guessed the oncomer [the farm-hand] was a spook.' And Forster went on to add: 'The story makes me happy. It gives bodily ecstacy [*sic*] outside time and place.'[62] In this strange tale of a 'chronic invalid', Clesant defies the authority of Dr Woolacott and his 'army' of nurses who do everything within their power to keep his erotomania under control (pp.84, 95). Indeed, 'Dr Woolacott' demon-strates that not only does homosexuality naturally resist those who would mobilize an 'army' to repress it, the story also shows how Clesant's dis-turbed mental state finally liberates him. Here his vivid fantasy is so pro-found that the love he feels for the imaginary farm-hand is as palpable as anything else in his life. It brings him to orgasm: 'They touched, their limbs intertwined, they gripped and grew mad with delight' (p.95). No wonder, given his anxiety about his ailing 'heart', Clesant is finally 'found . . . dead on the floor' (pp.84, 96).

The story had a purgatorial significance for T.E. Lawrence, not least because his own experience of being anally penetrated by another man is represented in highly conflicted terms in *Seven Pillars of Wisdom*:

There is a strange cleansing beauty about the whole piece of writing. So passionate, of course: so indecent, some people might say: but I must confess that it has made me change my point of view. I had not before believed that such a thing could be so presented – and so credited. I suppose you will not print it? Not that it anywhere says too much: but it shows far more than it says: and these things are mysteries. The Turks, as you probably know (or have guessed, through the reticences of the Seven Pillars) did it to me, by force: and since then I have gone about whimpering to myself unclean, unclean. Now I don't know. Perhaps there is another side, your side, to the story.[63]

Never before, it seemed to T.E. Lawrence, had a writer represented male homosexual love in such an unapologetic manner where death was a sufficiently high price to pay so that one's desires could achieve their full expression. Yet Forster was surely trying to accomplish something more than a moral of this kind. In 'Dr Woolacott', one of the most significant ideas is that the two lovers exist in the same psyche. The 'disease' that is supposed to keep Clesant apart from another man ironically provides the erotic connection. Later in life, Forster would look to another experimental genre to imagine how an older and a younger man might enjoy 'bodily ecstacy [sic] outside time and place'. By 1959, he was drafting science fiction to play out these insistent wishfulfilments.

Even though the central part of it is missing, the fragment entitled 'Little Imber' is sufficiently coherent for us to make an informed guess about the overall trajectory of the narrative. The story puts an altogether new angle on Forster's enduring concerns with the virilizing power of homosexual intercourse. The narrative culminates in a startling scene of male reproduction where a race of men at last have the means to survive without the interference of women. In fact, the story restages what has been a familiar set of sexual coordinates in Forster's writing from the closing scene of what might reasonably be called male breastfeeding at the end of *Where Angels Fear to Tread*. But at the end of his career Forster found an unusual outlet for his deep-seated anger at a hetero-normative world that still legislated against his desires. The plot is a simple one, the theory behind it less so. In a not too distant future, a group of women awaits the arrival of an aircraft which is bringing one of the few potent men left on the earth to impregnate some of the members of their remote community. No sooner has Warham been settled into the 'Birth House' than we discover 'he was profoundly concerned by the sterility that was nibbling into the human race'.[64] The 'shortage of males' is the main problem. Although Warham 'liked women' (even, in a misogynistic aside, 'to skilfully simulating acts of rape' (p.227)), heterosexual intercourse does not compare with the arousal he experiences in the company of Imber. The youthful Imber, who follows him on a later plane, is straight out of the 'Nursery' where he has been taught for years how to inseminate. Imber, not surprisingly, is the familiar embodiment of the virile male who stands at the peak of Forster's sexual hierarchy. Taunted by Warham that he is far too immature, Imber protests: 'I can fertilize and I've got my certificate with me' (p.228). 'I'm a rough man', he insists. 'Look!' he cries out, and displays his penis to the older man (p.230). Within seconds, they are wrestling, then intertwining, and finally ejaculating. What happens next completely stuns them. As their sperm mixes on the floor, they create a baby boy. But it takes them so long to realize what has happened during the 'wrestle-and-spill stuff' that all they can do is 'watch the enigmatic mass shrink, expand and shrivel up' (p.234). Next time, they agree, they will keep the baby warm, and so produce 'the new strain' that scientists have been 'hunting for in those test-tubes' (p.234). The final page of the story witnesses the homosexually-made baby cared for by the 'sorority' led by the Abbess. Yet rather than be mothered, what the child 'really desired was its own younger brother'. Hereafter, the world promises to be overrun by 'Romuloids and Remoids in masses'. Small wonder that, in the end, 'Males had won' (p.235).

Although we might read 'Little Imber' as a homosexual revenge fantasy – one that transfers all the horror of 'sterility' that Forster associated with male same-sex desire on to the heterosexual prerogative to reproduce – the story is so violent in its rage against femininity that one can clearly see how conflicted he was in his overidentification with it. In his case, this intense loathing was also a kind of loving. While he railed against the 'sorority' in 'Little Imber', in the same decade he was writing a biography of his influential female great-aunt, Marianne Thornton: a powerful member of the Clapham Sect, whose liberal values Forster was to inherit. Published when Forster was in his 70s, this engaging biography concludes with a chapter about his own babyhood, and the generous bequest made by Marianne Thornton to secure his success as a grown man:

> She died worth £20,000 . . . to me she left £8000. The interest was to be devoted to my education and when I was twenty-five I was to receive the capital. This £8000 has been the financial salvation of my life. Thanks to it, I was able to go to Cambridge – impossible otherwise, for I failed to win scholarships. After Cambridge I was able to travel for a couple of years, and travelling inclined me to write. After my first visit to India and after the first world war the value of the £8000 began to diminish, and later on it practically vanished. But by then my writings had begun to sell, and I have been able to live on them instead. Whether – in so stormy an age as ours – this is a reputable sequence I do not know. Still less do I know how the sequence and all sequences will end, with the storms increasing. But I am thankful so, and thankful to Marianne Thornton; for she and no one else made my career as a writer possible, and her love, in a most tangible sense, followed me beyond the grave.[64]

This striking tribute makes it only too clear that the bulk of Forster's career was based on the kindness of a public-spirited and liberal-minded female ancestor who recognized the needs of a fatherless only child left in the hands of a mother in whom many members of his family had not that much faith. It would not, I think, be unreasonable to claim that this final full-length work is going over already well-trodden ground that leads back to those anguished moments of his childhood where women exerted authority over practically every aspect of his life. They defined the literary, aesthetic, and cultured environment that Forster very closely associated with the domestic sphere, and from which he sought to escape. But what he called his 'domestic biography' of Marianne Thornton recognizes that he remained for years within her power. So one paradox assuredly vexed Forster's career right to the end. If he had not respected the feminine influence that Marianne Thornton symbolized, his courageous fictions could never have set out to virilize the misspelled 'effeminancy' that constantly troubled his sense of homosexual definition.

Notes

1 E.M. Forster, *Howards End*, ed. Oliver Stallybrass, Abinger Edition (London, Edward Arnold, 1973), p.43. Further page references appear in parentheses.

2 Forster, *Maurice* (London, Edward Arnold, 1971), p.204. Further page references appear in parentheses.

3 Forster attentively read the works of both Eliot and James, as is made clear in the several entries in his *Commonplace Book*, ed. Philip Gardner (London, Scolar Press, 1985), especially pp.13–15, 124.

4 Michael Levenson, *Modernism and the Fate of Individuality: Character and Novelistic Form from Conrad to Woolf* (Cambridge, Cambridge University Press, 1991), p.79.

5 This aspect of Forster's writing has drawn a great deal of critical attention. Notable essays include: Wilfred Stone, ' "Overleaping Class": Forster's Problem of Connection', *Modern Language Quarterly*, 39 (1978), pp.386–404; Barbara Rosecrance, 'Forster's Comrades', *Partisan Review*, 47 (1980), pp.591–603; and June Perry Levine, 'The Tame in Pursuit of the Savage: The Posthumous Fiction of E.M. Forster', *PMLA*, 99(1) (1984), pp.72–88.

6 Lionel Trilling, *E.M. Forster*, 2nd edition (London, Chatto and Windus, 1967), pp.9–23. Much of the early criticism of Forster's novels is preoccupied with his 'liberal dilemma'. See, for example, Frederick C. Crews, *E.M. Forster: The Perils of Humanism* (Princeton, NJ, Princeton University Press, 1962), pp. 19–36.

7 Richard Dellamora, 'Textual Politics/Sexual Politics', *Modern Language Quarterly*, 54(1) (1993), p.159.

8 Adrienne Rich, 'Compulsory Heterosexuality and Lesbian Existence', in Henry Abelove, Michèle Aina Barale and David M. Halperin (eds) *The Lesbian and Gay Studies Reader* (New York, Routledge, 1993), pp.227–54. This version of Rich's essay explains how and why it has been revised several times since it was first published in 1980.

9 Eve Kosofsky Sedgwick, *Between Men: English Literature and Male Homosocial Desire* (New York, Columbia University Press, 1985), p.21. Sedgwick develops

her model of homosociality in part from René Girard, *Deceit, Desire, and the Novel: Self and Other in Literary Structure*, trans. Yvonne Freccero (Baltimore, MD, The Johns Hopkins Press, 1966), pp.1–52.

10 On the feminization of the literary sphere during the *fin de siècle*, see Rita Felski, 'The Counter-Discourse of the Feminine in Three Texts by Huysmans, Wilde, and Sacher-Masoch', *PMLA*, 105 (1991), pp.1094–105.

11 On the development of these competing forces in Victorian thought, see David J. DeLaura, *Hebrew and Hellene in Victorian England: Newman, Arnold, and Pater* (Austin, TX, University of Texas Press, 1969).

12 E.M. Forster, 'Does Culture Matter?', in *Two Cheers for Democracy*, ed. Oliver Stallybrass, Abinger Edition (London, Edward Arnold, 1972), p.99.

13 Arnold, *Culture and Anarchy with Friendship's Garland and Some Literary Essays*, ed. R.H. Super (Ann Arbor, MI, University of Michigan Press, 1965).

14 [Fitzjames Stephen] 'Mr Arnold on Culture and Anarchy', *Saturday Review*, 6 March 1869, p.319. On Stephen's many criticisms of Arnold's works, see Merle Mowbray Bevington, *The Saturday Review 1855–1868* (New York, AMS Press, 1966), p.136–52. The wide-ranging debate provoked by Arnold's writings on culture is discussed in Sidney Coulling, *Matthew Arnold and His Critics: A Study of Arnold's Controversies* (Athens, OH, Ohio University Press, 1974), pp.181–216.

15 [W.H. Mallock] *The New Republic; or, Culture, Faith, and Philosophy in an English Country House*, 3rd edn, 2 vols (London, Chatto and Windus, 1877), I, p.45.

16 [Fitzjames Stephen] 'Culture and Action', *Saturday Review*, 9 November 1867, p.592. This critique of Arnoldian culture in many respects concurs with Frederic Harrison, 'Culture: A Dialogue', *Fortnightly Review*, NS 2 (1867), pp.603–14.

17 Alan Sinfield, *Literature, Politics and Culture in Postwar Britain* (Oxford, Basil Blackwell, 1989), pp.60–85; 'Private Lives/Public Theater: Noel Coward and the Politics of Homosexual Representation', *Representations*, 36 (1991), pp.43–63; and *The Wilde Century: Effeminacy, Oscar Wilde and the Queer Moment* (London, Cassell, 1994), especially Chapters 3–6.

18 E.M. Forster, 'A "Plot" 17/7/04', in *The Longest Journey*, ed. Elizabeth Heine, Abinger Edition (London, Edward Arnold, 1984), xlviii. Further page references appear in parentheses.

19 Alfred Tennyson, *In Memoriam*, V.8, in *The Poems of Tennyson*, ed. Christopher Ricks (London, Longman, 1969), p.868. Further quotation is taken from this edition.

20 Forster, 'Nottingham Lace', in *Arctic Summer and Other Fiction*, ed. Elizabeth Heine, Abinger Edition (London, Edward Arnold, 1980), p.7. Further page references appear in parentheses.

21 Forster, 'Ansell', in *The Life to Come and Other Stories*, ed. Oliver Stallybrass (London, Edward Arnold, 1972), p.3. Further page references appear in parentheses.

22 'Albergo Empedocle', in *The Life to Come and Other Stories*, p.10. Further page references appear in parentheses. For a detailed analysis of the homoerotic inflections to this story, see Richard Dellamora, *Apocalyptic Overtures: Sexual Politics and the Sense of an Ending* (New Brunswick, NJ, Rutgers University Press, 1994) pp.83–97.

23 Forster, *Where Angels Fear to Tread*, ed. Oliver Stallybrass, Abinger Edition (London, Edward Arnold, 1975), p.54. Further page references appear in parentheses.

24 In an interview with Forster, Angus Wilson remarks: 'He expressed pleasure later that I thought most highly of *The Longest Journey* of all his novels and said that he agreed and was at present "looking into the origins of it" ' – a retrospective that perhaps suggests the enduring power that the homoerotic dynamic between the scholarly young man and his athletic opponent had for Forster: 'A Conversation with E.M. Forster', *Encounter*, 9 (November 1957), p.56.

25 In *The Intermediate Sex*, Carpenter writes: 'Whitman constantly maintains that his own disposition . . . is normal, and that he represents the average man. And it *may* be true, even as far as his Uranian [i.e. homosexual] temperament is concerned, that while this was specially developed in him the germs of it *are* almost, if not quite, universal. If so, then the Comradeship on which Whitman founds a large portion of his message may in the course of time become a general enthusiasm, and the nobler Uranians of today may be destined, as suggested, to be its pioneers and advance guard'; *Selected Writings* ed. Noel Greig (London, GMP, 1984), I, p.238. To be sure, Carpenter viewed his comradely Uranian man as an advanced evolutionary type. Tony Brown has exhaustively researched Forster's earliest contact with Carpenter's writing; see 'Edward Carpenter and the Evolution of *A Room with a View*', *ELT*, 30(3) (1987), pp.279–300.

26 'Whitmania' titles a disparaging essay by Algernon Charles Swinburne in the *Fortnightly Review*, NS 42 (1887), pp.170–6. Symonds subsequently protested against Swinburne's imputations of 'vice, uncleanliness, and corruption against which every page of Whitman's didactic writing' was aimed: 'A Note on Whitmania', *Fortnightly Review*, NS 42 (1887), p.460. Sedgwick provides a searching analysis of the specific appeal of Whitman's poetry to English homophile readers: *Between Men*, pp.201–17.

27 E.M. Forster, *A Room with a View*, ed. Oliver Stallybrass, Abinger Edition (London, Edward Arnold, 1977), p.166. Further page references appear in parentheses.

28 Prejudice against spinsters was widespread. Sheila Jeffreys notes that 'spinster-baiting' formed a significant part of feminist factionalism during the struggle to secure the suffrage. The first issue of *The Freewoman* (23 November 1911) depicted the spinster as the 'barren sister, the withered tree, the acidulous vessel under whose pale shadow we chill and whiten'; *The Spinster and Her Enemies: Feminism and Sexuality 1880–1930* (London, Pandora, 1985), pp.94–5.

29 E.M. Forster, *The Manuscripts of* Howards End, ed. Oliver Stallybrass, Abinger Edition (London, Edward Arnold, 1973), p.26.

30 Peter Widdowson, *E.M. Forster's* Howards End: *Fiction as History* (Falmer, Sussex University Press, 1977), p.13.

31 Levenson, p.95.

32 Carpenter, 'The Intermediate Sex', in *Selected Writings*, I, p.189.

33 [A.N. Monkhouse] *Manchester Guardian*, 26 October 1910, p.5, reprinted in Philip Gardner (ed.) *E.M. Forster: The Critical Heritage* (London, Routledge and Kegan Paul, 1973), p.123.

34 There is, at the time of writing, no definitive edition of *Maurice*. A detailed evaluation of the problems with the text published in 1971 is provided in Gardner 'The Evolution of Forster's *Maurice*', and in Judith Scherer Herz and Robert K. Martin (eds) *E.M. Forster: Centenary Revaluations* (Basingstoke, Macmillan, 1982), pp.204–23.

35 Forster, 'Some Memories', in Gilbert Beith (ed.) *Edward Carpenter: In Appreciation* (London, George Allen and Unwin, 1931), p.74.

36 John Fletcher, 'Forster's Self-Erasure: *Maurice* and the Scene of Masculine Love', in Joseph Bristow (ed.) *Sexual Sameness: Textual Differences in Lesbian and Gay Writing* (London, Routledge, 1992), pp.70, 72.

37 Philip Toynbee, 'Forster's Love Story', *Observer*, 10 October 1971, p.32, reprinted in Gardner, p.463.

38 Jeffrey Meyers, for example, writes: 'There are no interesting characters in the book, for Maurice is a philistine youth surrounded by a thinly sketched cast of consummately dull mediocrities . . . Forster intended Maurice and Alec to have "the fullest possible knowledge of each other" but their puerile passions remain hollow and sentimental'; *Homosexuality and Literature 1890–1930* (London, Athlone Press, 1977), p.101.

39 Lytton Strachey, 'To E.M. Forster', 12 March 1915, in P.N. Furbank, *E.M. Forster: A Life*, 2 vols (London, Secker and Warburg, 1978), II, p.15.

40 D.H. Lawrence, 'To Bertrand Russell', 12 February 1915, *The Letters of D.H. Lawrence: June 1913–October 1916*, ed. George J. Zytaruk and James T. Boulton (Cambridge, Cambridge University Press, 1981), II, p.283, 285.

41 Trilling, p.9.

42 'Negative sentence structures, together with the words, "no", "not", "never" and in particular "nothing", predominate in the linguistic ordering of the novel', writes Gillian Beer, 'Negation in *A Passage to India*', in John Beer (ed.) *A Passage to India: Essays in Interpretation* (Basingstoke, Macmillan, 1985), p.45.

43 E.M. Forster, *A Passage to India*, ed. Oliver Stallybrass, Abinger Edition (London, Edward Arnold, 1978), p.98. Further page references appear in parentheses.

44 Edward W. Said, *Culture and Imperialism* (London, Chatto and Windus, 1993), pp.246–7.

45 Trilling, pp.16, 46.

46 Paul. B. Armstrong, 'Reading India: The Politics of Interpretation in *A Passage to India*', *Twentieth-Century Literature* 38(4) (1992), p.367. Armstrong proceeds to explore the ways in which Forster's novel exposes the limits to the famous Habermas–Lyotard debate about normative truth-claims, together with Richard Rorty's intervention in that debate in *Contingency, Irony, and Solidarity* (Cambridge, Cambridge University Press, 1989).

47 Homi K. Bhabha, *The Location of Culture* (London, Routledge, 1994), p.124.

48 Sara Suleri, *The Rhetoric of English India* (Chicago, IL, Chicago University Press, 1992), p.132, 136.

49 See, for example, Benita Parry, *Delusions and Discoveries: Studies on India in the British Imagination 1880–1930* (Berkeley, University of California Press, 1972), p.303. In a later essay, Parry briefly discusses how 'Forster's perceptions are in the tradition of Walt Whitman and Edward Carpenter, the one a passionate believer in popular democracy, the other a romantic socialist, both mystics and

homosexuals disassociated by temperament and conviction from the conventions of their respective societies'; but these important observations are not developed further; 'The Politics of Representation in *A Passage to India*', in Beer (ed.) A Passage to India: *Essays in Interpretation*, p.36.

50 Walt Whitman, *The Complete Poems*, ed. Frances Murphy (Harmondsworth, Penguin Books, 1975), p.429.

51 Betsy Erkkila, *Whitman the Political Poet* (New York, Oxford University Press, 1989), p.268.

52 Suleri, p.138.

53 Suleri, p.132.

54 E.M. Forster, *The Manuscripts of* A Passage to India, ed. Oliver Stallybrass (London, Edward Arnold, 1978), p.19.

55 Jenny Sharpe, 'The Unspeakable Limits of Rape: Colonial Violence and Counter-Insurgency', *Genders*, 10 (1991), pp.25–46. Sharpe's work provides a clear historical context for some of the observations by Brenda R. Silver in an intricate discussion of rape in the novel; see Brenda R. Silver, 'Periphrasis, Power, and Rape in *A Passage to India*', *Novel,* 22(1) (1988), pp.86–105.

56 Silver, p.88.

57 Silver, p.96.

58 Christopher Lane, 'Managing "The White Man's Burden"': The Racial Imaginary in Forster's Colonial Narratives', *Discourse*, 15(3) (1993), pp.95–6.

59 Frances B. Singh, '*A Passage to India*, the National Movement, and Independence', *Twentieth-Century Literature* 35(2–3) (1985), p.275.

60 Forster, *Commonplace Book*, pp.29–30.

61 Forster, 'Dr Woolacott', in *The Life to Come and Other Stories*, p.91. Further page references appear in parentheses.

62 Forster, 'To T.E. Lawrence', 17 November 1927, *Selected Letters of E.M. Forster*, ed. Mary Lago and P.N. Furbank, 2 vols (London, Collins, 1985), II, p.81.

63 T.E. Lawrence, 'To E.M. Forster', 27 December 1927', Garnett Collection, Northwestern University Library, Evanston, IL. Lawrence is alluding to how he was raped by the Turkish Bey in Chapter 80 of *Seven Pillars of Wisdom*. For an important analysis of the sexual fantasmatics at work in this scene, see Kaja Silverman, *Male Subjectivity at the Margins* (New York, Routledge, 1992), pp.328–34.

64 E.M. Forster, 'Little Imber', in *Arctic Summer and Other Fiction*, p.227. Further page references appear in parentheses.

65 E.M. Forster, *Marianne Thornton: A Domestic Biography 1797–1887* (London, Edward Arnold, 1956), p.289.

3

Firbank's exotic effeminacy

Ronald Firbank (a dingy lilac blossom of rarity untold).
(Firbank, *Prancing Nigger* 1924)

Let us follow these bright ornaments.
(Firbank, *Vainglory* 1916)

I

'To the historian', writes E.M. Forster in 1929, Ronald Firbank 'is an interesting example of literary conservatism; to his fellow insects a radiance and a joy.' Faced with Firbank's effeminate 'butterfly' intellect, his love of Roman Catholic ceremony, and his close affiliation with the 'decadent' styles of the 1890s, it should come as no surprise that Forster treated this near-contemporary to considerable disdain. 'Is he affected? Yes, always. Is he self-conscious? No; he wants to mop and mow, and put on birettas and stays, and he does it as naturally as healthy Englishmen light their pipes. Is he himself healthy? Perish the thought!'[1] But even if it becomes fairly clear that Firbank represented everything about homosexual identity that Forster loathed, it is undoubtedly significant that he was one of the few critics of Firbank's generation to pay this 'butterfly' serious attention.

Firbank died more or less in obscurity, and only intermittent amounts of critical interest have since been aroused in a writer whose eccentricities made him something of a cult. In fact, so little was known about Firbank even by those who claimed his close acquaintance that at the time of his death at the age of 40 in 1926 he was mistakenly buried in the Protestant Cemetery at Rome. Once the error had been discovered, his remains were promptly exhumed under his family's instructions and then deposited in a Roman Catholic grave. Rather like Wilde – on whom he partly modelled himself, to the point of converting to Rome – Firbank generated the kind of legendary status that many aesthetes achieved through their affected mannerisms. To be sure, Firbank was one of the main forerunners of those eminent post-1918 'Children of the Sun' – as Martin Green names them – whose 'dandyism provoked rebellion' among the generation of young men who saw themselves as the bearers of culture in the face of a philistine establishment.[2] In many ways, Firbank can be viewed as one of the most vital links between the 'decadence' associated with Wilde and the 1890s and the cult of the dandy-aesthete promoted by Harold Acton and Brian Howard, and which figures frequently in the fiction of Aldous Huxley and Evelyn Waugh. The respective worlds of *Antic Hay* (1923) and *Decline and Fall* (1929) owe much to the originality of Firbank's volumes which generated so little critical interest during his own relatively short lifetime.

Firbank's posthumous influence is borne out in a rather grudging review by Waugh, also written in 1929. (This was also the year in which Duckworth issued the eight-volume 'Rainbow Edition' of Firbank's works.) 'In quite diverse ways', remarks Waugh, 'Mr Osbert Sitwell, Mr Carl Van Vechten, Mr Harold Acton, Mr William Gerhardie and Mr Ernest Hemingway are developing the technical discoveries upon which Ronald Firbank so negligently stumbled.' Suggesting, indeed, that Firbank's innovations were largely accidental, Waugh underlines Firbank's derivativeness. This writer, he notes, fashioned himself on Wilde, if with one or two signal differences:

> It is the peculiar temper of Firbank's humour which divides him from the nineties. His raw material, allowing for the inevitable changes of fashion, is almost identical with Oscar Wilde's – the lives of rich, slightly decadent, people seen against a background of traditional culture, grand opera, the picture galleries and the Court; but Wilde was at heart radically sentimental. His wit is ornamental; Firbank's is structural. Wilde is rococo; Firbank is baroque. It is very rarely that Firbank 'makes a joke'.[3]

These acute observations make one thing very clear. Firbank, even if appearing to be perhaps the most frivolous writer of his day, was deadly serious in his art. If he made jokes (and he certainly did), they were never vulgar. He sought, at all times, to avoid the obvious. As Alan Hollinghurst observes, 'the typical Firbankian form is the innuendo-laden open remark, trailing off into the amoral possibilities of suggestive Sterneian punctuation'.[4] Anything likely to veer away from subtlety in Firbank's hands is always prone to dissolve in an ellipsis. So let us not be misled by Waugh: Firbank's writings were the result of neither negligence nor serendipity. Instead, they were the outcome of careful design. Intensely wrought, they were scrupulously executed, as detailed studies of his notebooks have revealed.[5]

Yet, given the characteristic impactedness of Firbank's fiction and drama, five decades passed before critics began to uncover the rationale governing the main bulk of his mature writings. So resistant did his fiction prove to conventional models of critical interpretation that it took until 1973 before a truly Firbankian critic, Brigid Brophy, began to make detailed sense of a series of demanding narratives which do not easily fit, stylistically or structurally, into the larger cultural patterns that we may discern in his contemporaries' works. Indeed, Firbank's life and art were so damagingly affected by his idiosyncracies – he was painfully shy; he cultivated an outrageous effeminacy; he had to pay established publishers to print and bind nearly all his works – that for much of his writing life he remained isolated from the metropolitan literary élite. His reclusiveness, typified most forcefully by his wartime years in Oxford, finally led him away from an England that failed to support him in a career to which he was profoundly dedicated. Significantly, his first work to be taken on by a publishers at their expense appeared in the United States. *Prancing Nigger* (1924) gained some popularity because its style and topic were consonant with several key developments in the Harlem Renaissance. In the wake of the First World War, there was barely any room in England for anyone to pursue with similar determination what I shall call Firbank's queer modernism. The discussion that follows examines in turn aspects of his perverse aesthetic. Beginning with an analysis of his assault on the realist tradition, I proceed to a discussion of two areas where his work is markedly transgressive. In Firbank's writing, we discover a deep fascination, not with male homosexuality, but with sexual love between women and with interracial eroticism.

II

In every sense of the word, Firbank's works are queer. No reader can avoid their insistent peculiarity. His fictional universe soon disabuses us of any illusion we may have had about time, manner, and place reverting to some conventional ordering. Here everything we might wish of a realist plot has been entirely obscured from view. Incidents, events, actions of any kind are constantly diminished by Firbank's emphasis on bizarre image and quirky idiom. 'Let us', his narrator insists in *Vainglory*, 'follow the ornaments.' No sooner has this announcement been made than the narrative becomes cluttered with those 'baroque' embellishments that Waugh rightly identified:

> Taking for granted the large, unwieldy furniture, the mournful carpet, the low-spirited draperies, the brown paper of the walls, the frieze, in which Windsor Castle appeared again, and again, and again, and which a patriotic landlady (a woman like a faded Giotto) would not consent to hide lest it might seem to be disloyal, let us confine our observations to the book, the candlestick, the hour-glass, or the skull.

In a litter upon the mantelpiece – some concert fixtures, a carica-
ture of Owen Nares, an early photograph of Andrew in a surplice, a
sketch of Mildenberg as Clytemnestra, an impression of Felia Litvinne
in Tristan, might be seen, whilst immediately above, usually quite
awry, was suspended a passionate engraving of two very thin figures
wandering before a retreating sea.[6]

Given the detailed attention each of these bright ornaments receives, one
should not in any way assume that their presence here lacks intellectual
purpose. Although Firbank is highly reluctant to deploy any image that
might stand as a symbol in some larger allegorical plan, his arrangement of
objects in these paragraphs makes one cultural contrast very obvious. The
landlady who rents a room to young Winsome Brookes subscribes to just
the kind of patriotic Englishness that Firbank always despised. Even if his
novels are populated by eminently wealthy individuals, these characters do
not hail from the jingoistic wing of the Liberal and Tory upper classes who
had taken Britain into the second Anglo-Boer War (1899–1902) and had
roused the nation into the Great War that was already claiming thousands
of lives when Firbank was writing these lines. Cultural value, in Firbank's
imaginary world, emanates not from conservative forces such as these.
Instead, he realized value in the eccentric attributes of highly individualized
ornaments. Like many of the *fin-de-siècle* 'decadents' of the previous generation, he furnished his writings with such a surplus of whimsical items that
his work in itself became, as it were, a 'passionate engraving'. Indeed,
significance, for Firbank, lies very much in superficial patternings.
Throughout his novels, there is a lasting absorption in intricate decorative
motifs. In much the same spirit, his writing persistently turns its gaze upon
spectacular displays and public pageants, like the operas and church services
that fascinate Winsome Brookes and his lover, Andrew. And, in every
instance, these 'ornaments' are taken to complete excess. So strenuous is
Firbank in assembling this 'litter' of trimmings and accessories that any
specificity of meaning evaporates altogether. The details keep amassing to
the point that one begins to wonder why his gorgeous interiors are filled to
the brim with such hordes of closely observed things. In fact, these fripperies and gewgaws often come much more to our notice than do the
beautifully accoutred people that inhabit this fictional domain. And they do
so because they are conspicuously 'awry', defiantly unusual in their
disposition.

Part of the reason, of course, for what may at first seem the puzzling
ornamentalism of Firbank's fiction lies in its wholesale attack on naturalism.
'Who among us to-day', remarks the Hon. Mrs Chilleywater in *The Flower
beneath the Foot* (1923), 'is carrying on in the tradition of Fielding? Who
really cares?' Besides herself, the only writer who strikes her as original is
'Madam Adrian Bloater' (p.560). In arranging this scene, Firbank was

obliquely satirizing Vita Sackville-West and Virginia Woolf who for him represented the contrasting poles of English realism and emergent modernism respectively (although it is perhaps difficult to see Sackville-West's work fitting properly under Firbank's rubric here). Yet he would also lightly mock himself in much the same manner. For while the members of the 'English colony' at Pisuerga are rummaging in their local library, Mrs Bedley suddenly exclaims: 'Is that one of Ronald Firbank's books?' and she adds: 'Ronald Firbank I can't take to at all.' Among her companions is Miss Hopkins, who observes: 'I once met him . . . he told me writing books was by no means easy' (p.532). This was certainly true for both himself and Woolf, since they were devising techniques enabling them to break with the realist tradition that stemmed from Fielding. But no matter how lightly Firbank ridicules his own novels in *The Flower beneath the Foot*, it is never the less noticeable that all his books have been borrowed from the circulating library at Pisuerga. It is surely a sign of his frustration of not having an engaged readership that Firbank went to such lengths to invent an audience for himself in his own fiction. This was the result of being so committed to putting – as his publisher, Grant Richards, remarked – such 'individuality' into his writing.[7]

Forever setting scenes, designing costumes, and equipping his sets with innumerable props, his theatrical imagination (which often evokes the flamboyance of the Restoration stage) by and large downplays plot. The same goes for his attitude towards the conventional regulating markers of time that punctuate most realist narratives. Although temporality is crucial to Firbank's fiction (*Caprice* (1917), for example, opens amid the clangour of Sunday church bells), his work rarely obeys anything remotely resembling a sustained train of thought. Everywhere, his stories are marked by interruptions, digressions, and hiatuses. He positively delights in telltale silences – so much so that his ellipses run on for line after line. Least of all do his stories and novels culminate in conclusive endings which serve to resolve the moral complications that preoccupy the majority of his high-Victorian predecessors. Not a word of moralism creeps into Firbank's prose. From what we can see in the extravagant parade of images that passes before our gaze, there are no large subjects on which his work wants to pontificate. To all intents and purposes, he would seem to be just the kind of writer Forster thought he was: frivolous, unintelligent, and very much a thing of the past. But Firbank, I must insist, was not a conservative writer in terms of technique. His work is expressly modernist in its marked self-consciousness, constantly prompting us to reassess how fiction can set about representing its imaginary worlds.

So opposed is Firbank's writing to its literary antecedents that it deserves to be understood as something more than a sustained and commercially unsuccessful joke. His seriousness of intent emerges once we accept that even in his apparently insubstantial juvenilia his creative mode is one of critique. Like all strong writers with a singular purpose of their own, Firbank was determined to revise the works of those from whom he had learned most. For him by far the most influential figure was Wilde, whom he emulated in his teens and early 20s. (In fact, Firbank eventually gained something of a sponsor in Lord Alfred Douglas.) To be sure, Wilde's presence haunts all of Firbank's works, finding its most honorific portrait in the figure of Reggie Quintus in *The Princess Zoubaroff* (1926). But already while busily preparing to go up to Cambridge, Firbank was producing short fiction and prose poems that made it clear that to relive the 1890s would inhibit his desire for an individual style. By the middle of the First World War, he was modernizing Wilde, making works such as *Salomé* much queerer than they had ever been before. Undoubtedly, it is within the realm of sexuality that Firbank's writing comes into its own. His whole aesthetic practice is based on a perversity that not only disorders the customary procedures of realist writing but also protests against the naturalized structures that regulate sexual relationships. Rarely do we find a writer who displays such contempt for the cherished social institutions of marriage and family. If one feature becomes increasingly accentuated with every book he completed, it is the strong emphasis on homophile relations – not just between men, but far more between *women*.

Much, indeed, could be said about Firbank's status as a lesbian writer. But before moving on to that polemical point, I wish to establish some initial ideas about Firbank's 'tacit apprenticeship with Wilde', as Brophy calls it.[8] Only by examining Firbank's early identification with and gradual distancing from Wilde can we define the unique homoeroticism of his work. It is equally important to make this our starting-point to show how and why there had to be – according to Brophy – a move from 'mauve' into 'fauve'.[9] (The technical innovations of the Fauvists, notably Georges Braque and Henri Matisse, can serve as a useful metaphor for Firbank's decisive break not only with Wilde, but also with the Belgian Symbolist, Maurice Maeterlinck, whose innovative drama, *Monna Vanna*, had been censored in England in 1902.) By the mid-1910s, Firbank had radically recoloured the empurpled 1890s with the altogether more varied palette of those Post-Impressionist painters. His affinity with this transformation in the visual arts is clear to see from the design of the novels which he paid Grant Richards to publish between 1915 and 1923. *Vainglory* is graced with a frontispiece by Felicien Rops. The work of Albert Rutherston and Albert Buhrer featured in *Inclinations* (1916) and *Odette: A Fairy Tale for Weary People* (1916) respectively. Yet, most important of all, drawings by Augustus John appeared in the first editions of *Caprice* (1917) and *Valmouth* (1919). In 1913, one art critic commented that 'Mr John's masterpiece, *The Girl on the Cliff*, is like nothing else in English painting for its pure keenness of imaginative invention.'[10] In many ways, John stood for all that the Philistines hated in those painters on both sides of the English Channel associated with Post-Impressionism. No wonder that the Tory *Daily Express* was outraged by the 1910 Post-Impressionist Exhibition. It found 'more shocks to the square yard at the exhibition . . . than at any previous picture show in England'. Post-Impressionism was, in other words, 'paint run mad'.[11] The same could be said for Firbank's mature prose style, which constantly alludes to these rapid developments in modern painting – ones that would enable him to expose some of the limitations to Wilde's aesthetics.

III

'To be artificial, and to be a little more improbable and impossible than one's neighbour is to be a perfect success', remarks Hester Q. Tail in one of Firbank's earliest stories, 'A Study in Temperament'.[12] This apophthegm appeared in his first book, which he presumably paid Elkin Mathews to publish in 1905, just before he went up to Trinity Hall, Cambridge. Firbank's echoing of Wilde is as clear as a bell. In his 'Phrases and Philosophies', Wilde exhorts: 'The first duty in life is to be as artificial as possible. What the second duty is no one has as yet discovered.'[13] But what is unusual in Firbank's rewriting of this maxim is that he places it in the mouth of a character who for Wilde represents the worst kind of moralizing. Hester Q. Tail, a successful American poetess, bears a name that reminds us of the high-minded Hester Worsley who, in *A Woman of No Importance* (1893), memorably delivers what her acquaintances consider a tedious and tactless 'lecture' on 'Puritanism' (p.453). So even as a teenager Firbank was remodelling his master. Indeed, all the way through the shorter pieces collected in *The Early Firbank*, Wilde's influence can be felt. For example, in 'A Tragedy in Green' (c.1907) – itself alluding to the subtitle to 'Pen, Pencil, and Poison' (1889) – Lady Georgia Blueharnis exclaims: 'To live solely for dress, or for what people so curiously misname "pleasure", to be spoken of invariably as "the aesthetic Lady Georgia" . . . is surely not to exhaust all the possible emotions of life?' (p.105). Lady Georgia, of course, is invoking Wilde's *The Importance of Being Earnest* (1895), where in the first act Algernon Moncrieff asks the man he thinks is Ernest: 'What brings you up to town?' 'Oh, pleasure, pleasure!', replies the disguised Jack Worthing. 'What else should bring one anywhere?' (p.322). In reminding us of *Earnest*, however, Lady Georgia is pointing out that to be known purely as an 'aesthetic' personage – such as Wilde – is not the be-all and end-all in life.

There were, without doubt, other 'emotions' that Firbank sought to express, and he gained access to them through a technique that in part shared the vision of those Fauvists – such as Matisse – who employed colour in completely unorthodox ways. This point is borne out at a later moment in Firbank's story where Lord Blueharnis can barely keep awake at the Foreign Office. The serious work of the Civil Service is interrupted by the entrance of a young man who asks whether Lord Blueharnis has 'noticed the colour of the sky'. Art, to be sure, is altogether more important here than state bureaucracy. Thus Lord Blueharnis replies with his own, delicately poised, question:

> 'Is it not the colour of the seventh veil of that remarkable Greek dancer, whom I once had the pleasure of seeing perform "Tea" in your mother's drawing-room? To be more precise, is the sky not blue?'
>
> It was one of Lord Blueharnis's idiosyncracies to address those younger than himself in the tones of a duke in a Jacobean melodrama.
>
> 'The sky is *not* blue', answered the young man in a strange voice, 'it is vert de paon', and with that he withdrew as quietly as he came. The sky had in truth undergone a metamorphosis. (p.111)

It is precisely at this moment that we can see how Firbank impresses his own distinguishing stamp on the 'aesthetic' world he largely inherited from Wilde. This incident contains an object-lesson in what Firbank was trying to accomplish. To call the sky 'blue' would be to literalize it – to lose any imaginative hold over its aesthetic possibilities. So to recognize the sky as 'vert de paon' is to take it to an altogether more exquisite level. This is not an unusual example. French words, especially proper names, always enable Firbank to allow the most plain and ordinary things to undergo their necessary 'metamorphosis'. This is especially the case when it comes to colour. Only can a painterly art achieve what the prosaic realist novel, in its stronger descriptive passages, sought to represent. 'If a painter were to paint such a sky', remarks Lord Blueharnis, 'everybody would say it was quite incredible' (p.111). So, presumably, would Wilde.

Among Firbank's early stories is one illuminating his acute awareness of being Wilde's self-appointed heir. In 'Lady Appledore's Mésalliance' (c.1907), the young gardener who tends his lady's 'mauve Orchid' is called Wildred (p.125) (a well-read, if not wild, reader of Wilde, perhaps). But in trying to develop the orchidaceous extravagances that he associated with Wilde, Firbank was also struggling to contest the charge of 'gross indecency' that landed his master in jail. This simple short story revolves around a conventional romance. But the love between Wildred and his beloved lady is regarded as a '*mésalliance*'. Even though Wildred comes from an upper-class background, he works for Lady Appledore as her gardener before she discovers his noble origins and marries him. He is, we are assured, 'no *ordinary* gardener' (p.142). Her neighbours, however, remain unconvinced. They roundly condemn her as 'frivolous', since she has betrayed the memory of Lord Appledore: 'a staunch Protestant' (p.148). So, in his portrait of how a landed lady defied social codes of respectability,

'Lady Appledore's Mésalliance' demonstrates how Firbank was using his newly developed Fauvist techniques to enable unacceptable desires to shape and define a world experiencing 'metamorphosis'. In this respect, one of Wilde's works more than any other empowered Firbank to create a homosexual aesthetic. *Salomé* (1894) paved the way for the first of his novels featuring those exotic, extravagant, and eccentric stylizations for which he would become known. Between 1909 and 1912 he was drafting 'Salomé or 'Tis a Pity that She Would', the narrative that would finally transform into *The Artificial Princess* (1915).

It is perhaps typical, in the light of Firbank's far from successful career, to discover that *The Artificial Princess* found no publisher during his lifetime. First brought to light in 1934, this fine novel provides the template for each of his subsequent works. The story, true to form, is very slight. Set in an unspecified European country, it introduces figures and places that are variously Germanic, Italian, and English in origin. This is not, after all, a realistic world but an emphatically artificial one which freely hybridizes different cultural sources. At the start, the Princess informs her friend, the Baroness Teresa Rudlieb, that because her horses are having a rest, her friend must deliver a note to her secret admirer, St John Pellegrin, by taking the omnibus. En route, the Baroness encounters her own paramour – a Baron whom her husband has promised to kill. So she craftily devises a way of spending a secret hour with him. In the meantime, she has entrusted the Princess's letter to the Baron's chauffeur. But the sulky driver out of malice fails to deliver the note. This, then, is about as far as Firbank gets in creating a plot. Altogether more to the point in this 'artificial' environment is the opportunity to make the world more than a little surreal.

Early in the story the wish to add unfamiliar colours to the setting catches our attention. The Queen exclaims how much she adores the paintings of the punningly named Minx. 'I like his pictures; they are so exquisitely unreal . . . I admire the fantastic grandeur of his backgrounds, his looped-back portières, and towering storm-clouds . . . so sweet!' (p.28). This insistent pursuit of the 'exquisitely unreal' extends to other elaborate accounts of the Queen's idiosyncratic behaviour, notably her 'passion for motoring'. 'She would', we are told, 'motor for hours and hours with her crown on' (p.30). Such was this spectacle that she was a 'delight' to those 'foreigners' who came to 'her Capital to study Art'. But the strangeness of her passion – as with most things Firbankian – has an underlying rationale that not even the narrator will reveal. Like so many of the members of the rich and aristocratic world of Firbank's invention, his characters have the prerogative to be as individualistic as they like, without having to apologize to anyone for their conduct. The Queen is no exception:

> The Queen always insisted while motoring on mending her punctures herself, and it was no uncommon sight to see her sitting with her

crown on in the dust. Her reasons for doing so were complex; probably she found genuine amusement in making herself hot and piggy;
but it is not unlikely that the more Philistine motive of wishing to
edify her subjects was the real cause. She had been called a great many
things, but nobody had ever said she was proud; this was her pride . . .
(p.45)

There is more to this passage than meets the eye. In making the Queen's
idiosyncratic conduct a matter of routine, the very idea of normal behaviour is wholly defamiliarized. But at the same time, the rationale governing her insistent desire to mend her own punctures remains a matter of
speculation. All Firbank will indicate is that her 'reasons' were 'complex'.
As with practically all his characters, their motivations, actions, and desires
cannot be easily referred to ready-made stereotypes. These are not people
whose intricate psychology absorbs us from beginning to end. Instead, his
novels patently refuse to allow anyone inside their characters' minds. Only
his protagonists' eccentricities, their unconventional choices, their highly
particularized mannerisms and affectations distinguish exactly who they are.
Even when a moral quality, such as pride, looks as if it will stabilize our
understanding of the Queen, it is promptly undermined. Although her
people dare not call her proud, they ought to bear in mind that she took
pride in her talent for vehicle maintenance. Likewise, although she is a pre-
eminently Firbankian creation, the Queen – for all his extravagant treatment – may turn out to be a Philistine. This is one more instance of how
Firbank regularly turns our expectations immediately upside down.

There is, of course, a descriptive term that captures the flavour of this
short vignette. It is, in a word, camp. And camp, of course, is one of the
defining features of male homosexual subculture. 'Just as he put into modern practice Oscar Wilde's aesthetic theory', writes Brophy, 'so Firbank
modernised Wilde's camp.'[14] But before pursuing this observation any
further, we need to recognize at once that camp, by virtue of its irreverent
striking of attitudes, proves remarkably resistant to serious-minded criticism. If we can at least concur that camp embraces a repertoire of parodistic
styles, we need also to be aware that it is not always an easily identifiable
structure. Without doubt, camp is not obvious to everyone, and to start
worrying away at definitions of what it might be does rather undermine its
frequent elusiveness. Following Susan Sontag's pathbreaking essay (dedicated to the memory of Wilde), Gregory W. Bredbeck beautifully teases
out much the same point:

Why has gay male culture embraced Wilde *as* Camp and Camp *as*
political? What might account for these conjunctions? These questions
seem to me to be effaced by the more typical questions – what *is*
Camp?; *is* Camp gay?; *is* Wilde Camp?; *is* Camp political? – questions
that overtly desire a determinism and degree of definition that betray

Camp itself. Certainly these latter questions demand attention, and my
own Camp response would be: *only her hairdresser knows for sure*.[15]

But what if we have *not* met her hairdresser? The only thing that we can say
for sure is that he is more than likely to be gay. Indeed, camp is very much
connected with kinds of subcultural knowledge about homosexual desire.
It is often said in gay circles (and not just in gay circles) that 'it takes one to
know one', and camp style is a significant conduit that can mediate a man's
same-sex interests when other social avenues would leave such desires
undisclosed. Yet, to return to Firbank, the camp that we discover in his
work is not purely about making homosexuality evident. If we take recourse to camp as a means of describing Firbank's style, then it is advisable
to see his love of excessive eccentricity within a broader formation of class
interests. 'The pseudo-aristocratic patrilineage of camp', writes Andrew
Ross, 'can hardly be understated.' Ross begs us to consider the 'etymologi-
cal origins of the three most questionable categories of American taste:
schlock, kitsch, and camp'. All of them, he adds, are not Anglo in proven-
ance. They are Yiddish, German, and French respectively. In one respect,
there is something distinctly unEnglish about camp. The reason may well
be that it acts derisively on the commonsensical outlook that one readily
associates with philistine Englishness. So, with this point in mind, it makes
sense that wherever we look in Firbank's writing, it is clear that he delights
in all things foreign. This is particularly the case when Firbank is writing
about England, since his vision of the nation is one in which everything
alien to a 'staunch Protestant' such as Lord Appledore makes its 'baroque'
presence felt. England, in Firbank's hands, becomes completely artificial to
the point of being almost unrecognizable. Yet *why* he is driven, so to speak,
to campify his world cannot be easily summed up. It is true that his refined
form of camp stands as the least debased of those terms that Ross mentions
when characterizing American idioms for what is synthetic, affected, fake.
Firbank's fiction never lapses into bad taste. But, to reiterate, camp is by
definition not always an obvious style. Its motivations can remain obscure.
Ross argues that what distinguishes camp – to those who can detect it – is
its capacity to locate some 'hitherto unexpected value . . . in some obscure
or exorbitant object'.[16] In other words, camp has the marked ability to
remove things from their seemingly natural order, and this process of
displacement is a source of comedy. Yet the comic results of such incongruous repositionings can vary greatly, since they depend on the subtlety or obviousness to which they are campily subjected. Moreover, there
are good reasons for making a cardinal distinction, as Ross does, between
intentional and unintentional modes of camp.

Firbank's camp, without doubt, is highly motivated. But if tangible on
the surface, it remains inscrutable to any further explanation. That this is
indeed the case emerges most clearly in those passages of *The Artificial*

Princess that invoke Wilde's *Salomé*. Take, for example, the moment where the Princess indulges in 'colouring her retrospect' (p.32). She is recalling how her father was assassinated at 'Montreaux seven years ago' (p.33). Soon the resemblances between Wilde's Herodias and Firbank's Queen become clear. Both have promptly married their brothers-in-law after their first husbands have been assassinated. (That is why, of course, the princess is 'artificial', since her royalty is the result of political trickery.) Not surprisingly, then, the Princess echoes Salomé's eerie lines that spell her doom at Herod's hands:

> How good to see the moon. She is like a little piece of money, you would think she was a little silver flower. The moon is cold and chaste. I am sure she is a virgin, she has a virgin's beauty. Yes, she is a virgin. She has never defiled herself. She has never abandoned herself to men, like other goddesses. (p.555)

Where Salomé fixates upon the cold and chaste moon to emphasize her resistant sexual desires, ones that refuse to comply with patriarchal authority, Firbank's Princess recalls the moon in radically different terms at Montreaux: 'I think the moon looked like a piece of Majolica-Ware as it hung above the trees, and I remember the fire-flies darting in the garden below were a new experience for me' (p.34). There is no room in Firbank's fiction for the least sombre tone, even when the moon has been adopted from Wilde's drama to signal that death is in the air. By making a goddess into a piece of crockery, Firbank may well appear to be indulging in derisive mockery. This is serious fun, however. Already the Princess has declared: 'How I should care to be a new Salomé!' 'Let us review the situation', she promptly adds, 'and you will see that all I need is to develop my style' (p.32). Here the Princess would seem to be taking Wilde at his word. In his 'Phrases and Philosophies', Wilde urged his young readers to remember: 'In all important matters, style, not sincerity, counts' (p.1205). And like the dandies whose style cannot go unnoticed in Wilde's elegant Society comedies, the Princess inhabits a world where everyone is judged by appearances – so much so that the Princess is always drawing our attention to the manipulative nature of artificiality. But Firbank's development of this 'new Salomé' pushes artifice to unforeseen extremes. As the Princess says of the Queen: 'She would often scold me for looking too old and said that no nice girl ever looked more than eight; and she would never take me about with her unless I carried a silly woolly lamb until I was past fourteen' (p.34). Not only do such observations serve as an appropriate reminder that artifice for Firbank always had to be taken to utterly implausible lengths, they also indicate how keeping up appearances relates at all times to the exercise of power. No wonder his interest often lies with those who conduct their affairs at court, in ecclesiastical circles, and among the landed gentry. But, more specifically, Firbank is absorbed by the power that emanates from his vision of a gloriously frivolous femininity. His princesses and ladies embody those superficial qualities that disregard the philistine orthodoxies that condemned his sexual and aesthetic preferences.

It was through his fixation on an expressly camp form of femininity that Firbank made his main break with Wilde. When Wilde sought to find an emblem for transgressive sexual desire, he located it in the rather compromised figure of the dandy. Wilde's dandies, after all, maintained their position as insider dissidents within the ranks of a familiar upper-class ethos. But Firbank's women, like the Princess, become for him the ideal icons for that capricious, whimsical, and exotic love of colour that patterns the surface of his works. If Wilde made Lord Illingworth insist that a 'well-tied tie is the first serious step in life' (p.459), then Firbank activates a spectacle where the dandy's dapper masculinity gives way to a feminine swishing of ceremonial robes which are positively aglitter. 'In a hurricane of silver, and swinging chains, leaning solidly on the arms of two of her most formidable critics', notes the narrator, 'the Mistress of the Robes approached the buffet; flushed and triumphant' (p.72). Even in the arms of her adversaries, this *grande dame* has pride of place. No one shall topple her. It is only too clear that the woman who controls the wardrobe of the court wields an enviable amount of power. It is she who has the prerogative to make the greatest impression.

Not every woman in Firbank's universe enjoys this privilege. At the end of *The Artificial Princess*, the Baroness is left 'wondering if her own fall from royal favour and grace would be equally rapid', since news has reached the court that the Princess's note has not been delivered (p.72). Musing that she should like to let her house and go abroad, she asks her companion, Sir Oliver (an 'elderly gentleman with a toothbrush-moustache and a sapphire ring'), whether he has ever been to Greece. Their conversation unfolds as follows:

'More than once', Sir Oliver dryly replied, 'I even married, *en secondes noces*, a Lesbian . . .'

'A native of Lesbos? Just fancy that!' The Baroness marvelled, appraising a passing débutante, a young girl in a mousseline robe of palest Langue de chat.

'*Née* a Demitraki.'

'A demi what?' the Baroness abstrusely twittered, blinking at the intermittent lightning in the sky.

'A Demitraki.'

'Hark.'

'What is it?'

'Only', the lady answered, raising her face into the soft dream morning, already pointing, '*a cock.*'

'A cock?'

'Chanticleer', she added suavely, for the sake of euphony: 'Chanti . . .'

★ ★ ★

'Cock-a-doodle, doooooooooooooooooooooooooooooooooooo
oooooooooooooooooooooooooooooooooooooooooooooo'
'(Cluck-cluck?)'
'Cock-a-doodle . . .'

The arrangement of this exchange bears all the hallmarks of Firbank's mature style. What distinguishes their conversation is the serious attention paid to its apparent inconsequentiality. Like the best Firbankian dialogues, this one is characterized by absent-mindedness, chance overhearings, and well-timed coincidences, all of which are carefully played off against one another. On the face of it, the Baroness is completely self-absorbed, and barely hears what Sir Oliver is saying. In fact, at one point it is fairly clear that she thinks she has heard him say 'demi-monde', not 'Demitraki'. Such a revelation would be scandalous indeed. But there is, of course, something much more sexually transgressive at work in this short episode. Here, for the first time in Firbank's canon, he introduces the clearest note of his queer modernism. True to form, he refuses to scandalize lesbianism. The Baroness's lesbian inclinations are treated with considerable tact. Rather than make Lesbos the subject of a titillating joke, he subtly indicates how the Baroness – who has hardly any interest in Sir Oliver – looks longingly at another woman while exclaiming, in a distracted manner, 'A native of Lesbos?' No sooner has this declaration been made than the 'cock' begins to crow. There are at least three reasons for his sudden appearance. For a start, Chanticleer heralds that dawn has brought an end to the all-night festivities of the court. Second, the extravagantly overextended 'cock-a-doodle' invokes the betrayal of Jesus Christ in the New Testament, signalling that the truth about the Baroness's behaviour will out. And finally, the 'cock' represents the phallic power which Firbank from now on readily confers upon sexual desire between women. Hereafter, the most significant relations in his writings will generally turn their attention to female homoerotic bonds. But why?

IV

Firbank's lesbians have their cultural origins in a French tradition of 'decadent' writing that stems from Théophile Gautier's scandalous *Mademoiselle de Maupin* (1835) and Charles Baudelaire's equally controversial *Les Fleurs du mal* (1857) – notably, in the suppressed poem, 'Lesbos', together with the two lyrics entitled 'Femmes Damnées'. Walter Benjamin remarks that for Baudelaire the classical Lesbian poet, Sappho, was 'the heroine of modernism'.[17] There are several reasons for this modernist attraction to Sappho's myth, and they have little connection with the contemporary lives of women-loving women. 'Given Baudelaire's detachment from lesbianism as anything but a lure useful as a promotional device,' writes Joan DeJean, 'it is hardly surprising that one tradition inspired by his Sappho portrays her as pure literariness, the absolute in art for art's sake.'[18] If, in the hands of a Symbolist poet like Baudelaire, the lesbian could embody pure art, she did so because her sexuality was seen as utterly divorced from naturalized understandings of femininity as domesticated, reproductive, and lacking in genius. But in modelling Sappho, in her unorthodoxy, as the doyenne of the modern age, Baudelaire and his followers represented her as a tormented poet who finally capitulated to a male lover. Betrayed by him, she committed suicide. 'Lesbos' thus culminates in a lament deploring the tragedy that befell her 'lovely body' when the 'brute['s] . . . arrogance avenged' her.[19]

This negative portrayal persisted into the early twentieth century, with important consequences for Firbank. In this respect, one writer who may have been important for him, and who internalized Baudelaire's vision of the lesbian as a *femme fatale*, was Renée Vivien. Always with a keen eye for speculative connections, Brophy explores the possible links between them:

> The furnishings of his lesbian fantasies Firbank probably borrowed from real life.
>
> No doubt the literary gossip of pre-1914 Paris directed his attention to two expatriates . . . who . . . chose to write in French: Natalie Clifford Barney, poetic-dramatist on the subject of Sappho; and Renée Vivien, poet and translator of Sappho into French, who (as her friend Colette later chronicled in *Ces Plaisirs*) dies young in 1909 (and Firbankianly) of drink and self-starvation.
>
> I imagine that Miss O'Brookomore and Miss Collins journey to Greece (in *Inclinations*), and that Mrs Thoroughfare sings (in *Valmouth*) of 'White Mit-y-lene' [p.429], in tribute to the sojourns of Natalie Clifford Barney and Renée Vivien in the villa Renée Vivien owned at Mitylene [on Lesbos].[20]

These conjectures are probably not so very far from historical fact. As Brophy points out, Vivien was living in Firbank's home village of Chistlehurst, Kent, in 1893, while being trained to become a proper young lady at the hands of an English gentlewoman. Even if these scant biographical details have no direct bearing on Firbank's novels, they do point up one important idea. His writing was part of a broader revision of the tragic Baudelairean mould into which Sappho had been cast. Where Vivien envisioned Lesbos as a sensuous utopia, Firbank took the opportunity to identify the lesbian not just with art. In his fiction, the lesbian becomes the ideal figuration of artifice. She embodied unnaturalness *par excellence*.

Firbank's artificial Princess bears some passing resemblances to his imaginary lesbians. Not only does she self-consciously model herself on Salomé, the archetypal *femme fatale*, she is also gamine, as we discover near the start: 'Like a Virgin in a missal her figure lacked consequence – sex. "My tall-tall schoolboy", her mother would usually call her in her correspondence' (p.28). This remark, however, is not complimentary. If the Princess's boyishness characterizes one aspect of her artificiality, it also threatens to make her rather undistinguished. It is only because her 'choice of gowns' is 'nearly always indiscreet' that the Princess manages to improve her appearance: 'Evidently she was not all plain; she looked like some radiant marionette.' There are, indeed, invariably ways and means for Firbank to give appropriate cosmetic treatment to the most ordinary things, making them altogether more appealing and interesting. Indeed, he did his utmost to effeminize himself by wearing red nail varnish long before it was an acceptable fashion for women. Equally outré was the white 'poudre-de-riz' that he applied to his hair. Yet, more than anything else, it was Firbank's bodily comportment that separated him out from the crowd, as Jocelyn Brooke observes:

> His figure was tall, very slender, and inclined to droop; in his movements, he affected a more-than-feminine *chichi*, walking with a willowy undulation which made him easily (and sometimes embarrassingly) recognizable at a considerable distance . . . In his clothes he favoured what was conventionally *chic*: dark, well-cut suits, a bowler, gloves and a cane; his physique, however, invested these accoutrements with an element of fantasy, and with his serpentine wriggling, his arch gestures and perpetual giggle, he had the equivocal air of a female impersonator rather than that of a conventional young man about town.[21]

For all his effeminate stylishness, however, he was no match for the lesbians of his marvellous invention. Since their sexuality was deemed so exquisitely peculiar, they were ideal representatives for his love of superficiality. Expressing their sublime individuality by donning the most glorious frocks, his lesbians held conventional manhood in considerable disesteem.

One novel that makes Firbank's distaste for masculinist authority expressly clear is *Inclinations*. The first part of this short tale concerns the Mediterranean travels of Geraldine O'Brookomore, a literary biographer, and her young companion, Mabel Collins. To Mabel, the very idea of being asked to journey abroad with such a disintinguished person as Gerald (as she is known) is 'like a fairy dream' (p.227). Gerald's sexual designs on the teenage girl are evident from the start. 'Was it Vampirism that made me ask her', she queries, 'or is it that I'm simply bored?' (p.229). Such reflections are very close to one of the familiar modern stereotypes of the predatory lesbian. If Gerald resembles a vampire, then Mabel is her quaking violet.[22] But no sooner have they stepped aboard their liner than Gerald's vampiric desires are quickly dashed when Count Pastorelli appears on the scene. Without further ado, he proposes to Mabel. No wonder Gerald insists that 'he's not so pastoral as he sounds' (p.237). Likewise, she later tells Mabel, 'You've yet to learn, I find, what frivolous things men are' (p.261). Mabel, however, does not heed this warning. Ever prepared to upset orthodox notions of scale, Firbank devotes the whole of Chapter 20 to Gerald's exclamations of grief:

> 'Mabel! Mabel! Mabel! Mabel!'
> 'Mabel! Mabel! Mabel! Mabel!' (p.284)

The lesbian lover, it seems, is a victim of these bitter circumstances. But if the pattern of the story at this point suggests that Mabel's conventional romantic longings have won the day, Part II of *Inclinations* returns us to her family estate where things are far from well. At Bovon – which has, of course, bovine connotations – the Collins family whiles away the time wondering whether Count Pastorelli will indeed arrive from Italy to collect his wife and newborn child. Rumours are already rife about the legal status of Mabel's marriage. That this is not a promising union arises at the end of Part II where doubts are cast on Mabel's domestic skills:

> Once the child and I were driving on the Via Appia Nuova when we saw a bunny peeping out of a tomb. Oh, such a darling! So I stopped the carriage and told Luigi, the footman, to run and dispatch it if he possibly could. He brought it back to me . . . And a few hours afterwards it was bubbling away into a fine chicken broth. Oio [her husband] had it all . . . But hardly had it passed his lips when he was seized with the most violent spasms. Whereupon he turned round and accused me of attempting to do what certain Renaissance wives are supposed to have sometimes done. (p.317)

Although Mabel quickly proceeds to itemizing her husband's delight in 'savoury' things – 'Zuccata . . . Zuccatini . . . soufflé' – enough hints have been dropped to suggest that her life is destined for nothing less than misery.

This is not the only incident where Firbank treats heterosexual love with suspicion. In *The Flower beneath the Foot*, Laura de Nazianzi shows concern for Olga Blumenghast ('whose exotic attraction had aroused not a few heart-burnings (and even feuds) among several of the grandes dames about the court'). Olga, like Mabel, is entranced by a male lover: 'He's such a gold-fish', Olga confides to Laura. 'I would give all my soul to him . . . my chances of heaven . . . How I envy *the men* . . . in his platoon.' But Laura cannot share her enthusiasm: 'Take away his uniform, Olga, and what does

he become? . . . Believe me, my dear, he's not worth the trouble!' (p.515).
Nothing could be more true where Laura's own love life is concerned. She
is betrayed by her beloved Prince Yousef, and decides to join a convent,
where she finds her spiritual home. In fact, *The Flower beneath the Foot*
presents itself as a work of hagiography. Equipped with a liberal number of
explanatory footnotes, it masquerades as the early life of Saint Laura. Such
tales of canonization, like so many aspects of Roman Catholicism, had great
attractions for Firbank. Like his own work, the lives of female saints have a
habit of taking human experience to implausible extremes. Their spiritual
struggles only too clearly express the most perverse sexual desires, which
are – in Firbank's bizarre universe – always much more enthralling than
anything offered by conventional heterosexual romance.

Firbank exploited these exaggerated tales of female saints renowned for
plummeting to the depths of sinful suffering at one moment only to scale
the heights of spiritual enlightenment at the next. One exemplary female
saint of his invention is Aurora de Vauvilliers, whose 'adventurous history'
is a constant source of inspiration to his artificial Princess:

> Aurora, who till the age of thirty-nine had been a celebrated courtesan
> when (by celestial design) an overturned carriage, and some injured
> limbs, had put a finish to her irregular mode of life. Aurora who had
> vowed (should she ever recover) to mend her ways, and make an
> expiatory pilgrimage as far as Palestine (with commissions to gather
> Roses at places of interest for the good Nuns of Forbonnais, and to fill
> bottles with water from well-known founts for the dear Monks at
> Istres). Aurora who had contemplated setting up shop . . . Aurora
> who had set sail one languid summer evening with just a faithful maid
> and a Book of Hours . . . Aurora who, before she had been at sea a
> week, was captured by Pirates, and after enduring untold horrors
> made her escape on a loose board disguised as a man. (pp.51–2)

As if such escapades were not enough to convince us of her extreme
agonies and joys, this recapitulation of the fictional Aurora's exceptional life
elaborates several more unlikely incidents. But that is the point. Firbank is
relishing how the most sacrosanct works of hagiography often have an
erotically sacrilegious subtext. If one Roman Catholic practice excited him
more than any other, it was ritual flagellation, especially when conducted
between women. 'Come, dear, won't you mortify my senses?' asks Sister
Ursula of the young novice, Laura, whose breathless answer is 'No, really,
no–!–!–!' Sister Ursula, however, reassures Laura that the mortification can
be done '[q]uite lightly' because, as she says: 'I was scourged, by Sister
Agnes, but yesterday with a heavy bunch of keys, head downwards, hang-
ing from a bar' (p.590). This, for Firbank, was where the greatest sexual
thrills could be enjoyed. Its utter perversity – lesbian, sado-masochistic,
and, for good measure, among a sisterhood bound to a vow of celibacy –

emerged from the wonderfully absurd idea that routine whippings of this kind could and did enjoy spiritual legitimacy.

Firbank, it has to be said, was not alone among homophile writers in being drawn to Roman Catholicism. Indeed, since the time of John Henry Newman's conversion to Rome in 1845, there was a discernible movement among men with homoerotic interests towards High Anglicanism, if not the Vatican itself. 'What were the reasons', asks David Hilliard, 'for this apparent correlation between male homosexuality and Anglo-Catholic religion?' In part, the attraction lay in the 'elaborate ceremonial and sensuous symbolism of Catholic worship'.[23] Among the evidence Hilliard rallies to prove this point is John Francis Bloxam's infamous short story, 'The Priest and the Acolyte', which was cited in court during the Wilde trials:

> I endeavoured to drown the yearnings of my heart with the ordinary pleasures and vices that usually attract the young. I had to choose a profession. I became a priest. The whole aesthetic tendency of my soul was intensely attracted by the wonderful mysteries of Christianity, the artistic beauty of our services.[24]

In this story, however, it turns out that joining the priesthood does anything but 'drown' his 'ordinary pleasures and vices'. The priest and the acolyte eventually die in each other's arms, their lips pressed together in a passionate embrace. Bloxam's tale, in many ways, serves as a model for Firbank's last completed work, *Concerning the Eccentricities of Cardinal Pirelli* (1926). Here Firbank depicts a Catholic Spain in all its baroque glory – and perversity. For, in the end, Cardinal Pirelli is seen chasing his beloved chorister through the cathedral chapels, stripping himself naked, and exclaiming 'Don't exasperate me, boy' (p.697). Little wonder that Brentano's, who had agreed to publish *Prancing Nigger* without a fee, declined this work on 'religious and moral grounds'. They feared that the 'outspokenness of the book regarding the life of the Cardinal and particularly church matters' would cause offence to booksellers.[25] So, once again, Firbank had to find a substantial sum to secure publication with Grant Richards, such were the risks of dedicating himself to the task of exploiting the perverse aesthetics that he and many other homosexual men identified with Roman Catholicism. None the less, it is important to bear in mind that not all men who became devoted to Catholic ritual were aesthetes. Many entered the Catholic priesthood because it offered a return to a true spiritual home whose traditions predated the punitive austerities of Protestantism. Yet, by the turn of the century there was a widely understood connection between Catholicism and male homosexuality. Less visible were the lesbians, like the collaborative poets Katherine Bradley and Edith Cooper, who enjoyed a limited sense of community among the many sexual outcasts who found a significant form of emotional expression within the Catholic church. But, as far as one can tell, they were not interested at all in the scourgings and whippings conducted among nuns. To them, the lesbians populating Firbank's fiction would no doubt have been wholly unrecognizable.

It is in *Valmouth* that his passion for whippings and scourgings among Catholic lesbians discovers its most unEnglish, exotic, and preposterous form. The lavishly dressed community of his imaginary estuarine town is populated by centenarians, many of whom are prone to perverse longings. In this respect, one episode is worth examining in some detail, for it points out exactly how Firbank's lesbians provide an outrageous critique of orthodox masculinity while at the same time bringing his delight in effeminacy to the fore. In Chapter 4, three old friends – Eulalia Hurstpierpoint, Lady Parvula de Panzoust, and Elizabeth Thoroughfare – are exchanging gossip about the elderly invalids who retire to Valmouth to convalesce. But their attitude towards the moneyed types who occupy their home town becomes instantly clear when Lady Parvula exclaims: 'So many horrid parliament-men come here apparently purely to bask.' Ever ready to seize on a pun, Firbank takes this as a prompt for Mrs Thoroughfare to make her own sexual preferences known. Her own passions could not be further from those honourable members serving in the British parliament. Given her propensity for Catholic ritualism of the highest and most elaborate kinds, she adverts immediately to her 'whips' (p.405). At Mrs Hurstpierpoint's country home, Hare-Hatch House, her life is a ceaseless round of scourgings, confessions, and complete devotion to the 'House-Basilica' dedicated to Nuestra Señora de la Peña. In this environment, the only men who arouse the interest of these women are unconventional, to say the least. Lady Parvula, at her ripe old age, has been thinking enviously of her daughter's desire for Mrs Thoroughfare's son, Dick. 'Men, men!' she remarks, ' "They're always there", dear, aren't they, as the Russians say?' But Mrs Hurstpierpoint is disinclined to agree. ' "Nowadays", she murmured, "a man . . . to me . . . somehow . . . oh! he is something wildly *strange*" .' To which Mrs Thoroughfare adds: 'Still, some men are ultrawomanly, and they're the kind I love.' This prompts Lady Parvula to interject: 'I suppose that none but those whose courage is unquestionable can venture to be effeminate' (p.406). Although she is the only heterosexual among them, Lady Parvula aches for the love of a 'shepherd' – a pastoral man, not a brute. And she recognizes only too well that for a man to behave in an 'ultra-womanly' manner is to take no uncertain risks.

Given the homophobic climate in which Firbank was writing, it remained almost impossible for him to represent his own queer effeminacy directly. Indeed, men rarely appear in *Valmouth*, and whenever they are glimpsed, their desires are just as iconoclastic as those of the three *grandes dames* who anticipate their whippings with glee. There is, for example, the gravestone in memory of Balty Vincent Wise, who – 'having lived and died – *unmarried*' – utterly bewilders Mrs Tooke, one of the local Philistines:

Oh what a funny fellow! Oh what a curious man! . . . What did he
mean by going off like that? Was no woman good enough for him
then? Oh what a queer reflection to be sure; what a slur on all her sex!
Oh but he should have settled; ranged himself as every bachelor
should! Improper naughty thing! He should be exorcised and
whipped: or had he loved? Loved perchance *elsewhere* . . .? (p.437)

From what we can gather, Balty Wise did his utmost to escape the heterosexual imperative to settle down into married life. But it is a telling fact that
Firbank employs Mrs Tooke's consciousness to speculate on Balty Wise's
queer desires when he is dead and buried. At no point in Firbank's works
do effeminate men get the opportunity to speak for themselves, even
through 'Sterneian' innuendo. Yet that is not to say that Firbank's exotic
effeminacy is in any way powerless. Instead, his whole aesthetic is shaped by
a protesting effeminate style that constantly displaced an inability to speak
for itself on to other perverse formations, such as lesbianism. Hollinghurst
claims that 'Firbank's interest in specifically Lesbian women . . . allows a
kind of transference, a half-transparent disguise, and also a possibility to
aestheticize – with clothes, make-up and jewellery – his cryptic subject'.[26]
Valmouth does everything within its power to break new ground in this
respect. This novel, however, not only concentrates on his highly stylized
lesbianism, it also explores the pleasures of interracial desire.

V

Towards the end of his career, Firbank turned his attention more and more
towards racial difference to elaborate his effeminate aesthetic. This fascination begins with the intricate depiction of Mrs Yajñavalkya, the masseuse
whose nimble hands relieve the aching limbs of the local community. No
sooner has Lady Parvula taken her painful corn to Mrs Yaj – the 'sole
proficient of the chiropodist's art at Valmouth' (p.413) – than she makes a
little light conversation with the 'negress'. 'Now and then', she remarks, 'an
interesting patient must wish to approach you.' Quickly grasping the sexual
implications to Lady Parvula's speech, Mrs Yaj replies: 'I always . . . decline
a gentleman. Often ze old greybeards zey say, "Oh, Mrs Yaj", zey say,
"include our sex". And I laugh and say, "I've enough to do wif my own"'
(p.415). Like all of Firbank's characters, Mrs Yaj cannot be easily placed
within a familiar frame of reference. Her racial disposition is treated to
exactly the same kind of disorientating details that we find among his
hybrid middle Europeans. Named after a Hindu goddess, she claims to
'miss a mosque . . . and de consolation ob de church' (p.439). No wonder
her cultural origins puzzle Lady Parvula. 'In what part, tell me,' she insists,
'is your home?' ' "Here!" the negress lisped.' Even if Mrs Yaj's family is, as

she puts it, '[g]eographically scattered', she belongs to Valmouth as much as any of her clients (p.416). Her patois is very much her own, sounding at times Caribbean, occasionally Italian, and vaguely Arabic. But if Mrs Yaj's unusual presence were not enough, then her charming and flirtatious niece takes Firbank's orientalist interests to altogether greater heights. This is Niri-Esther, on whom Mrs Hurstpierpoint and Mrs Thoroughfare have rival designs. 'Incontestably', the narrator assures us, 'she was of a superior caste to Mrs Yajñavalkya.' Like one of Paul Gauguin's portraits of Tahitian women, Niri-Esther is set before our gaze in all her exotic beauty: 'She wore a dishabille of mignonette-green silk and a bead-diapered head-dress that added several inches to her height; her finger-slim ankles were stained with lac and there were rings of collyrium about her eyes' (p.417). Excessively attractive, she is set to marry Captain Dick Thoroughfare. But not, it seems, before she has borne their second child. He, however, has not returned to Valmouth before the close of the novel. Sufficient hints are made to suggest that he never ceases from travelling abroad so that he can be close to his young 'middy-chum', Jack Whorwood, whose punning name makes their homosexual love-affair fairly clear. 'That little lad', he is reported to have said, 'upon a cruise, is, to me, what Patroclus was to Achilles' (p.398). No wonder that the liaison between Niri-Esther and Dick Thoroughfare prompts one of the servants to declare: 'I've seen a mort o' queer things in my day . . . but a *negress*' (p.461). Just as Balty Wise's '*unmarried*' life prompted Mrs Tooke's 'queer reflection', the idea of an interracial love affair which had led to two illegitimate children by a homosexual man strikes the conventional mind as very 'queer' indeed.

In August 1922, Firbank travelled to the Caribbean with the aim of writing a 'negro novel with a brilliant background of sunlight' and 'sea', which he would make as 'tropical' as possible.[27] Set in Havana, *Prancing Nigger* showcases Firbank's distinctly theatrical interest in 'negro' lives. Given the appeal of such material to fashionable white New Yorkers, it is not surprising that Firbank's permission was sought by Stuart Rose and Thurston Macauley of the Cherry Lane Theatre in New York to dramatize the novel as a 'Jazz Fantasy'. There was the possibility that George Gershwin might produce a score for it. But they aborted the project, according to Miriam Benkowitz, because 'the cost of staging and the financial risk of so *avant-garde* a comedy were too great'.[28] Yet, despite this setback, *Prancing Nigger* was the first of Firbank's books to yield financial rewards. By October 1924, he had received $695 from the American office of Brentano's. At last, as he informed his sister, the 'ball' seemed to be 'set rolling'.[29] For the first time, he had his eye on the market. Contact with Nancy Cunard, the American heiress whose name was most closely associated with the Harlem Renaissance, probably concentrated his mind as never before on a growing audience. Even more important, in this respect, was the American writer, Carl Van Vechten, whose novel, *Nigger Heaven*, would be a runaway bestseller in 1926. Participating in a symposium on 'The Negro in Art', Van Vechten celebrated 'the squalor of Negro life, the vice of Negro life'. But he was aware that this apparently natural resource of spontaneity was likely to be sapped dry by white opportunists. 'Are Negro writers', he asked, 'going to write about this exotic material while it is still fresh or will they continue to make a free gift of it to white authors who will exploit it until not a drop of vitality remains?'[30] Firbank was among the first whites to make the lives of African-Caribbeans conform to the racist stereotypes of primitive naturalness that white Americans readily conferred upon the flourishing jazz scene in New York. One episode from *Prancing Nigger* makes this undeniably clear. During the carnival that occupies the final chapter, Edna Mouth laughingly imitates 'a comedian from the Eden Garden' while she sits on her white lover's knee. 'Like all other negresses', the narrator observes, 'she possessed a natural bent for mimicry and a voice of that lisping quality that would find complete expression in songs such as: "Have you seen my sweet garden ob flowers?" ' To Vittorio Ruiz, Edna's 'self-importance and madcapery' are altogether more enchanting than 'his last mistress, an exotic English girl, perpetually shivering, even in the sun' (p.630). Edna positively glows with sexual warmth. And, like Niri-Esther and Mrs Yaj, she is yet another vehicle for Firbank's perverse aesthetic.

While Edna and Vittorio watch the pageant pass before them, the imaginary city of Cuna-Cuna becomes a spectacle of each and every transgressive desire that we have so far glimpsed in Firbank's works:

> Delegates of agricultural guilds bearing banners, making for the Cathedral square (the pilgrims' starting-point), were advancing along the avenue amidst applause: fruit-growers, rubber-growers, sugar-growers, opium-growers, all doubtless wishful of placating Nature that redoubtable Goddess by showing a little honour to the Church. 'Oh Lord, *not* as Sodom', she murmured, deciphering a text attached to the windscreen of a luxurious automobile.
>
> 'Divine one, here they are.'
>
> 'T'anks, honey, I best widdout', she replied, following the Bacchic progress of two girls in soldiers' forage-caps, who were exciting the gaiety of the throng.
>
> 'Be careful, kid; don't lean too far . . .'
>
> 'Oh, ki, if dey don't exchange kisses!' (p.641)

This 'Bacchic progress' unquestionably represents everything that white, civilized, Philistine England sought to banish from its shores. In Cuna-Cuna, it may well seem that Firbank had discovered a queer utopia where each and every prohibition on his desires was turned completely on its head. As Christopher Lane observes, Firbank 'used travel and foreign culture as a substitute for the problem of writing homosexuality from home'.[31] Yet, as with most European idealizations of race, his exorbitant representation of

Cuna-Cuna relies on the very forms of imperialist thought that on many occasions he seeks to attack. Even if, as William Lane Clark observes, Firbank's '*self*-identification with blacks carries over into . . . characterization' so that 'he can make fun of himself, his homosexuality, and his erotic attraction to other races, but not of the black man or woman', he does so at the expense of people who conform to demeaning stereotypes.[32] Here, as in *Valmouth*, Firbank uses lower-class servants – a 'yawning butler, an insolent footman, a snoring coachman' – to voice racial prejudice, since it is they who deplore the 'party of "b—d—y niggers" ' waiting outside the Ruizes' home (p.633). But this condemnation of proletarian bigotry masks the white supremacism that issues from the high cultural forms which turn Cuna-Cuna into such a display of perverse pomp and ceremony.

The apparently unEnglish environment of *Prancing Nigger* brings into view Firbank's conflicted attitude towards the empire he despised. In one respect, the 'Cunan Constabulary' and its 'handsome youngsters, looking the apotheosis themselves of earthly lawlessness, in their feathered sun-hats and bouncing kilts' are marvellously unconstrained in the sexual 'diversion' they create (p.641). On the face of it, nothing could be further from the soldiers marching through the streets of London. But, from another angle, this is an imperial pageant where all the wares of the colonies dazzle us with their wealth. Bearing this point in mind, one should greet what Brophy says about Firbank's handling of racial difference with some caution. 'Firbank', she writes, 'was a violently racially prejudiced man: in favour of the black races – perhaps partly because he saw the surface of their blackness as brushed by mauve, a colour dear to him . . . because it was the colour of the "decadence".'[33] Yet even if Firbank was drawn to the 'mauve' coloration of black skin, it was to support his desire to aestheticize a distinctly European world whose masculinist violence provoked his 'raging disgust' (p.671). So wherever we find traces of Firbank's profound Anglophobia, we discover his determination to create his own effeminate England. It was an alternative vision that sought to reappropriate the nation to his own ends. In the process, a parodistic conception of black minstrelsy and an idea of lesbian unnaturalness would become the two forms of extreme perversity that could mediate his otherwise unexpressed desires. Both were more familiar and permissible in their exoticism than the figure that the nail-varnished and hair-powdered Firbank cut in real life.

Noticeably, all his male homosexual characters remain in the background of his novels. When they do appear, as in the case of Claude Harvester in *Vainglory*, they are subjected to a little self-parody. 'In style', we are told, 'he was obscure, although, in reality, he was as charming as the top of an apple-tree above a wall' (p.82). This satire becomes somewhat harsher when we remember that Mrs Henedge could not stand Harvester's wife. To be a husband obviously carries with it certain disadvantages. As the Princess Zoubaroff reminds us in Firbank's only drama: 'A husband, one must remember, is something of an *acquired* taste' (p.710). Likewise, finding all of Firbank's books out of the library at Pisuerga, Miss Hopkins has to settle for '*Men Are Animals*' (p.533). There was surely something problematic for an effeminate writer such as Firbank in discovering he was erotically attracted to a sex whose gender he loathed. Only in *The Flower beneath the Foot* do we find something resembling a self-portrait of Firbank, and even then it proves dispiriting. The figure in question is the Hon. 'Eddy' Monteith, who is utterly devoted to his old school chum, Lionel Limpness. (Some critics, it should be added, contend that 'Eddy' is a satiric portrait of the poet, Evan Morgan.) 'Eddy', after all, is a Roman Catholic enthusiast. He not only has a portable altar, but he also whiles away his time penning odes to the scurrilous Swinburne. Only much later in the novel do we discover that he received a terrible shock by 'meeting a jackal while composing a sonnet' during his archaeological expedition to Chedorlahomor (p.581). It is perhaps the fate of the effeminate 'homo' to die in an exotic place whose name quietly encrypts his sexual preference.

Notes

1 E.M. Forster, 'Ronald Firbank', in *Abinger Harvest* (London, Edward Arnold, 1953), pp.138–9.

2 Martin Green, *Children of the Sun: A Narrative of 'Decadence' in England after 1918* (London, Constable, 1977), p.24.

3 Evelyn Waugh, 'Ronald Firbank', first published in *Life and Letters*, 1929, reprinted in *Essays, Articles and Reviews*, ed. Donat Gallagher (London, Methuen, 1983), pp.56–7.

4 Alan Hollinghurst, 'The Creative Uses of Homosexuality in the Novels of E.M. Forster, Ronald Firbank and L.P. Hartley', unpublished MLitt thesis, University of Oxford, 1980, p.115.

5 See Robert Murray Davis, 'Ronald Firbank's Notebooks: ". . . writing books was by no means easy" ', *Harvard Library Bulletin*, 25 (1977), pp.172–92. In his mature novels written after *The Artificial Princess*, Firbank thought 'nothing of fileing [*sic*] fifty pages down to make a brief, crisp paragraph, or even a row of dots!' ('To Stuart Rose', undated, cited in Miriam J. Benkowitz, 'Ronald Firbank in New York', *Bulletin of the New York Public Library*, 63 (1959), p.258). Davis remarks that this 'arduous process of composition helps to explain how, in very very short novels, he was able to create the effect of a full and busy world' (p.178).

6 Ronald Firbank, *The Complete Firbank* (London, Duckworth, 1961), p.106. Further page references appear in parentheses.

7 Firbank paid Grant Richards approximately £1000 over a nine-year period to publish his work, and by 1923 he was incensed that he had seen no financial returns at all. Richards' apologetic comments to the frustrated author are recorded in Miriam J. Benkowitz, *A Bibliography of Ronald Firbank* (London, Rupert Hart-Davis, 1963), p.40.

8 Brigid Brophy, *Prancing Novelist: A Defence of Fiction in the Form of a Critical Biography in Praise of Ronald Firbank* (London, Macmillan, 1973), p.81. It would

be difficult to write with any competence on Firbank's fiction unless one absorbed Brophy's exacting and very brilliant 'defence'. Her critical methods, however, are Firbankian to a degree that some readers might find (indeed, have found) infuriating. Martin Green, for one, remarks that *Prancing Novelist* is 'elaborate, pretentious, and . . . preposterous'; *Children of the Sun*, p.20. Brophy's study is equally detailed, scholarly, and tireless in its unravelling of Firbank's demanding canon of writing. The standard work on Firbank's life is Miriam J. Benkowitz, *Ronald Firbank: A Biography* (London, Weidenfeld and Nicolson, 1970). Brophy rightly remarks that Benkowitz's biography 'is a work of such conventionality of mind that it produces, when the conventionality is trained on the subject of Firbank, a riot of Firbankian irony' (p.115).

9 Brophy, pp.411–31.
10 James Bone, 'The Tendencies of Modern Art', *Edinburgh Review*, April 1913, pp.420–34, reprinted in J.B. Bullen, ed., *Post-Impressionists in England* (London, Routledge, 1988), pp.438–9.
11 Unsigned Review, 'Paint Run Mad: Post-Impressionists at Grafton Galleries', *Daily Express*, 9 November 1910, p.8, reprinted in Bullen, p.105.
12 Ronald Firbank, *The Early Firbank*, ed. Steven Moore (London, Quartet, 1991), p.26. Further page references appear in parentheses.
13 Oscar Wilde, *Complete Works*, ed. J.B. Foreman (London, Collins, 1966), p.1205. Further page references appear in parentheses.
14 Brophy, p.171.
15 Gregory W. Bredbeck, 'Narcissus in the Wilde: Textual Catharsis and the Historical Origins of Queer Camp', in Moe Meyer (ed.) *The Politics and Poetics of Camp* (London, Routledge, 1994), p.52. Susan Sontag's groundbreaking essay, 'Notes on Camp', dates from 1964, and appears in *Against Interpretation* (New York, Noonday Press, 1966), pp.275–92.
16 Andrew Ross, *No Respect: Intellectuals and Popular Culture* (New York, Routledge, 1989), pp.145–6.
17 Walter Benjamin, *Charles Baudelaire: A Lyric Poet in the Era of High Capitalism*, trans. Harry Zohn (London, New Left Books, 1973), p.125.
18 Joan DeJean, *Fictions of Sappho: 1546–1937* (Chicago, IL, University of Chicago Press, 1989), p.273.
19 Charles Baudelaire, 'Lesbos', in *Les Fleurs du Mal: The Complete Text*, trans. Richard Howard (Brighton, Harvester Press, 1982), p.125.
20 Brophy, p.366. For a useful account of Vivien's poetry, see Sandra M. Gilbert and Susan Gubar, *No Man's Land: The Place of the Woman Writer in the Twentieth-Century: Volume 2: Sexchanges* (New Haven, CT, Yale University Press, 1989), pp.226–30.
21 Jocelyn Brooke, *Ronald Firbank* (London, Arthur Barker, 1951), p.34.
22 On lesbian stereotypes in film and in fiction, see Andrea Weiss, *Vampires and Violets: Lesbians in the Cinema* (London, Jonathan Cape, 1992), and Paulina Palmer, *Contemporary Lesbian Writing: Dreams, Desire, Difference* (Buckingham, Open University Press, 1993).
23 David Hilliard, 'UnEnglish and Unmanly: Anglo-Catholicism and Homosexuality', *Victorian Studies*, 25(2) (1982), p.206.
24 John Francis Bloxam, 'The Priest and the Acolyte', *The Chameleon*, June 1894, reprinted in Brian Reade (ed.) *Sexual Heretics: Male Homosexuality in English*

Literature from 1850 to 1900 (London, Routledge and Kegan Paul, 1970), p.356.

25 Brentano's remarks on *Concerning the Eccentricities of Cardinal Pirelli* are recorded in Benkowitz, *A Bibliography of Ronald Firbank*, p.50.

26 Hollinghurst, 'The Creative Uses of Homosexuality', p.129.

27 Firbank, 'To Carl Van Vechten', 29 June 1922, cited in Benkowitz, *Ronald Firbank*, p.224.

28 Benkowitz, *A Bibliography of Ronald Firbank*, p.47.

29 Cited in Benkowitz, *A Bibliography of Ronald Firbank*, p.46.

30 Carl Van Vechten, 'A Drop of Vitality Remains', *The Crisis*, 32(11) (1926), p.219, cited in David Levering Lewis, *When Harlem Was in Vogue* (New York, Knopf, 1981), p.177.

31 Christopher Lane, 'Re/Orientations: Firbank's Colonial Imaginary and the Sexual Nomad', *Literature Interpretation Theory*, 3 (1992), p.274.

32 William Lane Clark, 'Degenerate Personality: Deviant Sexuality and Race in Ronald Firbank's Novels', in David Bergman (ed.) *Camp Grounds: Style and Homosexuality* (Amherst, MA, University of Massachusetts Press, 1993), p.145.

33 Brophy, p.174.

4

'No sign of *effeminatio*'?
Towards the military orchid

I

Near the start of Leslie Stephen's *Mausoleum Book* (1895), there is an oblique reference to a recent biography of John Addington Symonds. It is a curious allusion because Stephen was obviously troubled by what he knew about this distinguished contemporary man of letters. It disturbs him to think that anything remotely resembling Symonds's personal life might enter his own *Mausoleum Book*: a short work that seeks to preserve the memory of Julia Stephen for their children. To commemorate his late spouse, Stephen insists that 'to speak intelligibly it will be best to begin by saying something about myself'. But no sooner has he made this declaration than he instantly fights shy of the idea that he shall be led into making any undue autobiographical disclosures. 'I could give you', he remarks, 'none of those narratives of inward events, conversions or spiritual crises which give interest to some autobiographers.' It is in this context that Symonds – a respectable married man like Stephen himself – comes to mind:

> I was amused lately by reading Horatio Brown's life of Symonds, virtually an autobiography, and reflecting how little of the same kind of internal history could be told of me . . . I could give a history of some struggles through which I had to pass – successfully or otherwise: but I have a certain sense of satisfaction in reflecting that I shall take that knowledge with me to the grave.[1]

In these remarks, one feature is strongly apparent. Not only is the *Mausoleum Book* going to repress any truths that would cast Stephen in an unfavourable light, but in doing so, it shall also evade the form of conventional autobiography which obliges the author to wrestle with his tormented soul.

Yet there is even more to be made of these prefatory gestures. Stephen's urgent disavowals assuredly represent the Victorian patriarch straining to maintain an outward show of invulnerability. To reveal oneself in the manner that Symonds had chosen strikes Stephen as undesirable, if not altogether distasteful. But it was not in Horatio Brown's two-volume biography that Stephen would have found the most disturbing details about the 'internal history' of Symonds's life. In fact, Brown had drawn liberally on the intimate memoirs that Symonds had started writing in 1889 and pursued until the time of his death at the age of 53 in 1893. So dangerous were these documents deemed by Symonds's close associates that they remained hidden from the public for the best part of a century. Their existence, however, was known to various members of the literary élite. Stephen's daughter, Virginia Woolf, for example, recalls how Roger Fry admired Symonds for being the 'most pornographic person' he ever knew. Symonds was not, according to Fry, 'in the least nasty'. If 'very dogmatic and overbearing in discussion', Symonds expressed 'nice humane broad views of life'. Finding a companionable listener in Fry, he had 'become most confidential . . . over certain passages of his life'.[2] Oblique allusions such as these provide adequate evidence to suggest that Symonds's sexuality was something of an open secret to members of the Bloomsbury group. The important point is that Woolf's reflections on Symonds's personal life are clearly sympathetic where her father plainly was not. Given that Stephen began writing his *Mausoleum Book* when the Wilde trials were at their height, it is reasonable to claim that his reflections on Symonds were exacerbated by the appalling humiliation of another distinguished man of letters before the public. Symonds, after all, was associated with a kind of aestheticism that bore some resemblance to Wilde's interests in the high arts.

Comments made by contemporaries bear out this view. Gleaning information from Edmund Gosse, Henry James would note Symonds's 'extreme and somewhat hysterical aestheticism'. The idea of an artistic man married to a wife who thought his books 'immoral, pagan, hyper-aesthetic' provided James with the kernel of his short story, 'The Author of "Beltraffio" ' (1884).[3] Some nine years later, having received one of the few copies of Symonds's privately printed study of homosexual desire, 'A Problem in Modern Ethics' (1891), James thanked Gosse for bringing him 'those marvellous outpourings'. But, interestingly, James finds Symonds's work 'a queer place to plant the standard of duty'.[4] It is a striking statement. For James, it seems, there is something out of order, if not mistaken, in turning one's sexual longings for other men into such an extended form of protest. And yet, in another sense, James is suggesting – quite literally – that homosexual identification is indeed 'queer'. It is not at all unusual to find James at once revealing and concealing his homophile interests in this manner. We could well put James's reservations about planting the polite 'standard of duty' in an incongruously 'queer place' down to his fear that his own same-sex desires might become public knowledge. But there may have been – and it is certainly worth suspending judgement on this – other reasons for James's wary response to Symonds's sense of obligation. The same, it has to be said, goes for Stephen's worried remarks.

Symonds's memoirs were a potential source of embarrassment to his friends and family because they provided, not just a scrupulously detailed account of his homosexual liaisons during the course of his married life, but a polemic about the specific identity that attended his sexual habits. This autobiographical work was self-consciously political, since it sought to present a respectable image of male homosexuality at a time when the Labouchere Amendment – prohibiting all sexual relations between men, even in private – was already serving as a terrifying 'Blackmailer's Charter'. Symonds wanted to show that his homosexual practice made him 'more of a man than when he repressed and pent within his soul those fatal and abnormal inclinations'. But society, he declared, still insisted on deeming him a 'criminal'.[5] The same point is reiterated in 'A Problem in Modern Ethics' (1891) – one of the two pamphlets on homophilia that he published for private circulation – where he writes: 'sexual relations between males and males should not be treated as criminal, unless they be attended with violence (as in the case of rape), or be carried on in such a way as to offend the public sense of decency'.[6] Throughout his defence of male homosexuality, Symonds looks with admiration to the Code Napoleon established in France – a legal framework that did not interfere in private sexual behaviour between men. Such sentiments were toned down, if not eliminated, by Brown in his biography. Yet it was not just Brown who edited the contents of the memoirs with caution. In fact, from what we can tell, Brown used his utmost discretion to bring some of Symonds's homosexual truths to light. Instead, it was his publisher, Nimmo, that intervened in the name of censorship, preventing any incriminating information from appearing in the text.[7] These potentially explosive materials would remain in Brown's possession until his death in 1926, when they passed into the hands of his literary executor, Edmund Gosse. Thereafter, the large manuscript was deposited in the London Library, which immediately placed a 50-year ban on its publication.

The length of this ban seems inordinate, given that Symonds's acquaintances would not have needed to have read the memoirs to understand his homophile affiliation. In any case, he had for years been making his sexual preference as clear as he possibly could both in person and in writing.

Consorting with Angelo Fusato, his Italian lover during the early 1890s, Symonds had already caused controversy in 1877 when the final chapter of his *Studies of the Greek Poets* praised the 'genius' of Greek culture in the figure of an athletic young man. It was his enthusiasm for such 'clear and stainless personality' displayed by this noble Greek youth that instantly raised the suspicions of a moralistic contemporary.[8] Writing on 'The Greek Spirit in Modern Literature', St John Tyrwhitt infamously deplored the 'vices . . . which are not even named among us' that existed in ancient Greece.[9] The essay was a considerable source of controversy. Richard Dellamora has shown how Tyrwhitt's homophobic response played a central role in Oxford University politics at the time.[10] Once Tyrwhitt had launched his attack on the praise given by the likes of Symonds to homosexual 'vice', Symonds withdrew his candidature for the post of Professor of Poetry. (Equally worried by public opprobrium against his homophile interests was Walter Pater. His 'Conclusion' to *Studies in the History of the Renaissance* (1873) had already provoked contumelious responses. In the light of Tyrwhitt's remarks, Pater also retired from the professorial election.) But, in the face of such setbacks, Symonds remained irrepressible in seeking a forum in which readers could identify his sexual delight in the athletic male modelled on the Greek ideal. In 1891, for example, he published an article entitled 'Swiss Athletic Sports' in the liberal *Fortnightly Review*, which contains several barely coded allusions to homosexuality. Here is the most obvious example:

> I asked a young friend of mine – a stag-like youth from Graubunden, tall and sinewy, like the young Achilles on a fresco at Pompeii – how all the gymnasts in this country came to be so brotherly. 'Oh', he replied, 'that is because we come into physical contact with one another. You only learn to live with men whose bodies you have touched and handled'. True as I believe this remark to be, and wide-reaching in its possibilities of application, I somehow did not expect it from the lips of an Alpine peasant.[11]

Such comments are disingenuous, to say the least. In this excerpt, Symonds tactfully displaces the sexual implications of such 'brotherly' love on to someone as apparently lowly and innocent as a peasant. It would be left to his readers to discern the 'wide-reaching possibilities of application' arising from this sporting scene where close physical contact between men is surrounded by an aura of classical authority.

Sufficient evidence, then, exists to show that by alluding so quickly to Symonds's life, Stephen was defining his own upstanding Victorian respectability against the painful truth of another man's homosexual disposition. In other words, the *Mausoleum Book* begins by emphasizing how a respectable patriarch must publicly insist that certain facts about his life have to remain unrecorded because – if we are inferring rightly – a man's homosexual private life has been written down elsewhere. Stephen's fear, I suspect, is connected not so much with the horror that Symonds's homosexuality aroused in him; rather, his anxiety may well have stemmed from the thought that Symonds had done harm by producing a complex auto-biographical narrative which unsettled a much-needed silence about male sexuality in general. To start speaking about a man's desires – for women, for men, or for both – probably struck Stephen as creating an unnecessary problem, one that might perhaps draw his own sexual needs and desires into question by creating a discourse around them. For Symonds, by contrast, the anguished truth of human sexuality had at all costs to be articulated in his memoirs. He was absolutely determined to name and classify his specific sexual identity, to make his difference and distinctiveness known. And his reasons for doing so are less obvious than we may think. If homophile autobiographers promise to heighten our awareness of the naturalness of their erotic preference, they frequently discover that many men of their acquaintance fail to conform to their initial idea of a specific homosexual type – to the point, in fact, of becoming rather perplexed by male sexuality and its potential objects of desire.

This point emerges time and again in the significant examples of homosexual life writing produced after 1885 that I discuss in this chapter. In the process of chronicling their sexual histories, homophile autobiographers often perceive – sometimes to their own consternation, if not confusion – that a man's erotic attraction to women may not, for all its cultural privilege, be so very different in quality from the stigmatized longings expressed by one man for another. But, for some reason – as Symonds's memoirs set out to explore – a homosexual difference was demanded in late Victorian England, and it was a difference whose power was great enough to make subsequent homophile writers believe that the most highly prized models of masculinity that the culture produced were correspondingly the most desirable. Adamant to repudiate the least trait of effeminacy, each writer in this chapter in turn fixes his gaze upon military manhood: the erotic icon embodying everything that the literary life writer would like both to have and to be. Within this field of self-examination, these writers force themselves time and again to estimate exactly what it is about English culture that makes them necessarily distinct from heterosexual men.

Perhaps it was for the sake of resolving and containing the potentially anarchic fluidity of male sexuality that Symonds sought to make such a virtue of being such a singular and distinctive kind of man. Like the two pamphlets he circulated confidentially among friends – 'A Problem in Greek Ethics' (1873) and 'A Problem in Modern Ethics' (1891) – his memoirs count among the first modern documents to emphasize how human identity must primarily be understood in terms of sexual preference. The memoirs subsequently proved to be an important point of reference for readers concerned with modern conceptions of homosexual identity. In

1961, for example, E.M. Forster copied down various passages from Symonds's autobiography into his *Commonplace Book*. Recalling the famous incident at the age of 19 when Symonds 'denounce[d] his headmaster's homosexual practices to his father', Forster wrily notes:

> The above, all that follows, is in J.A.S.'s unpublished autobiography in the L.L. which may not at present be quoted from, nor I think referred to. *Will anyone who reads this remember that?* Publication possible in 1976. About 150,000 words in typescript. A complete life, the many 'literary' bits of which S. has published elsewhere. – He gave up all work to complete it.[12]

Symonds's memoirs assuredly had a special resonance for Forster. He recognized that the sexual truth was so urgent that Symonds gave over the final part of his career to revealing his relationships with an Alpine peasant, a British grenadier, and a Venetian gondolier. Symonds, therefore, undertook at great length to write what would still be deemed completely unquotable even after the Wolfenden Committee had made its recommendations for the decriminalization of male homosexuality in 1957. Only in 1984 did Phyllis Grosskurth's edition of the memoirs come into print, nearly a decade after the long ban on publication had eventually been lifted. This scholarly work represents all but a fifth of Symonds's lengthy manuscript.

Even if Symonds's memoirs comprise one of the first modern male homosexual autobiographies in England, it is noticeable that the word homosexual itself does not belong to their vocabulary. Although the *Oxford English Dictionary* lists Symonds as one of the earliest figures to use the term – and it recurs, to be sure, on many occasions in his later correspondence[13] – Symonds employed a different language in his work of life writing to specify his sexual selfhood. In this meticulous work of self-examination, his idea of the man-loving man belongs to a cluster of highly specific definitions derived from the emergent field of sexology, particularly the work of the German sex radical, Karl Heinrich Ulrichs. But sexology is not the only model upon which Symonds fashions his homophile ideals. This form of sexual typing overlays a very different form of thinking about sexual love between men which Symonds had for decades researched in detail, and without which he could not have applied himself to sexology at all. Before encountering Ulrichs's work – which would absorb him completely during the last few years of his life – he had developed an extensive number of studies of ancient Greece that were fired by the enthusiastic growth of Oxford Hellenism in the mid- and late-nineteenth century. Reform of the university classics syllabus in the hands of broad churchmen such as Benjamin Jowett brought with it the discovery that Greek *paiderastia* fostered male homosexual relations in the name of a martial ethic. Exploring the impact of this signal shift in university education, Linda Dowling sees how 'a counterdiscourse of male love' achieved admirable hegemony among men with strong homophile interests. 'The language of male love', writes Dowling, 'could now be triumphantly proclaimed the very fountain of civic health in an English polity imperatively in need, precisely as liberal theorists such as [J.S.] Mill and university reformers such as Jowett had all along been insisting, of some authentic new source of ideas and intellectual power.'[14] Certainly, Symonds and his peers, such as Pater, did all that they could to exploit the liberal ethos increasingly fostered by the transformed university. But even if emanating from an institution whose cultural authority in Victorian England cannot be underestimated, the Hellenism that Pater and Symonds were seeking to develop in terms of the Platonic 'spiritual procreancy'[15] that promised to regenerate the polity was only too aware – more so, I think, than Dowling is willing to admit – of the hazards that beset its bid for widespread legitimacy. Opposition there certainly was, not least from some ostensible Hellenists.

Symonds's essay on the minor poet, Edward Cracroft Lefroy, accentuates some of the competing and intriguing currents in the Hellenist engagement with male love. Here Symonds focuses on this writer's 'keen interest in boyish games and the athletic sports of young men'. 'These qualities', adds Symonds, 'were connected in a remarkable way with Hellenic instincts and an almost pagan delight in nature.'[16] In this essay, which first appeared in the *New Review* in March 1892, Lefroy presents a complex instance of what Victorian Hellenism could achieve in terms of the erotic ambience that Symonds wished to associate with it. Although admitting to a friend that he remained in 'closer affinity to Greek feeling than most people', Lefroy promptly insisted that he 'should be sorry to help on that Hellenic revival which some Oxford teachers desire'.[17] Lefroy, like the irascible Tyrwhitt, had written boldly against both Symonds and Pater when they stood as candidates for the Oxford Chair of Poetry in 1877, and yet – not quite as bewilderingly as we might at first think – he continued to compose poetry that was patently Uranian in its boy-loving Greek idealism. The curious thing about Symonds's essay is that it seeks to show how mistaken Lefroy was to consider himself only as a Christian Socialist, a belief expressed in an address on 'Muscular Christianity' that Lefroy had published in Oxford in 1877. Lefroy's problem, as Symonds saw it, lay in 'postulating the Christian faith as a divinely appointed way of surmounting the corruption and imperfection of nature' when, in fact, his poetry disclosed a very different set of interests.[18] In his sonnets praising male beauty, Lefroy 'proved it was possible to combine religious faith with frank delight in natural loveliness, to be a Christian without asceticism, and a Greek without sensuality'.[19] What, then, should we make of such a conclusion to an essay that cites at such length the works of a poet known to few outside the literary world of Oxford? It suggests, for one thing, that Symonds was bringing a sometime enemy back into the fold of the triumphal Hellenism that the minor poet –

for whatever reasons, his Christian faith among them – had assuredly repudiated in 1877. Eager to insist that Lefroy's 'neo-Hellenism is so pure and
modern',[20] Symonds has no hesitation in either comparing the poet's sonnets to Whitman's writings or characterizing these works as a type of
'democratic' art where the comrade in all his muscular girth figures the
regeneration of an athletic Hellenic ideal.

No doubt Lefroy was a valuable study for Symonds because his sonnets
of boy-love drew into question what exactly constituted same-sex desire –
the aspirations and disavowals upon which it might be built – for which
there was no ready-made answer. For Symonds, sexology provided a repertoire of terms that could perhaps come closer to estimating whether
Hellenism bore witness to specific types of sexual being, and whether
indeed there was some continuity between the Dorian armies, the Theban
Band, and the comrades embodying democracy in Whitman's national
epic. Pondering these topics, Symonds did not see his own sexual being
neatly complying with the sexologists' various typologies, and he was quick
to criticize many of the assumptions upon which Ulrichs's system of sexual
types was based. Likewise, he was distinctly wary of the emphasis he found
on congenital inversion among the sexologists, as shown in the following
passage from 'A Problem in Modern Ethics':

> It is now recognized by the leading authorities, medical and medico-
> juristic, in Germany, by writers like Casper-Liman and Krafft-Ebing,
> that sexual inversion is more than not innate. So far, without discuss-
> ing the physiological or metaphysical explanations of this phenom-
> enon, without considering whether Ulrichs is right in his theory of
> *anima muliebris inclusa in corpore virili* [the soul of a woman contained in
> the body of a man], or whether heredity, insanity, and similar general
> conditions are to be held responsible for the fact, it may be taken as
> admitted on all sides that the sexual diathesis in question is in a very
> large number of instances congenital. But Ulrichs seems to claim too
> much for the position he has won. He ignores the frequency of
> acquired habits. He shuts his eyes to the force of fashion and depravity.
> He reckons men like Horace and Ovid and Catullus, among the
> ancients, who were clearly indifferent in their tastes (as indifferent as
> the modern Turks) to the account of Uranodionings [i.e. bisexual
> men]. In one word, he is so enthusiastic for his physiological theory
> that he overlooks all other aspects of the question.[21]

An extract such as this one points up a productive incompatibility between sexology and Hellenism. Under this analysis, the Urning and the
Uranian are not quite the same thing, for they are based on different
assumptions about – to put it plainly – nature and nurture. Applying
considerable pressure to the tension between the two – between, that is, the
cultural acquisition of one's sexual identification and one's biological

determination to be a specific sexual type – Symonds remains highly ap-
prehensive about reaching hard and fast conclusions when discussing the
origins of a man's homophilia. Cultural and historical differences surely
served to cast doubt on the congenitality that Ulrichs wished to ascribe to
the inborn and unchanging invert, as Symonds saw it. But such thoughts
hardly made Symonds dismiss outright the often strange ensemble of terms
that Ulrichs devised to categorize gradations of homophilia in men. In his
account of his 'acquired habits', Symonds seeks to show – with scrupulous
qualifications – how he became, rather than was born, a particular kind of
Urning.

Symonds claimed to represent a sexual variant that had not as yet been
properly theorized, and which failed to fit into the exotic categories of
Ulrichs's invention. But, even if refusing to identify his sexuality with a
recognizable type, he none the less saw resemblances between himself and
some of the identities that Ulrichs had established. Indeed, he regarded the
'outlandish names' that Ulrichs used with some suspicion. The Urning, for
example, was subdivided into variant kinds: *Mannling* (male lover of effeminate men), *Weibling* (male lover of muscular men), *Zwischen-Urning* (male
lover of young men), and *Virilized Urning* (male lover of men who represses
his inborn sexual instinct by cohabiting with women). But for all his doubts
about the complete divisibility of these types, Symonds still put faith in
their 'technical value'˙ (p.65). 'With regard to Ulrichs, in his peculiar
phraseology', he comments:

> I should certainly be tabulated as a *Mittel Urning*, holding a mean
> between the *Mannling* and the *Weibling*; that is to say, one whose
> emotions are directed to the male sex during the period of adolescence
> and early manhood; who is not marked either by an effeminate passion
> for robust adults or by a predilection for young boys (p.65).

Yet Symonds asserted his sexual identity in this manner with no uncertain reservations about his moral disposition. Even if prepared to subscribe
to the theory, promoted by Richard Von Krafft-Ebing in *Psychopathia
Sexualis* (1889), that Urnings were 'inverts' – ones who possessed a female
soul in a male body, and vice versa – Symonds refused to believe, *pace*
Krafft-Ebing, that the Urnings were necessarily degenerate. Conceding that
as a teenager he 'exhibited many of the symptoms which Krafft-Ebing and
his school recognize as hereditary neuroticism predisposing its subject to
sexual inversion', he emphasizes that he has not been 'the victim of a
conceptional neurotic malady'. In no respect is he to be thought weak in
mind, body, or soul. If anything, his nervousness strikes him as a sign of his
intellectual strength. 'My literary achievement', he insists, 'is no doubt due
in part at least to a high degree of nervous sensibility; and compared with
the average of men, I may be pronounced to have exhibited an abnormal
strain of nervous energy' (p.64). The *Mittel Urning* thus embodies a sensitive

form of intellect with a prodigious capacity for literary endeavour, and it is this self-image that Symonds tries to impress on nearly every other page of what comprise his ultimate labour in this respect: the memoirs themselves.

Given the amount of self-analysis conducted in the memoirs, the influential distinction Michel Foucault makes between conceptions of the sodomite and the emergence of the homosexual as a specific kind of person in the late nineteenth century to a large degree rings true for Symonds – even if he adopted in this autobiography a set of terms that slightly predated what would become the rigid and conceptually restrictive hetero/homo binary.[22] Symonds's autobiographical reflections are largely the result of a wholehearted attempt to classify himself as a new sort of man – one who, as he would insist, 'dared to innovate' (p.249). In this respect, his innovations point up one of the main paradoxes of the identity politics established by those homophile writers who looked to sexology for models of self-confirmation. Sexology, writes Jeffrey Weeks, 'not only sought to regulate through naming; it also provided the springboard for self-definition and individual and collective resistance'. 'The theoretical seeds of this counter-discourse', he adds, '– what Foucault has called a "reverse affirmation" – were sown within sexological discourse itself.'[23] This is how Foucault remarks the paradox inherent to the discursive power that taxonomizes sexually deviant types:

> There is no question that the appearance in nineteenth-century psychiatry, jurisprudence, and literature of a whole series of discourses on the species and subspecies of homosexuality, inversion, pederasty, and 'psychic hermaphroditism' made possible a strong advance of social controls into this area of 'perversity'; but it also made possible the formation of a 'reverse' discourse: homosexuality began to speak in its own behalf, to demand that its legitimacy or 'naturality' be acknowledged, often in the same vocabulary, using the same categories by which it was medically disqualified.[24]

Just as the sexologists sought to define sexual behaviours that emanated from distinctive kinds of person – often with the purpose of establishing their debased nature – those emergent definitions were appropriated by homosexuals in the name of political empowerment, frequently by declaring that their sexual tendencies indicated the shape of more highly evolved and superior species, such as we would find in Edward Carpenter's writings. Never for one moment would Symonds claim that his special status as a *Mittel Urning* should be a mark of shame. This, indeed, is one of the chief results of Symonds's system of thought.

In his memoirs, however, Symonds is doing something more than insisting, as he informed Brown, on his unique identity as an innovative 'type of man who has not yet been classified' (p.289). Repudiating Krafft-Ebing's negative description of the invert, he sets out to establish that his vast quantity of admired literary work has been the result of his homosexual condition. The memoirs, then, are not just an account of a successful career driven by his 'abnormal strain of nervous energy'. Instead, they are very much a part of that career, proving once again that he is in a state of excellent mental and moral health while producing this sustained auto-biographical study. Occupying the last four years of his life, this exhaustive work of life writing marks the culmination of his tireless literary ambitions. To be sure, Symonds's innumerable tomes of criticism, biography, and translation – which he painstakingly lists as 'a large amount of work to accomplish in fourteen years' (p.281) – are overwhelming in their range and bulk. The memoirs, however, constitute his only narrative to reveal why he 'never ceased from scribbling' for the past quarter of a century (p.238). In this way, they stand as a metacritical work, since they constantly reflect on how they – like their predecessors – have come to be produced. Such levels of self-consciousness are hardly unusual in the diverse personal narratives that are often generically grouped together as autobiographies. But Symonds's memoirs are distinctive because they persistently focus on how literary production is the necessary outcome of a particular sexual inclination. Time and again, Symonds emphasizes how his writings have been directed by his 'unique' sexual temperament. Indefatigably, he poured his literary energies into projects that promised to sublimate his homosexual longings. Yet in preoccupying himself with such diverting forms of intel-lectual inquiry, his habitual industriousness tested his better nature. 'Trying to evade the congenital disease of my moral nature in work', he confesses, 'work has drained my nerves and driven me to find relief in passion' (p.239). At this point, Symonds's declarations of intellectual strength appear much closer than he has so far been willing to admit to his fear of sexual debility. Once he has stated that his publications were the product of his 'nervous energy', then he declares that the very act of writing on his chosen topics agitated his desire: 'The subjects with which I have been occupied – Greek poetry, Italian culture in one of the most lawless periods of modern history, beauty in nature and the body of man – stimulate and irritate the imagination.' Even worse, they 'excite cravings that cannot be satisfied by simple pleasures' (p.239). If Symonds's sexuality drove him towards litera-ture, therefore, literature forever forced him back to what he had been seeking to escape. It was an exemplary case of the cure becoming the cause of the original complaint. Indeed, scholarly writing and sexual craving chase one another throughout his memoirs. And the circuit of exchanges in which they are enmeshed is so intense that it can prove hard to extricate the literary from the sexual in Symonds's agonized imaginings. Taken together, his insatiable desires and his itch for scribbling enable and thwart each other throughout the course of his life. They cannot be divided, for they shape and define the main pattern of his career.

His memoirs expressly wish to divide them, however, for one good reason. Such itchings and cravings arouse in him appalling feelings of

excess, uncleanliness, and abjection: the very qualities he wished to dissociate from the image of the invert. More than that, these longings accentuate
the bestial and hydraulic model of male sexuality that had caught the
middle-class imagination in public debates about prostitution earlier in the
century, and which remained dominant for many years to come. W.R.
Greg infamously wrote in 1850 that in 'men, in general, the sexual desire is
inherent and spontaneous, and belongs to the condition of puberty'. For
this reason alone, the male of the species was recognized as the 'coarser sex':
there was no means of stopping this natural force thrusting itself forth from
a man's physiology. Greg would argue that, by contrast, in women 'the
desire is dormant, if not non-existent, till excited; always till excited by
undue familiarities'.[25] This model – which flatly insisted on an unbending
distinction between active masculinity and passive femininity – would have
a powerful bearing on the deeply felt horror of male homosexuality, since it
indicated the depths to which the 'coarser sex' could sink. It constituted
what campaigners against the Contagious Diseases Acts of the 1860s, such
as Josephine Butler, would call the 'double standard'. No wonder there was
such a drive among feminist campaigners and purity movements for male
continence. In fact, the second half of the nineteenth century in England is
marked not only by calls for self-control among men. Other voices were
exerting pressure on men to marry early so that they could find an immediate outlet for such wayward pulsations of male desire. Ed Cohen observes
that there was, unquestionably, a 'widespread divergence between conti-
nent "manly" ideals and profligate "male" practice'.[26] The middle-class
male body was certainly vexed by antithetical social imperatives to be a
chaste Christian figure of restraint while recognizing that a man's sexuality
was prone to surge forth of its own accord. It was within this field of
conflict that Symonds sought to convince himself that he was not an
inherently vicious and sinful person. If sexually different, with his own
inherent yearnings, he was also – as far he could see – morally sound.

Describing how his 'animal desire' was aroused by the sexual advances
made by a 'strongly attractive' grenadier, Symonds recalls how 'the wolf'
inside him often wanted to leap out in its 'undefined craving'. Instantly, his
mind turns to a moment of revelation where his sexual longings transform
from a 'ponderous malaise' into something altogether healthy:

> [A]t a certain corner, which I well remember, my eyes were caught by
> a rude *graffito* scrawled with slate-pencil upon slate. It was of so con-
> centrated, so stimulative, so penetrative a character – so thoroughly
> the voice of vice and passion in the proletariat – that it pierced the
> very marrow of my soul ['Prick to prick, so sweet'; with an emphatic
> diagram of phallic meeting, glued together, gushing]. But they had
> not hitherto appealed to me. Now the wolf leapt out: my malaise of
> the moment was converted into a clairvoyant and tyrannical appetite

for the thing which I had rejected five months earlier in the alley by the barracks. The vague and morbid craving of the previous years defined itself as a precise hunger after sensual pleasure, whereof I had not dreamed before save in repulsive visions of the night. (pp.187–8)

Even though this passage is striking in its powerful confrontation with the internalized oppression that can haunt the conscience of gay men to this day, the emancipatory dynamic of Symonds's prose belongs to a quite conventional structure. The transformation from neuropathic morbidity to healthy sensual appetite relies on the telltale verb 'converted'. The trope of conversion stands as one of the defining features of traditional auto-biographical narrative, as Stephen himself is quick to point out. In the narrative tradition of Christian enlightenment stemming from John Bunyan, conversion identifies those moments of spiritual awakening that are frequently recalled with one purpose in mind. Conversion, a word with strong religious resonances, provides the rationale motivating the subject whose model life is being written down. It marks the passage from igno-rance to wisdom, from shame to grace, from evil to goodness. And its characteristic mode is purgatorial. It may, then, appear odd that Symonds's conversion occurs in the context of reading an obscene graffito. But it is here where vice becomes virtue, where the 'obscene' is translated into a patent and deeply felt truth. How, then, was Symonds able to convince himself that 'prick to prick' could indeed be conceivably 'sweet'?

To this question, there was one clear answer. Symonds could pass through this conversion because his understanding of the labouring classes had radically changed. Earlier in his life, he associated his pulsating desires with insurgent forces that came from depths that were crude and filthy. Sexual feelings for him were marked as low, in complete antithesis to his respectable self-image as an upstanding public-school boy with a scholarly career ahead of him. Little wonder that working-class idioms were strongly connected to all that he loathed about the body. There were political movements afoot, however, that would enable him to transform his sense of sexual contamination into one of spiritual purity. Like those working men who were agitating in the 1860s and 1870s for the expansion of the franchise, Symonds began to understand his embattled eros as a natural force that demanded its rightful expression in a more democratic world. The increasingly vocal political demands of the Labour Movement un-doubtedly had a special resonance for the middle-class Symonds who en-joyed sexual contact with working-class men whose desires could be comprehended as refreshingly natural in their lack of social reserve. Later sections of his memoirs indicate exactly what was at stake in his moment of conversion: liberation from the Labouchere Amendment. It is not at all misleading to claim that this significant moment of politicization in Sym-onds's memoirs has a strong analogy with the agitation around the 1867 and

1884 Reform Bills. So Symonds's conversion not only means overcoming his self-disgust, it also brings with it an awareness that the proletariat shares his longings for personal freedom: nothing less than the practice of 'doing as one likes' that horrified Matthew Arnold when, in 1866, he witnessed the working-class 'Hyde Park rioter' making his protest for the franchise. 'The rough', Arnold condescends to note in *Culture and Anarchy* (1869), 'has not yet quite found his groove and settled down to his work, and so he is asserting his personal liberty a little, going where he likes, assembling where he likes, bawling as he likes, hustling as he likes.'[27] Within the course of three decades, the self-identified homosexual would have much the same sense of civil rights in terms of petitioning for freedoms. The link between working-class liberty and middle-class homosexual emancipation would emerge for Symonds in a figure whose labour offered an ennobling vision of a world that was not divided by class, and where men could embrace each other without shame. Not surprisingly, for such a literary man, Symonds located his ideal in a poet.

The poet was the American Walt Whitman. Like many homophile Englishmen reading the 'Calamus' poems of *Leaves of Grass*, Symonds was quick to appropriate the glorious depictions of muscular working men into his own idiom. In 'For You O Democracy', for example, Whitman's speaker declares:

> I will make divine magnetic lands,
>   With the love of comrades,
>   With the life-long love of comrades . . .
> I will make inseparable cities with their arms about each other's
>
>   necks.[28]

Such lines made perfectly manifest those brawny figurations of democratic eroticism between men that would excite so many of Symonds's homophile contemporaries. Eve Kosofsky Sedgwick has considered how and why Whitman had such a powerful appeal to sexual radicals such as Symonds and, after him, Carpenter:

> Imprecise but reverberant translations from the American to the English permitted Whitman, the figure, to embody contradictory and seductive attributes that would not have been combined in an Englishman. A 'working-class' figure himself, he nevertheless could seem by this translation both to practise and to sacralize something like the English homosexual system whereby bourgeois men had sexual contacts only with virile working-class youths.[29]

Consequently, after his conversion, Symonds remarks:

> if I were ever allowed to indulge my instincts, I should be able to remain within [Whitman's] ideal of comradeship. The dominance of

this ideal . . . contributed greatly to shape my emotional tendencies. It taught me to apprehend the value of fraternity, and to appreciate the working classes. (p.191)

To prove his point, Symonds later writes about the material results of such comradeship in his sexual affair with the Venetian gondolier, Angelo Fusato. Their intimacy enabled Symonds to support Fusato so that this working-class lover could obtain gainful employment 'in the P & O service': 'all this good, good for both Angelo and myself, has its taproot in what at first was nothing better than a misdemeanour, punishable by law and revolting to the majority of human beings' (pp.276–7). Undoubtedly, the Whitmanian ideal enabled Symonds to convert his former sense of sexual degradation in his liaisons with working men into a form of elevating philanthropy, for now he 'know[s] it is possible to bring forth good things out of evil'. Not surprisingly, he declares that the fulfilment of Whitman's democratic principle has 'given a healthy tone' to his 'feelings about masculine love' (p.277). The latter phrase provides the template upon which the unapologetic homosexual romance of Forster's *Maurice* would be set in 1913–14. But this was a utopian model elaborated by Symonds and many subsequent homophile writers to which Whitman himself refused to assent, as he made clear in a singularly bad-tempered item of correspondence.

Symonds elicited a letter from Whitman that roundly condemned him for putting an immoral gloss on the manly comradeship celebrated in 'Calamus'. In August 1890, Symonds cautiously tried to uncover what he regarded as the homosexual politics of *Leaves of Grass*. 'In your conception of Comradeship', Symonds apprehensively questions his idol, 'do you contemplate the possible intrusion of those semi-sexual emotions & actions which no doubt do occur between men? I do not ask, whether you approve of them, or regard them as a necessary part of the relation?' Obviously anxious not to cause offence, Symonds quickly notes that 'human nature being what it is . . . some men have a strong natural bias towards persons of their own sex'. But he can see that there are 'objections' to the idea that ' "Calamus" is calculated to encourage ardent & *physical* intimacies'.[30] Treading carefully, Symonds concludes by stating that he does not agree that such a view of 'Calamus' 'would absolutely be prejudicial to social interests'. By this point, he was no doubt hoping that his channel of communication was clear, and that Whitman would reciprocate by telling the homosexual truth. Whitman, however, fiercely declined. His reply is indignant:

Ab't the questions on Calamus pieces &c: they quite daze me. L of G. is only to be rightly construed by and within its own atmosphere and essential character – all of its pages & pieces so coming strictly under *that* – that the calamus [*sic*] part has even allow'd the possibility of such construction as mention'd is terrible – I am fain to hope the pages

themselves are not to be even mention'd for such gratuitous and quite
at the time entirely undream'd and unreck'd possibility of morbid
inferences – wh' are disavow'd by me & seem damnable.[31]

Having made his disavowal, Whitman then famously, if not bewilderingly,
remarks that although he has remained 'unmarried', he has sired 'six children' – none of whom any biographer has been able to identify. Given that
Whitman defines his procreative accomplishments against Symonds's 'morbid inferences', his scornful comments are not necessarily a defensive reaction against being exposed as homosexual. But that, precisely, is how
Symonds read them. Not surprisingly, Whitman's remarks cut deep, as
Symonds reveals in a letter to Edward Carpenter. (Carpenter, of course,
was espoused to similar wholesome ideals of homophile connection.) 'It
struck me', he observes, 'when I first read [Whitman's] p.s. that [he]
wanted to obviate "damnable inference" about himself by asserting his
paternity'.[32]

Perhaps Whitman was refusing to capitulate to the discourse of sexual
specification that could only be conceivably read by the dominant culture
as pathologically 'morbid'. Whitman may have had good reason for protesting that his comrades were not suitable candidates for homosexual
definition. Still that did not stop Symonds from commandeering them for
that purpose. Symonds's conversion never got him away from wanting to
write down the exact name of his sexual specification, and yet the categories available to him were a constant source of vexation. The sexual typologies in which he not uncritically believed – no matter how much he
strove to press them into the service of noble manhood such as he found in
Whitman's 'Calamus' – persistently connoted lust, craving, even sin, since
they were so undeniably a part of a male sexuality perceived as insatiable in
its desires. No wonder that he felt that 'the wolf' – as he called it – needed
to be carefully regulated. Throughout his memoirs, he constantly worries
away at the moral status of his past actions, fearing they may not subscribe
to any plausible code of honour. Much to his annoyance, homosexual
identification continually oscillates between literary culture and bodily anarchy – between cerebral aspiration and physical degradation.

Symonds never ceases to be irked by the thought that his erotics might
not have an ethics, since the two seemed completely discrete. In this
respect, the passage upon which Forster alighted in his *Commonplace Book* is
crucial. It concerns the memorable incident where Symonds recalls how he
betrayed his headmaster at Harrow, C.J. Vaughan, who had made advances
towards one of the boys. Symonds's highly conflicted response to his in-
crimination of Vaughan provides the clearest example of how his sense of
moral discipline led to the immoral disciplining of desire. The contradictions evident in this episode belong to a larger pattern of indecisiveness
where his homosexual wishfulfilment once again leads to its banishment:

My accusation rested solely upon the private testimony of an intimate friend, whose confidence I violated by communication of his letter to a third party. To complicate matters, I felt a deeply rooted sympathy with Vaughan. If he had sinned, it had been by yielding to passions which already mastered me. But this fact instead of making me indulgent, determined me to tell the bitter truth. At that period I was not cynical. I desired to overcome the malady of my own nature. My blood boiled and my nerves stiffened when I thought what mischief life at Harrow was doing daily to young lads under the autocracy of a hypocrite. (p.112)

This extract points up an undeniably complex chiasmus of identification. Symonds employed the headmaster's official methods of discipline to expose a man whose sexual affiliation he actually shared. So in punishing Vaughan, Symonds was – to some degree – punishing himself. His urgent and no doubt well-intentioned wish to bring an end to hypocrisy was based in his own hypocritical knowledge that he too could have indulged the sexual pleasures that he despised in the man he had condemned. Now the Whitmanian model of comradeship – embodying, as he thought, a healthy ideal of sexual relations between men – did not finally purge Symonds of his anxiety about the potential immorality of his homosexuality. Indeed, the confrontation with Vaughan shows that there is a very fine line between being 'indulgent' and 'tell[ing] the bitter truth'.

Throughout his memoirs, Symonds cannot escape the troubling idea that his unique sexual type may be just as debased as Krafft-Ebing claimed. Everywhere he lives in fear of indulging his desires. It is not just that he fears sexual excessiveness. In fact, he is made equally anxious by the inordinate lengths to which his literary endeavours might be taken, since they too aspire to high art only to be led back into the depths of depravity. Once more, body and brain interact on a model of mutual support and mutual destruction:

He who overworks any organ, whether brain, heart, lung, stomach or sexual apparatus, sins. The indulgence in excessive brain exercise, in excessive muscular exercise, in excessive or innutritious feeding, in excessive or libertine sexual pleasure, is wrong. The hierarchy of functions which compose us and on which society depends, forces man to regard one indulgence as more pardonable than another. Thus the indulgence in sex is so bound up with the first object of our physical being, propagation, that it cannot be viewed as more than venial. The indulgence in muscular activity is so serviceable as an example to the race at large that it appears almost to rank with virtues. The indulgence in cerebral tensions is so rare and aims at such high objects that even when it maims and kills, it passes for 'the last infirmity of noble minds'. The indulgence in food is either so harmless or

so ignobly detrimental to the individual alone, that it is almost over-
looked. (p.252)

One cannot help but notice how this diatribe reads like a sermon. But its
preachy style contains words of wisdom that undermine the didactic treatment of sinful 'indulgence'. Although Symonds asserts that it is vital to
exercise constraints on various forms of excess, at the same time he is
willing to acknowledge that what strikes one party as indulgent may seem
wholly acceptable and natural to another. Even though Symonds is attempting, once and for all, to lay down a code of 'natural law', he is
desperately seeking a regulative system precisely because the mind and
body are only too likely to spin out of control in their perpetual itchings
and cravings. In other words, it is not always easy for Symonds to make a
distinction between what is natural and what is indulgent. These apparently
dissimilar things reside in uncomfortably close proximity to each other. So
it remains undecided whether his 'unique type' has ultimately 'attain[ed] to
self-mastery and self-control' of his 'congenital malady' (p.282). Towards
the end of his deliberations, it comes as no surprise that Symonds feels
compelled to ask: 'What is the meaning, the lesson, the conclusion to be
drawn from this biography?' (p.283). Just at the point where we might
assume there is a clear-cut answer to this enquiry, his narrative lurches into
a long protesting paragraph that throws the paradoxes of his sexual being
into very sharp relief. The 'agony of this struggle between self-yielding to
desire and love, and self-scourging by a trained discipline of analytic reflection', he claims, 'breaks his nerve' (p.283). And yet, as the memoirs repeatedly insist, it is exactly his 'nerve' that has prompted him to make this
declaration in the first place. In the end, his sexual identity remains caught
in the tension between the natural restraints and indulgent desires contra-
dictorily attached to an ongoing disequilibrium of mind and body.
    Symonds would present a concise version of his autobiography in one of
the case histories he collected for the collaborative study of sexual inversion
begun in 1892 with Havelock Ellis. The research he collected appeared in
the volume Ellis and Symonds published as *Sexual Inversion*. Given the
controversial nature of its topic, this substantial work could not have been
completed at a more inauspicious moment. In 1895, Wilde's vilification in
court meant that any publication with obvious homophile interests was
likely to be prosecuted. So the first edition went out on sale, not in
England, but in Germany in 1896. The following year, an English edition
was prepared. Yet Brown, presumably at the prompting of Symonds's
family, did his utmost to buy up all the copies on which he could lay his
hands. Thereafter, Symonds's name did not appear on the title page. In any
case, Ellis had done much to underplay Symonds's role in the preparation
of the volume. In his study of the erotics of literary collaboration, Wayne
Koestenbaum has remarked on how Ellis edited and eliminated anything by

Symonds that seemed to lack scientific credibility because of its 'literary' quality. '[Ellis] performs', writes Koestenbaum, 'a symbolic castration on his dead collaborator, accusing him of collage, or worse, incoherence – a condition caused, in truth, more by Ellis's editing than by Symonds's lapses.'[33] Ellis, performing this deft 'castration' with the proficiency of a surgeon, then presents this study as a serious piece of scientific inquiry. Undoubtedly, Ellis was acting the role of a respectable man who was exercising a particular kind of patriarchal authority upon the 'invert' from whom he had learned so much, and whose sexuality was such a source of prurient fascination. Rather like Stephen, Ellis could define his masculine prowess against the fragmentary and incoherent truth of a homosexual identity that had emerged from a neuropathic condition.

Yet this is exactly the kind of authority that Symonds wished to exercise in his own right. In his case history – number XVII in the 1897 edition of *Sexual Inversion* – Symonds insists that he was 'certainly not passive and show[ed] no sign of *effeminatio*'. If he had appeared in any respect unmanly, then he would not have been able to defend himself as a distinguished 'type' who had been robbed of the 'most genial channels of self-expression' (pp.288–9). On this score, Symonds was presenting himself as a gentleman who felt he had the right, if not the noble bearing, to share the privileges of his bourgeois peers. At the same time, however, his strong sense of individuality – derived from his self-image as an 'artist and man of letters' (p.288) – meant that he wanted to be recognized as a class apart. If one lesson is to be learned from Symonds's memoirs, it is that sexological classification was taken up by homophile campaigners because it strongly appealed to their middle-class individualism. Even if the working-class comrade promised to fulfil his erotic longings, Symonds found in sexology a discourse that had continuities with earlier liberal ideals of self-sufficiency.

But the autonomy championed by such individualism often threatened to create structures of non-conformity that would fragment the middle classes. In the 1890s, as Henry James's letters show, there was still a great deal of doubt that it was a man's 'duty' to mark out his difference from every other man on the basis of his sexual needs. On what basis was this 'duty' truly necessary? If aiming to attack a law as pernicious as the Labouchere Amendment, would homosexual identification not surrender to those hostile forces that sought to uncover any such manifestation of 'vice'? Much subsequent homophile life writing would remain puzzled why a man's sexual object-choice, above all other things, should separate him so decisively from his own class. It was often difficult for these autobiographers to see that the values of self-expression promoted by their bourgeois upbringing ensured that they became outsiders to the group to which they belonged, and not just in terms of class. Repeatedly, these life writers recognize that they bear striking sexual resemblances to those men who did not openly identify as lovers of their own sex. This is the central preoccupation of J.R. Ackerley's *My Father and Myself* (1968) – a work that concentrates most of its attention on the late nineteenth- and early twentieth-century image of respectable manhood.

II

'I was born in 1896 and my parents were married in 1919.'[34] So begins the distinguished memoir that Ackerley began researching in 1933 and completed shortly before his death in 1967. (This was, not insignificantly, the year of the Sexual Offences Act that partly decriminalized sexual relations between men, and which precipitated a quick run of homosexual life stories, including Quentin Crisp's *The Naked Civil Servant* (1968).) Peter Parker observes that this stylish opening is of a piece with the tactics Ackerley had cleverly used in *Hindoo Holiday* (1932) and the astoundingly scatological *My Dog Tulip* (1956). 'Ackerley', writes Parker, 'unobtrusively employs the literary device of posing as an innocent narrator who blandly reveals the most surprising and shocking things, and with the professional insouciance of a showman, pulls aside curtains normally left drawn.'[35] Indeed, such supple prose could not be further removed in its poised and restrained style from Symonds's urgent 'outpourings'. But, then, Ackerley claimed *My Father and Myself* was not an autobiography: 'it is no more than an investigation of the relationship between my father and myself and should be confined as strictly as possible to that theme'. He feels obliged to make this point clear, since in earlier drafts he had 'fallen into the error of self-indulgence' by focusing far too much on his own 'sexual psychology' (p.209). Advised by a friend to rein in his self-analysis, Ackerley produced a memoir that tried not to present itself as a case history. To all intents and purposes, his narrative repels the sexological impulse to give a clear and detailed understanding of one man's struggles with his homophile identity. That, at least, is what Ackerley would like us to believe. And from the outset of the book, given its insouciant tone, we would imagine that everything that followed would remain perfectly unruffled. *My Father and Myself* is a highly polished piece of work that smoothly ironizes the scandal of his father's and his own – seemingly different – sexual lives.

But the calm and assured surface of Ackerley's prose is so understated in its handling of shocking facts that one begins to wonder whether this is a defensive strategy to control the trauma that set him writing the memoir in the first place. To be sure, *My Father and Myself* is a wholly unapologetic account of a middle-class man's homosexuality, and how it compares with the ostensibly respectable life of his father: the 'banana king', Roger Ackerley, who was a partner in a fruit importers, Elders and Fyffes. No-where does it seem that Ackerley endured any undue agony in coming to terms with his desires, although his reflections on finding himself 'sexually incontinent' – or suffering from premature ejaculation – are perhaps circumspectly consigned to an appendix (p.210). From what he tells us, it became a matter of habit not to discuss his sexual longings with his family, even if his parents were – at some undisclosed level – aware of what he was up to. Instead, the sexuality that causes greatest disturbance to Ackerley is his father's. Only on his father's death in 1929 did several painful truths emerge. To complicate matters, one or two troubling enigmas would follow, and it is these bewildering details that encouraged Ackerley to excavate what he could of his father's early youth. He would spend the best part of 35 years trying to make sense of this obscure paternal prehistory, only to remain ultimately baffled by it. In his will, Roger Ackerley revealed that he had not just been maintaining a mistress for many years, but that he was also the father to three girls who had been brought up separate from their mother. (His role as 'Uncle' to this second family has been detailed by one of his illegitimate daughters.)[36] No wonder Roger Ackerley had deferred his marriage to his second wife for well over 20 years. But what he failed to reveal to his son was his teenage companionship to Count James Francis de Gallatin, who had done everything within his power to establish Ackerley senior in business. The Count and Roger Ackerley had fallen out in acrimonious terms in the 1880s. From what Ackerley could gather, his father broke the Count's heart. A great deal of *My Father and Myself* is given over to the idea that Roger Ackerley had at one time belonged to the 'homosexual fold' (p.201). Yet, much to the son's frustration, no hard and fast evidence existed for Ackerley to confirm such speculation. All that remained was the memory of a father who had for most of Ackerley's life appeared utterly conventional in his bourgeois habits and outlook. The discovery of Roger Ackerley's 'secret orchard' forced him to reassess the obligatory silence that surrounded his own homosexuality (p.154). Was Ackerley's the only male sexuality that dare not speak its name?

If one question emerges more clearly than any other in Ackerley's memoir, it is the terms on which male sexuality ought to come into discourse. In this respect, *My Father and Myself* places its life writer in a paradoxical position. Declaring that he was 'generally regarded as an open, truthful man', Ackerley is constantly left wondering about how and why his own sexual interests and his father's 'secret orchard' simply could not be discussed. Consequently, much of this narrative provides the stuff and substance of a conversation between father and son that never took place in the 1920s or earlier. But whether this dialogue could – or even should – ever have occurred guiltily preys on Ackerley's conscience. '[I]f', Ackerley writes, 'he had ever evinced any curiosity about my private life I believe I would have told him, so long as he questioned me in an intelligent way' (p.145). Even when confronted with the truly obvious clues about his son's homosexuality – such as a key moment of dialogue in Ackerley's only and successful play, *The Prisoners of War* (1925) – Roger Ackerley politely chose to ignore it. (In this morbid drama, where practically all the male characters discreetly imply their homophile interests, the protagonist Conrad, having been betrayed by his younger lover, reacts sorely when he is addressed by the unsuspecting Mme Louis: 'I have heard you do not like much the fair sex.' 'The fair sex?' replies Conrad. 'Which sex is that?'[37] The doomed path for this man-loving man lies towards madness.) Only with hindsight can Ackerley begin to grasp how his father's silence on this dramatic exchange was something of a tactical evasion, which ensured that it was not so much Ackerley's own sex life, but more his father's private liaisons that had to remain obscured from view. Given these complicated circumstances, Ackerley is constantly prompted to think about his similarity to and difference from his father. Both, after all, had their secrets. But was there, he keeps thinking, an essential distinction between them?

One incident that probes this problem of identification between the two men concerns the brief advice on sex that Roger Ackerley delivered to his sons in 1912:

> He admitted, I remember, his own early participation in the practice in which he thought it advisable to counsel moderation, then took occasion to add – getting it all off his chest in one and providing for the future as well as the present – that in the matter of sex there was nothing he had not done, no experience he had not tasted, no scrape he had not got into and out of, so that if we should ever be in want of help or advice we need never be ashamed to come to him and could always count on his understanding and sympathy. (p.81–2)

Later in life, Ackerley admits this struck him as an 'excellent and friendly speech'. But he recalls how at the time he was 'embarrassed and shocked' by it. That sexuality was to be associated with his father offended his respectable sensibility. Clearly, he knew that the breaking of silence on sexual acts was not the done thing. It was, in a word, unnecessary. His father, however, realized that there was a place and a time when such matters had to be articulated. So it is with a strong sense of regret that Ackerley writes about his inability to seize the moment when male sexuality could have been a subject of discussion between his father and himself. Much to his subsequent annoyance and regret, his memoir develops a highly self-conscious discourse that repeatedly insists on the need to speak out about what could and should at one time have been spoken – if only he had known. Indeed, Ackerley's reflections on his father's sexual secrets communicate an immeasurable sense of grief at never entering into the conversation that was kindly offered by a man he never really cared to know.

One can see, then, that *My Father and Myself* elaborates the sexual knowledge that Ackerley's father momentarily raised in the billiard-room. It is as if father and son have over the course of time exchanged roles, as if the son gives back to the father a gift of knowledge and understanding that was once offered and never taken up. But like all gifts, this one circulates in a strange manner, oscillating between both parties as something that cannot be fully relinquished. This memoir, after all, recognizes that there should be some means through which the truth can be understood. And yet Ackerley is haunted by the thought that his father had a much greater understanding of this particular issue than he himself ever possessed, although his father's private thoughts remain completely inscrutable. Having assumed that his own life was the one rich in scandal, Ackerley eventually discovered that his father's secrets threw his own awareness of male sexuality into disarray. Consequently, Ackerley finds himself writing at length about something that never spoke its name. No wonder his father's life stands as the intriguing centre of this narrative, for it remains altogether more alluring by virtue of its hidden status than anything Ackerley may care to disclose about his rounds of cruising in the West End, along with the periods spent in a male brothel at 11 Half Moon Street. Ackerley's openness about his homosexuality holds for him – and us – altogether less fascination than his father's undisclosed and ultimately irretrievable desires.

So Ackerley's incessant interest in his father stems from the idea that his life in the homosexual underworld was not really as interesting as he had imagined all along. For example, once he has summarized his sexual contacts, he declares: 'Curiosity about myself has carried me somewhat further than I meant to go' (p.140). Time and again, he is eager to shock his readership with revelations about himself – ones that disconcerted those members of his family who, with some reservations, allowed this memoir to go into print. But he keeps displacing this impulse on to his father's 'secret orchard'. The same might be said for Ackerley's other sexual obsession – with his Alsatian, Queenie, who appears in fictional guise in *My Dog Tulip* and *We Think the World of You* (1960). In the latter novel, it is only too clear that the beloved dog becomes a figuration for an idealized sexual partner that Ackerley found neither in his father nor in his sexual contacts with soldiers and labouring men. Here the Alsatian Evie stands as the third term through which an older middle-class man can mediate his desires for a younger working-class bit of rough. Without doubt, Evie comes to embody the displaced longings for the manly youth whose style, wit, and intelligence mark him out as the ultimate – but correspondingly unattainable – object of desire: the aesthete and athlete in one. In the novel, we see how Frank, Ackerley's *alter ego*, discerns in Evie's appealing face an ' "intellectual" line' like 'that furrow . . . we see upon the brow of sages': it was this feature that made it seem as if she could cross 'the uncrossable barrier that separates man and beast'.[38] Evie, Queenie, Tulip – in all her various renamings – assuredly served as a substitute for the intellectual virile labourer that haunted Ackerley's imagination, and whom he never met in person.

Equally beyond his palpable reach, his father would continue to elude him. So in *My Father and Myself* several major contradictions come into view as Ackerley seeks out – and yet remains baffled by – Roger Ackerley's own obscure desires. It is not so much that Ackerley is worried about the propriety of what he is doing in exposing his father's adulterous behaviour. The book, without doubt, has no qualms whatsoever about sex. Instead, the ruse upon which he builds his memoir concerns his conflicted response to the construction of identity through sexuality. In other words, I am arguing that Ackerley cannot resolve whether he ought to be writing *My Father and Myself*, largely because he remains unsure that full knowledge of his father's sexual life story would, once and for all, bespeak the truth of the man. Knowing his father, like knowing himself, appears to subsist in sex, especially the unrevealed but eternally tantalizing homosexual history occupying the 1880s. But for all his faith in the power of sex to determine the character of a man, Ackerley's past actions certainly ran counter to this fundamental belief.

Conventional social behaviour for many years regulated Ackerley's homosexual dissidence. Take, for example, how he complied with the wishes of a business partner to burn his father's desk in 1929. 'I can scarcely believe I ever agreed to such an act', he remarks. 'Why did I agree?' (p.159). Poised to answer that question, he confuses matters further by suggesting a great number of possible reasons. Perhaps he wished to honour his father's posthumous wishes. Maybe the desk contained 'papers and letters unfit for filial eyes to see' (p.159). 'But', he concludes, 'perhaps the most likely formula for my feelings would be: I was then quite incurious about my father's history; I didn't want his gigantic roll-top desk, what on earth could I do with it?' (p.159). This last and most elaborate explanation sounds like the least plausible of all. But, then, the excuses he explores all point to his frustration at having relinquished the truth that might – and yet, in fact, may not – have existed among his father's papers. Sexual revelations about Roger Ackerley's various scrapes would without doubt define what kind of man he was – or so Ackerley wishes to believe. Time and again, the search for a clear picture of the paternal past makes his present circumstances altogether more opaque. In the process of uncovering his father's early manhood, Ackerley thought he would make some discoveries about his own sexual orientation, and how it was moulded by conventions of secrecy. The upshot of the memoir, however, shows how each of these men can only be understood through the sexual acts they kept hidden from each other, and which remain obscured from us as well. The one trait that made father and son so similar was undoubtedly what separated them. Worlds apart, they were – in a sense – much the same kind of man: equally respectable, with their own specific sexual mysteries.

So the sexual secrets that father and son actually shared could not, by definition, ever be shared at all. The paradox, which makes and breaks their relationship at once, endures in many areas of the memoir. Wherever Ackerley comments on the silence that shrouded his homosexuality from his father, he promptly mentions the resemblances between them. This point comes to the fore in Ackerley's account of how he went about picking up rent boys:

Evening after evening, for many years, when I was free I prowled Marble Arch, the Monkey Walk and Hyde Park Corner, or hastened from pub to pub as one unrewarding scene replaced another. Seaport towns also (sailors too were jolly short of cash) were often combed at weekends. The taint of prostitution in these proceedings nevertheless displeased me and must, I thought, be disagreeable to the boys themselves, accepting it as they did. I therefore developed mutually face-saving techniques to avoid it, such as standing drinks and giving cash at once and, without any suggestive conversation, leaving the boy free to return home with me if he wished, out of sexual desire or gratitude, for he was pretty sure to know what I was after. This, I suppose, was akin to my father's technique of bribery in advance for special restaurant service, for of course I too hoped for responsiveness to generosity and was annoyed if I did not get it. (pp.135–6)

It is only too clear that Ackerley behaved as any member of his class would to make the pick-up conform to his wishes without either party feeling any undue embarrassment. In making that point, however, Ackerley is questioning whether he was in fact an entirely different kind of man from his father. Both, after all, purchased services at a price. Eager to secure the transaction, they tried to make matters flow as smoothly as possible, without any distasteful outbursts that would cause offence. In other words, he was behaving as any gentleman would.

The whole movement of *My Father and Myself* is to question the considerable pressure that Ackerley felt to identify his sexual particularity in a way that would distance him from his class. This process began in his late 20s. Describing the 'energetic, derisive, iconoclastic mind and rasping demonic laugh' of Arnold Lunn, he recalls how this man fired the following 'mischievous question' at him: 'Are you a homo or a hetero?' Ackerley's subsequent comments are significant because they reveal that sexological definitions had not penetrated so very far into middle-class consciousness in the 1920s:

I had never heard either term before; they were explained and there seemed only one answer. He himself . . . was hetero; so far as I recall I never met a recognisable or self-confessed adult homosexual . . . until after the war; the Army with its male relationships was simply an extension of my public school. (p.117)

To clarify this question on object-choice, Lunn lent Ackerley the works of Otto Weininger, Edward Carpenter, and Plutarch – all of whom had a strong appeal to sexual radicals at the time. Thereafter, he claims, he found his place 'on the sexual map' (p.118). Yet even then he was resistant to being classified as a different species. 'I did not care for the word "homosexual" or any label, but I stood among the men, not among the women' (p.118). The importance of these statements lies in their contradictory impulse to find an orientation on the one hand, and reject labels, on the other. This ambivalence arises because he discerned a clash of interests between gender identity and sexual preference. Even if a 'homo', he insists that he is a masculine one, like the cast of characters inhabiting the military world of *The Prisoners of War*. Ackerley feels obliged to make this issue clear because he defines 'normal, manly' masculinity against its dreaded opposite – effeminacy – which the dominant culture had by this time indissolubly associated with male same-sex desire. He does everything he can to banish this stigma from his narrative.

On several occasions, Ackerley insists that effeminacy repelled him, no doubt because his homosexuality was readily associated with it. 'It should not be inferred . . . from . . . the nickname "Girlie" at my preparatory school that I was in the least effeminate' (p.111). Lest we remain unconvinced, he once again insists on his masculine identity: 'Certainly effeminacy in men repelled me almost as much as women themselves did' (p.118). His sexual interest lay in 'the normal, manly boy' (p.118) – his 'Ideal Friend', as he sometimes called him – who should be 'lusty, circumcised, physically healthy and clean' (p.125). But, as we discover later, the Ideal Friend in his own peer group did not exist. The best substitutes by far were working-class men. Why? Because, he reckons, they 'were more unreserved and understanding' (p.126). Needless to say, they were also more exploitable. Their virility was unquestionable, for they represented a powerful muscularity that could not contrast more starkly with the effeminate identity that Ackerley is at pains to disavow. Reviewing this memoir, W.H. Auden wittily explored the kind of homosexual that Ackerley thought himself to be:

> I conclude that he did not belong to either of the two commonest classes of homosexuals, neither to the 'orals' who play Son-and/or-Mother, nor to the 'anals' who play Wife-and/or-Husband. My guess is that at the back of his mind, lay a daydream of an innocent Eden where children play 'Doctor', so that the acts he really preferred were the most 'brotherly', Plain-Sewing and Princeton-First-Year.[39]

Auden's comments are significant, not least because they betoken one of the few places in which he makes his own homosexuality clearly known to the public. His observations certainly indicate that Ackerley was not being quite as frank about his sex life as we might be led to believe. If Ackerley's sexual contacts are described in his memoir, the sexual acts most definitely are not. But what seems more to the point is the manner in which Auden apprehends the dominant forms of active and passive homosexual behaviour in terms of heterosexual paradigms. Ackerley's interest in the 'Ideal Friend', the comradely lover, was seemingly unusual in the period about which he was writing. No wonder, perhaps, that his erotic projections on to a virile brotherly type remained a source of frustration and denial.

Auden's comments, then, suggest that the struggle Ackerley underwent to 'stand among the men' was a goal, not a given. In this respect, Ackerley's predicament was assuredly similar to that of his lifelong friend, E.M. Forster. This point is teased out in Ackerley's recollections of the novel he abandoned in the 1920s:

> The plot of *Judcote* (never finished) scarcely needs description, it can be guessed: a young, upper–middle-class, intellectual homosexual (myself of course), lonely, frustrated, and sick of his family, especially the women, his feckless chatterbox of a mother, his vain, quarrelsome and extravagant sister, and the general emptiness and futility of their richly upholstered life, becomes emotionally involved with a handsome young workman. (p.179)

The affinities of *Judcote* to Forster's *Maurice* are plain to see. No doubt Ackerley's acquaintance with Forster's suppressed novel brought his own endeavours with *Judcote* to an abrupt halt. Instead, the story that would absorb him for much of his remaining life concerned his father, who seemed to bear little resemblance to Ackerley's suppressed homosexual desires. Perhaps the most painful irony of his memoir is that he had something of an 'Ideal Friend' in his eminently 'normal' and 'manly' father – if only he had known it at the time. The very thought makes him wonder whether, in different circumstances, he might have become his father's lover. Having collected information about Roger Ackerley's years in the Blues at Albany Street Barracks, he ponders a photograph of his parent in military uniform. 'It is true that, studying the photograph of him in uniform, I decided that I would not have picked him up myself; but the picture was said not to do him justice, and the better one Uncle Denton claimed to have he never managed to find' (p.199). The ambivalence here is startling. In deciding that his father was not his type, Ackerley considers that other documents might prove the contrary. The very thought – as he himself recognizes – is both plausible and absurd. But, then, that is the characteristic mode of this memoir. Such equivocation points to the general pattern of unresolved identification and disavowal that shapes *My Father and Myself*. It strives to narrow the inevitable distance between two respectable men: a 'hetero' and a 'homo', in a pact of unacknowledged desires.

III

Symonds's and Ackerley's memoirs, if barely overlapping in time and context, share one feature that persists so far into the twentieth century that it is now appropriate to turn to one further writer to elucidate what can justifiably be claimed as the most resonant pattern of desire in homosexual life writing, and which becomes most visible – if in displaced and repressed forms – in E.M. Forster's fiction. The third section of this chapter, therefore, explores the erotic longings of the cultured man of letters who seeks to cleanse himself of the taint of effeminacy by virilizing himself through his sexual connection with brawny soldiers. This pattern of homosexual desire obtains its clearest outline throughout the prose works of Jocelyn Brooke. Between 1946 and 1963, Brooke produced a large and distinguished canon of life writing which critically and often amusingly reflects on the vicissitudes of male sexuality – in all its aesthetic and athletic manifestations – before, during, and immediately after the Second World War.

Writing in his early 40s, Brooke was obliged to offer his life story to the public as if it were fiction. Laws of libel dictated that names and giveaway allusions were tactfully altered. But there is no doubt that Brooke's stories are personal narratives whose details assuredly have their basis in fact. If one thing distinguishes his impressive record of the signal changes in English cultural life between the 1920s and the 1940s, it is Brooke's unswerving belief that his homosexuality is so ordinary and acceptable that no apologies whatsoever have to be made for it. This is, to say the least, a somewhat surprising feature in the writings of a man who in many respects regarded himself as an outcast, and who occasionally reveals his powerful sense of alienation from the respectable society in which he grew up. Hardly ever do we hear the voice of a homosexual who protests for his rightful place in a culture that was in the years immediately following the Second World War cracking down as never before on sexual activity between men. Weeks observes that between 1938 to 1955 the annual number of cases of 'gross indecency' in England and Wales rose sharply from 316 to 2,322.[40] It was an undoubtedly hostile climate. Consequently, more and more pressure would be put upon the government for legal reform. But to Brooke, in this inhospitable context, feeling agonized about one's homosexuality seems a rather dated attitude to strike. No wonder, writing in 1955, he treats D.H. Lawrence to slight contempt:

> Lawrence's 'secret' – if one can call it that – was, I suppose, that he was profoundly homosexual; but his lonely, puritanic, lower middle-class upbringing prevented him from coming to terms with his own homosexuality. Just how far he did, in later years, come to terms with it, we shall not know, I suppose, for some time – if we ever do now; but his crypto'queerness' seems to me to be the key to his complex and unhappy personality.[41]

Not only does Lawrence's sublimated homosexuality occur to Brooke as one of the most tiresome features of a previous generation, it also – and perhaps more importantly – strikes him as a product of a particular class background, one altogether lower than that in which the public-school-educated Brooke grew up. So Brooke defines his own sense of apparent sexual ease from a self-consciously modern and privileged perspective: one that is not at all troubled by the evangelical moralism that, as he saw it, haunted Lawrence's guilty conscience. Yet just what it might mean to be 'profoundly homosexual' constantly holds his attention. Crypto'queerness', to be sure, never ceases to engage his interest because – although he finds it hard to admit – it baffles him. Turning his gaze upon Lawrence, Brooke's all-too-knowing autobiographical persona performs a characteristic trick. He seeks to distance himself from the emotional torment that, from time to time, plagued the lives of many of the men he knew well. To this end, he focuses on the strategies that many male homosexuals employed to conceal, redirect, or refashion the 'queer' stereotype that had developed in the light of the Wilde trials. But, as the narratives unfold, we find that Brooke too is hardly free from the stigma attached to being queer, no matter how unapologetic he may appear about his homosexual identification. If one obsession emerges throughout Brooke's volumes of thinly veiled life writing, it is his sense of being haunted by the kind of effeminate literary identity that he feels he ought to repudiate. Even if he sees the 'wrestling match in *Women in Love*' characterizing the 'disingenuous, self-deceiving element' in Lawrence's novel, Brooke is involved here in an uncomfortable moment of self-recognition. His own life story indicates that he, like Lawrence, had been 'self-deceiving' when trying to imagine what kind of man he might in fact be.

On the face of it, Brooke's career from his late teens to middle age was quite uneventful. There is, indeed, some irony in the fact that he achieved a considerable reputation as a writer on the basis of seven short volumes of autobiography, beginning with *The Military Orchid* in 1948, all of which remind us of his failed dreams of becoming a man of letters in the years after leaving Oxford in 1929. There is a revealing moment in *The Goose Cathedral* (1950) where Brooke recalls the conversations he held with his close friend, Eric Anquetil, one summer in the early 1930s. Imagining their future fame, Anquetil remarked: ' "*you* might write a little monograph" . . . "Mr Brooke's acute and penetrating little study, dot-dot-dot." (We were both fond of quoting from reviews of each other's future works.)' Such literary accolades remained at a far remove from Brooke's present employment in the family firm at Folkestone. 'I'd rather', he tells Anquetil, 'be anything than a wine-merchant.' Watching a bunch of troopers leading some horses, Brooke exclaimed: 'I'd as soon be one of those soldiers.'[42] Anquetil immediately quips '*Housman*' (p.385). This allusion to the coy homophilia of *A Shropshire Lad* (1896) prompted Brooke to protest: 'It's not Housman in the least. I should rather like to de-intellectualize myself' (p.386). And this response, in turn, led to his friend's derisive suggestion: '*Lawrence*' – whose work Brooke obviously thought represented an embarrassing relic from the not so distant past.

In some respects, literary banter of this kind dissatisfied Brooke. Even though he relished aspects of these highbrow conversations – ones often peppered with allusions to the more obscure and funny sections of Ronald Firbank's fiction – he remained mesmerized by soldiering. It was not just that he, like so many aesthetes of his class, was attracted to the military. Brooke eventually realized that he could not only *have* the kind of man he desired, he could *be* one himself. The Second World War provided the ideal opportunity, and it is here that his life stories have their greatest subversive force. He first served as a private in a field hospital in 1939. Two years after being demobbed, he signed up – much to the bewilderment of his military colleagues – for a commission. But he soon bought his way out to return to 'Civvy Street' once his career as a writer and broadcaster finally came into its own. In *A Mine of Serpents* (1949), his equivocal attitude to military life – an environment that remains, to say the least, extremely inhospitable to lesbians and gay men – emerges on almost every other page:

> I felt, in fact, about the Army, much as I had felt, in early adolescence, about sex: it was something difficult, rather disgusting and ultimately inevitable, which I dreaded yet longed to experience. Soldiers, too, were linked in some way with my childhood-heroes – the people I feared and secretly adored. (p.254)

This ambivalence marks the driving force behind the three volumes collected in *The Orchid Trilogy*. The more we read about Brooke's progress from would-be author to private soldier, the clearer it becomes that his sexual identity is caught between the competing demands of being an aesthete on the one hand, and an athlete on the other. The disparity would never entirely disappear. Neither literary work nor military endeavour could wholly fulfil his needs. So even if Brooke makes no bones about his homosexuality, he remains troubled by the style of masculinity that suits him best.

Like Forster before him, Brooke was sorely antagonized by the effeminate aestheticism which shaped his Oxonian aspiration to be a writer. He assuredly followed Forster's interest in retaining the cultured sensibility of the literary man by combining it with the physical hardiness of the lower-class athletic male. But Brooke, born in 1908, belonged to a generation that had outgrown the comradely works of Whitman and Carpenter. Instead, he negotiated his path between the brains of his high-minded Oxford peers and the brawn of the working-class soldiers through his idiosyncratic life-long passion for nothing less than botany. Such a form of inquiry may appear remote from one man's struggle with different kinds of masculine identification. But in scouring the fields of England for unusual species Brooke discovered a repertoire of terms and images that promised to synthesize the competing styles of manhood that pulled him towards entirely antithetical forms of employment. In fact, one flower occupied his imagination more than any other – the military orchid.

This rare species becomes the emblem for his conflicted understanding of where his sexual identity lay in relation to other men. He was absorbed by the thought of this elusive breed at a very early age:

> The idea of a soldier, I think, had come to represent for me a whole complex of virtues which I knew I lacked, yet wanted to possess: I was timid, a coward at games, terrified of the aggressively masculine, totemistic life of the boys at school; yet I secretly desired, above all things, to be like other people. These ideas had somehow become incarnated in *Orchis militaris*. (p.21)

The military orchid symbolically brought together manliness and effeminacy in one. It spoke directly to the orchidaceous camp styles associated with Wilde, just as it invoked those grenadiers and guardsmen who had charmed the likes of Symonds and Ackerley. But, as Brooke continually reminds us, for all his botanophily, he never found this species as a child. In fact, he researched his subject so well that he began to discover that several botanists had confused it with similar strains. But still the military orchid evaded him. Only after a while do we begin to see that this flower is a figuration of Brooke's narrative persona. In this respect, he was remodelling Firbank's reflection on himself as 'a dingy lilac blossom of rarity untold'.[43] Brooke, without doubt, was making himself into a unique type of plant, one that was determined to flourish in a military context which continues to do everything within its power to uproot it. Part of the reason for this innovative act of self-fashioning concerned not just Brooke's own specific psychological make-up, but more general cultural shifts as well. The orchidaceous aesthete, he claims, was increasingly outdated by the late 1920s. Any man who by that time presented himself as a dandiacal heir to Wilde seemed nothing less than an anachronism. 'It was', writes Brooke, 'the real turn of the tide – already [Stephen] Spender and Auden were contributing to *Oxford Poetry*; in another few years, the full tide of Marxism would have swept away the last tremulous survivors of the Mauve Epoch.' But, for all that, 'the old two-party system survived; one was either a hearty or an aesthete' (p.196). Feeling the pressure to choose between them, Brooke threw in his lot with the 'unpopular party'. But this arty clique lacked the 'perfervid *chichi* of an earlier epoch'. They had, much to their chagrin, been superseded by history.

By the time war had broken out in 1939, it was the fate of some former aesthetes to don a soldier's uniform, and it would have a devastating effect. Much of *A Mine of Serpents* is given over to Brooke's memory of the once notorious Hew Dallas who had been depicted in an undergraduate magazine as 'an immensely tall, serpentine young man with a grave Roman profile and a lock of hair falling across his forehead' (p.196). Encountered some 10 years later, such artifice had been stripped away entirely. 'The uniform', writes Brooke, 'reduced him, as it does most people, to a kind of basic essence of himself. I saw a tall, thin young man on the verge of middle age; not very exceptional in any way, though he hardly looked like a regular soldier' (p.220). Dallas's history, in fact, is more intriguing than Brooke had at first imagined. Quite unexpectedly, he discovers that Dallas had recently left the Church to join the Army. So strange a figure does Dallas cut that Brooke feels compelled to designate him as 'a character in an unwritten Proustian novel, the projection of a self-created personal myth' (p.220). Only on reflection can we see that Dallas's fate as a military orchid, so to speak, would be shared by Brooke himself.

In producing his own 'self-created personal myth', Brooke turns time and again to men whose identities are equally riven between being arty and being hearty. In this respect, the figure of Basil Medlicott causes him the greatest confusion, for it proves impossible to locate the exact orientation of this affable man's desires. Even if Medlicott strikes Eric Anquetil as 'pure Wodehouse' (p.226), he too is not quite what Brooke had anticipated. Medlicott's extrovert masculine behaviour contrasts sharply with his high-minded literary tastes:

> When we arrived in the mess the next morning, Basil was as hearty and un-extraordinary as ever. But looking round the bookshelves in his room, while we drank sherry, I had my first surprise. There were all the things one would expect to find: regimental histories, text-books on infantry-training and so on; among them, however, I came upon *A Shropshire Lad*, a volume of Yeats and [Oscar Wilde's] *An Ideal Husband*. These were promising, I thought, but non-committal. A moment later, to my complete astonishment, I came on [Marcel Proust's] *Swann's Way*. (p.226)

No sooner, however, has Brooke alighted on the volume by Proust than his hopes that Medlicott might share his homosexual interests are quickly dashed. 'He's rather heavy-going, isn't he?' remarks this hale and hearty fellow. To all outward appearances, Medlicott remained a true son of empire. At least that was the kind of company he kept at the Trocadero in London. Only later would Brooke discover that Medlicott had been acting as a spy 'selling "information of national importance"' (according to the *News of the World*). The report in this scandal-mongering Sunday news-paper had 'lots of juicy bits about his visits to Berlin, and all the night-boxes he visited' (p.254). Although no explicit suggestion of Medlicott's homosexuality is made here, the allusions to Berlin and spying imply that he met his end through some unmentionable erotic goings-on. By the time Brooke was writing *A Mine of Serpents*, the Cold War encouraged the Western Alliance to perceive very close connections between queers and treachery. In 1951, it was discovered that the British diplomats, Guy

Burgess and Donald Maclean, had passed state secrets to the Soviet Union. It was at this point that the perceived political dangers of homosexuality reached fever pitch. One consequence of the persecution of homosexual men at this time was the strong link forged between the literary élite and state subversion. Alan Sinfield has documented how, during this period, many key figures such as Stephen Spender and Cyril Connolly were keen to exonerate themselves, since both had mixed in similar cultivated-artistic-leisured circles to the spies.[44] This configuration of queers, traitors, and arty types became something of a key component in the national consciousness of the early 1950s. But Brooke's portrait of Medlicott does rather go against the grain of the cultured man of leisure willing to betray his country. In fact, Medlicott was not the only hearty who failed to live up to the imperialist image he had created for himself, as Brooke shows in a later memoir.

In 'Gerald Brockhurst', from *Private View* (1954), Brooke provides a sustained and moving portrait of the homosexual man who identified, not as a sissy, but as a hearty athletic type. Yet Brockhurst too was a military orchid of sorts. It was only in later life that Brooke realized exactly the nature of Brockhurst's desires during their undergraduate years together at Oxford. Like Basil Medlicott, the very thought of Gerald prompted the aesthete Eric Anquetil to poke merciless fun. 'In novels', he remarked, 'people like that are *always* called Gerald. There's one in E.M. Forster.'[45] True to form, Anquetil was ironically referring to the robust figure of Gerald Dawes whose towering strength Forster mockingly cut down to size in *The Longest Journey* (1907). But Anquetil's view of Brockhurst, like Brooke's himself, is with hindsight subjected to a different kind of irony – one that makes their first impressions of Brockhurst look tragically mistaken. The problem for Brockhurst was that he had tried, and failed, to make contact with a homosexual grouping whose masculinity he found alien and strange. He could not bring himself to identify with those young men who, like Anquetil, donned 'a pale-grey suit, shantung tie and suede shoes' (p.42). In attempting to develop his friendship with Brooke, Brockhurst remarked: 'the people you know are all the same sort of type – awfully brainy and highbrow and all that . . . most of the blokes I've seen you around with look a bit sissyfied, if you don't mind me saying so' (pp.54–5). But although Brockhurst held Brooke's 'smarty-arty' friends in contempt, he remained repressively tolerant towards 'bloody nancy-boy[s]'. Indeed, he told Brooke that 'we're all of us a bit homo when it comes to the point' (p.59). This story sets out to show that Brooke, only too eager to make flourishes of his sexual knowingness, should have taken more notice than he did of that statement. So, once again, the effeminate life writer – with his exquisite literary manners – finds that he lacked the necessary awareness that could have helped a man who implicitly might have become Brooke's lover.

Although Brockhurst eventually marries, it comes as a shock when Brooke hears that the glamorous Veriny Crighton-Jones is obtaining a divorce so that she can wed a bisexual man (Teddy Boscombe) who had enjoyed an affair with her husband. Hereafter, the sexual plot thickens. A later encounter with Brockhurst reveals that he had been sexually involved with men at Oxford. In fact, he had ended up in bed with one of those sissies he had name-called with contempt. As he drunkenly told Brooke:

> 'Always a bit that way, I s'pose, an' didn't know it . . . Remember that night at Oxford, when you passed out at the House? Last I saw of you . . . Chap called Dallas was there – asked me back to his digs . . . Stayed the night – all rather sordid, really. Hew had a photo of Teddy . . . Liked women too, you know – sort of ambidextrous . . . Fancied me, though – went fishing together . . . Funny the way things turn out . . .' (p.111).

In fact, the tale goes from bad to worse. During the Second World War, Brooke learns that Brockhurst has been involved in a military scandal. 'You can', a friend tells him, 'guess what *sort* of trouble' (p.124). Placed under court-martial, Brockhurst apparently bribed a guard to obtain a revolver so that he could blow his own brains out. Chattering with gossip, Brooke's friend insensitively remarks that Brockhurst always seemed to him 'madly ungay' (p.126). Nothing could be further from the truth. Or could it? The question remains unanswerable. All that is left is the troubling thought that the hearty queer was driven to take his own life because he had little support among the effeminate arty types like Brooke.

Brockhurst's suicide is significant because it brings to a head one of the most paradoxical issues that never ceases to disturb the well-turned sentences of homosexual life writing after 1885. Although these autobiographers display a heightened awareness about male sexuality, they are frequently puzzled by it too. This point emerges forcefully in Crisp's drily humorous, urbane, and popular autobiography that became a *cause célèbre* when adapted for television in the 1970s. Although Crisp was public-school educated, he did not proceed to the collegiate life of Oxford and Cambridge. 'I have not spent my life hacking my way through the constraints of bourgeois existence', he insists. 'I was always free – appallingly free.'[46] An unsuccessful scholar, he at first made his way within a world of down-and-outs and streetwalkers, finally building up a career as a sometime commercial artist and artist's model. An heir to Firbank in his outrageous effeminate style, Crisp presented himself as an affront to the 1920s, an era in which '[m]anliness was all the rage'.[47] Defiant, he trolled the West End courting downright hostility from the passing crowd, not least the groups of young men who beat him up on countless occasions. 'The bravest man in the world I know', remarks an anonymous contemporary, 'is Quentin Crisp. Even we used to cross the road and walk on the other side when he was coming towards us! It's a terrible thing to say, but he was persecuted by us as much as he was persecuted by everybody else.'[48] No one can doubt the incredible risks Crisp took with his own life. But by inventing himself as a brazen effeminate homosexual, with his hennaed hair, red nail varnish, and shoes at least two sizes too small for his feet, Crisp did not for a moment identify with the leisure-class cultured circles in which Ackerley and Brooke moved. Although he was on friendly terms in the 1940s with the fashionable literati of Fitzrovia – notably Nina Hamnett – he thought of himself as 'an avowed enemy of culture' (p.132). Yet Crisp's oppositional stance was, as he recognizes in retrospect, not always as coherent as he wished to believe. Recognizing the working men down at the Labour Exchange as objects of both fear and desire, Crisp saw in them a masculinity that he regarded as antithetical to his own. At times, however, this cherished illusion broke down:

> I was over thirty before, for the first time, I heard somebody say that he did not think of himself as masculine or feminine but merely as a person attracted to persons with male sexual organs. A confession of this nature would still bewilder and, perhaps, anger some of my homosexual friends. Quite recently a male prostitute of my acquaintance, on one of his amateur nights, picked up a young soldier only to find at the crucial moment that he had lumbered himself with a passive sodomite. 'And, all of a sudden, he turned over. After I'd done – flitting about the room in my wrap, making him coffee. You know, camping myself silly. My dear, I was disgusted.' (pp.62–3)

In the swinging 60s, when dreams of sexual liberation were at their height, Crisp found himself inspired to write that it is now 'universally agreed that men are neither heterosexual nor homosexual; they are just sexual' (p.202). Wise as these words appear, developments during the next three decades would largely run against this view. By the time the Gay Liberation Front (GLF) exploded on to the scene in England in the early 1970s, the political imperative to identify as gay was so great in its emancipatory zeal that other styles of male sexual dissidence – such as bisexuality – were subject to extraordinary stigmatization from within homosexual campaigning groups, and almost ousted into oblivion. But in one assertion Crisp was surely correct. If in the late 1960s he felt that 'only obviously effeminate men' were 'ostracized' (p.202), it is certainly the case that violent effeminiphobia still remains rife throughout a gay subculture that has slowly been loosening itself from the identity politics that hardened around the GLF. It is still the case that many men insist on being 'straight-acting' when trying to make sexual contacts through the British gay press. The demand to conform to such strategies of acceptable impersonation is very great indeed. It cannot, however, be forgotten that the numerous outlets for making such contacts are the result of a much more commercially developed gay subculture than Crisp enjoyed for most of his life until the 1960s. There is no question at all that without Gay Liberation English society would not have been able to grow somewhat more tolerant in its attitude to male homosexuality, and Crisp's subsequent career as a public celebrity had played a significant role in a broad and diverse political struggle.

Reading the autobiographies of homosexual men across the course of a century does make one recognize that Gay Liberation placed such an emphasis on the specificity of homosexual desire that the fluidity of masculine eroticism proved too dangerous, if not puzzling, to entertain. Every oppressed group needs an imaginary other against which to define itself. 'GLF', writes Simon Watney,

> tended to base much of its theory (and practice) on the rejection of . . . [a] monolithic notion of Heterosexuality. Hence a picture of our own gayness emerged which was simply a reversal of all the norms, values, and institutions of heterosexual society, as if these were not riddled with conflicts and contradictions.[49]

Watney remarks that in its early heyday, GLF was split down the middle between the hippy 'life-stylers' from the 1960s and those 'actionists' whose political heritage came from hard-left Leninism. This conflict between libertarianism and communist moralism ensured that the political analysis of GLF remained incoherent. It pulled each grouping towards competing understandings that homosexuals were, on the one hand, emancipated by expressing their sexual instincts and, on the other, a class who had to be led forward in the revolution against capitalism. Both tendencies identified gays as an inviolable group with a distinctive identity. Neither position, as Watney insists, had anything resembling a developed theory of sexuality that could get beyond the illusion that 'our sexuality is the single most significant determining aspect of our entire existence'.[50] There were many men whose desires and subjectivities could not fit into this gay political mould, and whose histories these life writers were in part trying to uncover in the process of affirming the precise nature of their own homophilia. Each of the autobiographical works I have discussed begs us to question whether or not these homosexual writers are really so different from those men who held their desires in such contempt. Crisp puts this point well when recalling his response to the labourers with whom he queued to sign on for the dole. 'If I was busy trying to seem mysterious and aloof to them', he observes, 'we must not rule out the possibility that they were reciprocally engaged' (p.62).

Notes

1 Leslie Stephen, *Mausoleum Book*, ed. Alan Bell (Oxford, Clarendon Press, 1977), p.4. Trev Lynn Broughton kindly directed me to this passage; her forthcoming work on Victorian patriarchy analyzes Stephen's work in detail. Symonds and Stephen spent time in each other's company. Writing from

Davos in Switzerland in 1893, Symonds writes: 'We have got Leslie Stephen & 2 members of his family snowed up with us. Good company But I spend the days in bed alas!'; 'To Dr John Johnson', 3 February 1893, *The Letters of John Addington Symonds*, ed. Herbert M. Scheller and Robert L. Peters, 3 vols (Detroit, MI, Wayne State University Press, 1969), III, p.811. Stephen is alluding to the biography by Horatio F. Brown: *John Addington Symonds: A Biography Compiled from His Letters and Correspondence*, 2 vols (London, Nimmo, 1895).

2 Virginia Woolf, *Roger Fry: A Biography* (London, Hogarth Press, 1940), p.75.

3 Henry James, *The Notebooks of Henry James*, ed. F.O. Matthiesen and B. Murdock (New York, Oxford University Press, 1961), p.57.

4 Henry James, 'To Edmund Gosse', 7 January 1893, *Letters: 1883–1895*, ed. Leon Edel (Basingstoke, Macmillan, 1981), p.399.

5 John Addington Symonds, *Memoirs*, ed. Phyllis Grosskurth (Chicago, IL, University of Chicago Press, 1984), pp.182–3. Further page references appear in parentheses.

6 John Addington Symonds, 'A Problem in Modern Ethics', in Brian Reade (ed.) *Sexual Heretics: Male Homosexuality in English Literature from 1850 to 1900* (London, Routledge and Kegan Paul, 1970), p.271.

7 For relevant documentation about the production of Brown's biography of Symonds, see Timothy d'Arch Smith, *Love in Earnest: Some Notes on the Lives and Writings of English 'Uranian' Poets from 1889 to 1930* (London, Routledge and Kegan Paul, 1970), pp.14–15.

8 John Addington Symonds, *Studies in the History of the Greek Poets*, 2 vols (New York, Harper and Brothers, 1880), II, p.364.

9 Rev. St John Tyrwhitt, 'The Greek Spirit in Modern Literature', *Contemporary Review*, 29 (1877), p.552.

10 Richard Dellamora provides a richly detailed discussion of Symonds's and Pater's homophilia in the context of Oxford University politics in *Masculine Desire: The Sexual Politics of Victorian Aestheticism* (Chapel Hill, NC, University of North Carolina Press, 1990), pp.147–66.

11 John Addington Symonds, 'Swiss Athletic Sports', *Fortnightly Review*, NS 50 (1891), p.413.

12 E.M. Forster, *Commonplace Book*, ed. Philip Gardner (London, Scolar Press, 1985), pp.224–5.

13 Writing to Edward Carpenter, for example, Symonds remarks: 'Any good book upon homosexual passions advances the sound method of induction, out of which may possibly be wrought in the future a sound theory of sex in general. The first thing is to force people to see that the passions in question have their justification in nature'; 29 December 1892, *Letters*, III, pp.798.

14 Linda Dowling, *Hellenism and Homosexuality in Victorian Oxford* (Ithaca, NY, Cornell University Press, 1994), p.xv.

15 The term 'spiritual procreancy', frequently used by Dowling, is taken from the translation of the *Symposium* by Edith Hamilton and Huntington Cairns; Plato, *The Collected Dialogues Including the Letters* (Princeton, NJ, Princeton University Press, 1961), p.209a, cited by Dowling, p.xv.

16 John Addington Symonds, 'Edward Cracroft Lefroy', in *In the Key of Blue and Other Prose Essays* (London, Elkin Mathews and John Lane, 1893), p.89.

Dowling discusses the significance of Symonds's essay on Lefroy in *Hellenism and Homosexuality in Victorian Oxford*, p.116.

17 Symonds, 'Edward Cracroft Lefroy', p.90.

18 Symonds, 'Edward Cracroft Lefroy', p.94.

19 Symonds, 'Edward Cracroft Lefroy', p.109.

20 Symonds, 'Edward Cracroft Lefroy', p.101.

21 Symonds, 'A Problem in Modern Ethics', in Reade, p.265.

22 Michel Foucault, *The History of Sexuality: An Introduction*, trans. Robert Hurley (Harmondsworth, Penguin Books, 1981), p.43.

23 Jeffrey Weeks, 'Questions of Identity', in *Against Nature: Essays on History, Sexuality, and Identity* (London, Rivers Oram Press, 1991), p.75.

24 Foucault, p.101.

25 [W.R. Greg] 'Prostitution', *Westminster Review*, 53 (1850), pp.456–7.

26 Ed Cohen, *Talk on the Wilde Side: Toward a Genealogy of a Discourse on Male Sexualities* (New York, Routledge, 1993), p.69.

27 Matthew Arnold, *Culture and Anarchy with Friendship's Garland and Some Literary Essays*, ed. R.H. Super (Ann Arbor, MI, University of Michigan Press, 1965), p.122.

28 Walt Whitman, 'For You O Democracy' (1860), in *Complete Poems*, ed. Frances Murphy (Harmondsworth, Penguin Books, 1975), p.150.

29 Eve Kosofsky Sedgwick, *Between Men: English Literature and Male Homosocial Desire* (New York, Columbia University Press, 1985), p.204.

30 John Addington Symonds, 'To Walt Whitman', 3 August 1890, in Walt Whitman, *Correspondence: 1890–92*, ed. Edwin Haviland Miller (New York, New York University Press, 1969), p.72.

31 Walt Whitman, 'To John Addington Symonds', 19 August 1890, *Correspondence: 1890–92*, pp.72–3.

32 John Addington Symonds, 'To Edward Carpenter', 13 February 1893, *Letters*, III, p.819.

33 Wayne Koestenbaum, *Double Talk: The Erotics of Male Literary Collaboration* (New York, Routledge, 1989), p.51.

34 J.R. Ackerley, *My Father and Myself* (London, Pimlico, 1992), p.11. Further page references appear in parentheses.

35 Peter Parker, *Ackerley: A Life of J.R. Ackerley* (London, Constable, 1989), p.316.

36 Diana Petre, *The Secret Orchard of Roger Ackerley* (London, Hamish Hamilton, 1975).

37 J.R. Ackerley, *The Prisoners of War: A Play in Three Acts* (London, Chatto and Windus, 1925), p.68.

38 J.R. Ackerley, *We Think the World of You* (Harmondsworth, Penguin Books, 1971), p.76. Ackerley's life with Queenie is also recorded in *My Sister and Myself: The Diaries of J.R. Ackerley*, ed. Francis King (Oxford, Oxford University Press, 1990).

39 W.H. Auden, 'Papa Was a Wise Old Sly Boots', in *Forewords and Afterwords* (London, Faber and Faber, 1973), p.453.

40 Jeffrey Weeks, *Coming Out: Homosexual Politics in Britain, from the Nineteenth Century to the Present* (London, Quartet, 1977), p.158. Stephen Jeffery-Poulter provides an exceptionally well-documented account of campaigns for homosexual rights from the time of the Wolfenden Report: *Peers, Queers and*

Commons: The Struggle for Gay Law Reform from 1950 to the Present (London, Routledge, 1991).

41 Jocelyn Brooke, *The Dog at Clambercrown* (London, Cardinal, 1990), p.84.

42 Jocelyn Brooke, *The Goose Cathedral*, in *The Orchid Trilogy* (Harmondsworth, Penguin Books, 1981), pp.384–5. This volume also collects *The Military Orchid* (1948) and *A Mine of Serpents* (1949). Further page references appear in parentheses.

43 Ronald Firbank, *Prancing Nigger*, in *The Complete Firbank* (London, Duckworth, 1961), p. 631.

44 Alan Sinfield, *Literature, Politics and Culture in Postwar Britain* (Oxford, Basil Blackwell, 1989), pp.60–85.

45 Jocelyn Brooke, 'Gerald Brockhurst', in *Private View* (London, Robert Clark, 1989), p.43. Further page references appear in parentheses.

46 Quentin Crisp, *How to Become a Virgin* (London, Duckworth, 1981), p.7.

47 Quentin Crisp, *The Naked Civil Servant* (London, Flamingo, 1985), p.26. Further page references appear in parentheses.

48 Anonymous, 'A Remodelled Life', in Kevin Porter and Jeffrey Weeks (eds) *Between the Acts: Lives of Homosexual Men 1885–1967* (London, Routledge, 1991), p.140.

49 Simon Watney, 'The Ideology of GLF', in Gay Left Collective (eds) *Homosexuality: Power and Politics* (London, Allison and Busby, 1980), p.66.

50 Watney, p.72.

Coda: Effeminate
endings

I

In his Introduction to one of the first full-length studies of homosexuality and modern English writing, Jeffrey Meyers praised the 'clandestine pre-dilections of homosexual novelists' that purposefully led to 'a creative tension between repression and expression'. It was the 'cautious and covert qualities' characterizing writing of this kind, he believed, that made for the finest art. In his view, gentle hints and subtle suggestions were altogether preferable to anything resembling an explicit depiction of same-sex passion. No wonder that when the first liberated gay fiction was beginning to emerge, Meyers felt that the noble tradition of Oscar Wilde, E.M. Forster, and Marcel Proust had fallen disastrously from grace. 'When the laws of obscenity were changed and homosexuality became legal', he writes, thinking of the reforms of 1959 and 1967, 'apologies seemed inappropriate, the theme surfaced defiantly and sexual acts were grossly described. The emancipation of the homosexual had led, paradoxically, to the decline of his art.'[1] Not surprisingly, so distasteful are the examples he has in mind that he refuses to cite them. Such, to be sure, is Meyers's disingenuousness. Indeed, rarely have I come across a more absurd defence of the public condemnation of male homosexual desire in the name of maintaining the highest literary standards. Yet Meyers's pronouncements, in spite of themselves, remain significant because they reveal the uneasiness with which literary criticism could at one time praise the sexual interests of distinguished novelists while not facing up to the moralistic prejudice which dictated that homosexuality was indeed a topic fit only for blame. It is a sign of the welcome transformations in opinion that have occurred since the publication of Meyers's study in 1977 that his remarks would strike most liberal-minded readers in the 1990s as wholly unacceptable.

One reason for this change of climate has much to do with the impact of lesbian and gay studies, which dates from the mid-1970s when Meyers's regrettable statements passed into print. 1977 was not such a fated year, after all, since it also witnessed the publication of Jeffrey Weeks's pioneering inquiry into modern homosexual politics in Britain. If Meyers's book marked the end of an era of antiquated criticism that really loathed the object it strove to love, then Weeks's *Coming Out* ushered in a completely different epoch of politicized criticism that would lay the foundations for more specialized investigations of gay male culture and history.[2] The present study is a case in point. Needless to say, there is now a much more developed, politically engaged, and theoretically sophisticated canon of cultural criticism that falls within the field of lesbian and gay studies. Beginning with Eve Kosofsky Sedgwick's pathbreaking *Between Men: English Literature and Male Homosocial Desire* (1985), the study of modalities of homophile writing in European and American traditions has gathered such pace that it would be fair to claim that lesbian and gay studies, in all its diversity, has made one of the largest contributions to how we currently consider categories of sex, gender, and sexuality across a range of representational practices.[3] In the universities, it is now possible not only to state one's sexual dissidence in the workplace without complete fear of job discrimination (although prejudice can and indeed does exist in some quarters). Scholars can at last teach gay-themed materials in an academic environment that is far less hostile than it used to be. But on this score, one of Quentin Crisp's wisest maxims should be borne in mind. 'Tolerance', he claims, 'is the result not of enlightenment, but of boredom.' Only the 'constant repetition' of facts achieves the desired 'liberating effect'.[4] No one should labour under any illusion that at a time when lesbian and gay studies is in the ascendant, hetero-normative understandings of how we should, physically and morally, live our sexual lives have been finally dispelled. Homophobia still manages to displace its once brazen malevolence into other less conspicuous shapes and forms. It, too, has its 'clandestine predilections', even within the gay community itself. So in this coda some words about the signal shifts in gay politics and literary writing since the time Crisp published his autobiography are surely in order. Only by studying the rise and fall of Gay Liberation can we grasp how and why an epoch of homoerotic writing perceptibly reached what I shall explain as a recognizable effeminate ending.

Although the Gay Liberation Front did much to challenge self-oppression among homosexuals, reminding us – among other things – that while 'homosexual' was a term of clinical definition, 'gay' stood for political pride, it gradually lost its impetus so that in the early 1980s it seemed as if the movement had little or no direction – even though the commercial scene of bars and clubs, the broad network of helplines, and the various 'drop-in' centres around Britain were flourishing as never before. In 1980, Simon Watney argued that since gay politics had been 'politically hampered' by varieties of 'romantic leninist' or 'anarchist myth[s] of Total Revolution', it had been 'slow in making use of recent theoretical developments which, in the work of Michel Foucault, offer a broader range of the interactions between sexuality, the state, and our sense of our own identities as individuals'.[5] But no sooner had these words been written than some drastic changes in theoretical approaches to gay male sexuality would come into their own. Seven years later, Watney would be writing one of the foundational works on AIDS and the media that engaged Foucauldian paradigms to examine the regulative mechanisms being discursively exercised to present abhorrent images of the homosexual body. In *Policing Desire*, produced four years after the epidemic had been identified by the acronym by which it is now known, Watney would remind us that in 'a culture which is as thoroughly and pervasively homophobic as ours, AIDS can only too easily undermine the confidence and very identity of many gay men'.[6] Just at the point when male homosexuality seemed to have asserted itself sufficiently to retreat from the militant activism of Gay Liberation, AIDS inspired members of the Moral Right to declare that this epidemic was nothing less than the wrath of God coming down in true biblical form upon the inhabitants of Sodom. Not surprisingly, many gay men were moved – like Edmund White – to reflect that the rapid transformation from homophile reform to Gay Liberation and sexual emancipation, and then to death on a massive scale was almost impossible to negotiate at a psychic level:

> To have been oppressed in the fifties, freed in the sixties, exalted in the seventies, and wiped out in the eighties is a quick itinerary for a whole culture to follow. For we are witnessing not just the death of individuals but a menace to an entire culture. All the more reason to bear witness to the cultural moment.[7]

The process of bearing witness immediately prompted remarkably intense activity among gay male cultural practitioners, and the results of such labours have led to forms of literary production that have been greeted to huge acclaim – Thom Gunn's distinguished collection of poems, *The Man with Night Sweats* (1992), being a case in point.

The reasons for such cultural activity are obvious. Through the emergence of AIDS – together with the fear and fascination that it generated in the apparently infectious gay male body – the mid-1980s aroused such a homophobic backlash that it seemed that there would be no end to upping the ante against the purportedly promiscuous, sex-enslaved, and irresponsible lifestyles that were leading us, by the thousand, to our deaths.

Once HIV had been detected in bodily fluids, then campaigns to educate everyone in practices of safer sex were developed at national and local levels – often with very patchy and inadequate amounts of funding. To this day in Britain, the resources aimed at meeting the educational needs of gay men hardly correspond to the blatant statistical evidence that shows that we still comprise the largest proportion of people living with and dying from this epidemic. For the best part of 10 years, we have seen innumerable homosexual men – many of them celebrities – die from AIDS-related illnesses, to the point that by the mid-1990s their deaths appear little more than a matter of routine.

This preamble has been necessary because it provides an overarching context for comprehending one of the signal changes that has occurred within male homoerotic writing in England since the 1967 Sexual Offences Act. Responsive to the GLF, many writers in the mid and late 1970s were inspired to produce 'coming out' narratives. But in the late 1980s, there were signs that AIDS was bringing about the end of a distinctive kind of gay fiction, in part because of the overwhelming work of mourning that was being undertaken in the wake of the emancipated golden age that had been so briefly won. That, at least, was one perception of this cultural moment. On the more optimistic side, AIDS activism provided a vigorous and em-powering context for a different type of writing that broke free from the identity politics that Gay Liberation had made such a central core of its political agenda. Campaigns to meet the needs of people living with AIDS provoked dazzling styles of direct protest against homophobic prejudice, and this broad repertoire of well-staged forms of cultural activism moved a con-siderable distance from the models inherited from the GLF. The 'zaps' un-dertaken by ACT UP – the Aids Coalition to Unleash Power – devised distinctive and often highly visual forms of demonstration whose panache and inventiveness made it absolutely clear that people living with AIDS, their lovers and their friends, had nothing to be ashamed about, not least if they identified as lesbian or gay. One offshoot from the direct activism of ACT UP was the formation of Queer Nation in New York City in April 1990. Reclaiming the once stigmatized label 'queer' and then subjecting it to a parodistic resignification to transform it into a label of pride, this grouping aimed to diversify lesbian and gay political awareness so that a range of dissident sexualities – including heterosexual ones – could work within a civil rights movement that did not deny the questions of gender, class, age, and ethnicity that marked out the power differentials between their members.

So queerness requires an understanding of individual identity that re-mains alert and responsive to the endless variety of positions in which the very notion of identity might be articulated. Michael Warner writes:

> Every person who comes to queer self-understanding knows in one
> way or another that her stigmatization is connected with gender, the

family, notions of individual freedom, the state, public speech, consumption and desire, nature and culture, maturation, truth and trust,
censorship, intimate life and social display, terror and violence, health
care, and deep cultural norms about the bearing of the body. Being
queer means fighting about these issues all the time, locally and piece-
meal but always with consequences.[8]

Such an activist stance – where queerness is constantly reconfiguring itself,
open to provisional and postmodern self-reconstruction – could not be
more different from the lived experience of those men who in previous
decades often perceived their queer identities with feelings of guilt and
shame. Crisp, for one, wrily comments on his life in the 1920s:

My outlook was so limited that I assumed all deviates were openly
despised and rejected. Their grief and their fear drew my melancholy
nature strongly. At first I only wanted to wallow in their misery, but,
as time went by, I longed to reach its very essence. Finally I desired to
represent it. (p.33)

Rather than deny his difference, Crisp decided to embody it. He, too, was
fighting for his life. But there was no room in the hostile world he inhabited to attach any positive connotation to the word 'queer'. It should not
surprise us, then, that he bleakly looks upon his autobiography as 'an
obituary in serial form' (p.222). Undoubtedly, it is salutary to think that
Crisp has remained perhaps the most valiant survivor from an earlier era
that did everything within its power to ostracize him. Yet he remains an
icon of 'misery' to the end of his memoirs. 'No one', he remarks, 'forced
me into the role of a victim' (p.222). He voluntarily became one. Suffice it
to say that with such a legacy of bigoted attitudes towards our desires, it still
remains difficult for an innovative queerness to appear little more than the
fashionable posturing of a young metropolitan generation who have the
facilities, resources, and forms of education required to stylize themselves
with such radical chic. But that is not to disclaim that a decisive shift has
taken place in how we might think about the meanings of homosexuality –
to the point perhaps of rejecting the fixed identitarian assumptions that
underpin it. For 10 years, at least, there has been a growing bisexual
movement that has seriously questioned the privilege accorded to the
hetero/homo binary, demanding that a radical sexual politics has to recognize that to maintain such a rigid polarity can only serve to force men and
women to choose an exclusive monosexuality, as it were.

For all these transformations, however, it was still the case in the early
1990s that the old stereotypes of male homosexuality were being peddled in
the press, even – quite alarmingly – by gay men. Reading an article in the
Weekend Guardian such as 'Gay Abandon' by Rupert Haselden, I am struck
by how his image of men's sexual interest in each other is couched in an

apocalyptic tone that casts such a long shadow over the works that Oscar
Wilde produced after the Labouchere Amendment became law in 1885:

> There is an inbuilt fatalism to being gay. Biologically maladaptive,
> unable to reproduce, our futures are limited to individual existence
> and what the individual makes of it. Without the continuity of chil-
> dren we are self-destructive, living for today because we have no
> tomorrow. A gay man is the end of the line.
>
> Without offspring to make sense of life, we invite an indulgent
> outlook on life and literalize this in the clubs and bars, in casual promis-
> cuous sex, where the pink pound finds no better use than as an escape
> from a hostile world, and where AIDS dangles like a flashing neon sign
> in the midst of the gay community, becoming a metaphor for the self-
> destructiveness and the self-indulgence that accompanies it.[9]

This ridiculous and sensationalizing essay was understandably the source of
some heated subsequent debate in the gay press, so shocking did Haselden's
self-oppression seem. But the fact that a so-called 'quality' newspaper gave
such an irresponsible feature room for publication casts doubt on how
enlightened left-liberal journalists are in their selection of materials for
weekend consumption. To have a gay man reporting on the apparent
death-wish implanted in all gay men because of their lack of family com-
mitments presents an image that not only harks back to the worries that
vexed John Addington Symonds, fearful of indulging his irrepressible desires. It also attaches to the stereotype of the leisure-class queer, like Wilde's
disguised Jack Worthing, who went up to town for nothing but pleasure,
and had a great deal of fun leading a double life, until he had to be brought,
with the Army Lists in hand, back into the family fold.

There have, however, been much more intelligent and critical responses
to the grief that has come upon countless numbers of gay men who feel that
the epidemic has robbed them of their hard-won sexual rights. In the same
year as the Conservative government passed Clause 28 of the Local Government Act (1988), which banned local authorities from sponsoring any
materials that represented 'pretended family relationships', the finest gay
novel since the advent of the GLF went out on sale, receiving plaudits in
almost each and every review. The work in question is Alan Hollinghurst's
The Swimming-Pool Library. Since this novel sets out to examine a cultural
epoch that dates from 1885 and culminates in the arrival of AIDS in 1983,
it provides a fitting ending to *Effeminate England*. Hollinghurst's narrative
only by implication focuses on pre-AIDS life, since it was written at a time
when the very pressure of even mentioning the name of the epidemic often
proved too much to bear. In that respect, Hollinghurst's powerful novel
marks the terminal point of a specific type of homophile writing that
developed in England after 1885. In an elegant narrative whose greatness
was not fully recognized by the British press (nor, perhaps more

conspicuously, by the panel adjudicating the Booker Prize) when it was published in 1988, Hollinghurst traces some of the main contours of male homosexual desire that shape and define the persistent dynamic between the effeminate man of letters and those forms of rugged masculinity whose virility is thought to surge from their lower-class, oriental, or African origins. But in defining itself so explicitly against this palpably powerful tradition, both in its richness of allusion to gay literary history and in its almost Paterian stylistic poise, *The Swimming-Pool Library* finds itself unable to face the unutterable trauma that has brought its story into being. This complex novel, then, is both a tribute to a distinguished tradition of homophile writing and a troubling work of mourning for a brief period of liberated sexual practices that – in the light of the epidemic – came to an end.

II

The grief at the centre of *The Swimming-Pool Library* emerges only through its terrifying absence. No longer is it the 'love that dare not speak its name' that diverts and deflects the movement of this narrative. Indeed, Hollinghurst's novel joyfully celebrates explicit eroticism between men. Instead, the historical framework of the novel depends on a knowledge about an epidemic which remains implicit, and whose presence can only be inferred through the most oblique hints. Nowhere at all does AIDS surface in a narrative that recalls 'the last summer of its kind there was ever to be'. The eloquent but dislikeable first-person narrator, Will Beckwith, cannot bring himself to specify quite what it was that brought about this overbearing sense of fate casting its shadow across his life:

> I was riding high on sex and self-esteem – it was my time, my *belle époque* – but all the while with a faint flicker of calamity, like flames around a photograph, something seen out of the corner of the eye. I wasn't in work – oh, not a tale of hardship, or a victim of recession, not even, I hope, a part of a statistic. I had put myself out of work deliberately, or at least knowingly. I was beckoned on by having too much money.[10]

A member of the eminently idle rich who has no need whatsoever to seek out gainful employment, this wealthy protagonist remembers the sexual goings-on he enjoyed with a young black teenager and a muscular working-class waiter in days that he will never be able to recapture. But the 'faint flicker' surrounding the vibrant image that he depicts of his each and every sexual encounter – many of which are recorded in gorgeous and sensuous detail – remains little more than that. Like a speck of dust in the eye, he tries to blink it away. Yet its apocalyptic force is displaced and distorted in other parts of his story.

Perhaps the best example of this primary repression returning in sublimated form catches our attention when Will is loitering in the foyer of a porn cinema. To his surprise, Will finds himself transfixed, not by an 'endless circuit of video sex', but by a nature programme that the movie house attendant has chosen to watch to while away the time. This 'virtuoso footage' contained some shots of an anteater attacking a termite colony:

> First, we saw the long, questing snout of the ant-eater outside, and then its brutal, razor-sharp claws cutting their way in. Back inside, perched by a fibre-optic miracle at a junction of tunnels which looked like the triforium of some Gaudí church, we saw the freakishly extensile tongue of the ant-eater come flicking towards us, cleaning the fleeing termites off the wall. (p.48)

Only on a second glance might we see how the anteater is a violent figuration of an as yet unknown virus spreading throughout the metropolis. 'I felt a thrill', he eerily adds, 'at the violent intrusion as well as dismay at the smashing of something so strange and intricate' (p.49). So alluring is the termite colony that it has a visual potency that was altogether more mesmerizing than the 'relative banality of American college boys sticking their cocks up each other's assholes' (p.49). This nature programme, without doubt, signals the tidal wave of something still unnamed – and, in the narrative, wholly unnameable – that weighs heavily upon the retrospective time of writing about Will's bygone 'belle époque'.

What haunts this scene in the porn cinema is the spectacle of unsafe sex in the era of AIDS. Surely one of the most anguishing experiences for many gay men watching pornography produced before protected sexual activity became a matter of course is the staging of pleasures that belonged to a 'belle époque' where everything and anything could be physically enjoyed. Once a commodity that did much to affirm gay men's feelings of sexual self-worth in the light of Gay Liberation, pornography representing 'American college boys sticking their cocks up each other's assholes' would be, by the time AIDS-related illnesses had taken many of our friends and lovers to their graves, a subject of considerable emotional turmoil. Not only was the witnessing of unsafe sex a reminder of pleasures that were now beyond our reach, it also prompted the alarming thought that the very production of such films in the late 1970s and early 1980s may well have led to the deaths of countless porn stars. But Hollinghurst's novel only implies – and never states – this polemic. Without doubt, such calculated understatement makes the destruction of the termite colony look all the more alarming, for this powerful image of wanton destructiveness emphasizes how in 'the last summer of its kind' it was impossible to know that the virus was transmitted through the blood and semen that joyously passed between the bodies of men. The novel, then, communicates the uncanny sense that hindsight does not always have its benefits.

No one, in 1983, knew that such pleasures were leading – one ejaculation after another – to so many deaths.

Hollinghurst devises the upper-class Will Beckwith, aged 25, as an ideal subject for mediating the helpless ignorance in which so many gay men were caught at a time when it was only just becoming clear to scientists exactly what the epidemic was. In fashioning this rather repugnant and thoughtless protagonist – who has all the trappings of the English gentleman who has been through the marshalling-yards of public school and Oxford to join the cultured élite – Hollinghurst goes to considerable lengths to make Will paradoxically look as sophisticated and unenlightened as possible. Although Will clearly has the polished social manner we would expect of him, he is hardly as wise as he thinks among the members of the leisure class that characterize his milieu. Throughout the novel, readers are given more than a slight advantage over Will's lack of perspicacity when it comes to recognizing how his father was responsible in 1950 for sending to prison, on the grounds of gross indecency, the elderly gentleman he befriends at his gymnasium. It is in this athletic world of weight-lifting and locker-rooms, where Will steals glances at other men's bodies – evaluating the size of their pectorals, not to say their cocks – that any untoward sign of effeminacy is to be decisively eradicated.

Early in the narrative, Will becomes closely acquainted with Lord Nantwich after the old man has suffered a cardiac arrest at the swimming-pool belonging to the Corinthian Club in Central London which they both attend. Having invited Will to lunch at his gentleman's club, Nantwich discovers that his young friend is 'Beckwith's grandson' (p.43), and it does not take him long to discover – by means of various misogynistic comments – that Will shares his sexual interests. Little does Will, however, suspect that he is becoming slowly involved with an elderly peer whose shows of absent-mindedness are in fact carefully covering over his contempt for Beckwith senior. The trap that Nantwich deftly sets young Will comes in the form of an invitation to write the old man's biography: a task that will lead Will – and allow us – to see close parallels in the homosexual lives they have separately led two generations apart. 'My dear,' Nantwich says, 'what I want to ask you is this.' At this point, Will assumes that his elderly friend might have had 'some physical demand in mind' (p.81). But the request is simply to find a suitable narrative for the memoirs that Nantwich himself has never been able to assemble. It takes a while before Will – whose time, as his first name implies, is generally occupied with having sex with other men – capitulates to the idea of writing the life of his 'queer peer' (p.85).

The introduction of Nantwich's diaries – documents which occupy large sections of the narrative, and whose homosexual details are far from tame – makes one feature plainly clear to us. Hollinghurst's novel is contriving to produce a history that maps some of the cardinal shifts and transitions in gay men's lives in the twentieth century. Elegantly juxtaposed in this manner, Will's recollections of his '*belle époque*' in 1983 and Nantwich's voluminous records of his sexual contact with Sudanese natives in the 1920s tease out some of the main preoccupations of homoerotic writing after 1885. Reviewing the novel in 1988, the lesbian critic Catherine Stimpson instantly identified Hollinghurst's intentions in framing the two men's lives across the span of one century:

> Charles [Nantwich] is born in 1900, 15 years after the Labouchere Amendment, which criminalized homosexual behaviour, in public or private, between men. A subtle sign of the law's partial impotence is the name of one of Charles's gayest friends – Sandy Labouchere. Charles is a raped schoolboy during World War I, a colonial administrator in an Africa he adores during the 1920s, a homosexual adventurer in London during World War II, a homosexual victim during the repressive, cruel 1950s, a philanthropist in the 1960s.
>
> William is born in 1958, one year after the Wolfenden Report, which helped to liberalize English laws controlling homosexuality. He can gratify his appetites more freely, less secretly than Charles. He has also inherited a tradition of gay culture.[11]

In other words, Nantwich and Will in many respects serve as representative figures for larger political shifts as they affected homosexual men, decade by decade, from 1900 to the moment just before the acronym AIDS was invented. But the novel does not operate in quite the deterministic pattern that such a summary might suggest. To be sure, as Stimpson observes, there are on occasions rather amusing ironic touches that make the homophobic oppression suffered in the past look beautifully absurd. Not only is Nantwich's friend named after the politician who notoriously brought the charge of 'gross indecency' on to the statute book, the hotel in which Will's working-class lover works is called the Queensberry. So the man who turned out to be Wilde's ultimate adversary in court provides the name for the establishment in which two men enjoy truly raunchy sex. Indeed, many more wry allusions to a longstanding queer history turn up regularly only to be similarly ironized. They are, in fact, so numerous that the novel becomes an archive of gay literary history, one especially resonant for those who, like Hollinghurst, have undertaken graduate research into the lives and works of homosexual writers from William Beckford to W.H. Auden.

In fact, the carefully implanted list of references to homosexual history is almost unending. Just as Will's own name echoes the orientalist lover of boys, Beckford himself, so too do we find a schoolmaster bearing the surname of E.M. Forster's Leonard Bast in *Howards End*. But the figure who takes pride of place in this novel – not least because the epigraph is taken from his works – is the pre-eminently effeminate Ronald Firbank.

The book of Firbank's that matters most to this novel is *The Flower beneath the Foot* (1923), a story whose title signals how the orchidaceous flower of effeminate homosexuality is trampled by a ruthless society that refuses to witness the beauty of its bloom. In Will's hands, Firbank's pseudo-hagiography undergoes an equally symbolic transformation, for its pages are literally trampled beneath the boots of skinheads who pick a fight with him in South London. Apart from presenting a vivid picture of the kinds of queer-bashing that have injured innumerable gay men in the course of the past century, this carefully staged scene serves as a powerful reminder that the literary aesthetic type embodied in Will experiences a powerful sense of ambivalence towards these violent men who do not hesitate to intimidate him and then kick him to the ground. Drawn to the brutal masculinity that these young men embody, he is compelled to reflect:

> They were a challenge, skinheads, and made me feel shifty as they stood about the streets and shopping precincts, magnetising the attention they aimed to repel. Cretinously simplified to booted feet, bum and bullet head, they had some, if not all, of the things one was looking for. (p.172)

Here, unquestionably, is the age-old predicament of the leisure-class man of letters (Firbank's text in hand) discovering that his desires are directed towards an impossible object: the bit of rough whose homophobia characterizes his status as a 'real' man. Crisp puts this dilemma nicely. 'A man who "goes with" other men', he remarks, 'is not what they [homosexuals] would call a real man. This conundrum is without resolution' (p.64). Yet that is not to say that in Hollinghurst's novel the upper leisure-class gentlemen and the virile men of the labouring classes do not have sex with one another. Indeed, they enjoy sexual liaisons that stretch across those class barriers that to Symonds, to Ackerley, and to Brooke both defined and thwarted their desires. Even though in the world of *The Swimming-Pool Library*, Will is subjected to a form of violence that he finds most strongly emblematic of erotic masculinity, he is in many respects quite close to being the physical type of man that he most wishes to have. No matter how effeminate his cultural interests may be, Will – true to his punning name – is a sexual athlete, with the body to match. One could claim that Will himself figures both aspects to the swimming-pool library that titles the novel, perhaps suggesting that as a young gay man of the early 1980s Will has considerably narrowed the gap between once antithetical styles of masculinity.

Even though its specific origins lie in eccentric conventions of Will's preparatory school, the title of the novel – rather like Jocelyn Brooke's *The Military Orchid* (1948) – signals a desired synthesis between the work of the scholar and the physical exertion of the athlete. There are several instances where these divergent masculine styles come into a satisfying conjunction.

Take, for example, the moment when Nantwich recalls his time with the working-class Bill Shillibeer while they were both serving time in Wormwood Scrubs. It was in prison that the athlete tired of reading while the aesthete poured all his stamina into the library:

> Bill drew me out . . . and I have a clear and rather touching picture of him sitting opposite me, his powerful, stocky young frame transforming from the stiff grey flannel of his uniform so that he looks like a handsome soldier, in some poor, East European army . . . I have promised him that when he is released, early next year, I will find him something to do: a job in a gymnasium, if possible, where his feeling for men and physical exercise can be fulfilled . . . It was rather desperate to see him toiling for weeks over detective novels from the prison library: he doggy-paddled through books in a mood of miserable aspiration, but they were not his element.
>
> I took to the prison library with more duck-like promptness. (p.255)

Nantwich keeps to his word, and Shillibeer is settled in an East End boxing club for boys which holds an annual competition for the 'Nantwich Cup'. Not only are these cross-class interests shared by Nantwich and Will, the two men also share the same passion – one that features with equal prominence in homoerotic writing of this period – for black men. (By far the most influential document here is Richard Burton's account of the 'Sotadic Zone' detailed in his 'Terminal Essay' to his translation of *The Arabian Nights* (1885). Burton's enduringly bizarre account, one that remains extremely revealing in its handling of cultural categories, seeks to show how and why pederasty is influenced by 'geographical and climatic, not racial' conditions.)[12] Undoubtedly, in Nantwich's love for the Sudanese Taha and in Will's sexual encounters with the African-Caribbean Arthur – which have an important precedent, not just in Burton's essay, but also in the implied homophilia between Aziz and Fielding in Forster's *A Passage to India* (1924) – a longstanding pattern of interracial sexual desire between men is being carefully reworked throughout Hollinghurst's novel. Yet at no point does the narration defy the stereotypes attached to these erotic encounters between white and black males. The black men and working-class men of this pre-AIDS world are potently sexual, readily available for the upper-class man's sexual requirements. In representing these sexual episodes, Will remains in no respect apologetic about what turns him on. Having played a game of watersports with Phil, the barman at the Queensberry, he enthusiastically recalls how 'he went behind him, pulled down his trousers, pushed him to the floor and fucked him . . . like a madman' (p.163). Never once is any criticism uttered against the exploitative mechanisms that shape and define the pattern of Will's desires. Nor need there be.

The compelling ambivalence of Hollinghurst's novel lies in its refusal either to repudiate the spectacular pleasures of explicit eroticism enjoyed in an era of unsafe sex or to distance itself from the cross-class and interracial subcultural contexts that feature so largely in the tradition of English homoerotic writing to which *The Swimming-Pool Library* pays homage. Nothing about this novel is politically pure. Never does it capitulate to a didactic critique of the literary models to which it is so self-consciously an heir. Instead, this narrative positively embraces the stereotypical patterns of gay men's lives to remind us that they now belong to the past, and to which the present narrative marks an ending – an ending, I feel, to the longings of the effeminate literary man for his virile opposite. In this respect, the novel came to the public's attention – in White's words – as 'the best book about gay life yet written by an English author',[13] only to celebrate an era that had perceptibly been and gone. Among other things, the retrospective stance of Hollinghurst's story necessarily makes it a quite old-fashioned work that addresses a cultural ethos that is much closer to the concerns of the pre-Wolfenden queer world than the political militancy of Gay Liberation.

Bearing these points in mind, it is not surprising to discover that Ross Chambers reads this narrative as very much 'a novel of compromise' – since it exploits one of the main preoccupations of earlier homoerotic writing where the sexual dynamic between men is precariously inscribed in a homosocial patriarchal order. Chambers claims, quite plausibly, that in *The Swimming-Pool Library* to be 'oppositional . . . is to fail in performing the radical acts that would profoundly change the world, but to do so without, at the same time, enjoying full integration into or identification with the structures of power that make the world as it is'.[14] In other words, in this kind of fiction – one that also draws on the tradition of the urban *flâneur*, the poet of the asphalt celebrated by Charles Baudelaire – we glimpse a figure whose sexual life and aesthetic tastes, if clearly running against the dominant ideology of the day, none the less remain committed to many of the determining patterns of patriarchal law. To clarify this point, Chambers somewhat unfortunately figures Will as a 'parasite' within the larger system of homosocial relations, to suggest how this protagonist feeds off only to undermine the larger social order in which he both does and does not fit. But even if the disease-ridden connotations attached to the idea of parasitism are not apposite to any account of the novel in the current political climate, it is certainly the case that Will's sexual and social disposition place him at both the margin and the centre of the almost entirely male universe that occupies Hollinghurst's narrative. What Chambers identifies as the greatest compromise in *The Swimming-Pool Library* is its modelling of male–male sexual relations according to the triangulated structures of male homosociality where desire between men is traditionally mediated through men's rivalry for a subordinated female object. In this context, the athletic males who transfix the sexual gaze of gay men are often feminized in their beauty. So, as Chambers argues, 'these mediating men can be seen as stand-ins for the women who are absent from the novel . . . just as they are excluded from the homosocial world'.[15]

Chambers's astute observation drives at the centre of one of the main preoccupations that vexes much of the fiction and drama to which Hollinghurst's novel so frequently alludes. Homoerotic writing after 1885 repeatedly considers whether same-sex desire is necessarily different from the homosocial bonding sanctioned by a profoundly homophobic culture. To the radical queer politics of the 1990s, this may well appear an antiquated preoccupation. Only now is there increasingly wide acceptance among those of us who experience male same-sex desire that the hetero/homo binary is nothing less than a theoretical sham that has had devastating effects on separating men from one another. But, as I hope this book has shown, it is hard to not study the greater part of twentieth-century male homophile literature without bearing in mind that the division opened up by those prefixes 'hetero' and 'homo' was functioning to keep apart erotic formations that were altogether closer than the culture could for decades bear to imagine.

Notes

1 Jeffrey Meyers, *Homosexuality and Literature 1890–1930* (London, Athlone Press, 1977), pp.1–3.

2 Jeffrey Weeks, *Coming Out: Homosexual Politics in Britain, from the Nineteenth Century to the Present* (London, Quartet, 1977). Weeks subsequently published, among other works, *Sexuality and Its Discontents: Meanings, Myths, and Modern Sexualities* (London, Routledge and Kegan Paul, 1985), and *Sex, Politics, and Society: The Regulation of Sexuality since 1800*, 2nd edn (London, Longman, 1988).

3 Eve Kosofsky Sedgwick, *Between Men: English Literature and Male Homosocial Desire* (New York, Columbia University Press, 1985). This important study has been followed by *Epistemology of the Closet* (Hemel Hempstead, Harvester-Wheatsheaf, 1991), and *Tendencies* (London, Routledge, 1994). For some of the main developments in lesbian and gay criticism, see Henry Abelove, Michèle Aina Barale, and David M. Halperin (eds) *The Lesbian and Gay Studies Reader* (New York, Routledge, 1993); it has a very full bibliography listing a vast range of sources (pp.653–66). See also Diana Fuss (ed.) *Inside/Out: Lesbian Theories, Gay Theories* (New York, Routledge, 1991).

4 Quentin Crisp, *The Naked Civil Servant* (London, Flamingo, 1985), p.214.

5 Simon Watney, 'The Ideology of GLF', in Gay Left Collective (eds) *Homosexuality: Power and Politics* (London, Allison and Busby, 1980), p.73.

6 Simon Watney, *Policing Desire: Pornography, AIDS, and the Media* (London, Comedia, 1987), p.3.

7 Edmund White, 'Esthetics and Loss', in John Preston (ed.) *Personal Dispatches: Writers Confront AIDS* (New York, St Martin's, 1989), p.151, cited in John M.

Clum, ' "The Time before the War": AIDS, Memory, and Desire', *American Literature*, 62(4) (1990), p.660.

8 Michael Warner, 'Introduction', in Michael Warner (ed.) *Fear of a Queer Planet: Queer Politics and Social Theory* (Minneapolis, MN, University of Minnesota Press, 1993), p.xiii.

9 Rupert Haselden, 'Gay Abandon', *Weekend Guardian*, 7 September 1991, p.20.

10 Alan Hollinghurst, *The Swimming-Pool Library* (London, Chatto and Windus, 1988), p.3. Further page references appear in parentheses.

11 Catherine R. Stimpson, 'Not Every Age Has Its Pleasures', *New York Times Book Review*, 9 October 1988, p.9.

12 Richard Burton, 'Terminal Essay', from *The Arabian Nights* (1885), reprinted in Brian Reade (ed.) *Sexual Heretics: Male Homosexuality in English Literature from 1850 to 1900* (London, Routledge and Kegan Paul, 1970), p.159.

13 Edmund White, 'The Shimmer of Romance, the Sulphur of Confession', *Sunday Times*, 21 February 1988, p.G4.

14 Ross Chambers, 'Messing Around: Gayness and Loiterature in Alan Hollinghurst's *The Swimming-Pool Library*', in Judith Still and Michael Worton (eds) *Textuality and Sexuality: Reading Theories and Practices* (Manchester, Manchester University Press, 1993), p.212. Chambers describes 'loiterature' as the literature of loitering: 'a genre which, in opposition to dominant forms of narrative, relies on techniques of digression, interruption, and deferral and episodicity . . . to make observations of modern life that are unsystematic, even disordered, and usually oriented toward the everyday, the ordinary and the trivial' (p.207). For a comparable reading of Hollinghurst's novel, see Richard Dellamora, *Apocalyptic Overtures: Sexual Politics and the Sense of an Ending* (New Brunswick, NJ, Rutgers University Press, 1994), pp.173-91.

15 Chambers, p.213.

Bibliography

Abelove, Henry, Aina Barale, Michèle and Halperin, David M. (eds) *The Lesbian and Gay Studies Reader* (New York, Routledge, 1993).

Ackerley, J.R., *The Prisoners of War: A Play in Three Acts* (London, Chatto and Windus, 1925).

Ackerley, J.R., *We Think the World of You* (Harmondsworth, Penguin Books, 1971).

Ackerley, J.R., *My Sister and Myself: The Diaries of J.R. Ackerley*, ed. Francis King (Oxford, Oxford University Press, 1990).

Ackerley, J.R., *My Father and Myself* (London, Pimlico, 1992).

Ardis, Ann, *New Women, New Novels: Feminism and Early Modernism* (New Brunswick, NJ, Rutgers University Press, 1990).

Armstrong, Paul B., 'Reading India: The Politics of Interpretation in *A Passage to India*', *Twentieth-Century Literature*, 38(4) (1992), pp.365–85.

Arnold, Matthew, *Culture and Anarchy with Friendship's Garland and Some Literary Essays*, ed. R.H. Super (Ann Arbor, MI, University of Michigan Press, 1965).

Auden, W.H., *Forewords and Afterwords* (London, Faber and Faber, 1973).

Bartlett, Neil, *Who Was That Man? A Present for Mr Oscar Wilde* (London, Serpent's Tail, 1988).

Baudelaire, Charles, *Les Fleurs du Mal: The Complete Text*, trans. Richard Howard (Brighton, Harvester Press, 1982).

Baudelaire, Charles, *The Painter of Modern Life and Other Essays*, ed. and trans. Jonathan Mayne (New York, Da Capo, 1989).

Beckson, Karl (ed.) *Oscar Wilde: The Critical Heritage* (London, Routledge and Kegan Paul, 1970).

Beer, Gillian, 'Negation in *A Passage to India*', in John Beer (ed.) A Passage to India: *Essays in Interpretation* (Basingstoke, Macmillan, 1985).

Benjamin, Walter, *Charles Baudelaire: A Lyric Poet in the Era of High Capitalism*, trans. Harry Zohn (London, New Left Books, 1973).

Benkowitz, Miriam J., 'Ronald Firbank in New York', *Bulletin of the New York Public Library*, 63 (1959), pp.247–59.

Benkowitz, Miriam J., *A Bibliography of Ronald Firbank* (London, Rupert Hart-Davis, 1963).

Benkowitz, Miriam J., *Ronald Firbank: A Biography* (London, Weidenfeld and Nicolson, 1970).

Betjeman, John, *Collected Poems* (London, John Murray, 1970).

Bevington, Merle Mowbray, *The Saturday Review 1855–1868* (New York, AMS Press, 1966).

Bhabha, Homi K., *The Location of Culture* (London, Routledge, 1994).

Bredbeck, Gregory W., 'Narcissus in the Wilde: Textual Catharsis and the Historical Origins of Queer Camp', in Moe Meyer (ed.) *The Politics and Poetics of Camp* (London, Routledge, 1994).

Bristow, Joseph, 'Nation, Class and Gender: Tennyson's *Maud* and War', *Genders*, 9 (1990), pp.93–111.

Bristow, Joseph, *Empire Boys: Adventures in a Man's World* (London, HarperCollins Academic, 1991).

Bristow, Joseph, 'Wilde, *Dorian Gray*, and Gross Indecency', in Joseph Bristow (ed.) *Sexual Sameness: Textual Differences in Lesbian and Gay Writing* (London, Routledge, 1992).

Brooke, Jocelyn, *Ronald Firbank* (London, Arthur Barker, 1951).

Brooke, Jocelyn, *The Orchid Trilogy* (Harmondsworth, Penguin Books, 1981).

Brooke, Jocelyn, 'Gerald Brockhurst', in *Private View* (London, Robert Clark, 1989).

Brooke, Jocelyn, *The Dog at Clambercrown* (London, Cardinal, 1990).

Brophy, Brigid, *Prancing Novelist: A Defence of Fiction in the Form of a Critical Biography in Praise of Ronald Firbank* (London, Macmillan, 1973).

Brown, Tony, 'Edward Carpenter and the Evolution of *A Room with a View*', *ELT*, 30(3) (1987), pp.279–300.

Bullen, J.B. (ed.) *Post-Impressionists in England* (London, Routledge, 1988).

Butler, Judith, *Gender Trouble: Feminism and the Subversion of Identity* (New York, Routledge, 1990).

Butler, Judith, *Bodies That Matter: On the Discursive Limits of 'Sex'* (New York, Routledge, 1993).

Carpenter, Edward, *Selected Writings*, ed. Noel Greig (London, GMP, 1984).

Castle, Terry, *The Apparitional Lesbian: Female Homosexuality and Modern Culture* (New York, Columbia University Press, 1993).

Chambers, Ross, 'Messing Around: Gayness and Loiterature in Alan Hollinghurst's *The Swimming-Pool Library*', in Judith Still and Michael Worton (eds) *Textuality and Sexuality: Reading Theories and Practices* (Manchester, Manchester University Press, 1993).

Clark, William Lane, 'Degenerate Personality: Deviant Sexuality and Race in Ronald Firbank's Novels', in David Bergman (ed.) *Camp Grounds: Style and Homosexuality* (Amherst, MA, University of Massachusetts Press, 1993).

Clum, John M., ' "The Time before the War": AIDS, Memory, and Desire', *American Literature*, 62(4) (1990), pp.648–67.

Cohen, Ed., 'Who Are "We"; Gay "Identity" as Political (E)motion (A Theoretical Rumination)', in Diana Fuss (ed.) *Inside/Out: Lesbian Theories, Gay Theories* (New York, Routledge, 1991).

Cohen, Ed., *Talk on the Wilde Side: Toward a Genealogy of a Discourse on Male Sexualities* (New York, Routledge, 1993).

Cohen, William A., 'Willie and Wilde: Reading *The Portrait of Mr W.H.*', *South Atlantic Quarterly*, 88(1) (1989), pp.219–45.

Coulling, Sidney, *Matthew Arnold and His Critics: A Study of Arnold's Controversies* (Athens, OH, Ohio University Press, 1974).

Craft, Christopher, ' "Descend and touch and enter": Tennyson's Strange Manner of Address', *Genders*, 1 (1988), pp.83–101.

Craft, Christopher, 'Alias Bunbury: Desire and Termination in *The Importance of Being Earnest*', *Representations*, 31 (1991), pp.19–46.

Crews, Frederick C., *E.M. Forster: The Perils of Humanism* (Princeton, NJ, Princeton University Press, 1962).

Crisp, Quentin, *How to Become a Virgin* (London, Duckworth, 1981).

Crisp, Quentin, *The Naked Civil Servant* (London, Flamingo, 1985).

Croft-Cooke, Rupert, *Bosie: The Story of Lord Alfred Douglas* (London, W.H. Allen, 1963).

Danson, Lawrence, 'Oscar Wilde, W.H., and the Unspoken Name of Love', *ELH*, 58 (1991), pp.979–1000.

Davidoff, Leonore and Hall, Catherine, *Family Fortunes: Men and Women of the English Middle Class 1780–1850* (London, Hutchinson, 1987).

Davis, Robert Murray, 'Ronald Firbank's Notebooks: ". . . writing books was by no means easy" ', *Harvard Library Bulletin*, 25 (1977), pp.172–92.

DeJean, Joan, *Fictions of Sappho: 1546–1937* (Chicago, IL, Chicago University Press, 1989).

DeLaura, David J., *Hebrew and Hellene in Victorian England: Newman, Arnold, and Pater* (Austin, TX, University of Texas Press, 1969).

Dellamora, Richard, *Masculine Desire: The Sexual Politics of Victorian Aestheticism* (Chapel Hill, NC, University of North Carolina Press, 1990).

Dellamora, Richard, 'Traversing the Feminine in Oscar Wilde's *Salomé*', in Thaïs E. Morgan (ed.) *Victorian Sages and Cultural Discourse: Renegotiating Gender and Power* (New Brunswick, NJ, Rutgers University Press, 1990).

Dellamora, Richard, 'Textual Politics/Sexual Politics', *Modern Language Quarterly*, 54(1) (1993), pp.155–64.

Dellamora, Richard, *Apocalyptic Overtures: Sexual Politics and the Sense of an Ending* (New Brunswick, NJ, Rutgers University Press, 1994).

Dodd, Philip, 'Englishness and National Culture', in Philip Dodd and Robert Colls (eds) *Englishness: Politics and Culture 1880–1920* (Beckenham, Croom Helm, 1986).

Dollimore, Jonathan, *Sexual Dissidence: Augustine to Wilde, Freud to Foucault* (Oxford, Clarendon Press, 1991).

Douglas, Alfred, *The Autobiography of Lord Alfred Douglas* (London, Martin Secker, 1929).

Douglas, Alfred, *The True History of Shakespeare's Sonnets* (London, Martin Secker, 1933).

Dowling, Linda, 'The Decadent and the New Woman', *Nineteenth-Century Fiction*, 33 (1979), pp.434–53.

Dowling, Linda, *Language and Decadence in the Victorian Fin de Siècle* (Princeton, NJ, Princeton University Press, 1986).

Dowling, Linda, 'Ruskin's Pied Beauty and the Constitution of a "Homosexual" Code', *Victorian Newsletter*, 75 (1989), pp.7–10.

Dowling, Linda, 'Esthetes and Effeminati', *Raritan*, 12(3) (1993), pp.52–68.

Dowling, Linda, *Hellenism and Homosexuality in Victorian Oxford* (Ithaca, NY, Cornell University Press, 1994).

Eagleton, Terry, *Saint Oscar* (Derry, Field Day, 1989).

Egan, Michael (ed.) *Ibsen: The Critical Heritage* (London, Routledge and Kegan Paul, 1972).

Ellmann, Richard, *Oscar Wilde* (London, Hamish Hamilton, 1987).

Erkkila, Betsy, *Whitman the Political Poet* (New York, Oxford University Press, 1989).

Felski, Rita, 'The Counter-Discourse of the Feminine in Three Texts by Huysmans, Wilde, and Sacher-Masoch', *PMLA*, 106 (1991), pp.1094–105.

Firbank, Ronald, *The Complete Firbank* (London, Duckworth, 1961).

Firbank, Ronald, *The Early Firbank*, ed. Steven Moore (London, Quartet, 1991).

Fletcher, John, 'Forster's Self-Erasure: *Maurice* and the Scene of Masculine Love', in Joseph Bristow (ed.) *Sexual Sameness: Textual Differences in Lesbian and Gay Writing* (London, Routledge, 1992).

Flint, Kate, *The Woman Reader: 1837–1914* (Oxford, Clarendon Press, 1993).

Forster, E.M., 'Some Memories', in Gilbert Beith (ed.) *Edward Carpenter: In Appreciation* (London, George Allen and Unwin, 1931).

Forster, E.M., *Abinger Harvest* (London, Edward Arnold, 1953).

Forster, E.M., *Marianne Thornton: A Domestic Biography 1797–1887* (London, Edward Arnold, 1956).

Forster, E.M., *Maurice* (London, Edward Arnold, 1971).

Forster, E.M., *The Life to Come and Other Stories*, ed. Oliver Stallybrass, Abinger Edition (London, Edward Arnold, 1972).

Forster, E.M., *Two Cheers for Democracy*, ed. Oliver Stallybrass, Abinger Edition (London, Edward Arnold, 1972).

Forster, E.M., *Howards End*, ed. Oliver Stallybrass, Abinger Edition (London, Edward Arnold, 1973).

Forster, E.M., *The Manuscripts of* Howards End, ed. Oliver Stallybrass, Abinger Edition (London, Edward Arnold, 1973).

Forster, E.M., *Where Angels Fear to Tread*, ed. Oliver Stallybrass, Abinger Edition (London, Edward Arnold, 1975).

Forster, E.M., *A Room with a View*, ed. Oliver Stallybrass, Abinger Edition (London, Edward Arnold, 1977).

Forster, E.M., *A Passage to India*, ed. Oliver Stallybrass, Abinger Edition (London, Edward Arnold, 1978).

Forster, E.M., *The Manuscripts of* A Passage to India, ed. Oliver Stallybrass (London, Edward Arnold, 1978).

Forster, E.M., *Arctic Summer and Other Fiction*, ed. Elizabeth Heine, Abinger Edition (London, Edward Arnold, 1980).

Forster, E.M., *The Longest Journey*, ed. Elizabeth Heine (London, Edward Arnold, 1984).

Forster, E.M., *Commonplace Book*, ed. Philip Gardner (London, Scolar Press, 1985).

Forster, E.M., *Selected Letters of E.M. Forster*, ed. Mary Lago and P.N. Furbank, 2 vols (London, Collins, 1983–5).

Foucault, Michel, *The History of Sexuality: An Introduction*, trans. Robert Hurley (Harmondsworth, Penguin Books, 1981).

Furbank, P.N., *E.M. Forster: A Life*, 2 vols (London, Secker and Warburg, 1978).

Fuss, Diana (ed.) *Inside/Out: Lesbian Theories, Gay Theories* (New York, Routledge, 1991).

Gagnier, Regenia, *Idylls of the Marketplace: Oscar Wilde and the Victorian Public* (Aldershot, Scolar Press, 1987).

Gardner, Philip (ed.) *E.M. Forster: The Critical Heritage* (London, Routledge and Kegan Paul, 1973).

Gardner, Philip, 'The Evolution of E.M. Forster's *Maurice*', in Judith Scherer Herz and Robert K. Martin (eds) *E.M. Forster: Centenary Revaluations* (Basingstoke, Macmillan, 1982), pp.204–23.

Gilbert, Sandra M. and Gubar, Susan, *No Man's Land: The Place of the Woman Writer in the Twentieth Century – Volume 1: The War of the Sexes* (New Haven, CT, Yale University Press, 1987).

Gilbert, Sandra M. and Gubar, Susan, *No Man's Land: The Place of the Woman Writer in the Twentieth Century – Volume 2: Sexchanges* (New Haven, CT, Yale University Press, 1989).

Girard, René, *Deceit, Desire, and the Novel: Self and Other in Literary Structure*, trans. Yvonne Freccero (Baltimore, MD, The Johns Hopkins University Press, 1966).

Green, Martin, *Children of the Sun: A Narrative of 'Decadence' in England after 1918* (London, Constable, 1977).

[Greg, W.R.]* 'Prostitution', *Westminster Review*, 53 (1850) pp.448–506.

Guy, Josephine, *The British Avant-Garde: The Theory and Politics of Tradition* (Hemel Hempstead, Harvester-Wheatsheaf, 1991).

Harris, Daniel R., 'Effeminacy', *Michigan Quarterly Review*, 30(1) (1991), pp.72–81.

Harrison, Frederic, 'Culture: A Dialogue', *Fortnightly Review*, NS 2 (1867), pp.603–14.

Haselden, Rupert, 'Gay Abandon', *Weekend Guardian*, 7 September 1991, pp.20–1.

Hilliard, David, 'UnEnglish and Unmanly: Anglo-Catholicism and Homosexuality', *Victorian Studies*, 25(2) (1982), pp.181–210.

Hollinghurst, Alan, 'The Creative Uses of Homosexuality in the Novels of E.M. Forster, Ronald Firbank, and L.P. Hartley', unpublished MLitt thesis, University of Oxford, 1980.

Hollinghurst, Alan, *The Swimming-Pool Library* (London, Chatto and Windus, 1988).

Hyde, H. Montgomery, *The Trials of Oscar Wilde*, 2nd edn (New York, Dover, 1973).

Hyde, H. Montgomery, *Oscar Wilde: A Biography* (London, Eyre Methuen, 1976).

James, Henry, *The Notebooks of Henry James*, ed. F.O. Matthiesen and B. Murdock (New York, Oxford University Press, 1961).

James, Henry, *Letters: 1883–1895*, ed. Leon Edel (Basingstoke, Macmillan, 1981).

Jeffery-Poulter, Stephen, *Peers, Queers and Commons: The Struggle for Gay Law Reform from 1950 to the Present* (London, Routledge, 1991).

* The use of square brackets around authors names indicates that these works were first published anonymously.

Jeffreys, Sheila, *The Spinster and Her Enemies: Feminism and Sexuality 1880–1930* (London, Pandora, 1985).

Joyce, James, *A Portrait of the Artist as a Young Man* (Harmondsworth, Penguin Books, 1992).

Joyce, James, *Ulysses*, annotated student's edition, ed. Declan Kiberd (Harmondsworth, Penguin Books, 1992).

Jump, John D. (ed.) *Tennyson: The Critical Heritage* (London, Routledge and Kegan Paul, 1967).

Kiberd, D. (1994) 'Wilde and the English Question', *Times Literary Supplement*, 16 December.

Koestenbaum, Wayne, *Double Talk: The Erotics of Male Literary Collaboration* (New York, Routledge, 1989).

Koestenbaum, Wayne, 'Wilde's Hard Labor and the Birth of Gay Reading', in Joseph A. Boone and Michael Cadden (eds) *Engendering Men: The Question of Male Feminist Criticism* (New York, Routledge, 1990).

Lane, Christopher, 'Re/Orientations: Firbank's Colonial Imaginary and the Sexual Nomad', *Literature Interpretation Theory*, 3 (1992), pp.271–86.

Lane, Christopher, 'Managing the "White Man's Burden": The Racial Imaginary in Forster's Colonial Narratives', *Discourse*, 15(3) (1993), pp.93–129.

Laver, James, *Dandies* (London, Weidenfeld and Nicolson, 1968).

Lawrence, D.H., *The Letters of D.H. Lawrence: June 1913–October 1916*, ed. George J. Zytaruk and James T. Boulton (Cambridge, Cambridge University Press, 1981).

Levenson, Michael, *Modernism and the Fate of Individuality: Character and Novelistic Form from Conrad to Woolf* (Cambridge, Cambridge University Press, 1991).

Levine, June Perry, 'The Tame in Pursuit of the Savage: The Posthumous Fiction of E.M. Forster', *PMLA*, 99(1) (1984), pp.72–88.

Lewis, David Levering, *When Harlem Was in Vogue* (New York, Knopf, 1981).

[Mallock, W.H.] *The New Republic; or, Culture, Faith, and Philosophy in an English Country House*, 3rd edn, 2 vols (London, Chatto and Windus, 1877).

Meyer, Moe, 'Under the Sign of Wilde: An Archeology of Posing', in Moe Meyer (ed.) *The Politics and Poetics of Camp* (London, Routledge, 1994).

Meyers, Jeffrey, *Homosexuality and Literature 1890–1930* (London, Athlone Press, 1977).

Mikhail, E.H. (ed.) *Oscar Wilde: Interviews and Recollections*, 2 vols (Basingstoke, Macmillan, 1979).

Mosse, George L., *Nationalism and Sexuality: Middle-class Morality and Sexual Norms in Modern Europe* (Madison, WI, University of Wisconsin Press, 1985).

Nordau, Max, *Degeneration*, trans. from 2nd edn (London, Heinemann, 1895).

Palmer, Paulina, *Contemporary Lesbian Writing: Dreams, Desire, Difference* (Buckingham, Open University Press, 1993).

Parker, Peter, *Ackerley: A Life of J.R. Ackerley* (London, Constable, 1989).

Parry, Benita, *Delusions and Discoveries: Studies on India in the British Imagination 1880–1930* (Berkeley, University of California Press, 1972).

Parry, Benita, 'The Politics of Representation in *A Passage to India*', in John Beer (ed.) *A Passage to India: Essays in Interpretation* (Basingstoke, Macmillan, 1985).

Pearson, Hesketh, *The Life of Oscar Wilde* (London, Methuen, 1946).

Petre, Diana, *The Secret Orchard of Roger Ackerley* (London, Hamish Hamilton, 1975).

Poovey, Mary, *Uneven Developments: The Ideological Work of Gender in Mid-Victorian Britain* (Chicago, IL, Chicago University Press, 1988).

Porter, Kevin and Weeks, Jeffrey (eds) *Between the Acts: Lives of Homosexual Men 1885–1967* (London, Routledge, 1991).

Powell, Kerry, *Oscar Wilde and the Theatre of the 1890s* (Cambridge, Cambridge University Press, 1990).

Reade, Brian (ed.) *Sexual Heretics: Male Homosexuality in English Literature from 1850 to 1900* (London, Routledge and Kegan Paul, 1970).

Rich, Adrienne, 'Compulsory Heterosexuality and Lesbian Existence', in Henry Abelove, Michèle Aina Barale, and David M. Halperin (eds) *The Lesbian and Gay Studies Reader* (New York, Routledge, 1993).

Rorty, Richard, *Contingency, Irony, and Solidarity* (Cambridge, Cambridge University Press, 1989).

Rosecrance, Barbara, 'Forster's Comrades', *Partisan Review*, 47 (1980), pp.591–603.

Ross, Andrew, *No Respect: Intellectuals and Popular Culture* (New York, Routledge, 1989).

Said, Edward W., *Culture and Imperialism* (London, Chatto and Windus, 1993).

Sedgwick, Eve Kosofsky, *Between Men: English Literature and Male Homosocial Desire* (New York: Columbia University Press, 1985).

Sedgwick, Eve Kosofsky, *Epistemology of the Closet* (Hemel Hempstead, Harvester-Wheatsheaf, 1991).

Sedgwick, Eve Kosofsky, *Tendencies* (London, Routledge, 1994).

Sharpe, Jenny, 'The Unspeakable Limits of Rape: Colonial Violence and Counter-Insurgency', *Genders*, 10 (1991), pp.25–46.

Sieverking, A. Forbes, 'Dandyism', *Temple Bar*, 88 (1890), pp.527–34.

Silver, Brenda R., 'Periphrasis, Power, and Rape in *A Passage to India*', *Novel*, 22(1) (1988), pp.86–105.

Silverman, Kaja, *Male Subjectivity at the Margins* (New York, Routledge, 1992).

Sinfield, Alan, *Alfred Tennyson* (Oxford, Basil Blackwell, 1986).

Sinfield, Alan, *Literature, Politics and Culture in Postwar Britain* (Oxford, Basil Blackwell, 1989).

Sinfield, Alan, 'Private Lives/Public Theater: Noel Coward and the Politics of Homosexual Representation', *Representations*, 36 (1991), pp.43–63.

Sinfield, Alan, ' "Effeminacy" and "Femininity": Sexual Politics in Wilde's Comedies', *Modern Drama*, 37(1) (1994), pp.34–52.

Sinfield, Alan, *The Wilde Century: Effeminacy, Oscar Wilde and the Queer Moment* (London, Cassell, 1994).

Singh, Frances B., '*A Passage to India*, the National Movement, and Independence', *Twentieth-Century Literature*, 35(2–3) (1985), pp.265–78.

Small, Ian, *Conditions of Criticism: Authority, Knowledge, and Literature in the Late Nineteenth Century* (Oxford, Clarendon Press, 1991).

Smith, Timothy d'Arch, *Love in Earnest: Some Notes on the Lives and Writings of English 'Uranian' Poets from 1889 to 1930* (London, Routledge and Kegan Paul, 1970).

Sontag, Susan, 'Notes on Camp', in *Against Interpretation* (New York, Noonday Press, 1966).

[Stephen, Fitzjames] 'Culture and Action', *Saturday Review*, 9 November 1867, p.592.

[Stephen, Fitzjames] 'Mr Arnold on Culture and Anarchy', *Saturday Review*, 6 March 1869, p.319.

Stephen, Leslie. *Mausoleum Book*, ed. Alan Bell (Oxford: Clarendon Press, 1977).

Stimpson, Catherine R., 'Not Every Age Has Its Pleasures', *New York Times Book Review*, 9 October 1988, p.9.

Stokes, John, *In the Nineties* (Hemel Hempstead, Harvester-Wheatsheaf, 1989).

Stone, Wilfred, ' "Overleaping Class": Forster's Problem of Connection', *Modern Language Quarterly*, 39 (1978), pp.386–404.

Suleri, Sara, *The Rhetoric of English India* (Chicago, IL, Chicago University Press, 1992).

Swinburne, A.C., 'Whitmania', *Fortnightly Review*, NS 42 (1887), pp.170–6.

Symonds, John Addington, *Studies in the History of the Greek Poets*, 2 vols (New York, Harper and Brothers, 1880).

Symonds, John Addington, 'A Note on Whitmania', *Fortnightly Review*, NS 42 (1887), p.460.

Symonds, John Addington, 'Swiss Athletic Sports', *Fortnightly Review*, NS 50 (1891), pp.408–15.

Symonds, John Addington, 'Edward Cracroft Lefroy', in *In the Key of Blue and Other Prose Essays* (London, Elkin Mathews and John Lane, 1893).

Symonds, John Addington, *The Letters of John Addington Symonds*, ed. Herbert M. Scheller and Robert L. Peters, 3 vols (Detroit, MI, Wayne State University Press, 1969).

Symonds, John Addington, *Memoirs*, ed. Phyllis Grosskurth (Chicago, IL, Chicago University Press, 1984).

Symons, Arthur, *The Memoirs of Arthur Symons: Life and Art in the 1890s*, ed. Karl Beckson (University Park, PA, Pennsylvania State University Press, 1977).

Tennyson, Alfred, *The Poems of Tennyson*, ed. Christopher Ricks (London, Longman, 1969).

Tosh, John, 'Domesticity and Manliness in the Victorian Middle Class: The Family of Edward White Benson', in Michael Roper and John Tosh (eds) *Manful Assertions: Masculinities in Britain since 1800* (London, Routledge, 1991).

Trilling, Lionel, *E.M. Forster*, 2nd edn (London, Chatto and Windus, 1967).

Tyrwhitt, Rev. St John, 'The Greek Spirit in Modern Literature', *Contemporary Review*, 29 (1877), pp.552–66.

Warner, Michael (ed.) *Fear of a Queer Planet: Queer Politics and Social Theory* (Minneapolis, MN, University of Minnesota Press, 1993).

Watney, Simon, 'The Ideology of GLF', in Gay Left Collective (eds) *Homosexuality: Power and Politics* (London, Allison and Busby, 1980).

Watney, Simon, *Policing Desire: Pornography, AIDS and the Media* (London, Comedia, 1987).

Waugh, Evelyn, *Essays, Articles, and Reviews*, ed. Donat Gallagher (London, Methuen, 1983).

Weeks, Jeffrey, *Coming Out: Homosexual Politics in Britain, from the Nineteenth Century to the Present* (London, Quartet, 1977).

Weeks, Jeffrey, *Sexuality and Its Discontents: Meanings, Myths and Modern Sexualities* (London: Routledge and Kegan Paul, 1985).

Weeks, Jeffrey, *Sex, Politics and Society: The Regulation of Sexuality since 1800*, 2nd edn (London, Longman, 1988).

Weeks, Jeffrey, *Against Nature: Essays on History, Sexuality, and Identity* (London, Rivers Oram Press, 1991).

Weiss, Andrea, *Vampires and Violets: Lesbians in the Cinema* (London, Jonathan Cape, 1992).

White, Edmund, 'The Shimmer of Romance, the Sulphur of Confession', *Sunday Times*, 21 February 1988, p.G4.

Whitman, Walt, *Correspondence: 1890–92*, ed. Edwin Haviland Miller (New York, New York University Press, 1969).

Whitman, Walt, *The Complete Poems*, ed. Frances Murphy (Harmondsworth, Penguin Books, 1975).

Widdowson, Peter, *E.M. Forster's* Howards End: *Fiction as History* (Falmer, Sussex University Press, 1977).

Wilde, Oscar, *The Letters of Oscar Wilde*, ed. Rupert Hart-Davis (London, Rupert Hart-Davis, 1962).

Wilde, Oscar, *Complete Works*, ed. J.B. Foreman (London, Collins, 1966).

Wilde, Oscar, *Two Society Comedies:* A Woman of No Importance *and* An Ideal Husband, ed. Russell Jackson and Ian Small (London, Benn, 1983).

Wilde, Oscar, The Importance of Being Earnest *and Related Writings*, ed. Joseph Bristow (London, Routledge, 1992).

Woolf, Virginia, *Roger Fry: A Biography* (London, Hogarth Press, 1940).

Yeats, W.B., *Autobiographies* (London: Macmillan, 1955).

Index